GASLIGHT,
GHOSTS
& GHOULS

·BROECKER· ·19·

STEPHEN JONES' **MASTERS** OF **HORROR** SERIES

GASLIGHT, GHOSTS & GHOULS

A Centenary Celebration
R. CHETWYND-HAYES

Edited with an Introduction by
STEPHEN JONES

DIP

GASLIGHT, GHOSTS, & GHOULS
A Centenary Celebration

A Stephen Jones Book for PS Publishing Ltd.
Originally published in December 2019 by PS Publishing Ltd.
First Drugstore Indian Press edition published in May 2022
by arrangement with Stephen Jones & The Estate of R. Chetwynd-Hayes.

2 4 6 8 10 9 7 5 3 1

ISBN
978-178636-858-4

Design and Layout by Michael Smith
Cover design by Smith & Jones

Printed and bound in England by T.J. Books

PS Publishing Ltd.
Grosvenor House, 1 New Road
Hornsea HU18 1PG, England

editor@pspublishing.co.uk
www.pspublishing.co.uk

Contents

ACKNOWLEDGEMENTS

THE EDITOR WOULD like to thank Linda Smith, Peter and Nicky Crowther, Mike and Sheryl Smith, Marie O'Regan, Jo Fletcher, Marc Damian Lawler, Michael Marshall Smith, Val and Les Edwards, Randy Broecker, John and Liliana Bolton, Graham Humphreys, The Estate of Walter Velez, Jill Bauman, Mary Calvert [Danby], Aidan Chambers, Dave Brzeski, Peter Coleborn, Seamus A. Ryan, Caitlin Fleming (The University of Liverpool Library), Jean-Daniel Brèque, Brian Hughes, Steve J. Shaw, Jim Moon, Mark Yon, Mark Morris, Adrian Cole, Steve Lockley, Ian Taylor, Simon Cruise, and the late Dorothy Lumley for helping to make this collection possible.

"Although I published many of R. Chetwynd-Hayes' stories, I don't think we met many times. When I was Fiction Editor at Fontana Books, it was the early part of his career, and my main memory of him is that he had this rather mundane day job, selling furniture, but his head was full of ghosts and demons. I left Fontana at the end of 1971, and although I continued to edit the Fontana *Horror* and Armada *Ghost* series, amongst others, my main contact with authors was through the post. I do remember him as a kind and courteous man—very good to work with."

—Mary Danby
January, 2019

INTRODUCTION

DURING HIS WRITING career, Ronald Henry Glynn Chetwynd-Hayes turned out twenty-four collections, twenty-four anthologies, thirteen novels and more than 220 short stories. His work was adapted for the movies, television, radio and comics, and reprinted in various languages around the world.

One of his publishers called him "Britain's Prince of Chill" and, although his fiction has been described as "variable", his volumes of ghost stories and humorous tales of terror once filled the shelves of nearly every public library in Britain.

Given his prolific output, he ought to be a household name, as famous—or infamous—as those other masterful British exponents of the genre, such as M.R. James and Robert Aickman, or newer practitioners like Ramsey Campbell, James Herbert or Clive Barker. Instead, nearly two decades after his death, his work lingers in relative obscurity, with a few notable exceptions.

For many years he worked away in a house in the suburbs of London, surrounded by hundreds of books, continuing to churn out his urbane nightmares on an old battered manual typewriter. Apart from a couple of brief forays into the limelight when his stories were adapted for film audiences, he remained read by millions but known to only a few.

Ron came relatively late to writing fiction. His first book was not published until 1959, when he was about to enter his forties. Yet in a career that spanned the four decades until his death in 2001, he produced a prodigious amount of fiction that was widely published for both adults and children.

His highly original tales of terror and the supernatural invariably combined horror and humour in equal measure, giving them a style that was uniquely Ron's own. Not only was he happy to write about such genre standards as ghosts, demons, ghouls, vampires and were-wolves, but he also delighted in making up his own bizarre monster variations that managed to stretch the imaginations of both author and reader alike.

This is perhaps never more evident than in his most famous book, *The Monster Club*, in which he set out 'The Basic Rules of Mons-terdom':

> Vampire—sup; Werewolves—hunt; Ghouls—tear;
> Shaddies—lick; Maddies—yawn; Mocks—blow;
> Shadmocks—only whistle.

After eventually breaking into the booming paperback market of the early 1970s, Ron began a long and successful relationship with publishing company William Kimber in 1978 with the publication of his first hardcover collection. The title story from that book, 'The Cradle Demon', is included in this present volume.

Over the next ten years (until the imprint disappeared and he was forced to find another publisher for his work), Ron produced a further sixteen books for Kimber, which were aimed principally at the library market in Britain.

These books proved to be extremely popular, and Ron was always proud of the fact that each year he was one of the highest earners of the annual Public Lending Right (PLR), based on the number of times an author's books are loaned out from libraries in the UK.

When, due to failing health, Ron's stream of imaginative fiction began to dry up in the late 1990s, it was my honour to help him compile some new volumes of his uncollected fiction, which publisher Robert Hale produced in handsome hardcover editions that quickly sold out of their modest print-runs.

And now, to celebrate the centenary of his birth on May 30th, 1919, this present volume collects a sampling of some of his best fiction, along with the longest interview with the author ever published, the most complete bibliography of his work yet compiled, and a wealth of rare visual material.

From such early titles as 'The Day That Father Brought Something Home' and 'The Jumpity-Jim' to some of his most accomplished stories like 'The Coloured Transmission', 'Something Comes in from the Garden' and 'The Cradle Demon' from those now long out-of-print William Kimber volumes, all but two of the tales reprinted in this book have never previously appeared in any later collections of Ron's work.

'The Gatecrasher', 'The Door' and 'The Elemental' formed three of the four stories adapted for the 1973 film *From Beyond the Grave* and starred David Warner, Ian Ogilvy and a memorable Margaret Leighton, respectively.

The same year, 'Housebound' was the basis of the 'Something in the Woodwork' episode of the American television series *Rod Serling's Night Gallery*, featuring Geraldine Page and Leif Erickson, while Stuart Whitman was the hapless traveller who lost his way in 'The Humgoo' segment of the 1980 movie *The Monster Club*, which also featured horror film veteran John Carradine as author Ronald Chetwynd-Hayes!

Originally intended as the idea for a novel, 'Dopplegänger' was chosen by the author as one of his own favourite stories for Dennis Etchison's 1991 anthology *Masters of Darkness III*, while 'Acquiring a Family' was selected by acclaimed editor Karl Edward Wagner for the 1987 edition of his *The Year's Best Horror Stories* series.

For fans of "the world's only practising psychic detective" Francis St. Clare and his vivacious assistant Frederica ("Fred") Masters, I have included one of their early adventures together, 'The Gibbering Ghoul of Gomershal', and Ron's recurring haunted mansion, Clavering Grange, makes a cameo appearance in the aforementioned story, 'The

Door'. (In fact, the discerning reader may discover subtle connections between many of the stories in this book and also the rest of the author's work.)

As a bonus, 'Bits and Pieces' and 'A Walk on the Darkside' have never been reprinted since their original publications in 1974 and 1990, respectively, while 'Day School' was originally sent to *Fear* magazine in late 1989, where the editor considered running it over two issues. That never happen-ed, and this long-lost vampire story appears here for the very first time.

With this representative selection of the stories of Ronald Chetwynd-Hayes, it is my intention that readers familiar with his books will rediscover some old favourites, while those who are coming upon his fiction here for the first time will enjoy it enough to seek out more of his work.

Ron often stated that he was writing for posterity and that he hoped his fiction would continue to appear to entertain new generations after his death. It is my sincere pleasure to have helped make that aspiration a reality. And if this book is as well received as his previous collections, then I hope that you will see more of his stories reprinted in the future.

As Ron himself would have said: May you never hear invisible footsteps following you down the stairs...

Stephen Jones
London, England
May, 2019

A WRITER IN THE DARK LANDS

AN INTERVIEW WITH R. CHETWYND-HAYES

Stephen Jones & Jo Fletcher

"Fear of the Unknown is always tinged with curiosity."
—*The Dark Man (1964)*

THERE IS SOMETHING warmly reassuring about the fantasy fiction of R. Chetwynd-Hayes. It is not simply that, almost single-handedly, he kept alive the tradition of the typically British ghost story (which indeed he did), but when you dip into one of his collections you are transported back to a more genteel period of fantastic literature. Without doubt, it is this safe familiarity in his work that led to a string of successful hardcover collections published by William Kimber throughout the late 1970s and '80s, aimed almost exclusively at the library market.

However, the languishing author had mixed feelings about his limited success: "Kimber was always very good to me," he explained. "I had to cater for the public library trade, which is really middle-aged ladies and they like a gentle ghost story. I don't regret that. I'd love to get into paperbacks again—that's where the real money is, and of course, you get mass readership there as well. Still, you probably get as many readers eventually through library editions: I was averaging 18,000 borrowings per book per year."

Much of Chetwynd-Hayes' considerable output may be disarmingly prosaic, and he is often justifiably criticised for allowing his sense of humour to intrude upon the narrative. Yet his skill as a writer really lies in the out-rageous monsters he concocted and his ability to add a new—usually quite nasty—twist to a familiar theme. Take, for example, this extract from one of his best stories, 'The Jumpity-Jim':

> The skin split while Lady Dunwilliam screamed and a tiny wizened head peeped out from its cocoon, like a chick about to emerge from its cracked egg. It was rather like a shrivelled, pink balloon and it jerked around to stare at Harriet with microscopic red eyes. The girl gave a hoarse cry and jerked her hand from Lord Dunwilliam's loosened grip, before tearing wildly across the room in an effort to escape. As she did so the woman was flung on to her face, while something went leaping up to the rafters, then down to the floor again. A black, pink-tinted something that moved so fast it was only a blur that streaked up and down across the room. With her back against the far wall, Harriet saw it zig-zagging towards her, coming forward with high leaps that carried it up to the rafters and down again; then there was a glimpse of that wizened, deflated face, the long pink body and four many-jointed legs, before she seized a nearby chair and hurled it straight at the approaching horror.

Chetwynd-Hayes came relatively late to writing fiction. His first book was not published until 1959, when he was about to enter his forties. Yet in a career that spanned four decades, he published thirteen novels and twenty-four collections, edited twenty-four anthologies, and was the author of more than 200 short stories that have been reprinted in numerous languages around the world.

Despite his aristocratic-sounding name, Ronald Henry Glynn Chetwynd-Hayes was born into a working-class family at 7 Swan Street in the West London suburb of Isleworth on May 30th, 1919 (a date he rarely acknowledged, as he was always quaintly reluctant to reveal his age). Although his mother, Rose May ("Maisie") Cooper, was living with Henry Chetwynd-Hayes at the time, and he gave his surname to Ronald and his brother Len, he was not their natural father. When

Maisie died of tuberculosis at the tragically young age of thirty-two, the young Ronald was first put into foster-care before going to live with his maternal grandmother and, later, his aunt, Doris Cleghorn.

He left school in 1933 and for the next six years worked in a number of dead-end jobs, mainly as an errand boy for a variety of businesses, including a butcher's and a hardware store. The young Chetwynd-Hayes also appeared as a schoolboy extra in a number of pre-War British movies, including *A Yank at Oxford* (1938) and the Robert Donat version of *Goodbye, Mr. Chips* (1939), which started a life-long devotion to the moving pictures.

"I haunted the cinemas and fantasised film stories, with myself playing the leading roles," he remembered. "I cannot count the number of times I rescued Fay Wray from the clutches of King Kong!"

In 1939, at the outbreak of World War II, Chetwynd-Hayes joined the Army, rising to the "dizzy rank" (as he described it) of Sergeant in the Middlesex Regiment. He was one of thousands of soldiers successfully evacuated from Dunkirk in 1940, only to return to the beaches of France on D-Day, June 6th, 1944.

When he came out of the Army after the War, he wasn't even considering writing as a career. Instead he landed a job as a trainee buyer in the furniture department of Harrods, the internationally famous London department store in Knightsbridge. Four and a half years later he moved to the exclusive Peerless Built-in Furniture Emporium in fashionable Berkeley Street in Mayfair as a showroom manager. He also discovered his brother, Len, who had also been fostered out and whose surname had been subsequently changed to Cooper. He had been too young when his mother died to know that he even had a sibling, and the pair became close friends, quickly making up for lost time.

Chetwynd-Hayes lived in a basement flat in Richmond for many years, while scraping a living at these mundane trades, until his Aunt Doris died, when he moved into her house at Hampton Hill. Throughout this period he read voraciously and, soon, firmly convinced that he could do better himself, he began to churn out his own stories—everything from romances to his favourite genre, historical fiction. He sold his first story, 'The Orator', to *The Lady* magazine in 1953, but had infrequent success, garnering numerous rejection slips from periodicals and book publishers.

"For years I wasted my time," he recalled. "I used to turn out stories that pleased me, then send them out to magazines... and they'd send them back.

"I used to try to write the great novel, try to be another Brontë. But of course, nobody wanted to publish it. Then when I looked on the bookstalls and saw all these supernatural titles, I thought that was obviously the market to aim for. I'd always been interested in the supernatural anyway."

After noticing the profusion of horror titles on bookstalls, he promptly dashed off his own collection of short stories. "I thought I was clever," he said. "I sent one copy to Tandem Books and one to Hutchinson—and they were *both* accepted at the same time! So I told Hutchinson smugly, 'Don't worry, I've sold the paperback rights for you.'"

But Hutchinson had their own softcover line, Arrow Books, and they told the overzealous writer that he'd better let Tandem keep the collection. "It's a shame," he lamented, "I'd have liked to have been published by Hutchinson..."

The book was *The Unbidden* and although it had been accepted in just three days and was Chetwynd-Hayes' first commercial success, it was no overnight phenomenon—by the time it eventually appeared in 1971, he already had two published novels behind him.

"I wrote all the time," he explained, "except when I was in the Army—because I didn't think I was going to come out. But I used to come home from the showroom and turn out short stories in the evenings."

In fact, his first book was *The Man from the Bomb*, a science fiction novel that he was clearly embarrassed by and suggested is "put down to extreme youth." It was published in 1959 by John Spencer's now-legendary paperback imprint Badger Books. "I sent that all over the place," admitted Chetwynd-Hayes. "Badger offered to take it, so I let them have it. They paid me £25 for the novel and all rights to it. The layout and printing were terrible, but I was so delighted to see a book of mine in print, I was inclined to overlook those defects."

With a published book finally under his belt, the author followed it in 1964 with a novel from Sidgwick and Jackson about reincarnation, *The Dark Man*, but only after it was rejected by nineteen other publishers.

The Dark Man is still regarded as one of Chetwynd-Hayes' finest achievements, although it flopped when repackaged by Zebra Books as a romantic Gothic, *And Love Survived*, in America in the early 1980s. He was always genuinely bemused that in Britain copies of the original were being sold by book dealers for many times what he was paid to write it.

The novel tells the story of Anthony Wentworth, who faints on a crowded rush-hour train and for a few moments appears to be transported back in time to the First World War. Upon awakening, he discovers he has become "possessed" by the reincarnated spirit of Harry Wentworth, and the dual-personality is inexorably drawn into a web of mystery and intrigue that began many years before. The book finishes up with the protagonist solving his own murder.

Stories about possession became a recurring theme for the author. However, Chetwynd-Hayes was quick to point out that the finished novel was quite different from the tale he started out to write: "The story was going to be about a man who fell in love with the daughter of a dead girl whom he also loved—he identified her as the mother." However, that wasn't how the story worked out.

"When I write, I just sit down at the typewriter and type. I haven't a clue how it's going to finish. It all comes out quite naturally, without any planning on my part."

Chetwynd-Hayes also completed two other novels during this period, *Two Cheers for Cathy* (a kitchen-sink drama that wisely remains unpublished) and *World of the Impossible*. "In *World of the Impossible*," he explained, "I worked out a theory that the fairy stories we are taught in childhood are based on fact and they exist in another dimension. Some people from this world, armed with stainless-steel armour and Bren guns, go into the next universe and discover a walled city where beautiful women are taken and tied to an altar for the dragons who come down from the hills.

"A production secretary from Hammer Films described it as 'sort of

James Bond meets dragons' and they were actually thinking of making it into a film. But sex started to raise its ugly head at Hammer in those days, and that killed it. I think it's a lovely fantasy story..."

World of the Impossible was finally published by Robert Hale in 1998, after it had been recreated from the author's surviving manuscript pages. It was also his last published novel.

It was some years before Chetwynd-Hayes' tales finally made it onto the big screen, and in the meantime he found his niche producing short stories for *The Fontana Book of Horror Stories*, edited by Christine Barnard.

In 1970, Fontana asked him to compile his own anthology entitled *Cornish Tales of Terror*, and a few years later he followed up the success of *The Unbidden* with another original collection for Tandem, *Cold Terror*, and a second anthology for Fontana, *Scottish Tales of Terror*, edited under his regular pseudonym, "Angus Campbell".

"In those days, everything to do with the supernatural sold," he remembered fondly. "At one time I had six volumes with my name on them in bookshops."

Then, at another editor's suggestion, he took over the series of *Fontana Book of Great Ghost Stories*, beginning with volume nine. "Mary Danby told me they didn't much like Robert Aickman—he was concentrating too much on the old Victorian classics. So I started editing those, until the last one—volume twenty—came out in 1984. Sales stopped. The modern age doesn't want those sort of things."

He was sometimes bitter when talking about the current state of horror publishing in Britain and preferred to hark back to a more atmospheric period of history, often reflected in his own fiction: "Now the Victorians were the great ghost-story tellers. It was the age of ghosts, wasn't it? Gaslight, that sort of thing...But we haven't got it today—what with television and the electric light, the poor ghost doesn't stand a chance. I don't like this age very much," he added, "it's going to blow up sooner or later."

Now hailed as "Britain's Prince of Chill", Chetwynd-Hayes' highly original tales of terror and the supernatural invariably combined horror and humour in equal measure, giving them a style that was uniquely the author's own. "I've always got this terrible urge to send the whole thing up," he admitted. "It just slips in, I have never been able to stop it."

Despite his disarming humour and often with stark originality, Chetwynd-Hayes was still able to skilfully revitalise an old idea into a bizarre contemporary setting, such as in this opening sequence from 'The Elemental':

> "There's an elemental sitting next to you,' said the fat woman in the horrible flower-patterned dress with amber beads.
>
> Reginald Warren lowered his newspaper, glanced at the empty seat on either side, shot an alarmed look around the carriage in general, then took refuge behind his *Evening Standard* again.
>
> "He's a killer," the fat woman insisted.
>
> Reginald frowned and tried to think rationally. How did you tackle a nutty fat woman?
>
> "Thank you," he said over the newspaper, I'm obliged."

"I suppose you can have a ghost in a council flat just as well as in an old house," Chetwynd-Hayes mused. "I've had a ghost in a tape recorder, and even a haunted television—that story was done as a radio play," he added with pride.

Although he struggled to keep his writing attuned to the contemporary horror market, Chetwynd-Hayes freely admitted that he didn't really fit in, which is perhaps one of the reasons why he was never able to successfully break into America.

"The Americans understand horror—where you hit the walnut with a big sledgehammer—but the idea of something subtle, like a ghost, escapes them. That's the beauty of ghost stories really—the atmosphere that gradually comes into a personality. Horror always stands a long way off. If you come face-to-face with it, it's always an anti-climax."

An archetypal R. Chetwynd-Hayes haunting appears in 'Something Comes in from the Garden': the protagonist's first sight of the ghost is more mundane than macabre, but the author's skill lies in developing the sense of unease without resorting to the obvious genre clichés:

It was a month to the day before the unusual happened.

The sun was setting and Robert was looking out of the window, wondering where to put his summerhouse, when the man walked across the lawn. He was tall, with a red, hooked nose, and was attired in an old, faded army overcoat. Robert watched him for a few seconds with almost dispassionate interest. The man slouched—there was no other way to describe his loose-limbed action—across Robert's line of vision, with bent shoulders and lowered head, giving the impression he was treading a familiar path.

"They tell me my books are too subtle for the American market. Pyramid did three and said, 'Our critics say you're too English'—whatever that means," Chetwynd-Hayes smiled. He admitted that he "never really understood" the stories of H.P. Lovecraft, describing them as "heavy going", but readily admitted to a passing fondness for Stephen King's work:

"I've read all his stuff now, and some of it I didn't like. I didn't like *The Shining*, but the later ones, like *Firestarter*, I thought were ingenious. *Christine* was also clever, and I found *Cujo* quite enthralling. But when I met him, I said, 'You've only got one plot, haven't you?' and he replied, 'You've found me out . . .'"

Chetwynd-Hayes' own forays into fully-fledged horror were less successful: "I had a couple of stories in Bertie [Herbert] van Thal's *Pan Book of Horror Stories*," he recalled. "In one of them I had these people on the moors who would capture people; when they wanted an arm, they would amputate it, cook it and eat it. Then they would come back for another limb, and so on—you can carry on for a long time doing that. Pan loved it and wanted me to do some more, but I told them, 'No, I can't do any more like that.' I just proved to myself that I could write it."

The author most enjoyed writing for younger readers. Not only was he happy to write about such genre standards as ghosts, demons, ghouls, vampires and werewolves, but he also delighted in making up his own bizarre monster variations that managed to stretch the imaginations of both author and reader alike—the Wind-Billie, the

Mudadora, the Slippity-Slop, the Gale-Wuggle, the Cumberloo, and Ronald's own personal favourite, the Jumpity-Jim.

In 1976 he ghost-edited and wrote almost all of *Ghoul*, a one-shot magazine from New English Library, billed a "A Ghastly Giggle". He also edited a very successful and highly entertaining series of six juvenile anthologies, the *Armada Monster Books*, recalling: "I wrote to Armada at the time and said, 'There are too many books about giants and dragons—it's about time we had some new monsters.' The series was finally killed because the monsters were too tame for children today..."

More adult collections of his work appeared throughout the 1970s and into the '80s: *Terror by Night* (1974), *The Elemental and Other Stories* (1974), *The Night Ghouls* (1975), *The Monster Club* (1976), *Tales of Fear and Fantasy* (1977), *The Cradle Demon* (1978; "I still think it's the best") and *The Fantastic World of Kamtellar* (1980). He also continued to edit anthologies for Fontana ("I had a lovely time researching those") and other publishers. These included *Welsh Tales of Terror* (1973), *Tales of Terror from Outer Space* (1975), *Gaslight Tales of Terror* (1976) and *Doomed to the Night: An Anthology of Ghost Stories* (1978).

"I began writing supernatural fiction because it was the only genre I could break into," admitted Chetwynd-Hayes. "I could turn them out and everybody accepted them."

One of the reasons that he continued to enjoy writing about the macabre was his curiosity about what lay beyond death—a theme he returned to time and again in his fiction. He would have liked to believe that there is an afterlife, but he doubted it.

R. Chetwynd-Hayes' brief skirmish with the movies left him with two screen credits (neither of which came off entirely successfully), a couple of options and a pair of film novelisations.

In 1972, while still selling furniture in Berkeley Street, he was approached by Amicus Productions, who wanted to turn a number of his stories into a television series. "Just at that moment," he recalled, "we'd been taken over and I'd got the sack, so it was marvellous. I became a freelance writer on the strength of it. But it terrified me—I suddenly realised I had to live on my own wits, but it worked out." He never regretted his decision: "I was doing something I wanted to do—look at the books I turned out as a result of that!"

Former film editor-turned-director Kevin Connor had been flying to America when he picked up a copy of *The Unbidden* from an airport bookstall. Upon his return, he interested Amicus producer Milton Subotsky in filming Chetwynd-Hayes' stories. "Seventeen stories were scripted," revealed the author, "drawn from three of my collections: *The Unbidden*, *Cold Terror* and *The Elemental*. Alas, the television series never materialised, but Milton chose four stories—'The Gate Crasher', 'The Elemental', 'An Act of Kindness' and 'The Door'—which, when linked together, eventually became the film *From Beyond the Grave*."

Following the successful portmanteau format first introduced by Amicus back in 1965 with *Dr. Terror's House of Horrors*, the film starred Peter Cushing as the mysterious proprietor of an old antique shop called Temptations Limited, who delivers a gruesome surprise with every purchase.

"Needless to say, I was delighted with the all-star cast, and could scarcely believe that such famous names were actually going to give life to characters I had created, in the most part, in the small hours that separate midnight from sunrise," enthused the writer. "The film itself is a visual experience. That is to say, like most Amicus productions, there is very little dialogue and the plot depends mainly on informative actions, much like the old silent films. This is particularly effective when Donald Pleasence and his daughter Angela give meaningful looks out of ice-diamond eyes and undoubtedly make 'An Act of Kindness' the most terrifying story in the entire film.

"I think perhaps 'The Gatecrasher' could have been improved by a little more conversation from David Warner, as the point that I tried to make in the story—namely that the face in the mirror was the shade of Jack the Ripper—was completely lost."

With a strong cast of British character actors that included Margaret Leighton, Ian Carmichael, Ian Ogilvy, Diana Dors and Lesley-Anne Down, and an impressive directing debut by Kevin Conner, *From Beyond the Grave* deserved to do well, but failed at the box-office. Chetwynd-Hayes admitted that he was "bitterly disappointed" when he first saw the film, but added: "When I saw it again on television, it seemed somehow to look very much better."

To coincide with the film's release in the UK, Fontana published a tie-in edition of *The Elemental* but, as Chetwynd-Hayes explained, there were a few legal problems to be sorted out first: "There was a big fight between Tandem and Fontana about who was going to bring it out. Bertie van Thal got me into that mess: 'Don't worry', he said, 'I'm your agent, I'll handle this for you.' Then he dropped me in it and said, 'It's nothing to do with me.' The book finally came out from Fontana and Tandem brought one out at the same time as 'by the author of *From Beyond the Grave*'—that's how they got over it."

On the strength of that initial contact with Amicus, Milton Subotsky asked Chetwynd-Hayes to write the novelisation of *Dominique* (1978, aka *Dominique is Dead*). Published as a Universal paperback, the book was based on a script by Edward and Valerie Abraham, which in turn was based on a short story by Harold Lawlor, 'What Beckoning Ghost?', published in the July 1948 issue of the pulp magazine *Weird Tales*.

A psychological thriller with supernatural overtones, the film starred Cliff Robertson as a scheming husband trying to drive his wife (played by Jean Simmons) insane.

"We went to see it being filmed at Shepperton Studios," recalled Chetwynd-Hayes, "and I said, 'Milton, they'll never forgive you for what you've done here: you've got a ghost, and then you explain it away. But there is an answer—when it has all been explained, that door opens and out comes Dominique holding a rope, slithering towards the person who killed her.'

"Milton thought that it was a marvellous idea, but it was too late—the sets had apparently already been knocked down."

While he was writing *Dominique*, Chetwynd-Hayes was also approached to write the novelisation for *Damien: Omen II*, but regretted that he had to turn it down: "They wanted that in a fortnight; it's a shame, they were going to pay me $8,000..." However, he did get the opportunity to write another novelisation in 1980, when he adapted *The Awakening* for Magnum Books. Unaware that it was based on Bram Stoker's 1903 short novel 'The Jewel of Seven Stars' ("the only thing I'd read by him was *Dracula*") and—like the film-makers—ignorant of the 1971 Hammer version filmed as *Blood from the Mummy's Tomb*, the author was given just two weeks to write the book.

"It was marvellous," he recalled, "I got £2,000 for that. I read the script and pinched a bit from H. Rider Haggard, some from the *Arabian Nights*, and got a story out of it somehow. I found it was ridiculously easy. I also saw the film all by myself and thought it was stupid—why didn't they find an original idea? Anyway, it flopped, so I think I was right. I only found out afterwards it was based on Stoker's book because Arrow's original edition was selling better than my version. However, my book sold 15,000 copies, so Magnum was pleased."

If Chetwynd-Hayes was unhappy with *From Beyond the Grave*, he was even more disappointed with his next foray into the movies.

In 1980 the author was again contacted by Milton Subotsky, who by this time had a new production company, Sword & Sorcery, and wanted to make a horror film for children, based around Ronald's collection *The Monster Club*.

First published in Britain as a paperback original in March 1976 by New English Library, the volume was quickly reprinted in a number of foreign editions around the world. *The Monster Club* consists of five original stories linked by a Prologue, four "Interludes" and an Epilogue based around a dazzling and original array of monstrous creatures who gather in the titular establishment, situated somewhere off Swallow Street in London.

The book was moderately successful at the time, but Chetwynd-Hayes was soon back at work on his novels and compiling various collections and anthologies, and *The Monster Club* didn't get published in hardcover until 1992, when Severn House Publishers brought it out.

As the author points out in his introductory note:

I would like to stress that the Monstreal Table is only intended as a rough guide to the breeding habits of modern monsters. Inter-breeding between primates, secondaries and hybrids is not common, but not unknown. For example, if a *shadmock* should mate with a *vampire*, their issue will be known as a *shadvam*. A *mock* to a *ghoul* would produce a *mocgoo*, and so on.

In the third story I have crossed a *ghoul* with a *human*—or in monstreal parlance, a *hume*—and begat a *humgoo*.

Doubtless if the serious student of monstrumology keeps his eyes open, he will discover many strange mixtures walking about in out public places or strap-hanging in the Underground.

Chetwynd-Hayes readily agreed that he liked to "sit down and think up new monsters," and in case you were wondering what these creatures get up to, he thoughtfully included 'The basic rules of Monsterdom' in the same book:

"Vampires—sup; Werewolves—hunt; Ghouls—tear; Shodies— lick; Maddies—yawn; Mocks—blow; Shadmocks—only whistle."

The author had asked New English Library to revert the rights to *The Monster Club*, and they agreed. Then when Subotsky's Sword & Sorcery Productions announced it would be making a film of the book, the publisher wrote to Chetwynd-Hayes informing him that he would be delighted to hear that they were reissuing *The Monster Club* to tie in with the film. "I wrote back and said, 'Oh no you're not. You're going to give me a new contract and I want £4,000 advance . . .' and after a while they finally gave in."

Despite the all-star cast, with added rock music and humour for children, *The Monster Club* did not do well at the box-office. Chetwynd-Hayes believed he knew why the film was not successful: "There was no control over the adaptation." Scripted by Edward and Valerie Abraham, Chetwynd-Hayes blamed Subotsky for telling them what to write: "Milton Subotsky was the kindest man I ever met," continued the author, "but hates dialogue and should never have made a film. His idea of humour was silly. He had to crack a walnut with a sledgehammer. In *The Monster Club*, he had that business where Richard Johnson gets up out of his coffin and says, 'I was wearing a stake-proof vest', then turns to his wife and says, 'Look, ketchup!' They could have made it much funnier.

"Mind you," added the author, "Milton did me proud—look at the publicity he gave me."

The film was shot at Shepperton Studios and at various locations around Hertfordshire by director Roy Ward Baker. Chetwynd-Hayes visited the set during shooting and met the stars of the film, horror veterans Vincent Price and John Carradine (who was reputedly a replacement for Christopher Lee). "Poor old John Carradine played me in the film," explained the author. "That was Milton's idea of a joke because I had put him into the book as 'Lintom Busotsky', an anagram of his name.

"When I saw Carradine he was seventy-four years old and crippled with arthritis. At the preview, a lady came up to me and said, 'I'm so sorry you suffer from arthritis.' I said, 'I don't, that's John Carradine!'"

Released in 1981 by ITC Entertainment Group, *The Monster Club* starred an impressive supporting cast that included Donald Pleasence (again), Stuart Whitman, Britt Ekland, Simon Ward, Patrick Magee and Anthony Steel. Three of the author's stories were adapted for the film, of which only two—'The Humgoo' and 'The Shadmock'—were included in the original book. ('My Mother Married a Vampire' was in fact taken from a 1978 Chetwynd-Hayes collection.)

About the linking story, he recalled: "Vincent Price played a vampire in *The Monster Club*, and he was good. He was such a nice man, and he would tell me some wonderful stories about Hollywood."

ITC was so confident about the success of the film that they commissioned a thirty-page comic book adaptation, scripted by Dez Skinn and illustrated by John Bolton, to distribute as a promotional item, while New English Library issued a film tie-in paperback with a scene from the movie on the front.

Unfortunately, back in the early 1980s critics and audiences didn't know what to make of a horror film specifically targeted at children (today it constitutes the hugely successful YA or Young Adult sub-genre)—especially one that included some already-outdated songs (from B.A. Robertson, The Pretty Things and UB40, amongst others), not to mention a cartoon stripper who peeled off all her flesh!

In the end, *The Monster Club* was poorly distributed in the UK and was eventually released directly to television in America. However, over the years its reputation has continued to grow, and recent DVD and Blu-ray releases have cemented its position as a cult favourite amongst some viewers.

Another of Chetwynd-Hayes' books, *The Dark Man*, was optioned for filming in 1964, but nothing ever happened. As he explained: "A film producer took me to lunch and offered me £250 for the option—I thought, 'Good Lord, my fortune's made!' He said he'd need about half a million pounds to make the film, Dirk Bogarde would play Wentworth and who did I want as the female lead? So I suggested Mia Farrow, and he agreed. Then nothing happened. He paid his option for a year, then he renewed it, then he renewed it again, and then he dropped it. After *The Monster Club* came out, he started again and gave me three-month options; that went on for a couple of years… When I last spoke to him he said he still hadn't given up."

In *The Dark Man*, Chetwynd-Hayes first introduced readers to the haunted mansion Clavering Grange; he went on to write more than half a dozen other books about the building or the tainted ground on which it stood, spanning the ages from Elizabethan times to the far future. His dream was always for a producer to film *The Clavering Chronicles*: "We can work our way through the centuries then," he pointed out. "It would run for a long time."

In the late 1970s Chetwynd-Hayes began a long and successful relationship with publishing company William Kimber, starting with his first hardcover collection, *The Cradle Demon and Other Stories of Fantasy and Horror*, which he also considered to be one of his best.

Following the publication of *The Cradle Demon*, Chetwynd-Hayes returned to the publisher the following year with a science fiction novel, *The Brats: A Novel of the Future*. "I couldn't write science fiction now," he confessed. "They've got all sorts of complicated stuff." He preferred the Edgar Rice Burroughs school of SF/adventure, which he regarded as good, uncomplicated fantasy. Although he wanted to write a lost world-type yarn himself—his favourite film was the original *King Kong* (1933)—he acknowledged regretfully that there would be no market for it.

Kimber followed *The Brats* with another novel, *The Partaker* (1980), and over the next decade the author produced a further twelve original short story collections for Kimber, aimed principally at the library market in Britain: *Tales of Darkness* (1981; "That sold best, everyone likes that"), *Tales from Beyond* (1982), *Tales from the Other Side* (1983), *A Quiver of Ghosts* (1984), *Tales from the Dark Lands* (1984), *Ghosts from the Mist of Time* (1985), *Tales from the Shadows* (1986), *Tales from the Haunted House* (1986), *Dracula's Children* (1987), *The House of Dracula* (1987) and *Tales of the Hidden World: Four Episodes in the History of Clavering Grange* (1988).

R. Chetwynd-Hayes' stories have been adapted for films, television and radio; he has been published in Britain, America, Scandinavia and Europe (although in Germany they have managed to mistakenly credit him as both "Robert W. Chambers" and "Robert Chetwynd-Hayes"!) but—perhaps not too surprisingly—he was always rather dismissive about fame: "I don't think I have a reputation—who's ever heard of me?" he asked.

The first public acknowledgements of the author's long standing in the horror field came in 1989 when he won both the Horror Writers of America and The British Fantasy Society's Life Achievement awards for his services to the genre. The former gave the author his very first and only trip across the Atlantic, an experience that made almost as much of an impression on him as the accolades of his peers.

As he recalled: "I actually felt the trip across to be excessively boring, because I'd expected to be able to see the sea and all I could see were clouds! I'd even booked a window seat, but all that meant was that I had to climb over two other people every time I wanted to get out. But once I arrived in New York and my agent Cherry Weiner collected me, things improved. Everyone was excessively kind to me, and I thought New York quite a city."

However, when he found out that he had to give a speech at the awards ceremony, he admitted that he was a bit worried: "I made sure I didn't drink anything! I gave my little chat and that seemed to go down quite well, then I collected my award—a lovely thing. But the real point is that I couldn't believe it when they invited me over to the HWA meeting: I thought, 'Why me?' It was a very great honour.

"Of course, I wondered, when they said it was for Lifetime Achievement, whether they meant 'well, it's time to wind up now'; but I said, 'as I'm only thirty-five, the best thing to do is to call it half a Lifetime Achievement and I'd come back in thirty-five years' time to pick up another one!'"

A few months later, the annual British Fantasy Convention was approaching, and Chetwynd-Hayes received a phone call from his long-time friend and colleague Brian Lumley: "He said, 'You will be there, won't you? I shall want you to talk to some friends of mine.' Well, I thought that sounded a little suspicious, but I really didn't think much about it. So there I was, sitting next to Guy N. Smith, and Brian (who was Master of Ceremonies at that year's convention) started announcing the award. He was muttering away, and Guy turned to me and said, 'I believe he's talking about you.' I said, 'No, he can't be!' Then I listened a bit more, and he was! So I had to jump up and get another one—and they're both on my mantel-piece as we speak. I've been in this game so many years and to get two awards—my first two awards—in one year was unbelievable. In fact, they were the only good things that happened."

The 1990s did not begin well for the author. Thanks to William Kimber, Chetwynd-Hayes was building a solid library following in Britain when, hard on the heels of a two-book contract, came the publisher's sudden and unexpected dissolution, followed by an end to his recently revitalised American career.

"Kimber, my publisher for so many years, was marvellous. I never really had time to think about going to anybody else—as soon as one book was finished, they always sent me a commission and an advance for the next. Then they sold out to Thorsons, but that was all right. They gave me a commission for two books and I turned them out. I got the proofs back for *The Curse of the Snake God*, corrected them and all was going fine until I got a call from Amy Myers, my editor, who said, 'Ronald, dreadful news: Thorsons has been bought by Collins and they've cancelled your contract.'

It took the author a couple of years to begin to recover from that blow. Although originally sold to Piatkus, *The Curse of the Snake God* was finally issued under the Inner Circle Books imprint in 1991, while the other book from the Kimber contract, the collection *Shudders and Shivers*, eventually ended up coming out from Robert Hale in 1995.

Chetwynd-Hayes was always proud of the fact that each year he was one of the highest earners of the annual Public Lending Right (PLR), based on the number of times an author's books are loaned out from libraries in the UK.

"It was all looking pretty miserable a few months ago," he admitted. "I used to do very well in libraries: I have eighteen books available and I normally get around £1,000 a year from the public lending rate, so obviously a lot of people read me still. I keep talking about trying to move into the 'Stephen King market'—one of those colossal books—but I never get the time to start on it. I'd do anything that paid the biggest money.

"As far as America is concerned, it's a strange situation. Tor bought two books, *The Grange* (a re-titling of *The King's Ghost*) and *The Other Side*, and it looked as if they weren't selling very well at all. Then suddenly, I got a cheque through the post for American royalties over and above my advance. They weren't my first sales in America—that was my novel, *The Dark Man*—but they were my first in recent years. I've just heard that Zebra is going to reissue *The Dark Man* (as *And Love Survived*), but I don't get a penny as I'm still working off the unearned advance from last time around!

"The Tor books are obviously selling through, albeit slowly. I'd like to get another American publisher, as Tor has such a tremendous back-log that they are not taking any more books on. At least now I've got some hope again, with a new British publisher and proof of some US sales, however small."

Unfortunately, that much hoped-for resurgence in his career never happened. Except for a mostly retrospective collection, *The Vampire Stories of R. Chetwynd-Hayes*, which appeared from the small press imprint Fedogan & Bremer in 1997, and a pair of posthumous anthologies drawn from *The Fontana Book of Great Ghost Stories* series and compiled by Stephen Jones for Carroll & Graf in the early 2000s, that was the end of Chetwynd-Hayes' career in America.

Shocks, a four-story chapbook, was issued by The British Fantasy Society in 1997 to commemorate his appearance as a Special Guest of Honour at the 1997 World Fantasy Convention in London's Docklands; apart from that, Robert Hale remained the author's main book publisher in Britain for the rest of his career. Hale not only reprinted *The Vampire Stories of R. Chetwynd-Hayes* in 1998 under its original title, *Looking for Something to Suck and Other Vampire Stories* (which the US publisher had considered too racy!), it also issued two further— predominantly reprint—collections of the author's work.

There is no doubt that, later in his career, Chetwynd-Hayes began to slow down. Although he thought some of his stories from this period "not half bad", he also considered himself to be a lazy writer: "Writing a novel is far simpler than writing a collection of short stories—you've only got one plot. Edgar Wallace said, 'A novel is a lazy man's short story—any writer worth his salt can write a novel in a weekend'". When pressed on how long he took to write a novel, he replied with a smile, "A little longer than a weekend..."

Towards the end of his life R. Chetwynd-Hayes was beset with health problems, which eventually resulted in him having to go into a care home in Teddington in May 2000, where he died of bronchial pneumonia on March 20th 2001, less than a year later. He was 81 years old.

As with most authors, he always liked to believe that he was writing for posterity and hoped his stories would continue to appear, to entertain new generations after his death, but he was also worried that, "It's only a dream—I'll be forgotten... There's a story in *Ghosts from the Mist of Time* where an author stumbles and falls, gets up, and he's someone else 200 years hence. There he finds his works have been turned into a new Bible, a religion has been based on his fiction...

"That must be the dream of everyone who writes, mustn't it? I like to think I'm writing for the future: there's just a chance, with hardbacks of short stories, that in 100 years' time someone putting an anthology together will find one of my old stories on a bookstall and slip it in because there are no copyright problems. And so I shall live again.

In that respect, I suppose being a writer is very much like being a vampire.

"I shall never know whether it happens or not—or perhaps I will...? The truth is, I don't really know what the future holds for me. I'll just keep churning the books out like I always have, and hope they fill a vacuum somewhere. I think I have to write, even if nobody published it now. It's my life."

HOUSEBOUND

HE, IF INDEED that which remained of Charlie Wheatland could be designated as he, was most happy when he was in the woodwork. The wainscoting, the picture rails, the large wardrobe, the dressing-table, and sometimes the floorboards; the coarse-grained pine, the tough oak, enabled him to spread out, to become as water on blotting paper, to dim down his never sleeping consciousness to a gentle twilight. The walls were not so kind, the bricks and plaster did not absorb him so easily, and the thoughts of the room's occupants clung to the faded wallpaper like flies on a hot day. A certain measure of peace was to be found during the daylight hours when the bedroom was empty, and he could roll out across the woodwork in soft invisible waves and not be disturbed by the mental vibrations of living people. The man did not disturb him much, although his harsh passions sometimes seared Charlie's consciousness like a white hot knife, but the woman was a magnet that drew him towards her and some form of grotesque life. Charlie hated and feared her; the powerful raw power reached out tentacles that found him no matter where he might hide. Like a mouse chased by a cat he fled before them, sometimes drawing himself up into a tight ball, at others, spreading himself over every square inch of room and furniture, quelling the urge to submit and allow the power to make of him what it would. "I want to be nothing," the sobbing cry sometimes made itself heard in the form of a deep sigh, and the woman would pause in the midst of bed-making and look fearfully over one shoulder, "I want to forget, to sleep—to sleep."

"Surely you know," said Mrs. Hardcastle sipping her tea in a most lady-like fashion, "I mean the estate agent should have told you before actually selling you the house."

"Not a word," Celia Cooper breathed deeply and wondered when the woman would leave. She knew that her visitor's bright little eyes were valuing the furniture to the exact penny, and mentally noting her personal defects as to dress and hair style. "You see we were so pleased to get finally settled, you know what it's like trying to find a decent house at a reasonable price?"

"Do I not, dear," Mrs. Hardcastle waved her free hand and with practised skill balanced the tea cup with the other. "The trouble Arthur and I had before we found "Quiet Haven," but all said and done, the man should have told you."

"What is the story?" Celia did her best to sound interested, but she could imagine what was coming. A previous tenant who had loved well but unwisely; an outwardly respectable clerk who had absconded with the contents of his employer's safe; or perhaps something more sordid. She had long since discovered that the sins and misfortunes of the few give much joy to the many.

"My dear," Mrs. Hardcastle's eyes shone with pleasurable horror, "a man was shot dead in this house, in your front bedroom."

Celia Cooper did not move, refused to allow a single muscle to betray her, but the naked fear was now out in the open.

She said calmly:

"How terrible, was it—murder?"

"Not exactly. It all happened ten years ago, just after this estate was built, I'm surprised you don't remember the details, they were in all the newspapers."

"You forget," Celia managed to smile, "until last month Harold and I had not set foot in England for fifteen years."

"Of course," Mrs. Hardcastle tittered behind her hand, "how silly of me. Well, he was a little crook, the man that was shot, I mean, called

Charlie Wheatland, and he held up the bank in the High Street. He shot a clerk who managed to push the alarm button or whatever it is they do push, and made his getaway chased by a police car. They finally got him pinned down in this road, and he took cover in this very house which was empty as the builders had only moved out the previous day. There was a terrific gun battle which lasted for hours, until a police marksman got a bead on him from the house opposite. They found him in your front bedroom with a hole in his head. My dear, you've gone quite pale, I shouldn't have told you, but really, I did think you ought to know."

"Please don't mind me," Celia smiled again, "but it is rather a shock to find out your house was once the scene of a violent death. I gather this notoriety did not stop the house being sold, I mean it hasn't stood empty these past ten years?"

"Good heavens, no," Mrs. Hardcastle put down her cup and started to pull on a pair of black lace gloves, "Mr. and Mrs. Dowsett lived here until Mr. Dowsett was killed in a motor accident. Mind you, Jane did say to me on one occasion she never really felt happy in that front bedroom. But that's to be expected, I mean when one knows what happened there . . . Oh, how tactless of me, I do hope you won't . . ."

"I won't give it another thought," lied Celia, "I have no time to spare to worry about ghosts. Must you leave so soon, it has been nice meeting you . . ."

"Harold," Celia looked at her husband seated on the other side of the dining-room table, "did you know a man had been shot dead in this house?"

Harold Cooper put down his soup spoon and watched his wife with an appreciative eye as she took the plates of roast lamb from the heated food trolley. "Yes, I knew. The chap at the estate agents told me when I bought the place. I didn't see any point in telling you, it might have put you off, and I believe that what the ear doesn't hear, the mind doesn't worry over. Who told you?"

"A neighbour, a Mrs. Hardcastle. She paid me a visit this afternoon, superficially to make my acquaintance, but in reality I suspect to see what we had, and estimate its cost."

"Big mouthed old hussy," Harold grunted. "Well, now you know. I shouldn't let it worry you. Someone was bound to die in the house sooner or later; we shall probably die here ourselves one day. The manner of dying isn't all that important, the main thing is the little rat did die. It's a pity a lot more of his kind don't come to the same end. Shoot the lot, I say, there's too much moddle-coddling of these young thugs."

Celia said: "Yes, dear, you have mentioned the matter on various occasions," and then steered the conversation into more mundane channels until the time came for her to clear the table and wash up in the stainless steel and Formica panelled kitchen. When she had finished her work and hung the wiping up towel on the telescopic towel rail, she returned to the living-room and found Harold watching television, but not she noted with any great interest, for his head was already drooping and it would not be long before he was prone in his seat with fast closed eyes and gaping mouth. Celia turned off the set and took up a book, and every once in a while glanced at her sleeping husband. After twenty-five years of married life together she knew him as well as any one human being knows another; if she were attacked by a gang of thugs he would fight to defend her, even to the sacrifice of his life; if she were in some sort of trouble, no matter how dreadful, he would help her, for Harold was above all a husband, and she was his wife. But supposing she were threatened by a danger inconceivable to his practical turn of mind; if she were now to wake him and cry: "There is a—something in our bedroom, something horrible, wicked and pathetic, that torments me, floods my mind with unspeakable horror, fascinates me, please let us move away from here." He would, after the initial surprise, talk of tonics, rundown, pop along and see the old quack, and if she persisted, his thin lips would set in a straight obstinate line, and he would point out this was a good house in a nice neighbourhood, it suited him, he had done a lot of work on it, and be damned if he was going to move because of her hysteria and imagination. His unimaginative logic would become an iron wall, and if she continued to fight him, something vital in their marriage would die, to be replaced by fear, mistrust and finally hatred. This was one battle she must fight by herself, try to decide what was fact and how much of this terror was due to imagination. Of late Celia had come to believe that there was no such things as imagination, only fact viewed from different angles; what was life but a series of coloured lights reflected on a white screen.

"Harold," she called softly, "wake up."

"What's the matter?" he started and blinked foolishly, looking like a grey-haired schoolboy, "must have dozed off."

"You'll never sleep tonight," she smiled indulgently, "would you like a hot drink?"

"If you like," he yawned as she rose and went into the kitchen.

She lay beside Harold in the large double bed and listened to the even tempo of his breathing. He slept so deeply, encased in a cocoon of unconsciousness from which it would take five minutes of shaking to rouse him. She tried to keep her thoughts under control and not to let them wander round the darkened room, seeking, prodding, even as a mischievous child might goad a sleeping snake, aware of the danger, but drawn to that danger like a moth who must fly into a lighted candle.

He had spread himself out, along the wainscoting, over the wardrobe, into the dressing-table; a thin layer of whimpering, hate-streaked fear. Without being aware that she had exerted any effort, Celia found she had driven him out of the dressing-table, made him retreat from the wardrobe; now he flowed up the walls; she knew he hated the walls and pursued him relentlessly, and all the while her body shook with sickening horror. Now came the climax; she must change her tactics, draw him towards the bed and make him become a ball of pulsating life. He came, fighting every inch of the way; but he came, the walls and the woodwork were free, and he was there, on the floor at the foot of the bed. Celia shivered with intense cold as the power drained out of her, but there was no going back; whatever it was that crouched on the floor mingled with the life force that flowed from her body and grew into something tangible, rising slowly into view. The window curtains were drawn back and the top sash was open, for Harold had insisted that fresh air was essential in a bedroom, allowing the street lamp to light the room with a soft radiance. He was a black shadow that bore a rough resemblance to a masculine shape; the shoulders appeared to be bowed, a kind of oafish slouch, and Celia thought she could define the pale outlines of a face, but that may have been due to imagination. A whisper came to her, or so she at the time believed, although afterwards it seemed more likely that she translated some mental communication into sound.

"What do you want of me?"

It was then that Celia Cooper came face to face with truth; it came hand in hand with knowledge and stood beside the black shadow, and of the two truth was the more fearful.

"*What do you want of me?*" She knew why she had summoned this thing from the woodwork, why week after week she had developed the power, which until they had moved into this house she did not suspect she possessed. Celia Cooper, the placid, commonplace housewife of fifty was akin to Charlie Wheatland who had died in this room ten years ago. At that moment she could only think of the man who slept by her side; could only remember the dreadful boring years, his selfishness, his lack of imagination, his exasperating common sense; the fact that she had never consciously realised the extent of these shortcomings before, or knew how much she despised, even hated him for them, made this moment all the more terrifying—truth was relentless, more exciting. It was though she had been blind from birth and now saw for the first time. The fear dropped away like a dark heavy mantle, and a great sense of power flooded her being. Sitting up in bed she pointed to the sleeping form of her husband and cried in a loud voice:

"Kill him, make him as you are—kill him."

The figure moved slowly round the bed, grew more tangible until Celia could have sworn a living man was preparing to obey her command; then she saw the white little face, the blazing black eyes and screamed with renewed terror:

"No, I didn't mean it."

The figure stopped, turned his face to her, then disintegrated. Celia collapsed back onto her pillow and knew no more until the alarm roused her in the morning.

No one can say he or she is good or virtuous until they have been made to face temptation and found the strength to resist. Celia Cooper had never been tempted before; she never felt the urge to commit adultery; having always been blessed with sufficient money for her simple needs, there was no temptation to steal, and murder was a crime committed by depraved creatures who were beyond a middle class housewife's comprehension. This was still true; Celia could no more have physically murdered her husband than she could have set fire to her own house. But this was different, murder by necromancy was not by the laws of the realm murder at all. Celia fought her temptation; it was a battle that raged minute by minute, hour by hour, day by day, and worst of all night by night. As she lay beside the sleep drunk Harold the urge to summon that vile creature in the woodwork was nigh irresistible. The knowledge that it would obey her will overcame the loathing and terror, and made her realise in full her hatred for Harold, which once it had revealed itself grew rather than diminished as time passed. Celia could feel her character changing in the same way a man who has contracted a fatal disease can watch his body disintegrating, she could do nothing to slow down the process, let alone kill it. She toyed with the idea of running away; but where would she go, what could she do at her time of life? She had neither the ability nor the urge to earn her own living, whereas if Harold were to suddenly die she would find herself in very easy circumstances. His life was insured for a considerable sum, and despite their simple mode of living he had a respectable fortune in gilt-edged securities; there was also the widow's pension that the oil company for whom he had worked for over thirty years would pay her. Once this unwanted spouse was safely in the grave she could move far away and live under a golden umbrella.

Perhaps she might have successfully fought her battle, if not for ever, at least for a long time, had she not one afternoon walked into the bedroom and found Charlie Wheatland fully materialised and standing by the window. So accustomed had she grown to living with this horror, she felt no fear, only surprise as to how he came to be there. She had not consciously summoned him, and could only suppose that having once been called up he had waxed strong on his own account, or fed surreptitiously on her power, possibly while she slept. He turned slowly, his white face a mask of fear and hate, then whispered:

"When?"

Celia stood perfectly still and tried to absorb the knowledge that her eyes witnessed, and at the same time come to terms with the warning bells that were ringing in her brain. Would she be able to control this creature? If he were capable of murdering Harold, what of her? The apparition answered her unspoken question.

"You give me strength, without you I have no substance."

"But," Celia's thoughts were cold as steel, "suppose Harold were to . . . linger?"

Charlie Wheatland's lips did not move but the words came in a low, distinctive whisper.

"Only bad men are housebound."

"But what of me," Celia asked the all-important question, "when my time comes . . . ?"

There was a suggestion of a smile on the white face. "Can you not repent—afterwards?"

The last barrier collapsed and Celia breathed a deep sigh of relief, she surrendered completely to the great temptation that had dominated her for weeks, now she could face truth without flinching. Murder could be committed without fear of detection; she wondered how Harold's death would appear; heart failure possibly, and there need be no price to pay. As the phantom said, she could always repent afterwards.

"Tonight," she thought the answer to his first question, "must I be present?"

"No." The black eyes glittered with a joyful light. "But you must order me to do it."

"I order you to kill my husband."

"No, I cannot kill, only free your husband from his body. Order me to free your husband from his body."

"I order you to free my husband from his body."

Something essential went out of Celia as her mind formed these last words, she would have retained it if that had been possible, but it was too late, the fatal step had been taken, and now she stood face to face with her familiar, and knew that repentance was but a word; she must accept this new world where evil reigned supreme. There was pride in her voice when she said aloud:

"I will send him to you this evening."

She went out closing the bedroom door behind her.

The evening passed much the same as twenty-five years of evenings had passed, only this was the last one. Celia watched Harold eat his steak and kidney pie, served him the college pudding he liked so much, then washed up and put the dishes away neatly in the built-in dresser, and all the time she could feel the presence of the thing that lurked in the bedroom. Was it still standing by the window, the very window where its body had been destroyed ten years ago? Or was it resting in the woodwork, waiting for her summons; waiting for Harold to walk into the room?

Harold was sleeping in front of the television, his usual evening prelude to the nightly feast of sleeping; soon he would wallow in sleep; not the snorting, gasping sleep that had so often disturbed her rest, but a dignified cold repose that all the alarm clocks in the world would never break.

The hands of the clock slowly made their endless journey round the white dial; the television relayed its canned trivial entertainment, until Celia turned it off. Her hand was gentle as it shook Harold's shoulder, and her voice was that of a kind, indulgent mother.

"Harold, it's time for bed, wake up or you'll never sleep tonight."

"Wassat!" He opened his eyes, blinked and looked at the clock. "Ten o'clock, must have dozed off."

She made the cocoa and sat opposite as he sipped from his cup, talking of what he must do tomorrow, but his words made little impression upon her. She could feel the thing stirring in the room above.

"Time for bed-de-byes," he rose, stretched, then yawned, "coming, old girl?"

"In a moment, you go up, I'll be with you in a moment."

"Right," he walked heavily from the room, "don't be long, must be up bright and early tomorrow."

As he left the room she wanted to cry out, to take him by the hand and run from this house never to return, but even as her mouth opened she felt the power drain out of her. She sank into a chair unable to speak or move a muscle; the thing upstairs was building himself up, gathering strength for the supreme effort. She heard Harold climbing the stairs; he went into the bathroom and after a lapse of time pulled the lavatory chain, there was a roar of cascading water, then he crossed the landing, and opened the bedroom door.

"Forgive me, God forgive me," Celia was praying in a loud whisper, tears streaming down her face, "forgive me, don't let it happen . . ."

A loud scream pinned her back against the chair; a cry of indescribable terror followed by a crash that made the ceiling lamp swing gently from side to side, and light danced with shadows in a mad frenzy of horror. The power flowed back into her limbs, and Celia knew Charlie Wheatland no longer needed her strength, perhaps, this one terrible deed performed, he was now free to descend into the Hell from which he had so long been detained, or possibly he was now in some limbo where time and human values were without meaning. Whatever the reason, she could not feel his presence either in the room above or in any part of the house. She sat motionless, trying to accept the fact that Harold lay dead on the bedroom floor, killed by terror and his wife's mad, unsuspected hatred. She could not move, had not the strength or courage to ascend the stairs, only sit and realise that from now onwards she belonged to the damned.

The clock in the hall broke the silence by striking two, and as though this were a signal, Celia heard a sound from the bedroom above. The creak of loose floorboard, the slightly louder sound of a heavy body climbing to its feet, then a slow creak crossing the carpeted room; slippered feet moving out onto the landing; a banister groaning its protest when a hand pressed upon it, a loose stair rod rattling; a terrible harsh breathing growing louder by the second; Celia knew Harold was coming down. At first she experienced a sense of great relief, he was not dead, she was not a murderess; then she realised the foot treads were not Harold's; the harsh breathing was that of a man who has not breathed for a long time; whatever, whoever was coming down the stairs, it was not Harold.

She could not tear her eyes away from the closed door, for surely approaching it from the other side was a horror that rightfully belonged to some dark valley in Hades, and it was coming in to her. She tried to scream when the door handle turned, for to scream would let out some of the icy fear, but the vocal cords froze and no sound came; she clawed at the chair arms as the door swung slowly open, then became still as a corpse, only her eyes and ears continued to function. The body was Harold's, his face dead white, his arms hanging loosely; but the eyes burned with blazing hate, and the laboured breathing turned into rasping speech as he approached the armchair.

"Why couldn't you leave me alone—there was peace in the wood-work—peace . . ."

She found her voice and screamed once as the thing moved in, its arms outstretched.

THE GATECRASHER

SOMEONE SAID, "LET'S hold a séance," and someone else said, "Let's," and five minutes later they were all seated round a table. There was a lot of giggling, and any amount of playing footsie under the table, and it is possible that the entire idea might have collapsed if it had not been for Edward Charlton.

He was a tall, thin youth, with a hungry intense expression that is often peculiar to young men who embrace some burning cause. He had long-fingered hands that were never still, and his ears, which were rather large, stuck out like miniature wings.

"I say." No one paid much attention so he raised his voice, "I say, let's treat the matter seriously."

This had not been the original intention, and everyone looked at him with astonishment.

"I mean to say," he cleared his throat, "if one is going to do this kind of thing, one should do it properly."

Normally he would have been laughed down, but they were in his flat, and good manners, or what passed for good manners in that company, demanded the host be given some freedom in his choice of entertainment.

"What do we do?" asked a blonde girl.

"We all hold hands." He waited for the ribald comments to die down, then went on. "So as to form an unbroken circle. Yes, and I'll turn all the lights out except the table lamp."

They sat in the semi-gloom holding hands, and the occasional giggle was more an expression of uneasiness than one of merriment. Edward felt more confident now the lighting had been subdued, and his voice stronger.

"You must empty your minds," he instructed.

"That won't be difficult for some of us," a voice remarked.

"Then," Edward went on, "we must concentrate all our powers on the spirit world."

The young man cursed when a feeble wit asked: "Whisky or gin?", but nobody bothered to laugh.

"Now concentrate," Edward ordered.

They all obeyed him in their different ways, but an undisciplined mind is like a wild stallion when subjected to restraint. Under Edward's continued bombardment of whispered "Concentrate"s, several minds tried to chain thought, but mental pictures manifested in the void, and the senses would not be muted. Hand could feel hand, ears heard the sound of breathing; eyes saw the shaded table lamp; smell sipped at a whiff of perfume, and imagination was never idle.

"Is there anyone here?" asked Edward in a stage whisper.

"Only us chickens," the humorous one could not help himself, and now several voices ordered him to belt up.

"If anyone is there, come in," Edward invited, "don't be afraid—come in."

There was an ungrateful silence; the blonde girl shivered and tightened her grip on her neighbour's hand. Presently the shiver ran round the entire circle, passed from hand to hand, up arms, down legs, leaving behind a paralysing coldness. Consciousness fled, and was replaced by dreams.

Edward walked in the footsteps of a tall man; a great towering figure dressed in a black coat and matching broad-brimmed hat. The man stopped, then turned, and Edward looked upon the lean dark face, the deep sunken eyes, the jutting beak of a nose; the coat fell open revealing a row of knives stuck in a black belt. He heard the distant sound of carriage wheels, and tasted the bitter fog.

The room was like an ice chamber; the table lamp dimmed down to an orange glimmer, and the room was full of fog, and all around him he could hear the moans of his companions. Slowly, the fog lifted, rose to the ceiling and gradually dispersed, and the coldness went as the lamp grew brighter. Edward looked at the faces of his companions with astonishment that gradually merged into horror. It was as though they had all gone to sleep with their eyes open. The blonde girl had fallen back in her chair and was moaning as though in great pain; one young man had his face twisted up into a snarling grimace, another was opening and closing his hands while staring with unseeing eyes at the overmantel mirror. Edward whispered, "Stop messing about," but without much conviction; then he rose, went over to the wall switch and flooded the room with light. They all returned to the land of the living shortly afterwards.

The mass exodus began some five minutes later; no one said much, but eyes accused Edward of some unspeakable crime; a violation, an act of indecency, an unpardonable breach of human behaviour that was beyond normal reproach.

The last man to go out of the front door looked back at Edward with scornful, but at the same time, fearful eyes.

"I wouldn't be you, brother," he said, "not for all the tea in China."

He slammed the door, and Edward was left alone.

His bed stood on a dais situated in the centre of the far wall of his sitting room; during the day it was surrounded by a curtain, but at night he drew this back and by raising his head could see the entire room. As he lay on the bed and put out his hand to turn off the bedside lamp, the fear came to him, and he wondered, in the revealing moment, why it had not come before.

The fear was at first without form. It was just black, unreasoning terror, and he shrank back against his pillow and tried to see beyond the circle of light cast by his lamp. Then he knew. He was afraid of the dark. He lay awake all that night with the light on.

The next day was spent in anticipation of the night which must follow, and when he finally put his key into the lock and opened his front door there was a sense of fearful expectancy. But his flat was empty, was almost irritatingly normal, and he experienced a strange feeling of disappointment. As he ate a solitary meal before the artificial electric log fire, and later tried to read a book, his mind circled the canker of fear, like a bird flying round a snake. He toyed with the idea of going out; perhaps staying the night at a hotel. But this fear took him to the borderline of insanity. If he were to leave the flat, he would be haunted by the knowledge it was empty; his imagination would picture what was moving among his furniture; if his body slept, then surely his soul would return here and bring back some macabre memory to the waking brain.

He did not intend to fall asleep, but he had been awake the entire previous night, and unconsciousness smothered him unawares so he did not hear the book fall from his lax fingers. The icy cold woke him. The limb-freezing, hair-raising chill, and the wild thumping of his heart. He choked, cleared the bitter bile from his throat, gripped the arms of his chair, cried out like a frightened child as his sitting room door opened, then closed with a resounding slam. The overhead electric lamp trembled slightly, then began to swing to and fro, making a pattern of light circles dance a mad reel across the room. He looked up at the swaying lamp, and as though it had been caught out in some childish prank it suddenly became still; his gaze moved across the ceiling and travelled down to the overmantel mirror, then stopped. A man's face was staring at him out of the mirror.

A face that was long, lean, and dark. The sunken eyes, glittering pools of darkness, stared down at the shrinking figure and betrayed no emotion. Indeed, the entire face was a blank mask; the eyes moved, studied the room with the same unreasoning stare, then looked down again. The thin lips parted, and Edward read the soundless word.

"Come."

Like a sleepwalker, he rose and walked to the mirror.

Greek Street mumbled in the half sleep that falls upon Soho in the small hours. The after-theatre crowds had long since finished their late dinner and gone home; now only the night-club revellers, or more likely, seekers of esoteric entertainment, still moved like maundering snails along the pavement, glancing hopefully into darkened doorways, or looking upwards at lighted windows.

The girl came upon Edward suddenly. She materialised out of a shop doorway and gripped his arm, while gazing up at him with an air of one who has just stumbled upon an old and extremely dear friend.

"Hullo, darling, how nice to see you again."

One blue-painted lid closed in an expressive wink, and that part of Edward's brain that still worked took in the words, the expression, and the wink, then came to a decision.

"Let's start walking, darling." The full red lips scarcely parted, and the blue eyes were never still.

"You never know when a bloody copper is going to poke his nose round the corner."

"Let's walk," said Edward in a flat voice.

She took his arm, and together they walked along the pavement. The girl gave Edward a calculating sideways glance. "Like to come to my place, darling? Five quid and no hurry."

"I would like you to come to my place," said Edward.

"How far?" Now there was a hint of suspicion in her voice.

"Off the Edgware Road."

"Rather a long way. Have to make it worth my while."

"Shall we say thirty pounds?" Edward suggested.

Next time the girl spoke her voice sounded like a cash register.

"You a pussy, dear?"

"A pussy?"

"Yes, pussy—cat—do you go in for the rough stuff? If you do, count me out. I've got me other clients to think about. In any case I'd want more than thirty pounds."

Edward chuckled and the girl frowned. "Nothing like that. Just your company."

She relaxed. "All right then. Ten pound down in the taxi, and the rest when we say goodbye. Okay?"

"Okay," said Edward.

He opened his front door and, after turning on the hall light, stood aside for her to enter. Despite the carefully applied make up, tell-tale lines marred her face, and the muscles under her chin sagged slightly; the brash metallic blonde hair was brittle, while her calves were plump and streaked with extended veins. He helped her take off the light blue coat, noting with cold detachment the short, sleeveless, and very low cut black dress. He then guided her through the sitting room door and she gasped with pretend, or perhaps genuine, delight at the cosy surroundings.

"You are nice and comfy." She wriggled her bottom, and the action made her suddenly grotesque, and a mirthless grin parted his lips. "Do you thing I could have a little drinkie?"

"Of course." He walked over to the sideboard. "Whisky all right?"

"Luvely." She rubbed her well-corseted stomach. "Nothing like a drop of the hard stuff to turn me on."

He poured a generous helping of whisky into two glasses, then carried them over to the sofa where she sprawled, displaying a large amount of not particularly appetising leg. She gulped down the neat spirit with experienced ease, then glanced suggestively over one shoulder.

"I see you've got everything handy. Curtains and all. This is quite a treat after my place, and you know how to treat a girl. I always like dealing with gentlemen. At one time I had an extensive refined clientele, if you follow me. No riff-raff. But times are hard now, what with the Squeeze, and the Wolfenden Report, and all. Thank you, darling, perhaps I will have another. Tell me, have you anything special in mind?"

Edward's eyes were cold, devoid of expression.

"Yes," he said, "something very special."

"Well," she shrugged, "with one or two of these inside me, perhaps I won't mind. But I'll have to put my fee up." She suddenly shivered. "Strike a light, it's bloody cold in here."

He backed slowly to the window bay; an alcove lined with dark red curtains, and so masked with shadow the outward edge of a small mahogany table could only just be seen. With his eyes still fixed upon her face, Edward walked slowly backwards until he was stopped by the table; he reached back with his right hand and took something from it. Slowly he bought it out and the overhead lamp reflected its light on the steel blade. The woman, her wits dulled with whisky, giggled softly.

"Oh no, dear, not knives. I mean, there's a limit . . . "

Edward came out from the window bay, the knife clasped firmly in his right hand, and behind him strode a second figure. A tall, dark man, with a bitter lean face, his eyes masked by the shadow of his broad-brimmed hat; together they crept forward, the tall man's hands resting on Edward's shoulders. Their legs worked in unison. Breast to back, thighs to buttocks, legs to legs; the tall man's chin rested on Edward's head, and while his face was white, devoid of emotion, the stranger's lips parted in a joyous, anticipatory smile, his eyes gleamed with unholy joy, and his hands pressed down on his partner's shoulders, steering him . . .

"Gawd," the woman was sober now, and half-rose from the sofa, "not two of you . . . ?"

The tall man's eyes willed her to silence, forced her back on to the sofa, where she lay like a plump broken doll with a wide open mouth and glazed eyes. The four-legged, two-headed monster now stood over her; the two pairs of eyes, one cold, blue, dead fish, the other, black, glittering, stared down. Then the tall man raised his hand, and Edward raised his knife. The stranger's thin lips moved, and from between the tightly clenched teeth came one hissing word.

"Now."

Edward's hand flashed down—then up, then down, then up, then down, until the gleaming knife blade was an unbroken streak of red-blotched silver light.

There was blood everywhere, but no body.

Once the curtains had been pulled back and the early morning light flooded the room, his eyes refused to be deceived. There was a dark ominous stain covering the sofa and most of the surrounding carpet. In some places the stains were lighter in colour as though they had been scrubbed in a futile effort to remove them. His suit hung in front of the electric fire, shrunken and creased; it was still damp, and although it had clearly been washed, ugly dark stains darkened the coat front and trousers. His grey waistcoat was like a screwed-up house flannel, and his shirt was missing. He went up close to the overmantel mirror until his reflection filled it.

"Why?"

There was blood in his hair. His face and body had been washed, but the subconscious, or whatever had controlled his body during the dark hours, had not considered shampoo.

"How?"

That one was easy. In the bathroom he found a clean carving knife with blood-stained towel next to it; the subconscious had not bothered to empty the bath either. The water was pink, red-rimmed and foul; his missing shirt floated on the surface like the upturned belly of a dead fish.

"Where?"

That was indeed the master question. Where was the body that had given forth such a profusion of blood? He stumbled from room to room, searched the six-by-eight kitchen, even looked under the bed, opened cupboards; it took him a full five minutes to summon up the courage to open the blanket chest, but he did not find a body. His terror became flecked with anger, and he glared at the mirror.

"Where?" he hissed the word, "where did you hide it?" and instantly there came to him a thought. Maybe the victim had not died, but had managed to escape. If so, why had not the police paid him a visit long since? He went out to the landing, examined the banisters, stair carpet, even the hall door. There was no sign of blood.

He was about to open the front door when he realised he was still dressed in pyjamas, and the sound of the postman mounting the steps made him scurry back to his top floor flat. He dressed quickly, then like an unhappy ghost went out to haunt the city.

He walked all day. The sunlight burnt up the hours like a fire devouring the last frail barricade, and night was sending forth its first dark spears when sheer weariness forced him to come to rest, and enter a workman's café. The table at which he sat was situated by a mirror; a long oblong frame with its surface misty with steam, flyblown, and in some places the quicksilver had become blurred, but it still cast a reflection.

His coffee had grown cold, and the food on his plate congealed when that familiar face looked at him out of the mirror. He tried not to look into the eyes; made one futile effort to rise from his chair, then the great coldness froze him, and slowly his head came up, and then round.

The thin lips moved, and Edward did not have to read the word.

She was young this time, and walked with pathetic bravado along the pavement, swinging her cheap green handbag with childlike abandon, and recklessly eyeing the men who passed.

The tall young man with a white drawn face stepped out of the shadows, and the girl slowed her pace, and looked back over one shoulder.

"You a nosy?"

Her voice had a north-country accent, and her grey eyes, in that pitifully young, grossly over made up face, were hard. Like chips of grey flint.

"If you mean, am I a policeman, the answer is no."

"Oh, la-de-da," she relaxed and moved towards him, her hips swinging in what she considered to be a seductive walk. "Are you lonely, then? Looking for a friend, then?"

"You look as if you need one."

She eyed him up and down with some distaste. "You're not down on yer luck, are you? I mean, you've got some of the ready? I mean I don't do it for peanuts."

The young man smiled and took out his pocket book. The girl's eyes widened when she saw the thick wad of bank notes, and her smile flashed on like a neon sign.

"Oh, well," she patted her Elizabeth Taylor hair do, "looks as if this is my lucky night."

The young man nodded gravely. "It is indeed."

For the first time the girl betrayed signs of embarrassment.

"Look, have you got a car? Or maybe a place nearby? You see I haven't been in Fogsville long, and me landlady ain't a regular, if you get my meaning. She won't stand for anything."

"I was going to suggest you came back to my place. It's not very far."

She took his arm and he looked down at the bright red finger nails; the hand was small, plump, and not over clean; her false eyelashes were long, and stuck out like black spikes.

"We'll get a taxi," he said.

The flat looked like a well-furnished slaughter-house. There was blood everywhere; the bedclothes were sopping wet, again there had been a futile effort at washing; the old stains on the carpet were overlaid with fresh ones; blurred red fingerprints stood out on the pale blue emulsion paint on one wall; there were even red spots on the ceiling. Another ruined suit hung before the electric fire.

Edward stood against the door and surveyed the macabre scene with curious detachment. He was shocked to find his feeling of terrified disgust was less strong than yesterday. It was as though his senses were numb; his brain seemed to have absorbed its full capacity of horror, and now was willing to view the outrageous rationally. Terror, black dread, still smarting under the first healing skin, but it was just bearable. Tomorrow—next time—the pain would be less, and one day, perhaps when the room was a red cavern, and he paced a squelching carpet, there would be a strange peace that comes with normality.

For the second time—was it only the second time?—there was no body. At least almost no body. In the bathroom he caught a glimpse of his white, unshaven face; three long scratches curved down over one cheek. Three red lines that scarcely broke the skin, save in one place, just a little to the left of his mouth. A small fragment was embedded in the flesh. He pulled it out and stared down at the sliver of fingernail; it still retained traces of bright red lacquer, and the horror flared up, burnt away the healed scab, and gave him a brief moment of sanity.

"I must confess," he shouted the words, ran into his tiny hall and screamed defiance. "I'll give myself up. I'll make them lock me away."

The tall figure came out of the kitchen and moved towards him. The deep sunken eyes glared their awful anger from under the broad-brimmed hat, and the lips were stretched back in a mirthless grin.

"Never again," Edward was whispering now, a harsh madman's whisper, "I'll bring the police up here. I'll let them see it all . . . "

He stopped short as the gaunt head slowly moved from side to side. The voice spoke and his ears heard the word it uttered.

"Mine."

"I'm not yours. Not—not—not . . . "

The words came slowly, with great effort.

"Life—I—now—walk—in—daylight."

The teeth parted and he saw the black nothingness beyond. Then the laughter came, hollow, punctuated by silent pauses, like a faulty radio.

"Ha—ha—ha..."

He covered his ears with shaking hands, but the laughter echoed round the limitless caverns of his skull; then the figure was gone, and the laughter was his. Hollow, madman's laughter, that the walls absorbed, the very air contained, and whose vibrations still throbbed long after he had sunk to the floor in merciful oblivion.

The days passed and became weeks. In the world outside questions were being asked, but without great concert, for no mutilated bodies had been found and there were many reasons why a prostitute might find it good policy to disappear.

One person was perturbed, but for a different reason. Mr. Hulbert Jeffries stood on the landing outside Edward's flat and gently pressed the bell push. He waited for a few moments then pressed again. He heard a door open, then footsteps; a slow hesitant tread. A voice, muffled by the closed door, came to him; a tired, frightened voice.

"Who is it?"

"The chap from downstairs." Hulbert was irritated by all this security. In his world a fellow never spoke from behind a closed door, in fact if he had any sense he would never lock his door in the first place. There was no telling who you might lock out. "Can I have a word with you?"

For a while it seemed as if his request was going to be ignored, then the door reluctantly opened, and Hulbert gasped when he saw the skeleton face, the sunken eyes that flickered with a baleful light, and almost abandoned his self-imposed mission. Then he remembered what had prompted that mission, and hardened his heart.

"Sorry to bother you, specially if you're feeling under the weather, but I need to speak with you."

He paused, waiting for encouragement, but those awful eyes just stared at him, so he swallowed hastily and continued.

"I hope you'll take this in the right spirit, but I wondered if you would quieten things down a bit. I mean when you entertain your lady friends. I know a certain amount of noise is unavoidable, but there is a limit . . . "

Again he waited for some response; an excuse, even possibly an explanation, however feeble. But the bloodless lips only moved and muttered something that sounded like "Sorry", and the door began to slowly close.

"Here, wait a minute!" Hulbert's normally placid disposition became ruffled. "That's not the only thing. There's all that hammering, and if you must throw things, and spill stuff over the floor, for Pete's sake mop up the mess. I've got bloody great patches all over my ceiling."

The door jerked back, and a bony-fingered hand shot out and gripped Hulbert's shirt-front; a hollow voice croaked:

"What patches?"

"Watch it, matey." Hulbert gripped the slender wrist and wrenched his shirt free. "You're asking for a punch-up. The patches on my ceiling. It's beginning to look like the map of the world before we lost the empire. You must have knocked a couple of barrels of red port over to make a mess like that." He sniffed suddenly. "What the hell is that bloody stink?"

The door was slammed in his face, and he was left pounding out his rage upon its unresponsive panels. After a while he went back to his own apartment muttering angrily to himself.

He looked up at his disfigured ceiling. The dark red stains were deeper towards the centre; even as he watched, one swelled into a scarlet globule, it elongated, its tip became detached, then fell to a table top with a minute splash. Another red, glistening driblet yo-yoed down as Hulbert reached for his telephone.

Edward was ripping up his fitted carpet, an easy task for most of the tacks had been removed, and those that remained slid out of their holes at the first pressure. He rolled back the carpet, tore at the underfelt, and stared at the bare boards. They bore many bruises, made by a hammer wielded by an inexperienced hand, they were also blood-stained, and in some places not quite flat, like the lid of a suitcase that had been forced down on a too-full interior. Edward stood up as the tall man entered the room.

"Is this the end?"

"I fear so." The tall man bowed his head gravely. "And it is to be regretted that our fruitful association has to terminate. But," he smiled, or rather bared his teeth, "the vessel is, in more respects than one, full, and indeed, overflowing."

Fear had long since died, now only curiosity remained; an unsated lust for forbidden knowledge.

"What now?"

The lean cheeks were now tinted with colour, the lips full and red, the eyes bright with fully-charged life.

"Now I am replete, and the wheel has turned a full circle—almost. You alone can seal the circle, give me the power to walk abroad. Eighty years ago I suspected the truth, now I know. I too called forth a shade from the dark lands, and I gave him the seven sacrifices that are necessary, plus the ultimate."

"Your master," Edward asked, "he still walks the Earth?"

The eyes sparkled, and the deep voice took on a joyous tone.

"He walks, they walk, for we are legion. We sit in high places and fan discord until the guns begin to boom, and the bayonets flash. Your lovely wars are a feast, a banquet that charges us for twenty or thirty years. Once past the first barrier there is no reason why any of us should starve."

"What is the ultimate?" Edward knew the answer but he wanted the tall man to tell him. The strong, deep voice went on.

"It is important that the seven initial sacrifices be dispatched in a special way. You were an apt pupil, although at first your tiresome conscience wanted to cover up. That futile scrubbing and washing. But," he glanced round at the blood-spotted, in some places blood-coated, room, "you grew out of that in time."

He pulled his greatcoat open and lovingly selected a long-bladed knife; when he looked up his smile was gentle, his voice soft, comforting.

"How said Brutus on the Plains of Philippi?"

Edward looked into those shining eyes and knew he must follow the path of knowledge to the end—and beyond.

"Hold then my sword, and turn away thy face, while I do run upon it."

"That," whispered the tall man, "is the ultimate."

Edward moved forward and the knife came up; the blade quivered, then was still. The lean face turned and looked back over one shoulder.

"Grip my shoulders and thrust forward. You helped me to come here, it is only right that I should assist you to go there."

Edward gripped the powerful shoulders, then pulled with all his strength. The pain was cold fire that paralysed his body; he sank to the floor and watched his life-blood pouring out over the bare floorboards.

"Have patience," the tall man whispered, then threw wide his arms in a triumphant gesture. "Have patience; you have all eternity."

They tore up the floorboards and took away the bits and pieces. The room was stripped; the bed went to the flames, the furniture was dispersed, the wallpaper removed, but they left the overmantel mirror.

Time had no meaning, and perhaps a year passed before a new tenant took up residence in the flat; perhaps two, even five. But one evening that which had been Edward Charlton looked out of the mirror and saw that a new bed stood on the dais, a fresh carpet covered the floor, and unfamiliar furniture cluttered the room.

Night darkened the window, then the sun painted a golden bar across the carpet, and existence became a panorama of light and darkness; lamps that went on, then off, the murmur of far-off voices; the void waiting to be filled.

Tenants came, then departed, fashions changed, furniture became bizarre, strange contraptions entered the flat, but the overmantel, now a priceless antique, remained.

Young people dressed in outlandish clothes gathered before whatever had replaced Edward's electric fire; they danced, made love, ate, drank, and finally became bored. Suddenly the words rang out, a clarion call that brought Edward floating to the mirror; he gazed out at the crowded room.

A young man with pink hair and a spotty face asked: "What did you say?"

A girl's voice, young, fresh, impatient, repeated the long awaited call.

"Let's hold a séance."

The Day That Father Brought Something Home

ALEXANDER WAS SEVEN years old and saw much that seemed to escape the perception of his elders, but this he took for granted as the natural order of things. Granny, for example, had been very poorly for some time; merely sat in her chair by the fireside, looking frail and shrivelled, her transparent hands trembling slightly. She seemed totally unaware of the little old lady who was standing behind her chair. Alexander would have drawn her attention to this strange visitor, only he knew from experience such revelations were not accepted kindly.

"The boy gives me the willies," Aunt Martha had remarked on one occasion, "always talking about things that aren't there. Like that time he said he saw a dog following us down Powder Mill Lane."

That was the day Grandad died. Dropped dead in the woodshed while he was sawing wood.

"Fine imagination," Father remarked complacently, "takes after me."

"Lies, I call it," Mother said spitefully, "and that is certainly like you."

He thus came to accept that such manifestations were best left undeclared; a secret shared by himself and Tobias. Now, it must be clearly understood that Tobias was to all outward appearances a dog—a short-haired, sturdy animal of doubtful ancestry, but Tobias was a man in a dog's body. Where this information came from he was not aware. Tobias had certainly never mentioned it, neither had Alexander given the matter serious thought. He had never even said to himself, "Tobias is a man," but one day, the one when they had both seen a man with a badly scarred face peering down over the banisters, Alexander had known it was so. The fact was not important; merely another item of information to add to his growing store of knowledge.

Tobias was not kindly disposed to the little old lady who stood behind Granny's chair, for he eyed her with a wary look, even growled deep down in his throat, until Mother snapped:

"What's wrong with that dog?"

And Father asked: "What's the matter, boy, eh?" Thereupon, Tobias wagged his tail ten to the dozen, as though suddenly remembering that this was part of the dog-act.

"How do you feel, Granny?" Mother asked for the third time that day. They were almost the only words anyone ever addressed to Granny, and she always responded with one word: "Poorly."

"You'll soon be up and around," stated Father boisterously. "Come spring and you'll be chasing rabbits over the common."

Alexander saw the little old lady who stood behind Granny's chair smile, then shake her head.

Next day Granny died. She slumped in her chair, and Tobias howled, one long mournful howl, and Alexander watched Granny come out of her body rather like a chick breaking free from its egg. First a kind of mist poured out of Granny's ears, nose and mouth. This twisted and pulsated until finally a second Granny stood in front of the original; a perfect duplicate, right down to the carpet slipper that had a hole in the right toe. She looked weak, her little, faded blue eyes were narrow slits, and she swayed like a water fern when the river was in full flood, and there was a silver-coloured cord still joining her to the slumped body in the old rocking-chair, and this, the little old lady broke, and tied one half into a knot, which disappeared into a point just above Granny's bottom. Then she led Granny away, one arm about her waist, out through the parlour doorway, and Alexander saw them pass through the window. Tobias gave Alexander one eloquent look, and the boy said:

"Must have been her sister, the one she kept talking about."

Then Tobias went to sleep, apparently relieved that the unwelcome visitor was finally out of the house, and he could now dream peacefully of the time when he walked on two legs.

Mother of course had to scream, and Aunt Martha ran in from next door, and there was a lot of crying, and much mutual comforting, tea drinking, and utterance of statements.

"She's better off," said Mother after Father had removed what remained of Granny, "she's at peace now."

"A good innings," said Aunt Martha, "you've got to admit she had a good innings."

"That poor boy." With a stab of alarm Alexander realised he was the subject under discussion. "He saw it all. He was alone and saw her die."

And Mother surrendered to another storm of tears while Alexander watched a little man walk under Aunt Martha's chair, and daintily wend his way between her feet. He was not more than three inches high, clad in a little green suit and a tiny hat complete with a green feather. Alexander knew he lived with his family behind the wainscoting, and sometimes when the sun had set, and the firelight was making shadows dance a sombre reel across walls and ceiling, two minute children, so small they could have been little balls of fluff, came out to play hide-and-seek on the hearthrug.

Granny, Grandad and the little old lady all turned up for the funeral. They were attired in respectable black as befitted the occasion, and as there was no room for them in the following cars, they clambered up on top of the hearse, where they sat in a neat row with their legs dangling over one side. There was room for all in the church, the visible mourners consisting of Father, Mother, and Aunt Martha, plus a distant cousin who no one knew, but had turned up with a sympathetic smile and an eye for the refreshments that were to follow the sad proceedings. This meant the three uninvited mourners could make themselves comfortable in the front pew on the opposite side of the aisle to the family proper, and Alexander watched them wide-eyed which earned him a reproof from Father who said, "Keep your eyes to the front and be more respectful."

While the vicar expounded the virtues of Granny, who had been a constant source of irritation to him during her lifetime, having disapproved of his "high church" ways, the object of his discourse dabbed her eyes with a small black handkerchief, and Grandad blew his nose into a bright red one. However, when the misguided cleric genuflected three times before the altar, and moreover swung an incense burner over Granny's coffin, she shook a clenched fist in his direction, and Alexander saw Grandad and the Great-Aunt pleading with her to practise more self-restraint.

The north wind stabbed the live mourners with icy fingers as they huddled round the graveside, and Granny appeared to be completely overcome by the sight of her own internment, for she was escorted by her two companions away over the long, winter-bitten grass towards the lych-gate where they disappeared from view. Alexander knew he would not see them again until they returned for some later bereavement.

After the funeral, life soon sank to its normal level of ordinariness. Alexander went back to where he was careful not to acquaint Miss Everhard, his current teacher, with the indisputable fact that a little black man sat on her right shoulder and shook with grotesque joy whenever she considered it needful to slap a small girl's leg. In no time at all, spring breathed gently over the bleak countryside, and daffodils raised their yellow trumpets to a benign sky. Alexander, accompanied by Tobias, went down to the secret place well hidden in Martine Wood, where together they watched the outdoor-little-people as they crept out from their warm nest under the giant oak to perform a joyful dance to the new sun.

But spring did not enter the house on top of the hill, and Alexander became aware of a cold something which had not yet assumed a visible form, but lurked unseen in dark corners and the shadows on the landing. He knew, and this knowledge came to him uninvited, that someone in the house was the cause of this uneasiness. The little man and his family no longer came out from behind the wainscoting. Tobias wore a dejected air and whenever possible kept close to Alexander's side.

He found himself watching Father, and presently arrived at a surprising discovery. Father was not what he seemed. The big, jovial, rather silly man was a skin that hid someone quite different. Or perhaps not so much different, as older, with a face that was still familiar, but more deeply lined, which in turn hid a brain where swam thoughts, memories, emotions, that neither Mother nor Aunt Martha, nor even Alexander himself, had ever suspected. Sometimes, in the soft twilight, before it was banished by lamplight, Alexander detected a red glow surrounding Father's head. It was never still. It pulsated as though in time to his thoughts; sometimes it was pale pink, at others bright red, and it was then the cold 'something' was most evident. It filled the cosy room, came between Alexander and the roaring fire, made Tobias whimper, and Father's eyes became as window-panes reflecting the images of passing clouds. Stormy, sun-tinted, black, lightning-slashed, and Alexander watched, wondered, but was never, never afraid.

He lay awake in the thick darkness and listened to the sounds of the sleeping house. The muted sigh of the poor lady who had died here many years ago, and was now creeping down the stairs to roam through the lower rooms, searching for something she would never find. The soft flutter of wings on his bedroom windowpanes—the soul of someone closely connected with the sighing lady who must now fly through the night as a bird, even as Tobias walked the earth as a dog. Just before he slid into sleep Alexander heard a low cry by his bedside and he murmured sleepily: "Go away," and the man with the scarred face went back to the world from which he had strayed. Then the cold 'something', brought into being possibly by Father's dreams, invaded the room, but Alexander ignored it, just wrapped himself up more tightly in the bedclothes, and dreamed he was having tea with the little family behind the wainscoting.

Then one day Father brought something home with him, and the cold 'something' went away. Perhaps it had only been a pathfinder for the visible 'something', or maybe Father's thoughts, the red ones, had given it substance, so that now it was visible to Alexander's special vision.

Whatever the answer, and Alexander did not ponder on these matters, Father came into the parlour late one evening, and a great bear-like thing followed in his footsteps. It was all of seven feet tall; a rough, black fur covered the entire body from the neck downwards, and the face was jet-black with great red eyes that glittered strangely in the artificial light. A mass of black hair covered the head and framed the face, while the chin was hidden behind a thick, frizzy beard.

The evening meal was eaten in almost total silence, for although Mother could not see the Bear-Thing Father had brought home, it did seem she felt its presence. She watched Father from under lowered eyelids, and he toyed with his food, seemed oblivious to his wife and small son, and Tobias whimpered unhappily from his place on the hearth-rug.

But Alexander watched the Bear-Thing, and the Bear-Thing watched him, seeming unpleasantly aware it was visible to his special-eyes. It moved nearer to Father as though stressing that he was its particular property, and no interference would be tolerated; then as Alexander made no movement, only continued to eat a slice of Swiss roll, a delicacy to which he was most partial, it relaxed slightly, even moved back a few steps and examined the room with interest.

The overmantel mirror attracted Its attention, and after a single glance at Father as though to make certain he was firmly anchored to his chair, It lumbered over to the fireplace, and Tobias fled with lowered tail and dilated eyes to a position of comparative safety behind the sofa.

"What are you staring at?" asked Mother, and her voice was hoarse with fear.

"Nothing," Alexander replied and turned his attention to Father who was giving out scarlet thought-waves. After a while he thought it safe to look once again in the direction of the fireplace.

The Bear-Thing was pushing its head right into the mirror. Alexander stifled a giggle. It was clearly trying to fasten its fangs into the neck of its reflection. The reflected head retreated before that of the real one; red eyes glittered with grotesque hate, the bearded face grimaced, the mouth gaped, and Alexander wondered if the Bear-Thing supposed the mirror image to be a rival with designs upon its property.

Then Father got up and the Bear-Thing pulled its head out of the mirror, and swung round with surprising speed. Before he reached the door It was by his side.

"Harry!" Mother was half out of her chair. "What's wrong with you?"

"Me!" He stared at her in amazement, but his eyes reflected a terrible fear. "What are you going on about? I'm tired that's all. I want to go to bed."

"You haven't said a word all evening. And you haven't eaten a thing."

The scarlet thoughts were like lightning flashes against black clouds.

"Bloody hell, woman, I can't be chattering like a bloody monkey all the time, can I? Leave me alone."

He pulled the door open and rushed out with the Bear-Thing close behind. Mother remained at her place at the bottom of the table, the nagging worry rising from her head in the form of little green bubbles. Alexander thought they looked rather pretty, like decorations on a Christmas tree, then suddenly she began to cry, a terrible body shaking outburst that had nothing in common with her grief for Granny's passing. Alexander said "Mummy," and he tasted fear for the first time; it clung to his palate like nasty medicine. His voice broke through the wall of her anguish, for she stared at him with eyes that were fired by a sudden blast of terrible knowledge, and she sprung to her feet and rushed from the room.

Tobias came out from behind the sofa to push a cold nose into Alexander's hand, as he stared sadly into the fire.

"Why?" he asked after a while. "Why?"

Tobias did not answer.

The murmur of voices was like the sound of sea breaking on some wild shore. Sometimes it was soft, pleading. At others, it rose up into a battle of accusation and denial, but only an occasional word, a rare sentence, filtered through the dividing wall.

"You're mad."

"What have you done?"

"...tell..."

"...No...nothing..."

The Bear-Thing must be in there with them. Perhaps it was seated on the little upholstered bedside chair, or fighting its reflection in the dressing-table mirror, or maybe knowing its property to be safely in bed, it was roaming the house like a newly arrived cat, smelling out the dark corners, peering into cupboards, looking up chimneys.

"Shut up, blast you."

Father's voice was a scream of dark agony, and Mother's sobs a low cry of never-ending pain. Presently their bedroom door opened and heavy footsteps went down the stairs. The front door slammed, to be followed by a period of strange peace, such as comes during a lull in a violent storm. The house was unnaturally quiet, for the Bear-Thing had frightened the sad ghosts into uneasy retirement.

The word rang round the town and out across the surrounding countryside like a monstrous clarion call.

MURDER

It shrieked at Alexander from newspaper placards on his way to school, it tripped off the tongues of children when they collected together in groups in the playground, it was spat out by bright-eyed women as they gossiped over garden fences, it was vomited by drunken men as they lurched against walls on their way home for The Black Bull.

MURDER

Drab, grey lives received their need of colour. Fearful excitement rippled across the stagnant pool of urban existence, and the skies rained policemen. Words, sentences, harsh lust-ridden thoughts poured in from every direction, and only Alexander was unmoved. Faces became round blobs with mouths.

"No more than seventeen. Raped, strangled, she was."

"When they catch him, he ought to be boiled in oil."

"It's come so a respectable woman can't walk down the street in peace."

Alexander memorised the letters on the newspaper placard. He tactfully put the question to Aunt Martha.

"Please, what is a S-E-X-M-O-N-S-T-E-R?"

"Never you mind," Aunt Martha glared at him. "You don't want to know about things like that at your age."

But a little boy at school was more informative.

"Everybody knows that, stupid. It's a bloke who kisses a girl who don't want to be kissed, then does her in so she won't tell on him."

Alexander was not satisfied.

"What's he want to kiss her for?"

The boy shrugged.

"Because he's batty."

They came knocking at every door, mostly smart young men with polite smiles. They used such words as: Routing, co-operation, would you be so kind," but their eyes searched every new face with a kind of terrible, hopeful expectancy.

Alexander listened behind the parlour door.

"I am sure, Sir," the smart young man was saying, while his companion watched Father with an unblinking stare, "you wish this dreadful business cleared up, and the chap responsible brought to justice."

"Yes," Father agreed loudly, "I do indeed. Yes."

"Quite so. Then I would like you to cast your mind back to the night of May the nineteenth."

"That would be last Tuesday," Father said brightly. "Yes."

"As you say, Sir, last Tuesday evening. Can you recall where you were between the hours of seven and ten o'clock?"

"I was at home. Yes. Watching telly."

"Do you support this statement, madam?"

"What?"

Mother sounded as if she had been stung by a wasp.

"Can you verify. . . ? Was Mr. Palmer at home on Tuesday evening last between the hours of seven and ten o'clock?"

"Oh, yes. Yes, he was."

There was a short silence and Alexander patted Tobias's head. The suave voice spoke again.

"He did not go out at any time?"

"Beg pardon?"

"I said; your husband did not leave the house at any time between the hours of seven and ten?"

"No. No, he was here all the time."

"You are absolutely certain? If he did it does not mean we suspect he did anything—improper. We just want to know where he went."

"No." Mother's voice was a trifle too loud. "He went nowhere. Was here all the time."

"I see. Good. How old are you, Sir?"

"Forty-three."

"Right."

Alexander peered through the crack between the door and its lintel. The young man was writing in a small blue notebook; his companion was still watching Father.

"I think that's all." The man put his notebook away, then turned and walked towards the door. Alexander and Tobias beat a hasty retreat. Suddenly the voice spoke again.

"Just one little thing. Can you remember what programme you saw on television?"

There was an undercurrent of relief in Father's voice, rather like that of an examination candidate who has been asked a question to which he knows the answer.

"Yes, there was an old film which started at seven-thirty—*Carry on Smoking* I think it was, then a quiz show—Scotty Masters' *History is Knocking At Your Door*, then the news..."

The man cut him short with a low laugh.

"Same old rubbish each week. Scarcely worth the trouble of paying for the *T.V.* and *Radio Times*, is it, Sir? Well, thank you for your co-operation."

Father said: "Not at all, pleased to be of help. Hope you catch him soon," and the man replied: "Don't worry, Sir, we will," and the smell of fear was foul—like sour milk on a hot day.

When the men had gone, when the door was fast shut, and Alexander had crept back into the parlour, then, Mother removed the fixed smile from her face, loosened the muscles round eyes and mouth, so that her face crumpled like a balloon when the air has been let out, and she cried, and cried. And the face of Father was that of a man who has walked beyond hope, who has drunk deep from the cup of despair, and now sits in an ante-chamber of Hell where human emotions cannot enter. The Bear-Thing stood behind him, its face was raised and wore an expression of pain-ecstasy, so that for a moment Alexander though it looked strangely beautiful.

"Go to bed, Alec," Father said, "like a good boy."

There was a lump in his throat, and a strange liquid feeling in his stomach, and he recognised pity although he could give it no name. Tobias rubbed his rough coat against Father's leg, and whimpered softly, trying with all his might to explain the great riddle, but the unbreakable, and never-to-be-spoken-law, said he must always pretend to be a dog, and dogs do not explain only hide bones and christen lamp-posts. So Alexander drew him away, and together they ascended the stairs to take refuge in his bedroom, where sleep and forgetfulness lay waiting.

The two men came back the following evening, and they brought with them a third man, a much older, heavier person who was trying unsuccessfully to pretend he was someone's benign uncle. He shook Father's hand, seated himself, looked round the small room with extravagated ease, then rubbed his hands together as though he were Santa Claus paying his final visit on a cold Christmas Eve.

"Cosy, Mr. Palmer. Nice place you've got here. Real cosy eh, lads?"

The two young men nodded like puppets when the strings have been jerked."

"Cosy, Sir. Cosy."

Father had to say something. "You wanted to see me?"

Alexander, for the moment forgotten in his seat by the fireplace, watched the red thoughts flicker and smelt the stench of fear.

"What!" The big man looked painfully surprised. "See you . . . ? Oh, yes. There was one little matter, purely routine a damn nuisance really, but we do have to follow up every lead. You do understand?"

He appealed to Father who could only nod.

"You're very kind, very considerate. Many people aren't. I wonder, would you mind going over your statement again? The one you gave to these officers."

"Statement?"

Father let the word slide out of his mouth, like a plum stone that has aggravated a bad tooth.

"Yes, Mr. Palmer." The big man's voice was now low, caressing, soothing, inviting confidences, secrets, that would be forever locked in his brain. "Where were you between seven and ten o'clock on Tuesday evening last?

"I've told them already," Father insisted.

"Yes, I know. Dreadful pests aren't we? Just tell me, so I can get the record straight."

"I was home all the evening, watching telly."

"And you never left the house? Not even once?"

Father was looking for a pitfall, but the way ahead was dark, and he must go forward.

"No. No, not once."

"Thank you, Mr. Palmer. You've taken a weight off my mind. These two do a good job, but I like to get in on the act sometimes. Have to appear to be earning my keep. Eh?"

He laughed loudly, and the two young men tittered politely, and Father permitted himself a mild grimace, but Mother stared blankly at the big man, and pushed back a strand of hair with a trembling hand.

"I wonder, Mrs. Palmer," the big man was now pretending to be shy, afraid of overstaying his welcome, "could we trouble you for a cup of tea. The boys and I have been at it since lunchtime, and we're parched. Eh, lads?"

"Parched," said one.

"Dry as a bone," said the other.

"Of course." Mother was most reluctant to leave the room, but this appeal to her hospitality could not be ignored.

"And," the big man went on, "I should take this little chap with you. He looks tired. Long past his bedtime, I expect."

"Come on, Alec." Mother jerked her head slightly and Alexander could do no more than follow her out of the room. At the doorway he looked back. The Bear-Thing was leaning against the far wall. It looked very sad.

In the kitchen Mother gripped Alexander's shoulder tightly. Her eyes were wild, her voice a harsh whisper.

"Go back. Listen behind the door. Listen."

He went back to his former place behind the half-open door and applied his eye to the crack. He could see the big man's face; it was still benign.

"Before your good lady comes back, Mr. Palmer, there is one little matter I would like to clear up. We have recently interviewed a certain maiden lady by the name of..." He consulted a little black book "...yes, here we are, a Miss Sidgwich. A formidable old party, who apparently wanders round the common looking for what she calls evil-doers. She means snogging couples, of course. Turfs out any she finds and gives 'em a lecture on the evil of their ways. Know her?"

Father shook his head.

"Really!" The big man registered surprise. "I thought everyone in these parts knew Miss Sidgwich. Well she appears to know you. In fact she says she saw you walking across the common on Tuesday night."

"She lies," Father gasped, "lies."

"I think that is a bit strong, Mr. Palmer," the big man shook his head. "No, she's an oddity, a bit cracked, perhaps, but a respectable old body. Mistaken maybe."

"Well, then," Father grasped the offered straw, "she was mistaken."

"That then is your opinion, Mr. Palmer? The lady was mistaken if she states she saw you on the common between the hours of seven and eight on Tuesday last?"

"Yes," Father repeated, "she was mistaken."

Mother swept by Alexander with a loaded tray, and the big man insisted on helping her lay out the cups and saucers on the dining table. The two young men did not move.

"Some old crow says she saw me out on the common on Tuesday night," Father informed Mother.

She said, "Oh," quite sharply.

"Mistaken identity," pronounced the big man.

"I'll sue her for libel," Father stated.

"Slander," corrected the big man, "libel is written, slander is spoken."

"I'll sue her anyway," Father insisted, "I've got my good name to think of."

"Shouldn't let it worry you," the big man comforted, "a lot of what we hear goes in one ear and out the other." He chuckled. "As a matter of fact, she slipped up rather badly on Tuesday night. There was one young couple snogging away in the long grass, and she saw neither hair nor hide of them. I think you know them, Mr. Palmer, a Jack Binns and a Winnie Baun. They work at Garridges."

"I know them," Father admitted.

"I thought you must." The big man took a dainty sip from his cup. "Young Binns says he saw you running across the common at five minutes to eight."

"He can't have," Father protested weakly.

"That's what he says. In fact they both say so. Another case of mistaken identity, Mr. Palmer?"

"These kids will say anything." Father had backed to the wall, right up against the Bear-Thing. It placed its great paws on his shoulders as though trying to comfort him.

"True," the big man nodded, "very true. No sense of values. The country is going to the dogs." He stared sadly at his teacup as though pondering on the wickedness of the rising generation. "Do you know a Miss Eve Roberts, Mr. Palmer?"

"No."

Tears were running down the Bear-Thing's face.

"Or Miss Jane Gardner?"

"No, no."

"Strange." The big man looked up, his eyes cold. "They both stated you made—how shall I put it? Unwelcome advances to them?"

"Lies. I am a respectable, married man. Ask anyone."

"You would appear," said the big man slowly, "to be a much slandered man, Mr. Palmer."

"Well," he got up, "time's a'wasting, mustn't keep you good people up any longer. Thank you for the tea, Mrs. Palmer. Please, we will let ourselves out."

At the door he looked back, an apologetic smile parting his lips.

"I would think over our little chat, if I were you, Mr. Palmer. Try to think about why five people should be so very—mistaken. I'll see you tomorrow. Oh, one last thing. Take my tip, don't go out tonight. You'll be quite safe. I'm leaving a couple of chaps outside to keep an eye on things. Goodnight."

They left, but their darkness remained behind them, and the very walls of the house were sobbing with terror.

The scream pulled Alexander up from the pit of sleep and hurled him into a harsh reality, where, once the light was on, the room was a cold, cold place that was full of noise. The scream was repeated again, and the howl of a dog rose like a banshee's cry, also there was a loud banging on the front door, and the rising murmur of voices.

Down in the hall Alexander saw the Bear-Thing. It was slumped against the wall, and there was a look of naked terror in its red eyes. Alexander walked by it and crept into the kitchen. Father had been very clever. He had his head inside a plastic bag, the one Mother used to take the washing down to the laundrette, and after removing one of the gas burners, had connected a rubber tube to the pipe. The other end was in the plastic bag, which was tied tightly round Father's neck with a length of string. His body was very, very dead.

There was a sound of breaking glass, and presently the big man entered, followed by the two smart men. They pulled Mother to her feet and escorted her to the parlour where she sat in Granny's old chair, rocking to and fro.

"I didn't mean to fall asleep," she kept repeating. "I didn't mean to fall asleep."

"It's better this way," the big man said, "you must see, it's better this way."

The Bear-Thing had come in and was eyeing him with growing interest.

"Pity, Sir," one young man remarked wistfully, "he was near breaking point."

"He broke, lad," the big man replied, "broke. They always break."

The two young men looked at their chief with undisguised admiration; the Bear-Thing with pronounced consideration.

"Get the doctor," the big man ordered, "dig out the old party from next door, the woman will need someone to take care of her. I'll make out my report."

He left and the Bear-Thing went with him.

In the weeks which followed Alexander kept an eye open for Father, but he failed to materialise. Granny, Grandad and Great-Aunt turned up for the funeral, and the sighing lady returned to her haunting. Also, after a decent interval, the little man and his family made themselves heard behind the wainscoting. But no Father, nothing out of the ordinary.

Then one day Tobias brought home a small kitten. It was not more than a few weeks old, and was sopping wet. Alexander dried it on the kitchen towel, then made a home for it in a handleless shopping basket, well-lined with one of Father's vests. It accepted a saucer of milk, then after a short nap, woke up in time to see Mother, looking so old, so grey, as she cleared the table. It mewed piteously.

Alexander took the small bundle of fur up onto his lap and fondled the velvet ears. He looked at Tobias. The man-who-had-to-pretend-to-be-a-dog nodded.

They both knew.

THE DOOR

"WHY A DOOR?" Rosemary asked. "I mean to say, the house has a full complement of perfectly satisfactory doors."

William continued to run his hands over his latest acquisition, his eyes alight with that glow of pure pleasure that is peculiar to the ardent collector.

"I liked it, he explained, "besides it is very old. Three hundred years, if a day."

"But it doesn't match the paintwork or anything," Rosemary protested, "and it's so heavy."

She was right of course. The door was massive; made of solid walnut, fully four feet wide and seven feet high, the panels embossed with an intricate pattern that seemed to grow more complicated the longer it was examined. It had a great tarnished brass knob on the left side, and four butt hinges on the right.

"What are you going to do with it?" Rosemary asked after a while. "Hang it on the wall?"

"Don't be so silly." William tapped the panels with his knuckles. "I'm going to put it to its proper use. You know that cupboard in my study? Well, it's dead centre in the wall opposite my desk; I'll get the builders to take away the old door, enlarge the aperture, and hang this one in its place."

"A great thing like that as a cupboard door!" Rosemary gasped.

"Then," William went on, "I'll hang a large 16th-century print on either side, a couple of crossed swords over the top, and the result should be pretty impressive."

"Like a museum," Rosemary observed.

"It will inspire me," William nodded slowly, and Rosemary with a woman's inconsistency thought he looked very sweet. "It must be French polished of course, and the lock burnished and then lacquered."

"Where did you find it?" Rosemary asked.

"At Murray's. You know, the demolition people. Old Murray said it came from a 16th-century manor house he knocked down last year. I can't wait to see the door in position, can you?"

"No," Rosemary said doubtfully, "no I can hardly wait."

The builders made an awful mess, as she knew they would, but when the job was finished, and of course the study had to be completely redecorated, the effect was certainly very impressive. The entire wall was covered with red wallpaper, and in the exact centre was the door, now resplendent with polish, the brass knob and hinges gleaming like gold, giving the impression that behind must lie a gracious drawing-room instead of an eighteen inches deep stationary cupboard. On either side hung a Rembrandt print, each one housed in a magnificent gilt frame, and over the door were two crossed sabres with shining brass hilts. William sat behind his desk, his face wearing the look of a man well satisfied with the world and all it contained.

"Wonderful," he breathed, " absolutely marvellous."

"Well, as long as you're satisfied." Rosemary frowned, and puckered her lips into an expression of faint distaste. "Frankly I'm not certain I like it."

"What!" William scowled his displeasure. He liked people to share his enthusiasm. "What's wrong with it?"

"It looks very nice and original," Rosemary admitted, "but some-how..." she paused... "it's rather creepy."

"What utter rot!"

"Yes, I suppose it must sound that way, but I can't help wondering what lies behind."

"What lies...!" William stared at his wife with growing amazement. "You know what lies behind, an ordinary stationary cupboard."

"Yes, I know, and you don't have to shout at me. I keep telling myself it is only a door and behind is a shallow cupboard lined with shelves, but I can't really believe it. I mean, cupboards don't have grand doors like that, they have cheap ply-panelled ones covered with layers and layers of old paint, and they're sort of humble. If they could talk, they'd say: 'I'm a cupboard door, and I don't pretend to be anything else.' But that thing..." She jerked her head in the direction of the large door. "That wouldn't say anything. Just stare at you and wait to be opened by a butler."

"What an imagination," William pointed to his typewriter, "you ought to be doing my job. But you're right. I never thought about it. A door must take on the character of the room it guards, in the same way a face assumes the character of the brain behind it. Now..." He got up, walked round the desk, and moved over to the great gleaming door. "What kind of room do you suppose this once guarded?"

"A big one," Rosemary said with conviction, "yes, I'd say a big room."

"A reasonable deduction," William nodded, "large door, large room. What else?"

"I think it must have been a beautiful room. Sinister maybe, cold, but beautiful. A big expanse of carpet, a great fireplace, high blue walls, a big window with an olde worlde garden beyond... blue velvet chairs. I think it would have been a room like that."

"Could well be," William nodded again, "a large drawing room that hardly changed with the years. There again, it might have been a picture gallery—anything. Tell you what, I'll ring up Murray and find out what he can tell me."

"A big room," Rosemary murmured, more to herself than to her husband, "I'm certain it was a large drawing-room. Certain."

"Good morning, Mr. Seaton, what can I do for you?"

"About that door I bought," William pressed the telephone receiver closer to his ear, "I wondered if you could tell me something about the house from where it came."

"The house?" Murray sounded a little impatient. "Clavering Grange, you mean. An old place down in Kent. The last owner, Sir James Sinclair, died recently and the chap who inherited—Hackett was his name—had no use for it, falling to pieces it was, so he sold the lot to a building contractor. We had the job of clearing the site. Why do you ask?"

"Oh, my wife and I wondered what sort of room went with such a fine door. I suppose you wouldn't know?"

Murray chuckled. "Matter of fact I do. It came from the blue drawing-room. A great barn of a place, with a ruddy great fireplace. Very grand in its day I'm sure, but was a bit of a mess when we came to drive our bulldozer through it. You know, damp, the paper peeling from the walls. Can't tell you much else."

"Well, thanks anyway. My wife was right, she thought it was a large drawing-room, and strangely enough, she guessed it was blue."

"You don't say? What do you know about that? Must be psychic or something?"

"Probably something," William laughed. "Well, thanks again. 'Bye."

"So," William spoke aloud, "we have established a blue drawing-room should be behind you, but there isn't, is there? Only a horrible little cupboard, so you had better get used to your reduced circumstances, and be mighty grateful you didn't finish up as firewood."

The door ignored him.

William often worked late into the night, finding the peace and quiet of the small hours conducive to creative thinking. Usually there was a feeling of serene contentment when he settled down in his old chair, heard the muted roar of a passing car, and let his brain churn out a steady flow of dialogue. But once the door was installed he found his attention was apt to wander to it, or rather to what had once lain behind it. The blue room. Grand old country houses seemed to go in for that kind of thing. Blue rooms, red rooms, yellow rooms. Presumably if one had a lot of rooms, it was as good a way as any to identify one from the other. Also, decorating must be greatly simplified. Blue walls, blue hangings, carpet, upholstery—William chuckled to himself—there was really no limit. Why not have blue flowers just outside the great window, or perhaps a little blue creeper that completely surrounded the window and in fact gently tapped the glass panes on a windy night. He must get old Jem to cut it back.

William sat upright, dropped his pen, and frowned. Who the blazes was old Jem? It was all very well having a powerful, cultivated imagination, but he must keep it under control. But still . . . He stared at the door thoughtfully; there was a certain rather eerie satisfaction in creating an imaginary world for the door to guard. William lay back in his chair and half-closed his eyes. First of all the room; it must be reconstructed properly. You open the door, walk onto a thick, extremely beautiful, blue carpet, clearly made to measure, for it stretches from wainscoating to wainscoating, and in front of that great fireplace with its roaring log-fire, is a dark blue rug. So much for the floor, now the furniture. Situated some six feet back from the fireplace is a settee, at least so William supposed it to be, for it had a high back, a round arm on each side, would seat possibly four people at one time, and was covered with blue brocade. Six matching chairs were placed around the room, and William sank down onto one. It was very comfortable. He examined the wall. Blue of course, but the covering appeared to be some kind of material, embossed with dark blue flowers, and there were several pictures in blue velvet-edged frames. Indeed this is a blue room. Or was it. Funny this obsession for blue. What kind of man had he been . . . or was? There was a portrait of him over the mantelpiece, painted when he was a young man; his face still clean, not yet scarred by lines of debauchery and evil, but the eyes . . . By God and all his saints, the eyes . . .

William got up and walked towards the fireplace; he could feel the heat of the fire; a log settled and sent a shower of sparks rocketing up the chimney. An oval face with the dark beauty of a fallen angel, long, black hair that curled down to his shoulders, lace collar, blue velvet doublet, the epitome of a Restoration gentleman. The dark, terrible eyes watched him, and William pulled his gaze away, then walked to the window. The garden was a place of beauty, close-clipped lawns, islands of flowers, trees beyond, further still, blue-crested hills.

He turned and went over to the great desk; a quill-pen grew out of an ink-horn, a blue velvet-covered book lay upon the desk and his hand went down to open it, when . . .

Footsteps outside, just beyond the windows, slow, halting steps, punctuated by an occasional dragging sound, like a lame old man who is trying to overcome his handicap; drawing nearer, and the room was becoming colder. William shivered, then overcome by an unreasoning fear darted towards the door. He opened it, went out, closed it carefully behind him, then went over and sat down behind his desk.

He opened his eyes.

Five minutes passed. William got up, moved very slowly towards the door, turned the brass knob, then pulled. A cupboard, eighteen inches deep, filled with shelves on which nestled stacks of typing paper, carbons, ribbons, the familiar materials of his trade. He shut the door, then opened it again, finally closed it with a bang before returning to his desk.

He sat there for some time, then suddenly was seized by a fit of shivering that made his body shake like a dead leaf beaten by the wind. Gradually the spasm passed, leaving him weak, drenched with perspiration, but strangely at peace, like a man who has recently recovered from a brief, but serious illness. A dream, an illusion, or perhaps a rebellion on the part of an overworked imagination. What did it matter? It had been an experience, an exercise of the mind, and no writer worthy of his ink should be afraid of a journey into the unknown.

He watched the door for the rest of the night, and the door stared right back at him. Once he thought the handle began to turn, and he waited with breathless expectancy, but it must have been an illusion caused by his overstrained eyes, for the door remained closed.

The door became an obsession. His work was neglected, a bewildered agent telephoned at regular intervals, muttering dark threats about deadlines, broken contracts, and William tried to flog his brain back to its former production line, but to no avail. The door was always there, and with it the memory of a room; a study in blue, an anteroom to another age. "Next time," he told himself, "I will go out through the great window, and walk across the garden and rediscover yesterday."

He sat by the hour with closed eyes trying to recreate the dream, willing himself back into that armchair, gazing up at the portrait over the mantelpiece, but the 20th-century remained obstinately present, and several times he fell asleep. Rosemary was becoming worried.

"What's the matter?" Are you ill?"

"No!" He barked the denial, his irritation growing each time the gentle enquiry was made. "Leave me alone. How am I to work?"

"But you're not working," she persisted, "neither are you eating. William, this must stop."

"What?"

"You and that damned door." She glared at the door. "I do not pretend to understand, but ever since that lump of old wood came into this house, you haven't been the same man. It scares me. William, have it taken out, let's burn it in the boiler."

He laughed harshly, and experienced a pang of fear at her suggestion, and saw the startled expression on Rosemary's face.

"Don't worry so much. The truth is I've run dry, writers do occasionally. It's happened before and the old brain has always started ticking over once it was good and read. But it makes me a bit irritable."

"That's all right," she brightened up at once, "I don't mind you being a bit testy, but you're getting so thin. Are you sure that nothing else is bothering you?"

For a mad moment he toyed with the idea of telling her about the room, the dream, then instantly discarded it. She would not understand or believe, so he kissed her gently and said, "Absolutely nothing."

"Then pack it in for a bit," she pleaded, "and let me cook you a decent meal. One you will eat."

It was suddenly very important she be pacified, her mind be put at rest.

"All right. I'll give you a hand."

He helped her in the kitchen, was surprised to hear himself making small talk, while all the time his mind, his very soul hungered for the blue room and the fear that lurked in the garden. For that was the truth and the realisation burst upon him like a blast of light. The terror inspired by approaching footsteps, the heart-stopping, exciting horror of wondering what would come in through the great French windows, the craving for a new experience, even if fulfilment meant madness or worse.

They ate in the kitchen, two young, beautiful people, as modern as Carnaby Street. He tall, lean, dark, she petite, blonde, blue-eyed. His dark, clever eyes watched her, and he smiled often.

That night they retired to bed early, and long after Rosemary had fallen asleep he lay thinking about the room behind the door.

"It does not exist," he told himself, "maybe it did long ago, but not now. A bulldozer flattered the house, and only the blue room door remains. A flat piece of polished wood."

There was comfort in that thought, and presently sleep closed his eyes with soft fingers, and for a while he was at rest.

The room had not altered, the log-fire still spluttered, the chairs were in the same position as on his last visit, and the blue journal lay upon the desk. William found he was dressed in his pyjamas and his feet were bare.

"I must have sleep-walked," he whispered, "but now I am wide awake. This is not a dream."

He walked over to the door, opened it and stared into the gloom; a few yards away the outline of his desk shimmered softly, the door of his study was open, beyond was darkness. William closed the door, crossed the blue carpet and flattened his nose against the French windows. Back in his own world it was night, out in the garden it was sunset; long shadows lay across the smooth lawn, the trees were giant sentinels rearing up against the evening sky, and although it all looked beautiful and peaceful, there was something eerie about the scene. Suddenly William knew why. Nothing moved. There were no birds, the leaves did not stir, the flowers stood upright; it was as though he were looking at a three-dimensional picture.

He shivered, then turned and walked over to the desk. The blue journal lay waiting, and he fingered the soft velvet cover before sitting down, then with a strange reluctance opened the book. Crisp parchment, about fifty pages he estimated, bound together, the first one was blank serving as a fly-leaf. He turned it slowly, then read the clear, beautiful copperplate inscription.

THE EXPERIMENT IN DARKNESS
By
SIR MICHAEL SINCLAIR, BART.
of the county of Kent, Lord of the Manor of Clavering,
written in this the twenty-second year of the reign of his
gracious majesty, King Charles the Second.

It took a great effort of will to turn the title page, for the room
seemed suddenly to have become very cold, and the dying sun sent its
shafts of light through the window, making the shadows scurry like so
many disturbed mice. But he had to read on; the page went over with
a disturbingly loud crackling sound.

PART 1
INSTRUCTIONS AS TO THE ENTRAPMENT OF THE
UNBORN.

Having kept myself aloof from the troubles of the preceding
reign, I have devoted these many years to the pursuit of that
knowledge which fools call evil, and from which, even those men
that are dubbed wise, cover their faces, even as the night hides
from the rising sun.

To say that the knowledge I have confined to these pages is
the unadulterated fruit of my own labours would not be true, for
I have been helped by the old masters, such as Astaste and his
Book of Forbidden Knowledge, Conrad von Leininstein with his
invaluable *Transformation Of Living Matter Through Quickening
Time*, and many others. But I have gone beyond them, have
made myself as a seething-pot, created an essence of bubbling
truth such as no man has yet conceived.

Men avert their eyes rather than meet my glance, for I wear
my knowledge about me like a cloak; they whisper about me in
corners, and there is much talk of witchcraft, and were I not who
I am, I might fear the stake.

I prepared me the room after many years and the expense of
much blood, and the damnation of my soul should the Black

One whose name must never be uttered ever assume power over me. I brought me slaves from Africas; young persons whose disappearance would never be commented upon, although their screams have doubtless been heard, but such is the reputation of this house, the fools merely cross themselves and take to their heels. It was necessary to kill their body with a painful slowness, and draw off their soul or life essence while the blue room and all pertaining to it was imprinted upon their dying gaze. Thus did I make a *karma* or ghost room, kept alive by the life essence of those who had been sacrificed to it. But even as the body needs food, the earth needs fertilising, so the room from time to time, must be fed. Many of the Africans have a poor lasting quality, the power fades and my soul trembles lest *He* be able to enter. Therefore, I prepared me the door, seeping it in blood that was still warm, and making it into a trap that will function for a brief spell in the time that has yet to come. I pray that this be not destroyed in the centuries yet unborn, for without it will I be unable to acquire that which is needful, and be lost for all eternity.

The unborn must come in when the time is ripe, and should he be of the right mixture, then shall he give of his body and soul that I and the room many continue to be; or I will go forth beyond the door and find me a woman of his kind, which would be better, for a woman has a more lasting quality...

William slammed the book closed and looked about him with sudden fear. A sound had disturbed him and for a moment he could not be sure what it had been. Then it came again—a slow, halting footstep, just beyond the French windows. William seemed to be frozen to his chair; he wanted to get up and run back to the safety of his own world; at the same time, there was an irritating curiosity to know who—what, would shortly come in through the window.

Suddenly the overhead chandelier lit up; every one of its candles took on a yellow spear-shaped light, and beyond the window it was night, a black impregnable wall of darkness. But the slow, faltering footsteps continued to draw nearer, and it seemed as though the room shivered with fear at the approach of its dread master, for the coldness grew more intense, and William whimpered like a terrified puppy.

The French windows opened and slowly a black figure emerged from the darkness and limped into the room. The scarlet doublet was rotten with age, the blue velvet hat had long since lost its plume, the knee-breeches were threadbare, the black boots cracked and down-at-heel, and He—It—had no face. Just an oval-shaped expanse of dead-white skin surrounded by a mass of bedraggled white hair.

William screamed once, a long, drawn out shriek, then he was on his feet and racing for the door. He pulled it open, crossed the dark study in a fear-mad rush, barked his shins on a chair, then tore out into the hall, and up the stairs, to finally collapse on the landing where he lay panting and trembling like a hunted animal.

Slowly he recovered, fought back the terror, mastered his shaking limbs, and marshalled his thoughts. He crawled forward and peered down through the banisters to the dark hall below. He could see the pale oblong that marked his study doorway. The door was still open. Then another more terrible thought exploded and sent slivers of fear across his brain. *The door was open.* What had he read in the blue-covered book?

"Therefore I prepared me the door. . . making it into a trap that will function for a brief spell . . . or I will go forth beyond the door and find me a woman of his kind, which would be better, for a woman has a more lasting quality."

Rosemary! If Sir Michael was beyond the door, then he might be but a few feet away, hidden by the darkness, peering down at William with that face that was not a face, perhaps even moving silently towards the bedroom where Rosemary lay asleep.

William got to his feet, stretched out a hand and groped wildly for the light switch. He found it, pressed, and the sudden light blasted the darkness, shattered it into splinters, sent the shadows racing for protecting corners, forced imagination to face reality. The landing was empty; the familiar cold linoleum, the white painted doors, the brown banisters, the stairs . . . William peered down into the hall. The landing light did not extend to more than halfway down the stairs, the hall was still in total darkness. It took great courage to descend the stairs, and a great effort of will to press the hall switch. Light, like truth, is all-revealing; the hall table was in its proper place, the carpet he and Rosemary had chosen with such care covered the floor, two prints still hung on the green-papered walls, and all doors were closed, save the one leading to his study; and standing in the opening was something extra—a bedraggled, nightmare figure with no face. Almost no face, for since William had seen it last, it had acquired a mouth. Two thin lines that opened.

"Thank you," the voice came as a harsh, vibrant whisper, "thank you very much."

For the first time in his life William fainted.

Rosemary was crying. Sitting by his bed sobbing, but when she saw his eyes were open, a smile lit up her face, the sun peeping through the rain clouds.

"Oh, William, you're awake. Thank goodness, when I found you down on the hall floor, I thought...Do you feel better now? The doctor said you have a slight concussion. Hit your head when you fell."

He felt very weak, and his head hurt, a dull ache. There was also a nagging fear at the back of his mind, trying to remind him of something he wanted to forget.

"I feel fine," he said, "great, simply great. What happened?"

"I don't know," Rosemary was wiping her eyes, "I guess you must have walked in your sleep, and fell downstairs. I did not find you until this morning, and you lay so still..."

She began to cry again and he wanted to comfort her, but the nagging fear was coming out into the open, making him remember, causing him to shiver.

"You must leave this house," he tried to sit upright, "He is looking for someone—a woman who has..." he giggled inanely, "...who has a lasting quality."

"Oh, no," Rosemary had both hands clutched to her, mouth, staring at him with fear-filled eyes, "your poor head."

"I'm not mad," William clutched her arm, "please believe me. He—It, I don't know, but there is a room behind the door, and He made it—kept it alive and himself by the life essence—soul's blood, of living people. I know the door is a trap, is only active for a little while at certain periods, and *now* happens to be one of them. I don't know why sometimes I can go through, and at others I cannot, but it is so. But the point is, He—Sir Michael—has come through, He is on this side of the door, He wants a woman he can take back—make part of the room—take to pieces, tear soul from body, but you won't die, you won't be so lucky."

Rosemary ran from the room, raced down the stairs, and he heard the telephone receiver being removed; she was telephoning the doctor, convinced beyond all doubt he was mad.

Perhaps he was, or at the very best a victim of a walking hallucination. He was suddenly very confused. He had lived off his imagination for years—it could have rebelled, manufactured a sleep-walking nightmare. After all his first 'visit' had begun by him mentally building up the room item by item.

He pretended to be asleep when Rosemary returned.

The doctor said: "Run down," remarked sagely on the effects of overwork, strain, advised rest, wrote out a prescription, and then departed. William felt almost happy after his visit, quite willing to accept the certainty that his experience had been nothing more than a vivid and unpleasant dream. He would rest, stay in bed, then in a few days he and Rosemary would go away for a long holiday, and during their absence a builder could remove the door. That was the sensible solution.

"Sorry if I scared you," he told Rosemary, "but I had such a horrible nightmare—a sort of two-part dream, and it seemed so real. We'll go away when I feel fit."

She was delighted; chatted happily about where they should go, spent as much time as possible by his bedside, and left all the doors open when she went downstairs, so she could hear should he call out. The day passed and as the shadows of night darkened the windows, a faint chill of returning fear began to haunt his mind. Rosemary turned on the lights, drew the curtains, smiled at him, but there was an expression of unease in her eyes, and it was then he knew his hard-won peace of mind was merely self-deception.

"Anything wrong?" He tried to make the question sound casual.

"No," she straightened the counterpane, "no, nothing."

"Tell me," he whispered, fearful lest the very walls were listening, "please, tell me."

She averted her head.

"It"s nothing, only silliness on my part. But—that door—it won't remain shut. Every time I close it, the handle turns, and it opens."

"Then I was right, it was not a dream."

"Nonsense," she was pushing him back onto the pillows, "the door is shrinking, the warm air is making it contract, that must be the answer. It must be ... "

"Did ... did you see anything beyond the door?"

"Only the cupboard shelves, but ... "

She paused, and he did not want her to go on, tried to blot out her voice, but the words came to him, like echoes from yesteryear.

"I keep thinking there is someone else in the house."

He shook his head: "No ... no ... "

"I know it's pure imagination, but ... I thought I saw a face looking down at me over the banisters."

"Rosemary," he took her hand, "don't say anything more, just do as I say. Go downstairs, get the car out of the garage and wait for me. I'll pack a bag and will be with you in a few minutes."

"But ... " Her eyes were wide open, glazed with fear, and she made a faint protest when he clambered out of bed.

"Please do as I say. Now."

She ran from the room and William was reaching for his clothes when he had a glimpse of a figure gliding across the open doorway. For a moment he stood petrified, then he shouted once: "Rosemary!"

"What's the matter?" Her voice, hoarse with fear, came up from the hall. "What ... "

Her scream seared his brain like a hot knife and he raced for the landing, ran down the stairs, then stood in the hall, calling out her name, trying to master his fear, the weakness in his legs.

"William ...! "

The scream came from his study and for a moment he surrendered to the paralysing terror, stood trembling like a statue on the brink of unnatural life, then with a great effort of will he moved forward, staggered rather than ran through the doorway and took in the scene with one all-embracing glance.

He—It—Sir Michael, was complete, rejuvenated by the life force of the girl that lay limp in his arms. The face was now lit by a pair of dark terrible eyes, the nose was arched, cruel, the lips parted in a triumphant smile, the long hair only slightly flecked with grey, but his clothes were still ragged, old, besmirched with grave-mire.

The door was open but the room beyond was slightly out of focus, the walls had a shimmering quality, the chandelier candles were spluttering, making light dance with shadow; a chair suddenly lost one leg and it fell over onto the floor.

He watched William, eyes glistening with sardonic amusement and made no attempt to intervene as the young man stood in the open doorway, with the blue room behind him, the thin lips parted again, and the harsh voice spoke:

"I must thank you again. The woman may have a more lasting quality, but two bodies and souls were always better than one."

He moved forward, and Rosemary, now mercifully unconscious, lay in his arms, her head flung back so that her long hair brushed the desktop as they passed.

The door, William's brain screamed, *destroy the door*.

He would have given twenty years of his life for an axe. Then he remembered the crossed sabres hanging just above the door fame. He reached up and gripped the brass hilts, jerked and they came away, then he spun round to face the approaching figure.

Sir Michael chuckled as he slowly shook his head.

"Never. You will only harm the lady."

William swung the sabre in his right hand sideways; struck the door with a resounding crash, and instantly Sir Michael flinched, fell back a few paces as though the blade had been aimed at him.

"No-o-o." The protest was a cry of pain; William struck again, and red fluid began to seep out of the door panel, and something crashed in the room behind. Then in a fear-inspired frenzy, William slashed wildly at the door, and was dimly aware that Sir Michael had dropped Rosemary, was reeling around the study, jerking as each blow fell, emitting harsh animal-like cries, his eyes black pools of pain-racked hate.

The door shivered, then split; one half, now splintered, soggy, crashed to the floor; William swung his right-hand sabre and struck at the hinges, the door-frame, and did not cease until the brickwork lay bare.

Sir Michael disintegrated. The face dissolved into an oval featureless mask, the hair turned white, then seemed to melt into white powder, the entire body collapsed and became an untidy heap of rags and white bones. In a few minutes these too faded away and William was left staring at a dirty patch of carpet.

He had one last fleeting glimpse of the blue room. The walls and ceiling appeared to fall in, turn into a mass of swirling blue-mist; he saw a great jumble of faces; dark-skinned people with frizzy hair and large, black eyes, young fair-headed girls, children, even animals. Then the shelves of his stationery cupboard came into being, typing paper, ribbons, carbon paper, all merged into their proper place, and William turned his attention to Rosemary who was stirring uneasily.

He gathered her up into his arms.

The splintered remains of the door lay all around, crumbling, rotten with age.

THE ELEMENTAL

"THERE'S AN ELEMENTAL sitting next to you," said the fat woman in the horrible flower-patterned dress and amber beads.

Reginald Warren lowered his newspaper, glanced at the empty seats on either side, shot an alarmed look round the carriage in general, then took refuge behind his *Evening Standard* again.

"He's a killer," the fat woman insisted.

Reginald frowned and tried to think rationally. How did you tackle a nutty fat woman?

"Thank you," he said over the newspaper, "I'm obliged."

Then he tried to immerse himself in the exploits of a company secretary who had swindled his firm out of thirty thousand pounds. He had not progressed further than the first paragraph when the newspaper shook violently, and a little pyramid formed just above an advertisement for Tomkins Hair Restoring Tonic. He jerked the paper downwards and it was at once skewered on the sharp point of an extremely lethal ladies' umbrella.

"Look, madam," he spluttered, "this really is too much."

"And I really do think you should listen to me, ducks," the fat lady insisted, completely unmoved by his outburst. "This is a particularly nasty specimen—a real stinker, and he's growing stronger by the minute."

Reginald stared longingly at the communication cord, but he had been conditioned from birth to regard this interesting facility as something never to be pulled. Apart from which the old dear looked harmless. She was just batty.

"Have you been feeling weak, run down, rather tired lately?" the fat lady enquired solicitously. "Don't bother to answer that—I can see you have. He's been feeding on you. They do, you know, nasty, vicious things. I must say I haven't seen a homicidal one before. Sex-starved ones, yes, alcoholic ones, quite often, but killers, they are rare. In a way you are privileged."

"What . . ." Reginald felt he should display some interest, if only to humour her, "What exactly is an el . . . ?"

"An elemental?" the fat woman settled back and assumed the air of an expert revealing professional mysteries to a layman. "Generally speaking, it is a spirit of air, fire and water, but the 'orrible thing that's attached itself to you is something that's trapped between the planes. It sort of lusts after the pleasures of the flesh. It sucks—yes, that's the word—sucks the juices of the soul. You follow me?"

Reginald was incapable of coherent speech; he nodded.

"Good." She beamed, then fumbled in her handbag and produced a pair of spectacles. "Let's have a butcher's." She adjusted the spectacles firmly on her nose and stared intently at a spot immediately to Reginald's left. "Ah, yes, my word yes. Tut-tut. He's firmly embedded, I fear. His right arm is deep in your left shoulder—ah—he's not happy about my interest . . ." She shook a clenched fist. "Don't you glare at me, you dirty little basket, I've got your measure, me lad. Yes, I have."

A shocked expression made her lips pucker and she hurriedly removed the spectacles and replaced them in her bag.

"He spat at me," she stated.

"Oh dear, I am sorry." Reginald was completely powerless to subdue the urge to rub his left shoulder, and the fat lady smiled grimly.

"I'm afraid you won't rub 'im off, dear. Not in a lifetime will you rub 'im off."

The train roared into Hillside Station, and Reginald greeted its appearance much as a Red-Indian-besieged cowboy welcomed the arrival of the U.S. cavalry.

"My station." He pulled a suitcase from the luggage rack. "Thank you very much."

"Wait."

The fat lady was fumbling in her handbag. "I've got one somewhere."

She upturned the bag and its contents tumbled out on to the seat.

"Really, don't bother," Reginald had the door open "Must go..."

"Ah!" She produced a scrap of pasteboard. "My professional card. 'Madame Orloff, Clairvoyant Extraordinary. Séances, private sitting, palmistry, full psychic service guaranteed.' I can take care of your little problem in no time at all..."

Reginald snatched the card from her outstretched hand, slammed the door, and sprinted for the ticket-barrier. Madame Orloff jerked down the carriage window and shouted after his retreating figure:

"Special reduced rates for five sittings, and a bumper free gift of a genuine crystal-ball if you sign up for ten!"

Susan was waiting for him at the station entrance; she was white and gold and wore a backless sun-suit. He instantly forgot the fat lady, banished the last lingering thought of elementals to that dark world which had always lurked at the back of his mind, and drank in her cool beauty. The blood sang through his veins when he kissed her, and he wanted to say beautiful words, but instead: "It was hot in town."

"Poor darling." She slid her hand over his arm and they walked slowly towards the car. "You look tired. But never mind, seven lazy days in the country is what you need."

"Seven days of mowing grass, clipping hedges, hoeing, and chopping wood." He laughed, and the sound was young, carefree. "What have you been doing today?"

She opened the car door.

"Get in, I'll drive. Doing? Cleaning windows, Hoovering carpets, airing the bed, everything that's needed in a cottage that hasn't been lived in for three months. Did you remember to turn off the gas and lock the flat door before you left?"

He climbed in beside her and settled back with a sigh of content.

"Yes, and I cancelled the milk and papers, turned on the burglar-alarm, and flushed the loo."

"Good."

She swung the car out of the station forecourt and they glided smoothly under an archway of trees that linked arms over the narrow road. He closed his eyes and the occasional beam of sunlight flashed across his round, pleasant face.

"I shall sleep tonight. God, I feel tired, drained dry, almost as if..."

He stopped, opened his eyes, then frowned.

"As if what?" Susan cast an anxious glance sideways. "Look don't you think you ought to see a doctor? I mean it's not like you to be so whacked."

He forced a laugh.

"Nonsense. It's this hot weather and the stuffy atmosphere in town. No, give me three or four days of this country air, plus three square meals prepared by your fair hand, and I'll be raring to go."

"I don't cook *square* meals. They're very much *with-it* meals. But honestly, you do look peaky. I'm going to make you put your feet up."

He grinned. "I don't need any encouragement."

The car shot out from under the trees and the sunlight hit them like a blast from a furnace. Reginald opened the glove compartment and took out two pairs of sunglasses. He handed one to Susan and donned the other himself.

"We must have anti-glare windscreens installed. Bloody dangerous when the light hits you like that."

Susan changed gear.

"Don't swear, darling. It's not like you."

"I'm not swearing. 'Bloody' is a perfectly respectable word these days."

"But it doesn't sound right coming from you. You're not a 'bloody' type."

"Oh!" He grimaced, then sank back in his seat. Presently Susan's voice came to him again.

"Darling, I don't want to nag, but don't hump your left shoulder. It makes me think of the Hunchback of Notre Dame."

He jerked his head sideways and a little cold shiver rang down his spine.

"What?"

She laughed happily; she was gold and ivory in the afternoon sunlight.

"That made you sit up. 'Oh, man, your name is vanity.'"

They swept round a bend in the road, and there was the cottage nestling like a broody hen behind the neatly-trimmed privet hedge. Susan unlocked the front door and Mr. Hawkins barked happily and reared up on his hind legs, begging to have his ears tickled. "Down, you monster." She patted his silky head then went quickly through the little hall and disappeared into the kitchen. Reginald said: "Hullo, boy, how are you?" and Mr. Hawkins began to wag his tail, but after one or two cautious sniffs turned about and ran into the living-room.

"I think Mr. Hawkins has gone off me," Reginald said on entering the kitchen where Susan was examining a roast that was half out of the oven.

"About fifteen minutes more," she announced. "What did you say?"

"I said, I think Mr. Hawkins has gone off me. Seems I don't smell right or something."

"Probably thinks you need a bath. Why not have one before dinner? I've laid out a pair of slacks and a white shirt; you'll feel much fresher afterwards."

"Hey..." He crept up behind her. "Are you suggesting I stink?"

She looked back at him, her eyes laughing.

"If your best friend won't tell you, why should I?"

He was but two feet from her, his hand raised above her gleaming white shoulder, and he bellowed with mock rage.

"Is that the way you speak to your lord and master? I've a good mind to..."

She pulled a saucepan on to the gas ring, then reached up to a wall cupboard and took down two dinner-plates which she placed in the slotted plate-rack.

"Be a good boy and go have your bath."

"Right." He shrugged as he turned towards the door. "I'll wallow in soap suds and sprinkle *Eau-de-Cologne* under my armpits."

"Oh, don't! That hurt!"

He stared back at her in astonishment; she was rubbing her right shoulder, her face screwed up in a grimace of pain.

"What are you talking about?"

"Don't play the innocent. You know darn well—you hit me."

He laughed, imagining this to be some sort of joke, the point of which would become clear in due course.

"Don't be silly, I haven't touched you."

She was performing an almost comical convulsion in an effort to rub the afflicted shoulder. "Look, there's only two of us here, and I certainly didn't hit myself."

"I tell you, I was nowhere near you."

She turned back to the stove, adjusted the gas, then switched on an extractor-fan. "It's not important, so there's no need to lie."

Reginald took a deep breath, and made an effort to speak calmly.

"For the last time, I did not hit you, I was nowhere near you, and I don't like being called a liar."

She made a great business of opening and closing doors, her face set in angry lines. "Go and have your bath. Dinner will soon be ready."

Reginald stamped out of the kitchen. In the hall he almost trod on Mr. Hawkins, who yelped and streaked towards the living-room.

Dinner began in an atmosphere that would have gladdened the heart of an Eskimo; a thaw set in when the sweet was served, and warmth returned with the coffee.

"Darling," he murmured, "please believe me, I didn't ... "

She interrupted with a radiant smile.

"Forget it. If a man can't beat his wife, who can he beat?"

"But ... "

"Not another word. What are we going to do after dinner? Watch television, read, or go to bed?"

"Let's take Mr. Hawkins for a walk, then pop in the Plough for a quick one."

"Okay." She began to collect the empty coffee cups. "I'll wash up, then we'll be off."

"Give you a hand?" Reginald half-rose from his chair.

"No, you don't, this lot won't take me more than ten minutes. In any case, you always break something. Sit in the armchair and read the local rag—there's an uplifting article on pig-raising."

"If you insist."

He got up from the table, then slumped down in an armchair, where, after a fruitless attempt at interest in local events, he tossed the newspaper to one side and closed his eyes. The muted sounds made by Susan in the kitchen were pleasant; they told him all was well in his safe little world. They reminded him he had an adoring, beautiful young wife, a good job that he tackled with ease, a flat in town, a cottage in the country, money in the bank. He smiled, and this wonderful sense of security drew him gently into the quiet realms of sleep.

He came awake with a start. The rattle of plates still came from the kitchen; far away on the main by-pass a heavy van sent its muted roar across fields that dozed in the hot evening sun; Mr. Hawkins sat under the table and glared at his owner. Reginald blinked, then yawned as he spoke.

"What's the matter with you?"

The dog's usually placid, brown velvet eyes were fierce; his body was rigid, and even as Reginald spoke, he bared his teeth and growled.

"What the hell!"

Reginald sat upright, and instantly Mr. Hawkins retreated and took refuge under a chair, where he crouched, growling and watching his master with a terrible intensity.

"Susan!" Reginald called out, "what the hell's wrong with this dog?"

Susan came out of the kitchen wiping her hands on a towel, her face creased into an expression of amused enquiry.

"So far as I know, nothing. Why?"

"Well, look at him." Reginald pointed at the snarling dog, who backed farther away under the chair until all that could be seen was a pair of gleaming eyes and bared teeth. "Anyone would think I was Dracula's mother looking for her feeding bottle. I say, you don't suppose he's got rabies, do you?"

"Good heavens, no." Susan crouched down and called softly: "Mr. Hawkins, come on boy."

Mr. Hawkins ran to her, his tail wagging feebly, and he whimpered when she patted his head and stroked his soft coat.

"Poor old chap, has the heat got you down? Eh? Do you want nice walkies? Eh? Nice walkies?"

Mr. Hawkins displayed all the signs of intense pleasure at this prospect, and performed a little dance of pure joy.

"He's all right," Susan said, straightening up. "It must have been your face that put him off."

"Well, he put the fear of God into me." Reginald rose. "He hasn't been normal since I arrived. Perhaps we ought to take him to a vet?"

"Nonsense, he's fine." Susan went out into the hall and the dog scampered after her. "It must have been the heat that got him down. Do you think I need a coat?"

"No, go as you are and shock the natives." Reginald grinned, then frowned when he saw a six-inch-long mark that marred her right shoulder. "No, come to think of it, perhaps you'd better put on a jacket or something. It may be chilly before we get back."

She took a thin satin shawl down from the hall-stand.

"I'll wear this. There isn't a breath of wind, and I wouldn't be surprised if there's a storm before morning."

Mr. Hawkins was flattened against the front door, and when Reginald opened it, he growled low in his throat before scampering madly along the garden path and out through a hole in the hedge. Reginald smiled grimly as he closed the door and followed Susan towards the gate.

"There's something bothering that damned dog."

Out in the narrow road Susan took his arm and they walked slowly under a steel-blue sky.

"Don't be so silly. He's frisky. Just heat and sex."

"Ah!" Reginald nodded. "I know then how he feels. What a combination."

They left the roadway, climbed a stile and walked ankle-deep through lush summer grass, as the dying sun painted the far-away hill-sides golden-brown. Mr. Hawkins raced happily back and forth, sniffing at rabbit holes, saluting trees, reliving the days when his fore-bears acknowledged neither man nor beast as master, and Susan sighed.

"Heaven must be eternity spent in walking through an English field at sunset."

"And Hell," Reginald retorted, "must be eternity spent in a tube train during the rush hour."

They walked for a few minutes in silence; Susan adjusted her shawl, and Reginald watched her, a tiny frown lining his forehead.

"Susan, did something really . . . ?"

"Did something really what?"

He shook his head. "Nothing. Forget it."

"No, tell me. What were you going to say?"

"It wasn't important." He patted the hand that lay on his arm. "Just a passing thought."

The sun had set when they once again walked up the garden path, and a full moon lit up the cottage and surrounding countryside, painting the red-bricked walls, the neat little garden, with a cold silver hue. Susan was laughing softly, and Reginald was frowning; he looked tired and drawn.

"Honestly, you must admit it was funny." She inserted the latch-key, then opened the door and led the way into the hall. "That little girl . . . "

"Yes, yes, you've been through it three times before," Reginald snapped, but his irritability only provoked further laughter.

"But . . . " She opened the living-room door and switched on the light. "But in front of a crowd of beer-boozy layabouts this little mite pointed at you and said . . . " For a moment Susan could not continue, then she wiped her eyes . . . and said, 'Ugly man making faces at me'."

"All right," Reginald glared at Mr. Hawkins, who was watching him from under the table. "All right, so it was funny. Let's forget it, shall we?"

"But you should have seen your face. I thought for a moment you were going to be sick."

Reginald slumped into a chair and absentmindedly rubbed his left shoulder.

"Say, ugly face, you don't want anything else to drink after all that beer, do you?"

"No, and cut it out."

"Come on, now." She sat on the arm of his chair. "Where's your sense of humour? She was only a little thing, and probably tired out. I mean to say, you weren't really making faces at her, were you?"

"Of course not."

"Well then, why so grumpy?"

"I don't know," he spoke softly. "I honestly don't know."

"Let's go to bed," she whispered, "and dream away the dark footed hours."

"Yup." He rose, then smiled down at her; she slid an arm about his neck and laid a soft cheek against his own.

"You are the most beautiful man in the whole world," she said.

He nodded.

"I guess you're right at that."

Their laughter mingled when he carried her up the stairs, and Mr. Hawkins stood in the hallway and watched their ascending figures with worried eyes.

The curtains were drawn back, the soft moonlight kept shadows at bay, and they lay side by side and waited for the silence to summon sleep.

"Think of all the bunny-rabbits peacefully asleep in their burrows," she whispered.

"Or think of them eating Farmer Thing-a-bob's cabbages," he murmured.

She giggled.

"Are you sleepy?"

"Somewhat."

"Why do you insist on sleeping on the right-hand side of the bed?"

"That's a darn fool question." He stirred uneasily and widened the space between them. "Because it's man's prerogative, I guess."

There was a full minute of blessed silence.

"Darling, if you must hold my hand, don't press so hard."

His voice came from the half-world where sleep and consciousness hold an even balance.

"I'm not holding your hand."

"But, darling, you are, and you must cut your nails."

"Stop blathering and go to sleep."

Suddenly her body began to thresh wildly, and her cry of protest rose to a terrified scream.

"Reginald, what are you doing? No...oh, my God!"

For a second he imagined she must be playing some silly joke, that this was not a very subtle way of informing him she was not prepared to sleep, then the violent threshing of her legs, the choking gasps, made him sit up and fumble frantically for the light switch. As lamplight blasted darkness, hurled it back against the walls, she leapt from the bed and stood facing him, gasping, massaging her throat, staring with fear-crazed eyes. He was dimly aware of the faint smell, sweet, cloying, like dead flowers.

"What's wrong?" He climbed out of bed and she backed to the wall, shaking her head.

"Keep away from me."

"What the hell...?"

He moved round the foot of the bed then stopped when he saw her expression of terror deepen. At that moment, truth reared up in his brain, but he ignored it, crushed it under the weight of his disbelief, and he whispered:

"You know I would do nothing to hurt you."

Her whisper matched his and it was as though they were in some forbidden place, afraid lest a dreaded guardian heard their voices.

"You tried to choke me. Awful hands with nails like talons, and a foul breath that I can still smell."

He could scarcely utter the next words.

"Could that have been me?"

The awful fear on her face was dreadful to watch, and truth was uncoiling again, would not be denied.

"Then—who was it?"

"Get back into bed," he urged. "Please, I will sit on a chair. I won't come near you, I promise."

Beautiful eyes still watched him as she moved to obey, but the moment her hand touched the pillow, she recoiled.

"The smell—the stench, it's still here."

They went downstairs and seated themselves in the living room, far apart, like strangers who may never meet again, and his voice bridged the great gulf that separated them.

"There was a woman on the train. She said she was a medium."

She waited for his next words as though there were venomous snakes being offered on a silver tray.

"She said I had an elemental attached to my left shoulder. Apparently it is feeding off me, growing stronger by the minute."

Susan did not move or betray the slightest sign she had understood or even heard what he said.

"A few hours ago, I guess, we would have laughed at the very idea." Reginald was staring at the empty fireplace, even giving the impression he was addressing it rather than the silent girl who sat clutching her dressing-gown with white fingers. "It would have been a great giggle, a funny story to tell our friends over a drink. Now..."

They sat opposite each other for the remainder of the dark hours. Once, Mr. Hawkins howled from his chosen place in the empty hall. They ignored him.

Reginald found the card in his jacket pocket and read the inscription aloud.

"Madame Orloff, Clairvoyant Extraordinary. 15 Disraeli Road, Clapham, London SW4."

He dialled the telephone number at the foot of the card and waited; presently a voice answered.

"Madame Orloff, Clairvoyant Extraordinary, messages from Beyond a speciality, speaking."

Reginald cleared his throat.

"My name is Reginald Warren. I don't suppose you remember me— we met on a train yesterday..."

"Yes, indeed I do." The voice took on a joyful tone. "You're the man with the nasty little E. I expect you want me to get cracking on the 'orrible little basket."

"Well," Reginald lowered his voice, "last night he tried to strangle my wife."

"What's that? Speak up, my dear man. It did what?"

"Tried to strangle my wife."

"Yes, I expect it did. I told you it was a homicidal. Now look, stay put, and I'll have to belt down there. It's a bit of a bind because I had two table-tapping sessions and one poltergeist on the books for this afternoon. Still, it can't be helped. Let me have your address."

Reginald parted with his address with the same reluctance that he would have experienced had he given up his soul.

"The Oak Cottage, Hawthorne Lane, Hillside, Surrey."

"Right," the cheerful voice had repeated the address, word by word. "Be with you about 3:00. I wouldn't eat too hearty if I were you. He seems to be putting on weight if he's been up to his little tricks so soon. You may have a materialisation, although I doubt it at this stage. His main objective is to get inside you. Take over. Follow me?"

"Yes," Reginald swallowed, "I think so."

"Good man. See you at three. Can I get a cab at the station?"

"No, but I'll pick you up."

"Not on your Nelly." The voice assumed a shocked tone. "He'll most likely try to run you off the road if he knows I'm coming. I'll hire a car—and add the cost to my bill, course."

Of course," Reginald agreed, "anything at all."

Madame Orloff arrived at five minutes past 3:00; she crossed her fingers and waved at Mr. Hawkins, who promptly made a bolt for the stairs.

"Poor little dear," she sighed. "Animals always spot them first, you know. Animals and some small children. Now, let's have a butcher's."

She put on her spectacles and studied Reginald with keen interest.

"My, my, we have grown. Yes indeed, he's sucking up the old spiritual fluids like a baby at its mother's breast." She bent forward and sniffed, looking rather like a well-fed bulldog who is eagerly anticipating his dinner. "Pongs too, don't he?"

"How did it become attached to me?" Reginald asked, aware that Susan was watching the visitor with an expression that was divided between horror and amazement. "I mean, I was all right up to yesterday."

"Been in a tube train lately?" Madame Orloff asked.

He nodded.

"Thought so. That damned Underground is packed with them during rush hour. I once saw a bank clerk with six of 'em clinging to him like limpets, and he picked up two more between Charing Cross and Leicester Square. Wouldn't listen to me, of course."

She turned her attention to Susan, who cringed as the heavy figure came towards her.

"You're a pretty dear, and sensitive too, I fear. You must watch yourself, poppet, keep off animal foods—and I should wear a sprig of garlic if I were you. They can't stand garlic or clean thoughts. Think clean and religious thoughts, dear. Try to picture the Archbishop of Canterbury taking a bath. Now..." She rolled up her sleeves. "Let's see if we can get 'im dislodged. Sit yourself down, lad. No, not in an easy chair, this plain straight-backed one is the ticket, and angel love, will you draw the curtains? Light is apt to put me off me stroke."

Reginald was seated on a dining-room chair, the sunlight was diffused through blue nylon curtains, and the room looked cool, peaceful, a place where one might doze away the years. Susan whimpered.

"I'm frightened. Don't let her do it."

"Hush, dear." Madame Orloff twisted her head round. "We must dislodge the basket, or he'll be at your throat again, as sure as a preggers cat 'as kittens.

She put a large beringed hand on either side of Reginald's head, and closed her eyes.

"I don't follow the usual formula, so don't be surprised at anything I might say. It's just ways and means of concentrating me powers."

She began to jerk Reginald's head backwards and forwards while intoning a little rhyming ditty in a high-pitched voice.

> "Black, foul thing from down below,
> Get you hence, or I'll bestow
> A two-footed kick right up your bum
> That'll make your buttocks come through your tum."

She writhed, jerked, made the amber beads rattle like bones in a box, all the while jerking Reginald's head and pressing down on his temples, then gave vent to a roar of rage.

"No you don't, you black-hearted little basket! Try to bite, would you? Get out, out—out—out . . .

"Get right out or I'll bash your snout,
Go right under, or get your number,
No more kicks, or you'll pass bricks,
No more crying, it's no use trying,
Out-a-Daisy, you're driving me crazy."

Madame Orloff snatched her hands from Reginald's head and flopped down in a chair, where she sat mopping her sweat-drenched face with a large red handkerchief.

"Must have a breather, dear. Strewth, he's made me sweat like a pig. I've tackled some 'ard ones in me time, but he takes the biscuit." She clenched her fist and shook it in Reginald's direction. "You can grin at me like a cat that's nicked the bacon, but I'll get your measure yet." She turned to Susan. "Get us a glass of water, there's a dear."

Susan ran from the room, and Madame Orloff shook her head.

"You'll have to watch that one. She's hot stuff, attracts 'em like flies to cow dung, if you get my meaning. She's soft and pliable, and they'll slide into her as easy as a knife going into butter. You back already, dear? Mustn't run like that, you'll strain something."

She drank greedily from the glass that Susan handed her, then rubbed her hands.

"Thirsty work this. Well, as the bishop said to the actress, let's have another go."

She got up and once again took Reginald's head between her hands. Her face wore an expression of grim determination.

"Now, dear, I want you to help me. Strain. That's the word, dear. Strain. Possession is rather like having constipation. You have to strain. Keep repeating 'Old Bill Bailey' to yourself. It'll help no end. Ready?"

Reginald tried to nod but was unable to do so due to Madame's firm hold, so he muttered, "Yes" instead.

"Right—strain."

"Now nasty horsie that's had no oats,

This little bunny ain't afraid of stoats,

(Strain man—Old Bill Bailey)

Coal black pussy, he's no tom,
He's had his op, so get you gone."

Madame raised her voice to a shout, and a large blue vase on the mantelpiece suddenly crashed onto the tiled hearth.

"Strain—Old Bill Bailey—come on, we've got 'im! Out—out—get your skates on . . .

"Out of the window, out through the door,
There's no marbles here, he'll keep you poor,
Don't grind your teeth . . ."

A chair went tumbling across the floor, books came hurling from their shelves, a rug left the floor and wrapped itself round the ceiling-lamp, and a cold wind tugged at the window curtains. Madame Orloff lowered her voice, but it was still clear, unexpectedly sad.

"Lonely wanderer of the starless night,
You must not stay, it is not right,
Blood is for flesh, and flesh is for blood,
We live for an hour, then are lost in a flood
That sweeps us away into a fathomless gloom,
We spend eternity in a darkened room."

"Please stop!" Susan's voice was lost amid the howling wind, but Madame Orloff's cry of triumph rang out.

"Strain—strain . . . he's coming out. Aye, he's coming out as smooth as an eye leaving its socket. He's fighting every inch of the way, but old Ma Perkins was one too many for him. Out you go, my beauty, out you go, down to the land where black mountains glow with never-quenched fire, and white worms crawl from the corrupt earth, even as maggots seethe from a carcass on a hot afternoon. Go . . . go . . . "

The cold wind died, hot air seeped back into the room; all-around lay wrecked pictures, scattered books, broken furniture. An ugly crack disfigured the polished surface of a table. Susan was crying softly, Reginald was white-faced, looking like a man who has survived a long illness. Madame Orloff rose, pulled open the window curtains, then looked about with an air of satisfaction.

"A bit of a ruddy mess, but then, as someone once said, you can't make an omelette without breaking eggs. "'Fraid me services, come a bit high, dear. I'll want fifty nicker for this little do."

"Worth every penny." Reginald Rose somewhat unsteadily to his feet. "I can't thank you enough, Madam, I feel like . . . "

"A feather, eh?" Madam Orloff beamed. "A great weight lifted off yer shoulders? I know what you mean. I remember an old geezer down in Epsom; he had a nasty attached to him that was as big as a house. Ruddy great thing, had a lust for rice puddings, made the poor old sod eat three at one sitting. When I got shot of it, he leapt about like a two-year-old. Said he felt like floating. Well . . . " She took up her handbag. "Mustn't keep that car waiting any longer—the fare will cost you a fortune." She put a hand under Susan's chin and tilted her head; the blue eyes were bright with tears.

"Cheer up, ducks. It's all over now. Nothing to worry your pretty little head about any more."

"You must stay for dinner," Susan said softly. "We can't let you go like this . . . "

"Thanks all the same, but I've got a sitting laid on for six o'clock, so I'll leave you to clear up the mess. Don't trouble to see me out. I'm quite capable of opening and closing a door."

From the hallway she looked back.

"I should keep away from the Underground during the rush hour, Mr. Warren. The place is a cesspit—everything from a damn nuisance poltergeist to a vampire-elemental. See you."

The front-door slammed and Reginald gathered Susan up into his arms; he patted her shaking shoulders and murmured: "There, there, it's all over now. It's all over."

They sat in the twilight, younger than youth, older than time, and rejoiced in each other.

"You are wonderful," she said.

"True," he nodded.

"And awfully conceited."

"Self-confidence," he corrected. "The weak are vain, the strong self-confident."

"And what am I?"

"White, gold and tinged with pink."

"I like that." She snuggled up to him and Mr. Hawkins dozed peacefully on the hearth-rug.

Presently—

"What's that?"

She sat up. Fear was in waiting, ready to leap into her eyes.

"Nothing." He pulled her back. "Just nerves. It's all over now."

"I thought I heard someone knocking."

"There's no one to come knocking at our door. No one at all."

Mr. Hawkins whimpered in his sleep, and somewhere above, a floor-board creaked.

"The wood contracting," he comforted her. "The temperature is falling, so the wood contracts. We must not let imagination run away with us."

"Reginald . . ." She was staring up at the ceiling. "Madame Orloff—she got it loose from you, and I'm grateful, but—suppose—"

Another floorboard creaked and a bedroom door slammed.

"Suppose—it's—still here?"

He was going to say 'nonsense', laugh at her fears, but Mr. Hawkins was up on his four legs, his coat erect, growling fiercely as he glared at the closed door. Heavy footsteps were on the landing, pacing back and forth, making the ceiling lamp shake, breaking now and again into a kind of skipping dance. Susan screamed before she collapsed into merciful oblivion, and at once the sound ceased, to be replaced by a menacing silence.

Reginald laid Susan down upon the sofa and crept on tip-toe towards the door. When he opened it a wave of foul-smelling cold air made him gasp, then, with courage born of desperation, he went out to the hall and peered up into the gloom-haunted staircase.

It was coming down. A black blob that was roughly human-shaped, but the face was real—luminous-green; the eyes, red; a bird's-nest thatch of black hair. It was grinning, and the unseen feet were making the stairs tremble. Reginald, aware only that he must fight, picked up a small hall table and flung it straight at the approaching figure. Instantly, something—some invisible force—hurled him against the front door, and he lay on the doormat powerless to move. The Thing moved slowly down the stairs, and for a hell-bound second the red eyes glared down at the prostrate man before it clumped into the living-room. The door slammed, and Mr. Hawkins howled but once.

Minutes passed and Reginald tried to move, but the power had gone from his legs. Also, there was a dull pain in the region of his lower spine, and he wondered if his back were broken. At last, the living-room door slid open, went back on its hinges with a protesting creak as though wishing to disclaim all responsibility for that which was coming out. Susan walked stiff-legged into the hall, white-faced, clothes torn, but her face was lit by a triumphant smile, and Reginald gasped out loud with pure relief.

"Darling, thank heavens you're safe. Don't be alarmed—it flung me against the door, but I think I've only sprained something. Give me a hand up and we'll get the hell out of here."

She moved closer, still walking with that grotesque stiff-legged gait. Her head went over to one side, and for the first time he saw her eyes. They were mad—mad—mad... Her mouth opened, and the words came out in a strangled, harsh tone.

"Life...life...life...flesh...flesh...flesh...blood..."

"Susan!" Reginald screamed and tried to get up, but collapsed as a blast of pain seared his back; he could only watch with dumb horror as she swung her stiff left leg around and began to hobble towards the broken table that lay on the bottom stair. She had difficulty in bending over to pick up the carved walnut leg, and even more difficulty in straightening up, but she gripped the leg firmly in her right hand, and the grimace on her face could have denoted pleasure.

"You...denied...me...life," the harsh voice said. "You...denied...me...life..."

She, if the Thing standing over Reginald could still be so-called, looked down with red-tinted eyes, horror in ivory and gold, and he wanted even then to hold her, kiss away the grotesque lines from around the full-lipped mouth, murmur his great love, close those dreadful eyes with gentle fingers. Then the carved walnut leg came down and smashed deep into his skull, and the world exploded, sending tumbling over and over into eternity.

Presently the Thing which had been Susan went out into the evening that was golden with the setting sun. It drank deep of the cool air, for storm clouds were pouring in from the west and soon there would be rain.

It went stiff-legged down the garden path, and out into the roadway. There was still much killing to be done.

THE JUMPITY-JIM

"KEEP YOURSELF NEAT and tidy at all times," Father said, "and learn your duties."

"Read a portion of Holy Scriptures every night before retiring," Mother instructed, and Father nodded his agreement.

Harriet waved to them from the coach window, more than a little frightened if the truth be told, for this was the first time she had been away from home and she was going into an unknown future. The coachman whipped up his horses, the guard blew a blast on his horn, and they were away, drawing clear of the village, leaving the happy years of childhood behind.

"You look distressed, my dear," a kindly-looking matron on the opposite seat said. "You are leaving home for the first time?"

Harriet nodded while patting her eyes with a nice clean handkerchief, freshly laundered by Mother that morning.

"Never mind," the good lady consoled, "you'll soon get used to your new surroundings. It's good for youngsters to break away from the apron-strings. Going into service, I expect."

"Yes, ma'am," Harriet nodded again. "Begging your pardon but how did you know?"

The lady laughed. "Can always tell. Fresh young thing like you, all done up in your Sunday best. Service, I said to myself the minute you put foot inside this coach."

The four other passengers had been listening to this conversation with varying degrees of interest, and one young man who wore a beautiful waistcoat, smiled a rather supercilious smile.

"And what household is to be honoured by your service? Buckingham Palace?"

"Oh, no!" Harriet gasped. "But I am going to a nobleman's house. Lord Dunwilliam's."

"Are you, indeed!"

The young man produced a quizzing-glass and examined Harriet carefully for a few minutes, as though she were some rare specimen he had not encountered before. At length he dropped the glass, which dangled on the end of a gold chain, and pronounced his verdict.

"You should fit into Dunwilliam's establishment very nicely," he said. "Very nicely indeed."

Harriet stood in the courtyard of the Royal George and watched the departing mail-coach rumble its way up a slope and out onto the main highway. The last link with home had been broken and she was now alone, subject to the caprice of total strangers. She sat down on her black box, not daring to enter the inn, for Father had often stressed the evil which lurked in such places, and wondered what she should do. Father had said someone would be waiting to meet her, but so far none of the loungers that were clustered round the inn door advanced to claim her.

Presently, however, a tall, dark man, dressed in a cassock, entered the courtyard. His coming seemed to alarm everyone in sight, for they dispersed, scattering like corn husks before the wind. Harriet saw the priest had a long, harsh face—a visage she knew to be right and proper for a man of his calling—and she got quickly to her feet, performing a little bob, thus displaying a seemly respect for the cloth and a sense of righteous humility.

The reverend gentleman interrupted his journey towards the inn, which, if his expression was any criterion, boded ill for its occupants, and scowled down at the girl.

"And pray, child, what is a girl who displays all the outward signs of a proper upbringing doing in this place of iniquity? And unattended? Eh!"

He barked the 'Eh' with such ferocity that Harriet trembled before bowing her knee into another bob, an action her mother had often stressed was most pleasing to the quality.

"If you please, sir, I'm waiting to be picked up."

"What!"

The roar made Harriet realise she had not perhaps chosen her words well, and she hastened to explain.

"Begging your pardon, sir, but someone is to collect me. I am to be kitchen-maid, if it so please you, at Dunwilliam Grange..."

She stopped in mid-sentence, for the dark, awful eyes that glared down at her now held an expression that left no doubt she had again, inadvertently said the wrong thing.

"Repeat," the priest said, his jaw muscles quivering. "I say, if you have the brazen effrontery, repeat what you have just said."

"If you please, sir, I am to be kitchen-maid at..."

"Yes, go on. Where, child? Where?"

"Dunwilliam Grange, sir..."

One hand seized the front of her dress, the other tilted her chin, and the raucous voice rang out.

"The face is fair. Eh? I grant you the Devil has grown cunning and now hides his evil under a pretty—nay—even an innocent mask. But I am not deceived. Eh? The form is shapely, well-calculated to inflame men's senses, but I warrant that somewhere the great beast has left his mark. Eh? Tell me, wench, where is it?"

"I don't know what you mean, sir."

Harriet dared not struggle, for she saw the reverend gentleman was sore afflicted; saliva was trickling down the corners of his mouth and his eyes were dreadfully bloodshot. She recalled that Gaffer Cheeseman had a similar appearance after he had drunk two gallons of cider on an empty stomach. The priest tightened his grip.

"Not know what I mean, eh? Going to Dunwilliam Grange and pleading the innocence of a lamb that has just seen the light of day? I would as lief believe the sun rose at midnight and the Devil bathed in holy water. Now, I ask again, girl. Where is the mark? The secret tit from which the beast takes substance?"

"I have no mark, sir." Harriet was crying. "When you have slept, I am certain you will regret abusing me so. My father says cider breeds madness . . ."

The roar of rage was like that of Farmer Giles's bull when it spotted Mistress Jarvie crossing the field in a red cloak. The priest spun her around and, gripping her dress at the neck-line, ripped it open to the waist. Harriet felt the cold air on her back, and she pulled away, only to have her hair grabbed. The now-spluttering voice shouted: "The flesh is white. Eh? So is the leper that is cast out from the haunts of men. But I will find the mark. Eh, I will find it."

"Enough!"

A sharp voice cut across the priest's tirade like the blade of a knife, and Harriet was suddenly released, to go sprawling face-down on the cobblestones, where she lay sobbing for a few moments then, remembering her half-nude state, scrambled to her feet. A man was just dismounting from his horse, and tossing the reins to a nearby ostler. He sauntered over to the sobbing girl and glaring priest. Harriet, despite her distress, thought she had never seen such a beautiful gentleman before. He was tall, with a lean, bronzed face, and a pair of dark, penetrating eyes. His hair was jet-black, save for a single white streak which ran from the centre of his high forehead to the base of his skull. He was dressed all in black, relieved only by the silver trimmings on his cloak. He smiled, revealing even white teeth.

"I admire your taste, parson. But in public! Whatever would the dear Bishop say?"

The clergyman crossed himself, then backed away a few paces.

"*Avaunt*, Satan."

The gentleman laughed. "I will be gone when the mood suits me. I will not ask why you molested this pretty creature, for you are as crazed as a cracked jug and I have not the time for the prattle of a madman. Where were you bound, girl?"

Harriet would have dropped a curtsy, but she suspected such an operation might cause her to release her torn dress, so she meekly bowed her head instead.

"To Dunwilliam Grange, if it so please you, sir."

"Another of your imported devil spawn?" the priest growled and the gentleman raised his hand in mock horror.

"You malign me. I rarely snatch from the cradle, but I grant you, she is a delicious morsel. What post are you to fill in my house, child?"

"You are—Lord Dunwilliam?" she gasped.

He sighed deeply. "I fear so."

"I am to be your kitchen-maid, my lord."

"Indeed? I was not aware that we needed one. It must be you that rogue Hackett was supposed to collect, but he ran the dog-cart into a ditch. Drunk as a priest at a bishop's convention."

He made an ironic bow in the parson's direction.

"Your pardon, Mr. Dale, I forgot—you prefer stripping girls to opening a bottle."

"The day of reckoning is coming." The Reverend Dale shook his fist. "I know of the obscenities that take place in that proud house, but I tell you the time will come when its stones will be levelled to the ground."

"You'd best ride before me, girl." Lord Dunwilliam smiled down Harriet. "'Twould not be wise to leave you here with that poor, mad fool, and Heaven above knows when Hackett will be sober enough to drive the cart."

He beckoned to the ostler: "Take the girl's box into the inn. Someone will call for it later."

He mounted the great horse, then, leaning down, pulled Harriet up. She sat side-saddle, trying hard not to lean against him and very mindful of the strong arms that railed her in on either side when he took up the reins. They rode out of the courtyard and the Reverend Dale's voice followed them.

"God is not mocked. He will send forth his legions and they will crush the forces of evil. Cursed be ye that walk by night, for darkness will be your lot for all eternity..."

"The home of my fathers, said Dunwilliam in a low tone. "See girl, the nest in which I was hatched."

The grey-stoned house stood before a screen of trees; turreted, a face with many eyes, it was a structure of rare, if somewhat grim beauty. Harriet wondered if she dare enter such a grand place with a torn dress and a dirty face.

"It's very nice," she said.

Lord Dunwilliam chuckled.

"I doubt if there are many hereabouts who would agree with that description. How, in the name of sanity, did you ever become engaged as my kitchen-maid?"

"Mother, who was in service before she married, wrote to an agency in London. For she knows her letters, and writes as good a hand as Parson himself. They sent someone down to see me, and I am to be on a month's trial."

"Um." His lordship grunted as they rode down one hill and then another, finally to pass through the great iron gates of Dunwilliam Grange.

Mrs. Browning was a woman of large proportions and such a grim aspect that Harriet almost wished herself back in the inn courtyard facing the Reverend Dale. The housekeeper allowed her cold gaze to travel slowly down from the girl's auburn head to the tips of her laced-up boots.

"How are you called, girl?"

"Harriet, ma'am."

"Most unsuitable. From now on you will be known as Jane." She called abruptly over one shoulder. "Mary, come here."

An extremely pretty girl left the kitchen table where she had been slicing potatoes and came quickly over to Mrs. Browning, before whom she stood motionless, her head bowed.

"Yes, ma'am."

"Mary, you will take Jane upstairs and see that she returns suitably attired. She is to share your room."

"Yes, ma'am. Thank you, ma'am."

Harriet followed her guide up some very steep and winding stairs and presently came to a small room that overlooked the back garden. It was furnished with two narrow beds, a washstand and a large cupboard. Mary was brimful with curiosity and, scarcely had she closed the door, when questions came tripping off her tongue.

"How did your dress get all tore like that? And Jem the gardener says you come here on his lordship's horse. Did he tear your dress?"

"No." Harriet shook her auburn curls. "It was a horrible old parson."

"Ah, the Reverend Dale. He hates this place something cruel and says all of us who live here be limbs of Satan."

"Why?" Harriet had removed her tattered dress, which she was examining rather ruefully, and Mary opened the cupboard door and produced a black skirt and white blouse.

"Well, they do say all sort of weird goings-on took place in this house back in his lordship's father's time. There's a big room, right up under the roof, and people saw flashes of light and heard terrible cries. Then one morning his old lordship was found dead. 'Twas said he took poison or some such thing."

"How awful!" Harriet shuddered. "Aren't you frightened?"

Mary shook her head.

"No. I pay no heed to talk like that, only I wouldn't care to go wandering around the upper storey after nightfall. Besides, the pay's good, and although Mrs. Browning is a tartar, the work ain't all that hard."

While they had been talking, Harriet had dressed, and now she wore a costume corresponding to Mary's; a long, black serge skirt and an off-the-shoulder blouse. She was not happy with this last item, Mother having on more than one occasion stated that the face and hands were the only parts of the body a respectable woman bared for public gaze.

"It don't seem right," she began, but Mary laughed.

"You'll soon get used to it. 'Tis only the shoulders. Why, some ladies leave parts of their boobs there and aren't thought none the worse. It's a fad of her ladyship's. Indoors, we young 'uns have to wear this get-up. Don't do no harm. But it makes the parson howl."

She laid Harriet's torn dress out on the bed and sighed.

"Shame. But a needle and thread should soon put it to rights. Now, we best get down, or Mrs. Browning will be raising old Cain and her tongue be sharp enough as it is."

Back in the kitchen Mrs. Browning gave Harriet a quick glance, then said: "There's an overall hanging up behind the door. Put it on, then go into the scullery and start cleaning out the saucepans. We're all behind like a donkey's tail."

During the days that followed, Harriet began to realise to some degree why the Reverend Dale entertained such pronounced misgivings about the household at Dunwilliam Grange. With the exception of Mrs. Browning, all the female staff were young and extremely pretty. Another disquieting piece of information was that few completed their month's probation. The turnover in female staff was alarmingly high. Once, when washing-up in the scullery, she heard Jem the head gardener and Hackett, a bearded, morose individual, talking as they sat drinking beer at the kitchen table.

"The new 'un be shapely. 'Twould be a good tumble in the 'ay."

Harriet wondered what this remark might mean, but, realising that she was the 'new 'un' under discussion, wiped her hands dry and stood listening.

"Won't last long," Hackett stated. "They never does. After a little chat with 'er ladyship, out they goes."

"That be a strange thing." Jem refilled his glass from an earthenware jug. "Why be that? Right as a trivet, until they 'as a little heart-to-heart with 'er ladyship. The number of boxes and blubbering wenches you've driven down to the Royal George... Don't they talk right or summat?"

"Maybe," Hackett murmured gruffly. "Maybe."

There was a full minute's silence and Harriet wondered if the conversation had come to an unsatisfactory conclusion. Then Hackett spoke again, but this in a low, though perfectly audible tone.

"Jem, if I tells you summat confidential like, will you promise to keep it under your 'at?"

"I'll be as silent as the grave," Jem promised. "I'm not one to blab, you knows that."

"Well," Hackett said and cleared his throat, "perhaps I shouldn't tell you, as his lordship gave me a gold piece to keep me mouth shut, but it's lain on me conscience and I'd like to unburden, if you knows what I mean."

"Aye, man. Get on with it."

"Well, about two years back, do you remember that red-headed piece, Clara? Only her real name was Jenny Binns. Well, she went upstairs for her little chat with 'er ladyship. Excited she was, thought maybe she'd get promotion to above stairs, and I didn't tell 'er no different. It must 'ave been about half-past six when 'is lordship comes over to the coach-house; looked a bit down in the mouth 'e did. He sez: 'Hackett, Clara has been taken ill. I wants you to take 'er to the good Sister,' 'e sez. 'I'll ride over and see the Mother Superior.' Well, I thought that a bit funny, see? Any road, I went up to 'er ladyship's room, and there was the girl looking as if she's had a fit. Speechless she was, with 'er face all twisted up, and 'er eyes—strewth! You'd think she'd seen Old Nick 'imself."

"Do you think, maybe," Jem asked in a low, quivering voice, "she 'ad?"

"No, man. I don't 'old with that nonsense. But I tell you summat else. There were three ruddy scratches down 'er back."

"No!" Jem gasped. "You're 'aving me on."

"True as I sit 'ere. 'Er blouse was all tore, and scratches, like claw marks, down 'er back. Don't know what they thought of it up at the convent. Mad dog, mayhap. Anyway, 'er ladyship was furious. Kept muttering about 'er almost being the one."

"What do you think she meant?" Jem asked.

"Gawd knows. But...Not a word mind. 'Ere comes old Ma Browning."

Harriet went back to her washing-up, trying to understand what the conversation had implied. Above all, what sort of person was Lady Dunwilliam?

"Mary, have you seen Lady Dunwilliam yet?"

"Once or twice."

Mary was bathing her feet in an earthenware bowl. "She walks in the small garden sometimes. Why?"

"I just wondered. You haven't been up to see her?"

"Oh, I see what you mean." Mary wiped her feet on a towel then, opening the window, emptied the contents of the bowl onto the garden below. "That'll make the cabbages grow. No. Mrs. Browning said her ladyship would want a few words with me some time. But nothing's happened yet."

Mary climbed into bed and blew out the candles before snuggling deep down into the feather-mattress. She grunted with complete satisfaction.

"Never slept on a feather-mattress 'til I came here. Do you proud they do."

"What's she like?" Harriet asked.

"Who?"

"Lady Dunwilliam."

"Oh, I've never spoken to her. She's got a lovely face, but she's deformed."

"Deformed!"

"Yes." Mary turned over, making her bed creak. "She's got a hump. Terrible it is. A great bulge that comes up to her shoulders. I never seen anything like it."

"We had a hunchback in our village," Harriet said, "and the boys used to poke fun at him. He was a nasty man who beat his donkey."

"If you poked fun at Lady Dunwilliam, Mrs. Browning would most likely beat you. Now go to sleep, do. We've got to be up early tomorrow."

The following morning Mrs. Browning summoned Harriet from the scullery and handed her a stiff brush and dustpan.

"Nora is down with the flux. You must stand in for her. Get upstairs to the first landing and brush the carpet. Don't make a mess."

Harriet took the dustpan and brush and, not without some trepidation, for she had never been in the upper part of the house before, made her way upstairs. Lord Dunwilliam had been kind when he had rescued her from the clutches of the Reverend Dale, but she instinctively knew it was the kindness he would have bestowed on a tormented dog, had the mood so moved him. Her parents had taught her to fear and respect people of quality, and fear was uppermost as she mounted the grand staircase.

The carpet was thick; her feet sank into the soft pile and she was trying hard to look in all directions at once. Massive gilt-framed pictures lined the walls; a magnificent chandelier was suspended from a high ceiling that dominated both staircase and hall. A footman, resplendent in a plum-coloured brocade livery and a powdered wig, minced his way across the first landing and stared at her with supercilious scorn.

"What are you doing up here, girl?"

"I am to clean the carpet." Harriet raised her head, not in the least impressed by brocade or wig, knowing the man's status to be little above her own.

"Then get on with it," he instructed, "and don't make any noise. Her ladyship is still asleep."

She poked her tongue out at his retreating figure, then sank to her knees and began to brush the carpet. In fact, it needed little attention and she found the work pleasant after a week of washing-up, scrubbing the kitchen floor and other menial tasks. She had reached the centre of the landing when a quiet voice asked: "Who are you?"

Harriet was afraid to look up. The voice was low and had that well-bred quality which told her it was one of authority. It spoke again.

"Stand up, girl, when I am speaking to you."

Harriet laid aside her dustpan and brush, then obeyed, to find herself facing the most beautiful woman she had ever seen.

"I am Lady Dunwilliam."

If she had said she was the Queen of England, Harriet would have felt no surprise, for the lovely fair-skinned face was regal, even arrogant. A mass of waving, ash-blonde hair tumbled down to her shoulders, a glorious cascade that Harriet wanted to touch. Her eyes were possibly the most outstanding feature, for they were dark brown and contrasted dramatically with her dazzling fairness. But all this beauty was ruined by the grotesque hump that swelled out in a gradual curve from the small of her back to just above her shoulders. The weight, or perhaps the ungainly bulk of this awful deformity, made it impossible for Lady Dunwilliam to stand upright, and she stooped, reminding Harriet of the coal man preparing to empty his sack into Father's cellar. The dark, wonderful eyes were bitter, and lines of suffering were etched round the full mouth.

"It would seem you are deaf," Lady Dunwilliam said. "I asked who you were."

"Harriet—I mean Jane, my lady. The kitchen-maid, if it please you."

"It does not please me," the cold voice stated. "I am at a loss to know what the kitchen-maid is doing upon this landing. Surely you should be scouring pots, or something."

"Nora, the housemaid, is ill. And Mrs. Browning said..."

"Never mind." A long-fingered hand waved aside the explanation as a spasm of pain passed over the lovely face.

"Leave off doing whatever you're supposed to be doing and come with me."

She turned quickly and led the way into the bedroom. Harriet followed and found herself in a charming blue room that was in a state of chaos. Articles of clothing littered the floor, were draped over chair backs and even the dressing-table. The bed was unmade; the sheets and blankets were twisted up and one pillow was ripped open: a great gaping wound from which feathers seeped like maggots from the belly of a dead horse.

"Clear this lot up," Lady Dunwilliam ordered, then sank down onto a dressing-stool, from where she watched the girl with sombre eyes. Harriet began to collect the clothes together, piling them on a chair.

"How long have you been here?" Lady Dunwilliam asked.

"A week, my lady."

"You can drop the ladyship business. Ma'am will suffice."

"Yes, my... Yes, ma'am."

An uncomfortable silence prevailed for some five minutes before Lady Dunwilliam spoke again.

"Do you like working in the kitchen?"

Harriet thought it good policy to express satisfaction with her mode of employment.

"Oh, yes ma'am."

"Then you must be either mad or stupid—and you appear to be neither." Her ladyship spoke sharply, and Harriet shivered. "Scouring saucepans, scrubbing floors. Being bullied by the excellent Mrs. Browning. I am sure you must enjoy that."

Harriet did not answer, but turned her attention to the bed which she proceeded to strip before kneading the mattress. As she leant forward her eyes caught sight of a book. She quickly read the title: *Unnatural Enmities and Their Disposal* by Conrad von Holstein. She must have gasped or betrayed some sign she was startled, for instantly Lady Dunwilliam asked: What is it, child?"

"Nothing, ma'am."

"Don't lie. Was it that book? Can you read?"

"Yes, ma'am."

"An unusual accomplishment for a kitchen-maid. Who taught you?"

"My mother. She was in service at Sir William Sinclair's house and Lady Sinclair allowed her to study with the children."

Lady Dunwilliam pointed to a chair.

"Come and sit down and bring that book with you."

Harriet crept forward, clutching the book with moist hands, not at all sure she should obey. Mother had been most indignant when a milkmaid had once sat down in her presence. Besides, the invitation might be a test to see if she knew her place.

"Thank you, ma'am, but I'd rather..."

"Great balls of fire, girl, sit down."

Harriet perched on the very edge of the chair and waited.

"Open the book at page two hundred and seventy-two," her ladyship ordered.

Harriet found the book almost fell open at that page; the paper was well-thumbed and had quite obviously been re-read many times.

"Let us see how well you can read," Lady Dunwilliam invited.

Harriet cleared her throat and began.

"'Chapter Eight. The Jumpity-Jim...

"'We are blind men groping in eternal darkness, not knowing who or what is attendant upon us, or the pitfalls that are waiting for our stumbling feet. Many and diverse are the creatures that can be raised by those who have dipped a spoon in the unlimited sea of knowledge, but having once clothed them with a semblance of life, even the great Solomon would seek in vain for the power to control them.

"'Let it be known to all those who would follow the path of forbidden lore, that there is no creature more gruesome to behold, or more hell-binding in its relationship to the flesh, than the Primate Horrific, or, as it is known among the unlettered peasantry, the Jumpity-Jim.

"'The natural habitat of this creature is the third lower plane, and it can only be raised by a magician of the first order. But once brought into being, then I say woe unto him who has not protected himself with the three circles of light, or cannot speak the words that are written in the blue book.

"'It is of foul aspect, having the face and form of an unborn monkey, yet is there a fearful parody of a human in its lineaments. It can leap to great heights and with mighty speed, and if he who has called it forth has protected himself, then will it find another...'"

"That is enough," Lady Dunwilliam"s voice cut short the recital. "You read well, child, and are a credit to your mother's tuition."

Harriet gladly closed the book and looked at her employer with certain astonishment.

"'Tis most fearful reading, my lady, and, begging your pardon, I wonder why..."

"Why I interest myself in such things?" Lady Dunwilliam smiled. "Perhaps a crooked body breeds a crooked mind. 'Tis nonsense anyway. The poor fool who wrote it had but listened to tales babbled by peasants as they huddled round their fires on a dark night. None of them know the truth or can be expected to."

She rose and made her way towards the door, talking as she went.

"When you have finished here, come into my withdrawing room. There is another service I require of you."

It took Harriet some twenty minutes to put the rooms to rights, then she went out onto the landing and, seeing an open door some little way along, went towards it. In the room that lay beyond she found Lady Dunwilliam seated behind a table, with a strange contraption made of polished walnut in front of her. It had a mass of wires and glass tubes rising up from its flat surface and curving down to disappear on either side. Two perpendicular, polished metal rods were fixed to left and right at the front, while a sheet of smoked glass, set in the metal frame, made a kind of screen at the rear.

"Come and sit beside me, girl," Lady Dunwilliam ordered, "but first remove that hideous overall, I would see if you have the appearance for the kind of work I have in mind."

Harriet unbuttoned the offending garment and draped it carefully over a chair back; Lady Dunwilliam was watching her with a strangely intense look.

"Turn round."

Harriet did as she was told, turning her back to the lady, who appeared to be in a state of mounting excitement.

"Good, white shoulders," she muttered, "and a strong back." She raised her voice. "Come and sit beside me. Hurry."

As soon as Harriet was seated, Lady Dunwilliam pointed to the contraption and said: "This was invented by Lord Dunwilliam's father, and is meant to test a person's aptitude."

"Beg pardon, ma'am?"

"Great balls of fire!" Lady Dunwilliam appeared to grind her teeth, but hastily regained self-control. "Test your intelligence, girl. Never mind. This is what I want you to do. Grip those metal rods and stare straight at the glass screen. Now, do that."

Harriet, with some reluctance, gripped the metal rods as she had been bidden, and found they vibrated slightly. Lady Dunwilliam's voice was rather hoarse when she spoke again.

"Now, press them down. Gently... press down gently..."

Harriet felt the rods sink slowly downwards and as she pressed them, a reddish liquid began to bubble up through the glass tubes, while the machine gave out a faint humming sound.

"Good... good..." Lady Dunwilliam was whispering. "Now, listen carefully. Stare at the glass screen and empty your mind of all thoughts. I know it is not easy, but you must be a good girl and try. Empty your mind. There are no thoughts at all. Just emptiness."

Harriet found it very difficult indeed to think of nothing at all, but Mother had taught her always to obey her elders and betters, so she tried. And as she tried, the glass tubes filled with fast-moving red liquid, the machine hummed like a kettle just on the boil, and my lady was breathing heavily. The smoked-glass screen was getting bigger—or so it seemed—and its surface was most certainly becoming brighter, was developing a pulsating silver sheen that would have alarmed

Harriet had she not been so enthralled. Suddenly, the screen cleared and became a three-dimensional picture, portraying a terrible, gloomy valley, illuminated by flickering flames that flared up from the peaks of flanking mountains. The valley and mountainsides were covered with dead trees; twisted shapes that reached out black, skeleton arms towards a red-tinted sky. Something moved on the topmost branch of the nearest tree: a small, long-legged, long-armed something, that dropped to the ground and went bounding down the valley in great, effortless jumps. It looked like a cross between a deformed monkey and a monstrous spider, but the swift, leaping jumps were its most horrible aspect.

Harriet screamed as she relaxed her grip on the metal rods, and instantly the picture disappeared to be replaced by the original smoked glass. The girl was in hysterics, screaming, then laughing, and Lady Dunwilliam was clawing at her arm, slapping a face, shaking her. "What did you see, girl? Stop it... stop it... tell me what you saw..."

"It was awful, ma'am," Harriet began, then lapsed into another fit of sobbing and my lady's patience snapped like an over-stretched cord.

"Talk, you stupid, hysterical slut... What did you see?"

"I saw a dark valley, and..."

"Yes... yes... go on," Lady Dunwilliam urged.

"There was something dreadful that went jumping..."

She was not allowed to continue, for Lady Dunwilliam suddenly hugged her, kissed her on both cheeks, then sat back and watched as though she was some long-sought-for treasure that had, against all expectations, come to hand.

"You have it." She giggled like a very young girl, and clapped her hands in an ecstasy of pure joy. "The true essence... you have it. You wonderful, wonderful child."

Harriet wiped her eyes, gradually coming to understand that she had recently displayed some unknown gift, or virtue, that might be to her advantage.

"Beg pardon, me lady, but what exactly have I... got?"

"Good heavens, child," Lady Dunwilliam was looking from side to side as though searching for a plausible explanation. "You have intelligence and imagination. The aptitude machine demonstrated that beyond all doubt. Who but an intelligent and imaginative girl could have created a dark valley and a funny little thing that jumped up and down on a piece of ordinary smoked-glass. I am very pleased with you, my dear."

"Thank you, ma'am." Harriet blushed with pleasure.

"I have been looking for a suitable companion with whom I can converse," Lady Dunwilliam went on, "for, as you can see, I lead a very lonely life, and really, I see no reason why you should not fill the post. What do you say to that?"

"Oh, my lady…" Harriet began, but Lady Dunwilliam cut short her thanks with an imperious wave of her hand.

"That's settled then. There's a nice little room next to mine and you might as well move in right away."

"What will my duties be?" Harriet asked.

"Duties?" Lady Dunwilliam appeared to be at a loss for words for a short while, then, as though struck by a sudden thought, said: "Reading. You may read to me and keep my rooms tidy."

"I will endeavour to give satisfaction ma'am," said Harriet.

For no apparent reason, Lady Dunwilliam suddenly began to laugh.

Youth is adaptable and Harriet soon got used to doing practically nothing at all. That is not to say her erstwhile companions of servitude either accepted the situation or failed to show their shocked surprise. Whenever Lady Dunwilliam was out of sight and earshot, Harriet was winked at, sneered at, scowled upon, pinched, kicked and, on one occasion punched in the ribs by Mary, who seemed to regard her as a deserter. She was also envied—and, by those who said they knew more than they were prepared to reveal, pitied. One morning, while dusting the china in Lady Dunwilliam's withdrawing room, she looked up to find Mrs. Browning staring at her with cold, expressionless eyes.

"Do you know why her ladyship has taken you to her bosom, girl?"

"She required a companion," Harriet stated boldly, for of late a feeling of self-confidence had moved in with the pretty dresses and her mistress' constant esteem.

"One of ten poor relations would have filled the post," Mrs. Browning retorted with a sound that was as near a snort as was possible to a person of her demeanour. "'Tis no affair of mine, but pride goes before a fall, and I've not walked about with closed eyes and blocked ears these past ten years. Do you say your prayers at night?"

"Of course," Harriet expressed surprise at the question.

"Good," Mrs. Browning nodded. "I would say them at twilight, just before the sun sets, for it is said the good Lord is most receptive then. Another thing." She paused in the doorway. "I wouldn't go roaming around on the top landing after nightfall. It was there, in the locked room, up under the roof, his late lordship—may his soul rest in peace—used to conduct his experiments, whatever they were. They still talk in the village about the horrible cries that could be heard a mile away. There's no servants left that was here then, and that's a fact a sensible girl would think about. So watch yourself, wear a crucifix, keep what I've said under your bonnet—and think about it."

Such revelations were as stones thrown into a placid pool; they caused unpleasant ripples of alarm, but then, warmed by Lady Dunwilliam's affability, well-fed, comfortably bedded and with no arduous toil to mar her days, the feeling of well-being soon returned to Harriet. So pleasantly, in fact, did the days pass, she quite forgot there was such a person as Lord Dunwilliam, and therefore it came as a shock when she entered the with-drawing room one morning, with her arms full of flowers, to find him seated in an armchair, his dusty boots propped up on a small table. He eyed Harriet with some surprise, then raised a slim eyebrow.

"The damsel in distress? You appear to have made yourself at home."

Harriet curtsied and almost dropped her flowers in the process.

"Her ladyship . . . she said I was to be her companion . . ."

Lord Dunwilliam seemed to uncoil like a handsome snake; he towered over her, his eyes suddenly alight with a gleam of dawning joy.

"She made you . . . her companion! Well, that is marvellous news."

Harriet had not thought his Lordship would greet her elevation with anything but complete indifference, but here he was displaying all the emotion of a man who has been told he has just inherited a large fortune. He seized her roughly by the shoulder, kissed her soundly on both cheeks, then rushed from the room and tore upstairs.

For the first time she experienced a cold wave of apprehension. She remembered the story Hackett had related, Mrs. Browning's sinister warning. Why should Lord Dunwilliam express undisguised joy when he learnt the kitchen-maid had been promoted to lady's companion? What should have been an unthinkable thought struck her. Was she to play Hagar to Lady Dunwilliam's Sarah? The very idea was extremely sinful and she decided not to think about it. Instead she went upstairs to her bedroom, where she sat by the window and looked out over the garden. Jem was pruning roses. A tall, ungainly figure who looked solid and matter-of-fact; a man of the soil, the kind of person Harriet had known all her life. She was about to go down and speak with him when she heard raised voices. They came from behind the closed door which led into Lady Dunwilliam's bedroom. The deep voice of Lord Dunwilliam was quite distinct, that of his wife a blurred murmur, but Harriet felt sure it was of the uttermost importance for her to hear as much of their conversation as possible. She bent down and applied her eye to the keyhole. His lordship was striding up and down, clearly much agitated; Lady Dunwilliam reclined in a chair and was tapping the palm of her hand with an ivory fan as though stressing her impatience.

"Are you absolutely certain?" Lord Dunwilliam was speaking. "You know what happened last time."

Harriet could not hear her ladyship's answer, then the man spoke again. "We must get her accustomed to the idea. God knows how. She seems simple and perhaps money and the promise of a life of ease might reconcile her. We can but try. There must be no talk. That mad fool, Dale, is already shouting 'witchcraft' at the top of his voice—if he were to know the truth . . ."

The lady began to cry and Dunwilliam was about to put his arm around her shoulders, but, as though repulsed by the hideous hump, took one of her hands instead.

Harriet stood up, then walking over to the window, looked down at Jem, still peacefully pruning his roses.

"How long 'ave I been 'ere?" Jem sat on his wheelbarrow and lit an old clay pipe. "Well now, let me think. Must be nigh on eight years. Just after old Sir 'Ilary Sinclair died, 'eard 'is lordship was in need of a 'ead gardener, and so 'ere I comes."

"Was Lord Dunwilliam married eight years ago?" Harriet asked, tapping her front teeth with a rose-stem.

"That 'e were," Jem nodded, "and 'ad been for two years. Poor lady, must be cruel 'ard for 'er being afflicted the way she is. 'Specially with that pretty face."

"His Lordship must be a very kind man," Harriet spoke with assumed artlessness. "I mean it's not every great gentleman who would marry a cripple."

"I guess 'e be kind enough," Jem agreed, "but they do say she wan't a hunchback when he married 'er. Sweet sixteen she were, and as straight as a larch. Some sickness took 'er after they'd been married nigh on a month, and when she was up and about she were as you see 'er now."

"No!" Harriet gasped. "Honestly?"

"So they say. Mind you, this was back in the old master's time and there were no servants 'ere now that there was then. But it sounds right. I can't see a up-and-bucko like his Lordship marryin' a humpy. Must 'ave been a sickness affected 'er spine. Made it all crooked like."

They dined together that evening. Lord Dunwilliam sat at one end of the table, his lady at the other and Harriet in the centre, while the pleasantly-shocked footman relayed news of this startling arrangement back to the kitchen.

"She looks very pretty, does she not, Charles?" said Lady Dunwilliam, and the gentleman nodded as he sipped his port wine.

"As a picture that has escaped from its frame."

"What white shoulders." Her ladyship laughed so joyfully, and looked so beautiful, one was inclined to forget the awful hump, and Lord Dunwilliam chuckled as though she had said something very witty.

"With a strong back to support them." He nodded gravely. "A veritable column of ivory."

This was too much for her ladyship, who shook with helpless merriment, so that the hump seemed to jump up and down, and her face was a mask with narrowed, gleaming eyes and gaping mouth. Then, suddenly, the laughter was strangled by a gasp of pain, and the lady was bending forward, shaking her golden head, while making a series of animal-like cries. Lord Dunwilliam sat back in his chair and closed eyes that were bleak. His voice was scarcely above a whisper.

"Sit still, my darling. It will pass."

"What is wrong?" Harriet's pity was aroused, as also was her alarm, for her mistress seemed to be in mortal agony, what with the terrible groans that were being forced out from behind her clenched teeth, and the way her long fingers gripped the table edge. "Is there aught I can do?"

Lord Dunwilliam sat perfectly still, his eyes still closed, but the ghost of a smile creased his mouth.

"Nothing, child. 'Tis but a gripping pain."

The spasm passed as quickly as it had come and presently Lady Dunwilliam was smiling faintly, apologising for the alarm she had caused.

"Do not be frightened, my dear. I have these attacks if I get excited. I should never become excited."

"It must be soon," Lord Dunwilliam said, and his lady nodded.

"Aye, it must be soon. If I am to remain sane, it must be soon."

A day passed.

"You will wear this."

Lady Dunwilliam's eyes were bright and her hand shook as she tossed the dress onto the bed. Harriet said: "Yes, ma'am. Thank you, ma'am."

"And," Lady Dunwilliam added, "you will wear nothing underneath."

"But, my lady," Harriet gasped out her horror, "'twould not be decent."

"Great balls of fire!" An expression of anger passed over the beautiful face. "I am not concerned with your opinion of decency. I said, you are to wear nothing—nothing underneath."

"But, ma'am..." A tinge of colour tinted Harriet's pale cheeks, "I am a respectable girl..."

Lady Dunwilliam gripped the girl by both shoulders and shook her until her head rocked.

"Listen, girl. Listen. I have put up with your simpering face for nigh on four weeks. I have pampered you, listened to your childish prattle, and now you will do as I say, or by God's wounds I'll have his Lordship strip you himself. Do you understand?"

Harriet was crying, sobbing, so that her body trembled like a wind-rocked tree, and so great was her fear she could only gasp: "Yes, my lady."

"Very well." Lady Dunwilliam went to the door. "We will come for you in ten minutes."

Left alone, Harriet reluctantly disrobed, then put on the dress, her horror growing when she viewed herself in the wardrobe mirror. The dress was black and completely backless. She turned around and looked back over one shoulder. Her back, save for a tape that held the dress in position, was bare from neck to waist.

She ran to the door, pulled it open and went racing down the stairs, determined to take refuge in the kitchen, trusting that Mrs. Browning or some of the servants would protect her from the madness of Lady Dunwilliam.

The kitchen was empty. The fire was out, all the saucepans were piled neatly on their racks, the doors and windows were locked. She called Mrs. Browning's name and, receiving no answer, went tearing up the stairs to the servants' quarters. She flung doors open, scampering like a trapped animal from room to room, but there was no one. Terror came racing down the empty corridors and she screamed, shriek after shriek that gave birth to an army of mocking echoes, like cries of the damned when the lid of Hell has been raised. She fled back through the echoes, stumbled down one flight of stairs, fell down the next, picked herself up, then tore out into the main hall. The great front doors were locked and she pounded on the unresponsive wood, tugged at the gleaming handle, then sank down to the floor, sobbing like an abandoned child.

Footsteps came over the paved floor. A shadow moved over her and she looked up into the face of Lord Dunwilliam. Never had he appeared more beautiful; a wonderful gleam of compassion softened his sombre eyes, making him the lover-father, the dream-master who would love and chastise, order and protect. He reached down and pulled her up, then held her to him, murmuring softly.

"She should not have been so cruel. There now, don't cry so. She does not mean to hurt you, but it has been such a long time. Think of it—ten long years. She was younger than you when it happened and she was so sweet, soft and gentle, and so very, very beautiful."

"Please, my lord, let me go."

Harriet felt sure when she looked up into that beautiful, kindly face, her request would be granted, but he shook his head, while he smoothed back the tumbled hair from her forehead.

"I can't do that, child. You must surely understand that. I love her. Love demands so much. Honour, pity, the common decencies that enable a man to walk upright under the sun; all these must be sacrificed when the one we cherish cries out for help. You do see?"

"I am so frightened," Harriet said as he began to lead her across the hall and up the grand staircase. "Please, I'm frightened."

Lord Dunwilliam had an arm about her waist, and he held her left hand in his. The deep voice went on, carefully manufacturing words that had no meaning.

"One can learn to live with fear, so that after a while it is as natural as the air we breathe. Resignation and acceptance are the two words you must learn, then when you carry your burden through the darkest valley, there will always be a gleam of light ahead."

They went up two flights of stairs, then began to ascend a third and Harriet started to struggle, but the iron grip tightened around her waist and the deep voice gently protested.

"Do not struggle, my little bird. You will only break your wings against the bars, and you must not waste your strength. See, there's but a short way to go, and my love is waiting for you."

They came up to the top landing, and there, like the mouth of a ravenous beast, was an open doorway. He led the now speechless girl into the room beyond, and, after seating her on a straight-backed chair, he went back and locked the door. The room was little more than a vast attic that possibly covered most of the rooms below. Above were cobweb-festooned rafters supporting the roof. Dormer windows lined the walls on either side. Glass vats, jumbled heaps of wire and glass tubes littered the floor, and there were signs of a long-ago fire, for some of the rafters and floorboards were charred. The only furniture Harriet could see was a large table and a few wooden chairs.

Lady Dunwilliam came slowly forward, her burning stare fixed on the girl's white face. She wore a loose, flower-patterned dressing-gown and her hair was piled up high on her head.

"No delay!" She spat out the words. "Let's get on with it."

"No!" Her husband's voice was like a whip-crack. "No. She must be prepared."

"Was *I*?" The woman glared at him, hammering her hips with clenched fists. "When your father trapped me, was I prepared? He but led me under the rafter..." She pointed to a charred beam. "...Tore the dress from my back and..."

"Stop!" Lord Dunwilliam thundered. "She is young and untutored."

"What was I?" Lady Dunwilliam shrieked back. "A mature woman of the world? I was sixteen, fresh from the schoolroom, and happy to have suddenly acquired a kind father and a handsome husband. Father!" She laughed, a mad shriek that made Harriet whimper. "A devil incarnate. A monster."

"He but sought knowledge," Lord Dunwilliam murmured. "He followed the dark path and found it had no end."

Lady Dunwilliam sank down on to a chair and lowered her head.

"Tell her what you must," she said in a low tone, "but in the name of mercy, hurry."

Lord Dunwilliam took up a small black book from the table and handed it to Harriet. She recognised the title.

Unnatural Enmities and Their Disposal by Conrad von Holstein.

"My wife tells me you can read, Harriet."

She nodded.

"Now, I want you to turn to page two hundred and seventy-three and read from the top of the page. Will you do that?"

"Yes," she whispered.

"Very well. Begin when you are ready."

She turned over the yellow-edged pages and presently came to the place. The page stared up at her, the words mutely demanding a voice. She began to read.

"'The Primate Horrific or Jumpity-Jim hath little intelligence, being but a form of low existence that doth demand life essence and warm blood. Once it hath been raised it will leap about with much speed and agility, and, if that which it needs be not to hand, will depart with a mighty explosion.

"'But should there be within the radius of twenty feet, who hath the right essence, and should the flesh of her back, that which lies between the neck and the upper portion of the loins, be bare then will it leap thereon, and will become as part of the poor wretch, as doth the legs and other members that did God in his bountiful goodness provide.

"'Once the abomination has mounted the steed, it can in no wise be removed, unless a light-virgin, cursed with the same essence, can be induced, or forced, to accept the loathsome burden...'"

"That is enough, Harriet."

Lord Dunwilliam gently took the book from her limp hands and laid it on the table. She raised tear-filled eyes; never had he seemed so handsome, so kind.

"You have the right—essence, my dear. The instrument my father perfected told us that. You are also a virgin, or the glass screen would not have portrayed the dark valley. 'Twas our wedding eve when my father... But enough of that. You do understand what is expected of you?"

"No." She shook her head violently. "In God's name... No... "

"There is no other way," his gentle voice insisted, "for we have searched for so long. One girl had a little power and it did move, causing my wife much pain and injuring the girl. But you are the one. For you the transportation will be easy and there will be a life of ease for you and your parents, for as long as any of you live."

Harriet could not speak. She was watching Lady Dunwilliam who was unfastening her robe, loosening the girdle, all the while smiling like one who has at last seen the gates of Heaven through the smoke-clouds of purgatory. The robe fell to the floor and she was as Venus in her naked glory, a vision of white curves and moulded breasts. Then she turned round and Harriet tried to scream, but her vocal chords refused to function.

A hump? A promontory? A protuberance? Rather a curvature that arched up from the base of her spine, then terminated in a kind of craggy ridge which unnaturally deepened the thickness of the shoulders.

"Come," Lord Dunwilliam pulled Harriet to her feet. "You must stand side by side."

"No!" She screamed and his face grew grim. "No . . . !"

"Do not force me to tie you down."

The threat did much to command her obedience, for there was an added terror in the thought of being tied up, helpless, while—something—leapt upon her. She allowed him to lead her, unprotesting, to Lady Dunwilliam's side, flinched as a cold hand gripped hers, then she stood still and waited. Lord Dunwilliam took up a position in front of them and, after closing his eyes, began to chant a jumble of words. From far below there came the sound of splintering wood, but the three occupants of the room ignored it.

"Darkness, shadows that flow in a black stream, hear me. May that which feeds upon one, come forth and take nourishment from another. May that which has come from the nether-world and can never return, having taken on the flesh of the meat-eater, see the light of day and jump upon the waiting vessel."

"Aye, upon the waiting vessel," Lady Dunwilliam repeated.

"She is young and hath much strength," Lord Dunwilliam raised his voice to a higher pitch. "And she hath the right essence . . . "

Lady Dunwilliam began to writhe and moan, her grip tightened on Harriet's hand, so that the girl automatically turned as the sudden pain shot up her arm. The hump was moving. The skin was heaving, tremors were passing across the taut surface and on the crag-like ridge little eruptions were taking place. Small, ragged holes appeared, accompanied by little popping sounds. The voice of Lord Dunwilliam had a triumphant ring.

"The shoulders are white, aye, and the back is strong; the blood is thick and sweet and she is rich with essence . . . "

The skin split while Lady Dunwilliam screamed and a tiny, wizened head peeked out from its cocoon, like a chick about to emerge from its cracked egg. It was rather like a shrivelled, pink balloon and it jerked round to stare at Harriet with microscopic red eyes. The girl gave a hoarse cry and jerked her hand from Lady Dunwilliam's loosened grip, before tearing wildly across the room in an effort to escape. As she did so the woman was flung onto her face, while something went leaping up to the rafters, then down to the floor again: a black, pink-tinted something that moved so fast it was only a blur that streaked up and down across the room. With her back against the far wall, Harriet saw it zig-zagging towards her, coming forward with high leaps that carried it up to the rafters and down again; then there was a glimpse of that wizened, deflated face, a long pink body and four many-jointed legs, before she seized a nearby chair and hurled it straight at the approaching horror. Chair and thing collided and what appeared to be a pink ball went rolling over the floor to bounce against the nearest wall.

It lay there, a pulsating beach-ball, artistically striped with black where the legs were coiled tightly about its gleaming roundness and it began to rock slightly as though gathering momentum for another leap.

Lord Dunwilliam had laid his wife flat upon her back before dragging her under the table, where she lay moaning softly. He turned to Harriet and shouted his rage and fear.

"You must let it mount, otherwise it will go back to her. There is no door or wall that can hold it—"

His words were cut short by a sudden and violent interruption. The door first quivered, then splintered under a powerful blow; a second crash sent it hurling inwards and the Reverend Dale stood on the threshold, a thick beam of wood in one hand and a crucifix in the other. He was attired in a white surplice and a ferocious smile.

"Dunwilliam, the day of reckoning has come." He advanced into the room, crucifix held high. "Ye have mocked and practised abominations, but Hell is hungry for your soul and I have come to make an end. Aye..." he tilted his head to one side and glared down at Harriet. "...An end to you and the foulness that has assumed human form."

Dunwilliam faced him, a thoroughbred stallion squaring up to a mad bull.

"Get out. This is not the place for ranting, insane fool. You have not the slightest conception of what..."

"I have eyes." The priest pointed to the naked form of Lady Dunwilliam, then at Harriet. "They tell me all I wished to know. When you send your servants packing for the day, where did you suppose they would go? Eh? To the village, where they prattled of the foulness you be practising with yon wench. You are cursed, Dunwilliam, you and your Devil-bedded wife."

Dunwilliam struck the white face, then gripped the not-so-white surplice and punched the priest about the body. All the while shouting obscenities, bellowing out his mad rage. As the Reverend Dale struggled violently there came the sound of ripping cloth and he went hurtling backwards, the surplice split from neck to waist, baring his scrawny back. Dunwilliam retreated a few paces and looked down at his fallen adversary. A look of indescribable horror was dawning on the clergyman's face; a stupefied glare. His mouth fell open and a gurgling, retching sound emerged from his constricted throat. It slowly and painfully dissolved into words.

"What . . . foul . . . thing . . . is . . . on . . . my . . . back?"

He came up from the floor like a boxer at the count of nine; his questing hands went back and gently caressed that which crouched on his shoulders. He quickly withdrew them, then stared at his moist fingers with a comprehending glare. When he spoke again his voice was a low, hoarse whisper.

"I say again, Dunwilliam, what foul thing is on my back?"

Dunwilliam began to laugh. He roared, slapped his thighs, shook with uncontrollable merriment, while tears ran down his cheeks. Harriet could only watch the Jumpity-Jim. It was perfectly at home on the reverend's back; the head was nestling sideways a little below Mr. Dale's neck; the legs were folded neatly under the pink, narrow torso and a slimy excrescence, oozing out from every part of the body, was rapidly congealing into a chalk-white skin. Lord Dunwilliam at last gave utterance.

"Your 'holiness' has condemned you, Dale. A virgin! A virgin whose flesh is bare from neck to waist."

"What in God's name is it?" Dale was trying to shake his dreadful burden off. He twisted, jerked, then gasped when the creature tightened its hold.

"You must not get excited," Dunwilliam warned. "It's a Primate Horrific—a Jumpity-Jim." He grinned. "I should take it to a monastery. It will find many changes of abode there."

The Reverend Dale backed away towards the door, then after vainly trying to speak, turned and went staggering out on to the landing. They heard him stumbling down the stairs. Five minutes passed before Harriet's strength returned and she too was able to creep from that room of horror. She left Lord Dunwilliam holding his wife and rocking her gently. They were both laughing softly.

Down on the lawn they were waiting. Terrified men with blazing torches and they shrank from the Reverend Mr. Dale as though he were a leper. One man, braver than his fellows, approached the hump-backed figure and asked in a strangled whisper:

"What is it?"

The clergyman grinned, a terrible bearing of teeth, and he beckoned the man nearer.

"Are you a virgin?" he whispered. "Eh? Are you a virgin? If so, take off your shirt and we'll dance a merry jig."

The man retreated, muttering, "Witchcraft . . . they have bewitched him and put the Devil on his back."

"Witchcraft!" The word leapt from mouth to mouth as they moved with uplifted torches towards the house. Harriet, they spat at, beat about the face and back, before she managed to escape from the garden and ran out onto the dusty road that led to the village. When she walked over the narrow bridge she did not look down into the dark waters of the river and did not therefore see the figure of Mr. Dale floating, face downwards. She did, however, look back and see great scarlet tongues trying to lick the steel-blue sky. Dunwilliam Grange was burning.

She went on down the road, a pathetic, bowed figure, wandering the short but perilous path that separates the cradle from the grave. Her white back gleamed in the sunlight.

A little way back, something was zig-zagging across a meadow, leaping over hedges, swinging from the lower branches of an occasional tree. It came to a gate that barred the entrance to a dusty road. There it paused, deflated, wizened head tilted to one side. Tired, hesitant footsteps came shuffling along the road, they passed the gates and went on behind a low hawthorn hedge.

The Jumpity-Jim jumped.

THE COLOURED TRANSMISSION

MISS CHARLOTTE BLESSINGTON had fallen in love with Errol Flynn at seventeen when she first met him in *Captain Blood*: she deserted him for Robert Montgomery whose suave flippancy won her fickle regard while he was being charmingly rude to Norma Shearer in *Private Lives*. Alas, time marched on, and as Miss Blessington matured, Messrs Flynn and Montgomery were discarded, and Ronald Colman reigned in their stead, having stolen her heart while wandering through a complicated plot in *Random Harvest*. For the next thirty years Miss Blessington was a veritable Jezebel; she tossed the seed of her affection over a wide field. Her lovers were as the sand of the desert, ranging from Van Johnson to David Hemmings, although at one time she did consider the possibility of settling down with Charlton Heston.

Then midway through the 1960s a terrible thing happened. Films went way out. The handsome heroes of yesteryear gave place to hollow-cheeked young men who mumbled coarse four-letter words; instead of bright-eyed young heroines who displayed proper gratitude for being rescued from a fate worse than death, there were brazen young women who seemed reluctant to assume an upright position, and whose clothes floated from them like leaves from a tree in an autumn wind.

For a while Miss Blessington felt betrayed, jilted. She recalled with pathetic nostalgia that the enchanted time she spent with Charles Boyer in the Kasbah, before being lured to his death by Hedy Lamarr. Then she discovered television and the hot surge of romance flowed through her veins once again.

One had to be careful of course. The journey through the channels could be a perilous one. One came upon unexpected pitfalls in the shape of *Play of the Month*, which sometimes served up cold slabs of reality garnished with a spicy sauce of improbability that left a nasty taste in the mouth. But there were lovely, seemingly unending serials, which left one hanging weekly to a tiny cliff of suspense. Would Margaret make up her quarrel with Jim? Could it be that handsome Doctor Fortescue was taken in by that bold-eyed Clara? And why had Mr. Derby given old Mrs. Jones that bunch of violets?

The square-eyed god adequately filled the void left vacant by the silver screen; more, it reached out invisible tentacles and bound Miss Blessington to its altar. From 7:30 to around midnight she was its devoted slave. Party political broadcasts, panel games, quiz shows, old films (she sighed softly when a young Mr. Flynn paid a fleeting visit), all were consumed by an insatiable appetite, and the hunger was still unappeased when a suave announcer murmured his final goodnight.

Sometimes Miss Blessington found herself watching the sparkling blank screen and wondering, like Oliver Twist, why there wasn't any more. On occasions, although Miss Blessington would never admit such a possibility, the late-night programmes were—well, a little dry for a maiden lady whose interest in art and politics was so limited as to be practically non-existent. Then, soothed by the flickering light and the murmur of a pedantic voice, her head would sway, her eyelids close, and she would be lost in a cosy world of unawareness.

One evening in early November, when the first autumn mists were drifting like unformed ghosts beyond the velvet-curtained windows, Miss Blessington sat contentedly relaxed in her TV chair, while a lean, bespectacled gentleman propounded the merits or otherwise of some particularly revolting modern paintings, and after a while her head drooped, her eyes rolled up, and a gentle lady-like snore merged with the speaker's rumbling voice.

She came up from the deep, dark waters of sleep with a rasping snort; she said "Wassat?" in a startled voice, then opened bleary eyes and stared owlishly at the television screen. The gentleman with views on modern art was gone, and in his place was a scene so extraordinary, Miss Blessington at first was inclined to believe she was still asleep. To begin, the scene was in colour, which in itself was more than a little surprising, for Miss Bessington's set only accepted black and white transmissions. She rubbed her eyes, blinked, stared, then pinched herself so as to be absolutely certain she was not dreaming. There was no manner of doubt; her old two-channel, portable set was presenting a scene in beautiful crystal-clear colour, and no matter how many times she pinched herself remained disturbingly real.

She was looking into an empty room; a cosy, luxurious room, with bright-red wallpaper, snug upholstered chairs; a mahogany table stood against one wall, and the entire scene was lit by a beautiful cut-glass chandelier.

Her thoughts were tumbling over one another, like raindrops running down a windowpane, and there was a great joy such as comes to a child who finds a brightly-coloured toy in a plain parcel. Perhaps her set had always been a coloured one, but up to now, due to some unexplainable fault, it had never functioned properly. Or maybe, those clever television people had perfected a new device that permitted any set to pick up coloured transmissions. Miss Blessington crooned with undiluted pleasure, and waited with bubbling expectancy for the action to begin.

A door opened in the left-hand wall, and a tall, dark-haired man entered; he walked over to the table, took a cigarette from a brass box, lit it with an elaborate silver table-lighter, then sauntered slowly towards the camera. He pulled up a chair, sat down, his face half-filling the screen. Miss Blessington sighed. Just her type. Not too young, in his forties, with a dark sardonic face and brooding brown eyes, and— yes—a thin pencil-line moustache. He looked as if he might be a distant relative of both Ronald Colman and Errol Flynn, and be on nodding terms with Vincent Price. He raised the cigarette to his lips, inhaled deeply, and let the smoke trickle out through his nostrils.

"Good evening." He had a deep masculine voice, rather like breaking chocolate. "I do hope you are nice and comfortable, for you and I are going to have a little chat. Or rather, I'm going to talk and you are going to listen."

Miss Blessington gave a sigh of content; she liked to be talked to by handsome men, always supposing they had something interesting to say, and were safely confined to a shining screen.

"Are you lonely?" he enquired. "Do you feel shut off, isolated?"

"An advertisement," Miss Blessington nodded, "toothpaste."

"Can it be," the man leant back and his face assumed an almost dreamlike expression, "that you have been deprived, shut off from the intimate relationships that make life worth living? Watched the companions of your youth—I will not call them friends—disappear behind the fortress of marriage, from where their sated giggles have mocked you? Have you watched the lights go on behind nylon-clad windows, and allowed your imagination to dwell on what went on in that gnome-guarded retreat? In short . . ." He leant forward until his face filled the screen. "Are you starved?"

"Goodness gracious!" Miss Blessington jumped as though her Relax-Easy TV chair had suddenly been transformed into a nest of hornets. "I do hope this isn't going to be something awful."

The man, having made his point, relaxed back into his chair and smiled so gently. He looked so like a combination of all the film stars that had ever toyed with Miss Blessington's heart, her dire suspicions went into temporary retirement. His voice sank into a low, caressing tone.

"You have never known the pain that raises the soul into the realms of ecstasy, or that pleasure born from the womb of indescribable sadness. You have lived in the half-world where flickering shadows wear flimsy masks of reality; your unborn children reach out ghostly fingers for a shrivelled breast."

"Really!" Miss Blessington exclaimed, but the deep voice went remorselessly on.

"And your soul is smothered by the pestilence of frustration, scarred by the whips of ridicule, starved by a famine of emotion."

For an eternity-filled moment the dark eyes stared straight at Miss Blessington, and she suddenly realised her body was trembling.

"Love," said the man, "is deep blue; when it sours it turns first pink, then bright red. The first stage is called dislike, resentment, the second . . ." He paused, and bitter lines appeared around his mouth, his eyes glittered. "The second is called—hate."

Miss Blessington said, "Oh dear," several times.

"Open the flood-gates of memory," the man insisted, "dig down into the black soil of the mind, then ask yourself one question."

The camera moved in, the dark handsome face filled Miss Blessington's world.

"Can you afford not to hate?"

The coloured scene dissolved and was replaced by the familiar silver mist, and Miss Blessinton burst into tears.

Next morning presented a day that was as drab, as commonplace as any that had preceded it, and Miss Blessington's television set stared at her with its blank grey eye, as though the impossible prospect of a coloured transmission had never crossed its cathode tube. She had not slept well. That dark, sardonic face had come between her and sleep; there had been a hint of cruelty around his well-shaped mouth, and his voice had become a well-honed knife, cutting away the protective layers from her subconscious mind, allowing the memories to come fluttering up, like flies from a disturbed midden.

Miss Blessington took a bath, and her naked body mocked her; slenderness had become lean, legs had become serviceable, bone, muscle, covered with dull-white skin; her stomach bulged slightly, a ridiculous extra, out of keeping with the sparse frame. She dressed quickly, then was drawn to the dressing table like a moth to a lighted lamp.

Deep creases on either side of the mouth, china-doll blue eyes, they had always been her best feature; the skin was tired, the auburn hair was faded, flecked with grey. The face and form of a middle-aged woman, neither attractive nor repellent, a carbon copy of many who packed the tube trains, pounded a typewriter five days a week, and changed their library books on Saturday morning. But there was one horrible, terrifying difference: Miss Blessington had been asked a question. "Can you afford not to hate?"

Harry Cooper stood by the bedroom door; dapper, red-haired, young as he had been twenty-five years ago.

"Sorry, I guess it's no go. I mean . . . " He hung his head, not wanting to hurt, but determined to be cruel. "I can't get through to you. I guess I can't compare with all those film chaps."

"You didn't try."

Miss Blessington swung round, but the doorway was empty, so she turned again to the mirror and sparingly applied lipstick.

Hell is a green cool passage running through a maze of small, cosy torture chambers. The beginning had always been so wonderful.

"I think we have so much in common."

It was Giles Harrington now who stood in the bedroom doorway; his fair hair tousled, his blue eyes shining, rather like a young Burt Lancaster, and there was a taste of joy in Miss Blessington's mouth, and she wanted to cry lovely saccharine tears, like she did when Greta Garbo died in *Camille*. But she smiled instead, a sad little twisted grimace that she had borrowed from Bette Davis.

"Others have the moon, we have the stars."

Then, in no time at all, they were in a torture room, and she recognised the all-too-familiar sly look, the lowered eyes, the stammering voice.

"The other girl . . . Helen . . . didn't want it to happen. We'll be great friends of course . . . "

"Why?" she mentally screamed at him. "Why?"

Giles did not answer for the very reason he was no longer there, and Miss Blessington set the neat little sensible hat firmly on her head, took up the brown handbag, and let herself out of the flat.

Her mother, safely dead these past twelve year, was waiting for her at the bus stop. She wore that "I'm determined to be unpleasant for your own good" expression.

"When I was your age I had a string of boyfriends as long as your arm. But then, I had a bit of life in me, didn't go about with a face as long as next week."

Pride demanded she assume an air of indifference; hint of an unspecified number of breaking masculine hearts.

"I don't chase men. I don't have to."

A bus came along and so terminated immediate need for further explanation, but her mother squeezed herself between a fat man and Miss Blessington, and the thin mouth opened and shut like a nut-cracker.

"You're no beauty, no one could say that, wouldn't matter so much if you had a bit of personality; had something to say for yourself. Them pictures will get you nowhere."

"Oh, shut up." Miss Blessington was stung into a rare act of rebellion.

"I beg your pardon!" The fat man was staring at her; his eyes were angry behind the horn-rimmed spectacles.

"I'm sorry," Miss Blessington felt her cheeks burn, "I was thinking out loud."

He grunted and she was aware he was watching her out of the corner of his eyes for the rest of the journey.

The tube was packed, but even so Miss Blessington recognised her father who had passed away a little before Mother; she woke up one night and found him dead beside her; his face with its long, drooping moustache, was as sad as it ever had been. He was wedged in between two chattering office girls, and a tall, strange-looking woman, who was glaring at everybody.

"Don't pay too much heed to yer mother. She means well, but you've got yer own life to lead, and what is 'appiness to one, is downright misery to another. I mean if you don't fancy settling down with some chap, well, don't force yerself because yer mother says you ought. Going to the pictures is no crime; tell the truth I'd just as soon go to bed with a good book meself, but yer mother says I ought to be up and doing. Don't cry, lass. It'll be all forgotten in a hundred years."

It was just as the escalator crested the hill at Green Park she spotted Him, or someone very like Him. He was walking towards the ticket barrier, the one facing the bookstall, and as He flashed a season ticket, He turned His head. The same dark, sardonic good looks, those magnetic brooding eyes seemed to seek out Miss Blessington as she stepped off the escalator, and her suspicion hardened into certainty. It was the man from the coloured transmission. She broke into a run, pushing her way through the crowd, and faces began slowly to assume expressions of pained surprise.

"Don't go chasing dreams, lass," Father said, "you won't see the pitfalls."

"Ticket, lady," the ticket collector snarled.

To find a season ticket in an overfilled handbag takes time, and she could see the man making for the Piccadilly exit; being drawn away, like when the switch is turned off and the picture shrinks inwards until it becomes a tiny dot of light, and it was no use Father looking at her with those worried kindly eyes, and saying over and over again: "Don't go chasing dreams, lass", because what else was there to chase, but dreams? And Miss Blessington went stumbling up the steps with her heart beating so fast, and people were now muttering angrily because she was pushing them to one side, each body an obstacle between her and the ultimate Him.

The pavement was crowded with scuttling ants, each one secure in the knowledge it had a hole into which to hide, but He, the Master, was nowhere in sight, and Miss Blessington turned blindly into Berkeley street, lost in a mist of unreasonable grief.

The morning passed with Miss Blessington's fingers flying over the typewriter keys; the routine of thirty years could not be easily broken, but once the lunch period was over there came a sense of mounting excitement, time was eating up the hours that separated her from His next appearance.

Then a sudden doubt struck her like a bullet; suppose there were no more coloured transmissions! Worse, suppose there had never been a first one. A cold wave of sanity came rolling over her beautiful dream garden, washing away the tiny fantasy-seedlings that had only just begun to rear their heads. An old black-and-white television set did not, could not, suddenly present a coloured picture. It was a rank impossibility. Miss Blessington looked out of the window and noticed that rain was sheeting down. She looked at the office clock. 5:25. In five minutes it would be time to go home, and she had not brought an umbrella. She would get wet. Catch cold. No one to look after her. This terrifying prospect drove all thoughts of men on coloured television programmes right out of her mind.

made a great business of trying to put his arm around her vast waist. His smile was suddenly an obscene smirk.

"A cuddlesome armful her. Aye, love?"

Mrs. Jenkins giggled and Miss Blessington covered her burning face.

"Oh, he is a one. Honestly he is."

"Now," Scotty Masters removed his arm and assumed a mock stern expression, "you are ready to answer three tweeny, weeny little questions. Aren't you, love?"

"I don't know," Mrs. Jenkins hung her head. "I'd rather play three games with you."

"Oh, how could she?" Miss Blessington exclaimed. "Has she no shame?"

But Mr. Masters appeared to be delighted with the prospect, for he grimaced, twisted his thin shoulders into a parody of pure ecstasy, then finally planted a resounding kiss on Mrs. Jenkins's cheek. Miss Blessington shuddered.

"Listen carefully," Scotty Masters was saying, "take your time. Who—this is for five pounds—who was king of England during the reign of Henry the Eighth?"

"Oh dear," Mrs. Jenkins screwed her face up into an expression of intense concentration, "let me think."

"Take your time," Mr. Masters instructed.

"You silly thing," Miss Blessington shouted, "it was King Henry the Eighth. Henry the Eighth."

The camera was suddenly focused on the audience, and there, right in the front row, were Mother and Father. Mother was shaking her head as though in some doubt as to the propriety of the question and Father was staring mournfully at the camera.

"'It's really too bad," Miss Blessington complained, "they've no business to be there."

But as the camera panned the studio her anger deepened, for there in the third row, sitting together if you please, were Harry Cooper, Giles Harrington and Jimmy Harris, and two rows back was a boy whose name Miss Blessington could not remember, but he had once tried to take liberties with her on Wimbledon Common. She seemed to recall he had been killed in North Africa in 1943.

With grim determination Miss Blessington strode over to the television set and pushed a button; a mighty roar, a crazy jumble of black and white lines, and the other channel revealed Mr. Montgomery Clift having words with Miss Elizabeth Taylor. Miss Blessington returned to her chair and sank back while giving vent to a loud sigh of relief. Willpower had triumphed again.

She watched the film right through, thankful that she had switched over just after it had begun, closed her eyes when the news followed, then involuntarily slipped into the realms of sleep.

"Evil is all around us, and we must be forever on our guard."

Miss Blessington opened her eyes and blinked at the image of a clergyman who was staring benignly at her from the television screen.

"Goodnight," said the clergyman, and promptly dissolved into grey mist, to be almost immediately replaced by Miss Blessington's favourite announcer who informed her that BBC television was closing down and would be on the air at 11:30 tomorrow morning.

The mist came back bringing with it an atmosphere of fearful expectancy. Should she switch over to the other side? Would He not feel more at home on a commercial channel? Then came an awful thought. Perhaps her newly found willpower had banished him forever; her earlier disbelief in a coloured transmission could well have disbanded its atoms and sent them hurtling across the immensity of time-space, each one now a tiny spot of gleaming colour. She had already driven Mother and Father, Harry, Giles and Jimmy, not to mention the forgotten-name young man, into a black-and-white Hell, where they would possibly sit for all eternity watching a Scotty Masters' quiz show.

"Please, please come back." She was down on her knees before the television set; pouring out her prayer at the altar of make-believe, calling upon the new gods for help. The screen remained obstinately blank, although the grey mist pulsated like a pot of seething porridge, and she sent forth her thoughts as thin ghostly fingers, probing the ether, trying to discover what she must do to bring Him back.

Then it came to her as a wordless thought and exploded in her brain. She stammered in her effort to give utterance.

"I hate . . . I hate . . . I cannot afford not to hate."

The screen was alive with colour; she chuckled and crooned with pure delight, tasting the so far denied and forbidden pleasures the room offered, then went down on all fours like a dog who has sighted a long absent master when He entered and walked slowly towards the screen. A high-backed chair was moved by invisible hands; it took up a position in front of the screen and He seated himself upon it, studied the kneeling Miss Blessington with a burning, melancholy gaze while lighting a cigarette.

"Let us be comfortable," he said.

Miss Blessington went back to her TV chair, and there, sitting bolt upright, waited.

"You have taken an important step forward. A long step. You at last realise you cannot afford not to hate. Hate. What a world of wonder there is in that little word. You could say loathe, detest, abominate, but hate is so much more satisfactory. It's rather like a snake bite, don't you think? One can imagine the word coming out of the mouth as a forked tongue. The point is of course—who do you hate?'

He blew thoughtfully on the end of his cigarette, it gleamed bright red.

"Can't it be your mother? She dominated, browbeat, ripped the protecting veil of make-believe aside and made you face the unthinkable but, alas, the inevitable. She sensed your 'apartness' and confused it with her own frustration. Can you afford not to hate your mother?"

"I hate her,' Miss Blessington screamed. 'I hate her, hate her..."

"Then there is your father," he went on, "a pliable man. Think of putty, a rubber ball, water, a leaf blown by the wind, a sounding board, an echo. Think of your father. Can you afford not to hate your father?"

"I hate him," Miss Blessington sobbed. "He could have protected, defended me. I hate him."

"The young men." He looked very sad now. "They came out of the rose-tinted dawn and left in the fog-shrouded evening. They touched your heart with passion-warm fingers, caressed your forehead with chaste kisses, then struck your mouth with a blow of contempt. Can you afford not to hate them?"

"I hate them," Miss Blessington was on her feet, her fists clenched, her face a mask of snarling hate. "I hate...hate...hate..."

"And you condemn them?" he asked softly. "You pass judgement on them all?"

Miss Blessington nodded, "On them all. All, all."

He inclined his head.

"You have spoken."

The chair on which He sat moved smoothly to one side, and in through the doorway trooped a single file of people who approached the screen with bowed heads and dragging feet, while on either side walked two Hollywood-style gangster characters armed with sub-machine guns. The procession lined up in front of the screen, and Miss Blessington saw Mother was on the extreme right, looking so fright-ened, and Harry, who glared out of the screen and muttered something that sounded suspiciously like "cow", and next to him was Jimmy Harris, who looked as if he were pretending he didn't give a damn. The forgotten-name young man was also there, also four young women who Miss Blessington supposed were the wives they had taken after jilting her.

"You wicked, ungrateful girl," Mother waved her fist, "after all me and yer father did for you."

"Yer didn't ought to do this to yer mother," Father complained, "I mean it ain't natural."

"And what about me?" Giles demanded. "Why have you got it in for me? I can't help it if I didn't fancy you."

"Or me," Harry shouted.

"I hate," Miss Blessington thumped clenched fists down upon her knees. "I hate the ridicule, the sneers, the lies, the shutting off, the taking away."

"Let them be taken away."

He came into view, stood on the right-hand side of the screen, and the men in black suits and matching shirts waved their machine guns, then barked: "About turn."

The file turned their backs on the screen; Father was a little slow, being rather awkward on his feet, and then began to drift towards the far wall, rather like those dream sequences they film in slow-motion. The wall parted in the centre, then both halves drew slowly apart, reminding Miss Blessington of the curtains in the Luxor

Cinema, revealing a scene that froze her to the TV chair with shuddering horror.

Hell was in black and white. It was moreover a Hell designed to suit all tastes. There were whipping posts, racks, bubbling cauldrons of boiling oil, iron maidens, racks of thumbscrews, leg irons, nasty-looking pincers, scold bridles, choppers, chains, to say nothing of a number of sinister attendants, who looked like a cross between Frankenstein's monsters and Count Dracula after a particularly dry night.

Miss Blessington said, "No" several times, and He turned an enquiring glance in her direction.

"No?"

"No," Miss Blessington insisted. "No, not that."

He waved a hand and the scene froze; Father looked very funny poised on one leg, and Mother really horrible with her terror-scarred face glaring back over one shoulder.

"But you hate," he said gently, "and hate demands revenge. Hate is an acid that if it is not tossed into a face, will burn the hand that made it."

"I do not hate that much," Miss Blessington tried to explain.

He shook his head, "One does not hate a little, no more than one commits a little adultery, murders a little. You hate with all your being."

"I hate."

"Then with fierce joy in your heart, let them go into the fire."

"No."

His face expanded, filled the screen, his eyes were suddenly pools of gleaming light, and Miss Blessington whimpered.

"Who do you hate?"

Miss Blessington closed her eyes, covered her ears, but the voice would not be denied.

"Who do you hate?"

"Not them."

When the question came for the third time, she knew she must answer.

"Who do you hate?"

Her voice was a whisper lost in the awful emptiness of eternity. "Myself."

Miss Blessington turned off the television set, then went back to her chair and waited. Presently the door opened, and they entered. First Mother, then Father who looked somewhat distressed. Harry, Giles, and the others followed, the small room was rather full when the last one closed the door. Mother said: "Thank you for nothing," and Father said: "You ought to have had more respect for yer mother," otherwise they all stood round and watched her in silence.

Presently Miss Blessington got up and went into the kitchen to make herself a cup of Ovaltine; there wasn't much room for all of them in the tiny kitchen, so some watched from the doorway, but Mother was close to hand, tut-tutting when Miss Blessington took three lumps of sugar. She tried to shut them out of her bedroom; slammed the door in Mother's face, but they got in somehow, and their low laughter made her shiver. However, the silence was alive when she went to the chest of drawers and took out Father's old cut-throat razor. It was already at her throat when she saw the expression on their faces. It was gloating, evilly joyful, the expression of a starving hunter who at last sees a succulent prey walking into his line of fire. Miss Blessington screamed and dropped the razor. The look of extreme disappointment confirmed her fears.

With a sigh of resignation she got into bed and turned out the light. Their faces gleamed like slabs of moonlight in the darkness.

R. CHETWYND-HAYES:
Photo Gallery

*THIS PAGE: Portraits of the writer
as a young man, circa 1930s–1960s
© The Estate of R. Chetwynd-Hayes.*

LEFT: R. Chetwynd-Hayes (bottom left) with fellow members of the Middlesex Regiment during World War II. © The Estate of R. Chetwynd-Hayes.

BELOW: As a trainee buyer in the Harrods department store in London, circa 1950s © The Estate of R. Chetwynd-Hayes.

ABOVE: R. Chetwynd-Hayes with his Aunt Doris in August 1982 © The Estate of R. Chetwynd-Hayes.

LEFT: Signing books in London, 1983 © Peter Coleborn

RIGHT: At home in Richmond, London, May 1985 © Jo Fletcher.

BELOW: R. Chetwynd-Hayes and Karl Edward Wagner at the 1988 World Fantasy Convention in London © Peter Coleborn.

LEFT: R. Chetwynd-Hayes with his HWA Lifetime Achievement Award during his one and only visit to New York, June 17th 1989 © Andrew I. Porter.

BELOW: Special Award-winner R. Chetwynd-Hayes with fellow British Fantasy Award winners in Birmingham, October 8th 1989 © Peter Coleborn.

ABOVE: R. Chetwynd-Hayes with Stephen Jones, Di and Mike Wathen and Kim Newman in London, summer 1990.

RIGHT: R. Chetwynd-Hayes and Brian Lumley signing at Fantasy Centre, London, on June 12th 1992 © Fantasy Centre.

RIGHT: R. Chetwynd-Hayes at FantasyCon XVII, Birmingham, in October 1992 © Andrew I. Porter.

BELOW: Another book signing in London alongside Peter James, Clive Barker, Brian Stableford, Christopher Fowler, Stephen Jones and Kim Newman, November 1992 © John Menzies.

ABOVE: R. Chetwynd-Hayes, Islington, London, 1997 © Seamus A. Ryan

BITS AND PIECES

ALFRED CAVENDISH HAD successfully escaped the bonds of matrimony for forty-two years, and was a source of constant irritation to his friends and relations. His position could be likened to that of a healthy man in a leper colony. The family gathering at Christmas time had much in common with the worst aspects of the Holy Inquisition.

"Not tied-up yet then?" His brother in-law, who suffered from the dual afflictions of ulcers and a watchful wife, never failed to question the obvious. "Dodging the column! Eh!"

An ancient aunt who had buried two husbands and still entertained hopes of trapping a third, shook her head sadly. "You'll be sorry. Wait 'til you're old."

"I expect," observed a distant female cousin, with the face of an inquisitive parrot, "Alfred hasn't met Miss Right yet."

"Damned selfishness, I call it," snapped a tomato-faced uncle. "All take and no give. Suppose we all decided to remain single and enjoy life? What about the next generation? Eh!"

This question never failed to produce a thoughtful silence, while everyone pondered on the prospect of a generationless future. However, it was the extremely ancient grandmother who finally pushed Alfred over the precipice into the ravine of matrimony. Ninety-five and the possessor of a mouth-watering fortune, she ruled the family with the twin rods of hope and greed.

"If," she pointed a bony forefinger at the shame-faced Alfred, "'e was to get wed, I might leave 'im that what everybody expects, but won't get. But I'll not 'ave my money wasted by a shiftless bachelor."

The afflicted brother-in-law looked thoughtful. "Perhaps he's a bit set in his ways. I mean to say, there is such a thing as a confirmed bachelor."

The entire family nodded, with the exception of the extremely ancient grandmother.

"Think about it," she instructed.

Alfred began to think.

The lady's name was Sarah Butcher. She was fiftyish, inclined to stoutness, had one or two extra chins, a complexion that bore some resemblance to raw putty and walked with a strange, stiff-legged gait. But her smile was rather nice, and she was blessed with a comfortable, if not particularly interesting bank account. Alfred, after much deliberation, came to the conclusion that he could do far worse.

This key to the extremely ancient grandmother's strongbox, had moved into the ground floor flat some two weeks after Christmas, and from the very first day, appeared to be a gift from a suddenly benevolent providence. She smoothed the path that led from the quick-sands of "Good Evening" to the bedrock of "I will," with skill and considerable tenacity.

First came a timid knock on his front door. "So silly of me, I seem to be out of sugar. I wonder...?"

Then: "What a nice flat you have! Could I look round...?"

Naturally this was followed by: "My television has broken down. Do you suppose...?"

There was much talk of two halves making a whole; loneliness shared is loneliness forgotten; half-humorous misquotations: "Better wed than dead." In next to no time, the date was fixed.

The family, far from greeting this proposed union with joyful acclaim, began to display signs of cynical distrust.

The afflicted brother-in-law said it was not so much a marriage as a merger. The ancient aunt wept and remarked it was taking the food out of the mouths of innocent children. The tomato-faced uncle loudly proclaimed that the entire proceedings were a damn scandal. The extremely ancient grandmother summoned her lawyer.

Alfred felt like a newly arrived member of a chain-gang who has not been properly convicted.

The wedding was a very quiet affair.

The bride wore a shocking pink dress, the bridegroom a dark blue suit, and those members of the family who bothered to attend, frustrated frowns. The registrar clearly realised that this was a marriage of convenience, for he raced through the ceremony with the speed of a man who has been pulled away from a hot dinner. Alfred was relieved when Sarah suggested there was no need for a wedding-breakfast, for the prospect of feeding, cheek to jowl with a pack of expectation-bereft relatives, was not a cheering one. In fact, once the deed had been done, the fatal words spoken, and the alleged happy couple were alone in his seventh-floor flat, he had serious misgivings about the entire business.

True, the sacrifice of his freedom could be looked upon as a solid investment, for was not the extremely ancient grandmother's fortune now a certainty? Or was it? For the first time he realised that the family must now be mounting an all-out counter-attack on the fortress of expectation, and although the old lady was as obstinate as a pig-headed mule, who could say that there might not be a change of heart? Then he would be saddled with some very solid stock in a bankrupt enterprise.

At that very moment the solid stock was seated in his best armchair, wearing an expression of growing impatience.

"A cup of tea would be nice," she said.

Alfred thought it would be nicer still if she offered to make it, but being basically a peace-loving man, he went into the kitchen and put the kettle on. Five minutes later he returned to the living-room carrying a loaded tray and a growing sense of grievance.

"I expect," he said pointedly, depositing the tray on a low coffee table, "you can't wait to get established in your own kitchen. Get settled in."

"I'm delicate," she protested in a gentle voice, "and need a lot of attention. I hope, dear, you are adaptable."

Alfred waited for his bride to pour the tea, but as there was no indication that she intended to do anything of the kind, he did it himself.

"You did not mention you suffered from ill-health." He could not help feeling that this was a dirty trick. Had he known there was the slightest risk of being lumbered with an ailing wife, expectations or not, he would have taken the first train to Brighton—the ultimate refuge for harassed bachelors. "I always thought you looked," he had to say it, "pretty solid."

Sarah reached for her cup of tea and took an experimental sip. "There's nothing wrong with my health. I said—I was rather delicate. Now we are married there's no point in my hiding this distressing fact from you. You will need a lot of strength, both physical and mental. Particularly mental."

Alfred muttered, "Bloody hell!" and envisaged years of running from bathroom to bedroom, loaded down with bedpans and bread-poultices. Then a spark of hope lightened his gloom.

"It's nothing—fatal?"

Sarah chuckled, a fat, gurgling rumble. The spark was extinguished by a cold blast of despair.

"Gracious me, no. Why, bless your heart, I'll live to close your eyes, don't you fret. But I have a condition, that can be a little alarming until you get used to it. Did I mention I had been married before?"

Alfred sat upright and violently shook his head. "No, you did not. Most certainly you did not."

Sarah emptied her teacup and placed it gently down on the coffee-table. "That was very remiss of me. I'll have another cup, dear. But not quite so much milk. If you have a fault, it is that you are a bit heavy-handed with the milk jug. Yes, thank you, that will do very nicely. Don't worry, you'll learn in time. Now, what was I saying?"

"You were married before."

"Oh, yes. I have been blessed by three short—but while they lasted—happy marriages."

Alfred said: "Three! Stone the crows!"

"You have, dear," Sarah went on, sipping from her second cup of tea with ladylike daintiness, "a terse, but pungent way of summing up a situation. Yes—three marriages. Triple unions. A thrice bonding of flesh and spirit. One might say, a hat-trick—but one shouldn't. When I remember that some women never even get to the starting gate, I realise how fortunate I've been."

Alfred could do no more than ask a certain question, even though he was not at all sure he wanted it answered.

"What—what happened to them? All—all three of them?"

Sarah sighed. A vast intake and exhalation of breath, that made her substantial bosom rise and fall, like twin mountains riding a minor earthquake.

"Day must be followed by night. Summer must give way to winter. Happiness is so often followed by sorrow. My three darlings all shared one common failing."

Alfred recognised his cue and asked the second question.

"What was it?"

Sarah gently dabbed her eyes with a silk handkerchief.

"They all jumped from a seventh-floor window."

Alfred did a simple calculation and came to an alarming conclusion.

"This . . . this flat is on the seventh floor."

Sarah smiled bravely. With an air of quiet determination, she put her handkerchief away.

"Yes, I know. Isn't it a strange coincidence? I suppose it's because I do admire men with elevated principles. But I'm not going to think about the past. What has gone down, never can be brought up again, particularly when it has been flattened on a pavement. In any case, I know that you are strong-minded. You would never dream of jumping from a seventh-floor window."

"Too true!" Alfred nodded vigorously. "I don't know what made your first three husbands do such a daft thing, but . . . " He stopped, because the third question had slipped into his brain and refused to go away. "Why . . . why did they jump?"

Sarah looked at him with some surprise. "Didn't I explain that? They refused . . . simply refused to accept the unusual. They could not adapt. Their sweet, but silly little minds . . . broke."

Alfred pondered on this completely unsatisfactory explanation for some time, and he could have wished for further elucidation, but he had temporarily run out of questions. Or maybe, he had no wish to add to his stock of disturbing answers.

"Isn't it about time you prepared our dinner?" Sarah asked gently.

The hall clock struck twelve.

Despite coy suggestions, thinly veiled hints, smirks, meaningful looks at the bedroom door, Alfred had so far pushed the inevitable from him. Now he had reached the end of the road.

"Let us," said Sarah rising, "retire."

The recently installed double bed crouched against the far wall, like a hungry monster waiting for the virginal sacrifice. The sheets were turned down, the pillows kneaded into plump white mounds, but there was no sign of night attire. Beside the bed stood a yellow plastic bucket.

"What," enquired Alfred, pointing to this ill-placed object, "is that for? The bathroom is only just across the hall."

"But you won't be able to reach the bathroom," Sarah explained, locking the bedroom door. "And even if you could, experience has taught me that you'd never make it in time. Now, let us get down to essentials. Help me to undress."

"Why have you locked the door?"

Sarah dropped the door key into a dressing-table drawer, which she also locked, then tucked that key under the mattress. "So we won't be disturbed, silly. Now, please, no more questions. Help me to undress."

"But . . . ?"

"I said . . . *help me to undress*!" The final four words were shouted, and the accompanying glare, plus the sight of two clenched fists, made Alfred obey without further argument.

The pink dress buttoned down the back. Alfred was not inexperienced in the art of undressing ladies, having served a long and varied apprenticeship during his misspent youth. But he had never worked with the kind of material that stood before him. It was rather like peeling an onion. After much fumbling, the buttons were eased through their holes and the pink dress fluttered to the floor like a discarded skin. Alfred was now faced with a blue slip. This too surrendered to his reluctant assault and he was left staring open-mouthed at the next line of defence. As he had never been required to surmount this obstacle before, he could only stand perfectly still and wait for instructions.

"You will have to unlace my stays," said Sarah softly.

Made of canvas, reinforced by whale-bone, they could well have deflected an armour-piercing bullet. As Alfred unlaced, he was aware of a gradual expansion, a swelling out, a slow overflowing; the release of much that had been compressed into a small space. He heard the groaning of concealed springs, the cracking of disturbed whale-bone, the gasping sighs of relief, the soft *flop-flop* of freedom-loving flesh.

The stays were finally removed. They fell to the floor with a resounding thud and somehow managed to lie there in an attitude of glowering resentment. The last two frail barriers were removed without too much trouble, and Alfred was at last able to view the full abundance of all that had been hidden. When Sarah turned round, he realised that she was more than generously endowed. Nature had not been backward in coming forward. Her breasts quivered, bulged, heaved, and threatened suffocation to he who came too close. There was a hint of disbelief in Alfred's fascinated gaze.

"I'd better remove *these* myself," said Sarah in a low voice.

She reached up and pulled the left one. It came away with a faint sound. She laid it gently on the bedside table. Alfred's eyes watched the operation, then stared wonderingly at what had been removed. It might have been mistaken for a gigantic milk-jelly, topped by a succulent cherry.

Sarah then removed the right one and laid it beside its fellow. Their previous place of residence was marked by two little red holes. Possibly a full minute passed before Alfred's stomach started its rebellion, but when it did Sarah silently handed him the yellow plastic bucket.

Alfred's partial recovery was followed by a period of unpleasantness.

He kicked the locked door, pulled frantically at the handle, then made a mad dash for the window. Sarah tripped him with her left foot, and floored him with a masterly karate chop across the back of the neck. He was much more amenable after that.

"Please get a hold of yourself," she ordered. "Try to see my point of view. It takes all sorts to make a world, and I'm quite willing to admit that my sort is rather unusual. But that is no excuse for you carrying on like a spoiled baby. Now, when you are ready, I'll get you to give me a hand with my legs."

"Legs!" One might have supposed that Alfred had never heard of these useful and sometimes decorative members. "Hand . . . with . . . legs!"

"Yes." Sarah sat down on the bed and stretched out a podgy, chalk-white leg and thrust the foot under his chin. "Catch hold and pull. I can't rest properly unless I'm fully dismembered."

Alfred required further forcible persuasion before he could be induced to carry out this simple task. But eventually he placed the foot under his arm, took a firm grip on the swollen calf with both hands— and pulled. The leg stretched, assuming the shape of a long, white sausage; it cracked, appeared to belch, then finally came away with an obscene sucking sound. Alfred fell backwards and lay still for a while, while he contemplated the detached leg. He noticed a neat little knob on the thigh end. Then he got up and paid another compulsory visit to the yellow plastic bucket.

There is no doubt that practice makes perfect. It is also an indis-putable fact that familiarity blunts the senses, so that eventually the most grotesque situation assumes the appearance of normality. Having removed the left leg, Alfred was able to detach the right without too much bother, although he was quite unable to avoid making an inter-esting sound, that rather resembled a gurgling scream. He placed his latest acquisition beside its counterpart and tried not to think of what came next.

"That's marvellous." Sarah sighed with evident satisfaction. "It's such a relief to get shot of them for a bit." She raised her head and peered down her nose at him. "Well, don't just stand there. Arms. Get the arms off."

He shook his head. "I can't. Honestly. I would if I could . . . "

"Nonsense." Her face set in a ferocious expression, and an extraor-dinarily long tongue darted out from between parted lips. "Do you want me to come over there? Don't imagine for one moment I can't get around without my legs. Because I can. The loose flaps . . . "

"I'll do it. I'll do it." Alfred was in no condition to witness novel means of transportation. "Which one shall I start with?"

"The left. Always work from left to right, then you don't get the bits and pieces mixed up. Just a minute—I'll take me hair off."

The mop of black hair came away with a faint tearing sound, and Alfred hoped it was a wig, although by now he was almost past caring.

"Hang it on the door knob," Sarah instructed, handing him the limp mass, which bore an uncanny resemblance to a long-dead cat. When he returned to the bedside, she held out two little hairy strips, that were not unlike squashed caterpillars. Only her naked brows explained their purpose more eloquently than words.

"And we don't want this old thing getting in the way," she added, pulling her nose off and pushing it into Alfred's trembling hand. He dropped it into the plastic bucket and had the hell's own job in getting it out again.

"Butter fingers," Sarah complained. "While we are about it, you might as well have these." She detached her ears and tossed them to him with such a nonchalant air, he began to wonder if perhaps, he had been a little over-sensitive. When all the smaller items were laid out on the dressing-table, they made a picturesque, if somewhat thought-provoking display.

It is pleasant to record that there was nothing sinister about Sarah's teeth. When she had removed them, they were revealed as a set of ordinary National Health choppers, such as can be found in a glass, beside many suburban beds. She tucked them under the right pillow and gave Alfred a black-gum smile.

"Now—for my arms."

He grabbed one arm and pulled, thereby earning himself a bellow of rage.

"Don't pull, you stupid ox. Push and twist. They have bayonet fittings."

So they had—a long red plug with two little prongs on either side. Had Alfred been in a calmer frame of mind, he might have admired the ingenuity that had gone into the fitting of his bride's arms. As it was, he could only stare at what was left.

A torso with two, large red holes up, and two down. Two small holes north of the stomach. A toothless, noseless, earless, browless, hairless, dead-white head. Frankenstein had started with less. Perhaps Alfred could have eventually come to accept the entire situation—for one can get used to anything, given time—had not Sarah made that final, soul destroying statement. She raised her head and said with a gummy, simpering smile:

"I'm ready when you are."

Alfred went head-first through a closed window, bounced off three balconies, then seriously impeded the progress of a cruising Aston Martin.

It took Sarah almost an hour to pull herself together again.

SOMETHING COMES IN FROM THE GARDEN

"THE HOUSE WILL suit me down to the ground," Robert Erwin stated, then instantly regretted his too apparent enthusiasm. "I mean of course if we can come to some agreement regarding price."

The house agent smiled one of those enigmatic smiles that are peculiar to his kind. "I am sure we can reach a satisfactory agreement, Mr. Erwin. However, there is just one piece of information that I have been instructed to pass on to any prospective buyer. The house is haunted."

There was a short silence while Robert looked out of the window, then back at the agent again. Presently he said: "You mean that?"

The man nodded. "I have reason to believe my client fully believes what she says. You of course are at liberty to draw your own conclusions."

"What..." Robert coughed, then went on bravely, "...what form does the alleged haunting take?"

"I have no further information. My client has stipulated that the prospective buyer spends a probationary month in the house before signing the contract. I find this to be ethical, if not very business-like. I would of course ask for a deposit as a sign of your good faith, on the understanding that it be refunded, should you decide to vacate the premises at the end of the stated period."

"I'll think it over," Robert promised.

He moved into Ennerdale House on the first of October. Edna and the children liked the house, the garden—an expanse of green lawn, surrounded on three sides by tall yew trees—the neighbourhood, the air, and everything about it. He knew this was the enthusiasm that comes with change and that familiarity would dull the keenness. But he was content. The ghost he had dismissed as a shadow phantom created by a senile or disturbed mind. He himself had decided that he would believe only what he saw. Disregarding the probationary period, they moved all their furniture in, and gave the house a new coat of paint so that soon it smiled happily out across the moors. Robert ran a motor-mower back and forth across the lawn until it resembled a smooth green carpet, while Richard who was twelve, and Joan, ten, did things with spades and forks in the borders. Then the time came when there was really nothing else to be done and they sat back and gazed upon their work with a smile of achievement.

"Not bad," Robert said, drowning a pint of brown ale.

"Super," Joan declared.

"Spiffendous," Richard announced, having arrived at an age when the manufacture of words was considered to be a necessity.

"Make sure you wipe your feet before you come in," Edna warned.

They decided to give a house-warming party.

The sky rained relatives, for it was rumoured that Robert was well-endowed and had a sympathetic ear for those in need. Aunts came from the suburbs; pretty nieces and distant cousins drifted in from Chalfront-St-Giles. Edna was in her element, handing out strangely-shaped sandwiches, sausages on sticks, bits and pieces on biscuits and answering the never-ending calls for coffee. Robert contented himself with serving sherry and a concoction of white wine and gin he had invented. After the third glass even he rather liked it.

Voices became blurred; the room appeared through a faint mist, and he was warmed by a delicious feeling of well-being. Even his mother-in-law assumed a kind of golden glow, and her acid-tipped barbs glanced off his armour of reinforced self-esteem.

"Bit remote, I should have thought," she stated, sipping from a glass of grapefruit juice.

"Distance," he said airily, "is a great protector."

"And personally," she went on, "I find the house much too large."

"But the question is," he wagged a forefinger at her, "would the house find you too large?"

She disappeared into the deepening mist and was replaced by one of the pretty nieces, who had a long-haired boyfriend in tow.

"Uncle Robert," she said, showing him more leg and bosom than is usually considered an uncle's just due, "this is Jason. He's in the dress-designing business."

"Good for Jason." Robert nodded with ponderous solemnity. "May his designing never grow less."

"That is to say, he is thinking of going into the dress-designing business," the niece corrected.

"Tell him never to think," Robert advised, "it's bad for the liver."

"If only he had a little capital," the niece went on, nudging Jason, who appeared to have indulged in the gin concoction rather too well, "I am certain he would make a fortune."

"Tell him to try Dublin." Robert gave her one of his lop-sided smiles and moved on. He was beginning to feel rather bored when he spotted the young girl in the white dress. She looked sad, lonely and very pretty and his heart warmed to her. He found himself looking down on the rich auburn hair, which was tied back with a white ribbon, and adjusted the room by swaying gently back and forth.

"Hullo," he said.

She looked up and presented a long pale face. Her hazel eyes were the most beautiful and sad he had ever seen. Her face crumpled into a wavering smile.

"Hullo."

"Are you enjoying yourself?"

She looked round the crowded room. The mother-in-law was talking most earnestly to Edna and kept glancing in Robert's direction.

"It's all rather frightening."

He nodded very slowly. "Too true. This lot are enough to frighten the living daylights out of anybody."

She seemed rather surprised. The smooth forehead was creased by a tiny frown and the beautiful eyes widened.

"Are you frightened too?"

"Sweet child," he swung his arm out in a gesture that embraced the entire room, "this room is full of vampires, and they are all after my blood."

A fleeting look of alarm crossed her face, then she smiled.

"You are joking? You are—what is the expression—pulling my leg?"

"It's not such a joke," he said, thoughtfully, just as he was captured by a middle-aged aunt who wanted him to meet her new son-in-law. A little later when he remembered to look round, the girl in the white dress had disappeared.

It was a month to the day before the unusual happened.

The sun was setting and Robert was looking out of the window, wondering where to put his summerhouse, when the man walked across the lawn. He was tall, with a red, hooked nose, and was attired in an old, faded army overcoat. Robert watched him for a few seconds with almost dispassionate interest. The man slouched—there was no other way to describe his loose-limbed action—across Robert's line of vision, with bent shoulders and lowered head, giving the impression he was treading a familiar path. Robert turned and, going quickly to the door, shouted across the hall.

"Edna, have you hired an old rough to do some gardening?"

She came out of the kitchen, wiping her hands on a glass-cloth.

"No, I haven't engaged anyone. I leave the garden to you."

They went outside, and after looking around rather anxiously, proceeded to search the garden with methodical care, occasionally making a weak joke as to the possibility of invasion. Neither of them wanted to admit the unthinkable suggestion, the secret fear. Their search revealed nothing out of the ordinary; no sign of the man or a trace of his passing. Once back in the house there was a ridiculous urge to keep looking out the window and start at every passing shadow. Presently Edna said; "I will begin to believe in the ghost if this sort of thing goes on," and then they both laughed. But when a few days had passed, the incident was pushed into the back of their minds, where memories lay, waiting to be recalled.

A week later the children found the girl in the white dress standing by the front gate and requested she be allowed to come in. Robert was delighted: Edna was not so pleased.

"What does she want?" she asked.

"Probably lives nearby," Robert said, "and has come to say thank you for the party."

"But who is she?" Edna demanded, watching the white figure being led up the garden path.

"God knows." He grinned. "But then, I didn't know half the crowd that came to the house-warming. It was a free-for-all for most of London and the suburbs."

She came into the sitting-room like a stray kitten, uncertain of its welcome. Joan and Richard both wore an expectant expression, as though contemplating praise for a novel discovery. Edna advanced and held out her hand, creasing her face into a polite smile of welcome.

"So pleased to see you, my dear."

The girl allowed her hand to be shaken, then gravely presented it to Robert. He was much more effusive.

"Delighted. We don't get many visitors, especially young and pretty ones. Do you live hereabouts?"

"Yes." She nodded and the long auburn hair danced. "Yes, I used to live here."

"Did you hear that, Edna?" He appealed to his wife who still wore her fixed smile. "Eh—what is your name?"

"Julia."

"Julia used to live here."

"I heard," Edna said, adjusting her smile to one of pleased surprise.

"It must be rather sad to see other people living in what used to be your home," Robert observed.

"Yes," Julia answered with rather sweet simplicity.

"She didn't want to come in," Richard stated, "but we made her."

"I think she did, really," Joan added, "but was too shy."

"I came the other night," Julia raised her beautiful eyes and looked at Robert, "because lots of other people were coming in and it seemed to be all right."

"Indeed!" Edna exclaimed.

"The lady who lived here before you," the girl went on, "never welcomed me."

"You must feel free to come any time you like," Robert ignored Edna's look of disapproval. "We will always be pleased to see you."

"Absolutely," Richard hastened to add. "You can tell us all about the ghost."

A look of bewilderment clouded the young face and she turned her head slowly from side to side as a gesture of denial.

"Ghost! This house was never haunted when I lived here. It was a happy place."

"There you are." Robert grinned at Edna. "I always said it was a lot of piffle." He again addressed Julia, whose face wore an expression of rather fearful bewilderment. "The house agent relayed a message from the last owner, who warned us that the place was haunted. Why should she do that?"

"Mrs. Ames," Julia said slowly, "was a lady who was easily frightened."

"Rattling windows, wind in the chimney, and shadows at sunset." Robert nodded. "Imagination can do the rest."

Edna was still watching the girl with some concern, and her eyes narrowed when she asked: "Why did you say the lady was easily frightened?"

Julia shrugged. "I don't know but she was. Once she screamed when I came in by the window."

"Perhaps," Edna observed drily, "she wasn't expecting you. If someone were suddenly to appear uninvited, I would possibly scream."

"But I'm always around," the girl protested. "I wasn't a stranger."

"Well, no one will scream when you come in now," Robert promised. "What would you say to a spot of tea?"

Julia nodded. "I would like that. It's been a long time since anyone invited me to tea."

"Well, talk to the children while I get it ready," Edna instructed. "Robert, come and give me a hand."

He made a face but dutifully followed his wife into the kitchen, then looked surprised when she closed the door.

"What's the idea? She'll think we are talking about her."

"We are." Edna filled the kettle and placed it on the stove. "Robert, who is that girl?"

"I don't know. I saw her at the party and thought she looked a bit lonely so I spoke to her. She seems a nice enough kid."

"Kid my foot." Edna unwrapped a sliced loaf, then proceeded to butter each slice. "Get the jam out of the cupboard. She's a minx if you ask me. Sliding in when she's not invited. And that meek, 'I am so easily hurt,' expression! That might go down with you men but it cuts no ice with me."

"Oh, be your age." He slammed two pots of jam down on the table. "Surely you don't think I . . . ? Look, she's just a child who wants a bit of company. So far as I am concerned she can come here as often as she likes."

Edna appeared unmoved by his outburst.

"She's not so much a child as you seem to imagine. Don't be taken in by that unlined face and innocent eyes. I bet my best cotton socks she's every day of twenty-five."

"Rubbish," Robert ejaculated. "I'd say sixteen—certainly not more than seventeen. Honestly, you women, once you get it in for one of your own sex, you cover the impossible with a thick layer of imagination and call it logic. Why don't you like her, anyway?"

"She never looks you in the eye," Edna pronounced.

"Oh, for heaven's sake. It's not everyone that goes around staring into your eyeballs. It's embarrassing, anyway."

Edna did not answer but loaded the tea trolley while Robert made the tea. When he wheeled the trolley into the sitting-room, the two children were bubbling over with excitement.

"Daddy," Joan grabbed his arm, "Julia has been telling us about the pimpkins. They are little people who live behind the skirting boards and under the floor. And they come out to play when we are in bed."

"Indeed!" Edna, who had been following close in Robert's footsteps, frowned. "My name for them is mice."

"No." Richard sounded a little scornful. "Julia says pimpkins go for rides on mice. But what I like best is the horrible little thing that lives in an oak tree, and on windy days, jumps down on people's heads and tangles their hair."

"I think you'd all better get on with your teas," Edna said. "Julia appears to have a very vivid imagination."

"No I haven't. Mother used to say I had no imagination at all. I just see things that other people don't. I have sort of special eyes."

Edna frowned again. "Joan, pour out the tea, there's a good girl. And Richard, see that your guest has everything she wants."

Robert sat back and closed his eyes. The rattle of teacups was soothing. The children's chatter was a comfortable reminder that his life ran along well-ordered lines. Someone nudged his arm, and he opened his eyes and blinked as Joan said: "Your tea, Daddy."

He smiled indulgently, then took the offered cup and saucer, while his glance automatically went to the young girl seated on the sofa. She was holding her cup with limp fingers and staring at the window with an expression of horror.

"What is it, my dear?" he asked.

She turned a white face towards him, and there was great fear in the lovely eyes.

"There is . . . there is someone in the garden."

"What?" Edna rose quickly and shot the girl an impatient glance. "How can you possibly know? You are too far away from the window to see."

"I know." She dropped the cup and an ugly brown stain began to spread over the new carpet. "Someone is walking across the garden. There is an awful loneliness—I am frightened."

Robert walked quickly to the window, where he pulled back the curtains and looked out into the gathering gloom. At first he saw only the long shadows cast by the trees as they reached out for the last golden rays of the dying sun. Then he stiffened as he saw the reason for her fear. The man in the old army overcoat was once again walking across the garden.

For a while Robert could only stand by the French window, with his nose flattened against the glass and watch the brown figure as it walked very slowly across the grass and into the shadow of the first tree. Then Edna's voice, its tone sharp with anxiety, cut into his consciousness.

"Robert, what on earth is the matter? Who is it?"

He knew he must take some form of action. Cover his rising fear with a light blanket of anger, reinforce his courage—such as it was—with cynical disbelief.

"I've had enough of this. Bloody layabouts using the place as though it were the main road."

Edna was still calling after him when he flung the windows open and stepped out into the garden. "Don't go out . . . come back . . . come back . . ." As though he dared not go out; could possibly live with the knowledge that he was afraid to find out who—what—walked across his green, well-tended lawn at sunset. The memory of those beautiful, fear-bright eyes went with him as he moved out into the Gothic-grey of expiring day. The soft breeze that heralds the coming of night caressed his face with cold kisses. But the garden, save for deepening shadows, was as empty as a dead man's brain, and although he ran back and forth with desperate courage, even into the blackness that lurked beneath the trees, no trace of the intruder did he find. Finally he stopped and listened. A bird twittered in its nest far overhead; some small creature scampered among the plants that grew against the tall, red-bricked wall; the leaves muttered as the breeze disturbed their peace—but otherwise all was still in the garden. He could do no more than go back to the house, and once there, laugh away the atmosphere of gloom.

"No one there. The old devil must be able to move fast when the mood takes him."

"You must report this," Edna insisted. "We can't have some horrible old tramp coming and going as he pleases."

Robert grinned ruefully, and marvelled that he was able to act so well. "I suppose I must. But I'd like to know how he gets out. The wall surrounds the entire house and he walks away from the front gate."

"Perhaps he shins up the wall," Richard suggested.

"But he's too old . . ." Robert began, then realised he was entering a maze where questions and conjecture led to a central point that he had no wish to find. "Where's Julia?" he asked.

There was a turning of heads and questioning glances, before Joan spoke for them all. "I don't know. She was very frightened, and must have slipped out when we were at the window."

"If you must ask me," Edna said, "that girl is not all there. I am not at all sure she should be encouraged to come here again."

Both Richard and Joan protested and Robert gave way to a sudden surge of unreasoning anger.

"Why must you condemn anyone who does not toe your line of mundane normality? Maybe she is a bit eccentric. But I'd rather have that, than the 'thank you very much and I'd love to come again' types you go for. Sometimes you make me want to throw up."

The ensuing silence told him he had stepped out of character. He had showed a depth of feeling unusual to a man who prided himself on being cool and collected at all times. Edna's face was a picture of hurt surprise.

"I'm sorry I spoke. I had thought I was entitled to express an opinion as to who should be a guest in my house. It seems I was wrong."

She turned and hurried from the room and presently they heard the kitchen door slam, a sure sign that although a retreat had been effected, peace overtures were expected from the antagonist. The children looked decidedly uncomfortable. Presently Richard asked: "What are we going to do about the man, Dad?"

"What man?"

"The one that walks in the garden."

Robert went to the window, then resolutely pulled the curtains. "I'll think of something."

When Joan asked the next question, it was like a hot needle on a raw nerve. "Daddy, do you think the man is a ghost?"

"Don't be so damned silly," he snapped.

The house agent was as urbane and non-committal as ever.

"My client was most insistent that her identity and whereabouts should not be revealed, Mr. Erwin."

"But I am also your client," Robert pointed out, "and I consider it essential that I contact the late owner of my house."

The man seemed a little uneasy. "To be frank, I have never met the lady. All business was transacted through a firm of solicitors."

"May I suggest then, that you write to them and say I would be most grateful for an interview."

"Yes. I can do that."

Robert rose and looked down at the round, red face.

"You are very kind," he said.

"Not at all," replied the house agent.

Edna was waiting for him in the hall. She was pale and seemed to have forgotten the atmosphere of polite restraint which had lain between them for the past twenty-four hours. She put a hand on his arm and whispered loudly: "I've seen him again."

Robert hung his hat on the hall-stand, then carefully placed his umbrella in the rack.

"Who?"

"The man. He came into the kitchen, did something at the sink, then went out again."

He frowned. "Then why on earth didn't you speak to him? Ask him what the hell he was playing at?"

Edna gripped his arm and shook it, while she struggled for words to describe her fear.

"I did...I did. I yelled...said, "get out...get out..." but he ignored me...then went out through the door."

He was trying not to understand, doing his utmost to put off the final moment of realisation, but then Edna screamed out the four terrifying words.

"*The door was shut!*"

He led her gently into the dining-room and poured her a generous measure of whisky. She emptied the glass with the dutiful obedience of a child. Then she burst into tears.

"Now, now," he comforted her with the awkwardness of a man who is embarrassed by displays of emotion, and patted her rather heavily on the shoulder. "Tell me about it. Were you in the kitchen when...he entered?"

She sniffed, dabbed her nose with a ridiculous scrap of white linen, and gradually returned to a state of coherency.

"No...When I went into the kitchen, he...it was walking towards the sink. I was too astonished to speak for a minute...it was such a shock...then I shouted: "What do you want? Who are you?" He took no notice, but went to the sink and did something there. It looked as if he was washing his hands."

She collapsed again and while Robert continued with his shoulder patting, he was surprised to find that his fear was giving way to a feeling of growing excitement. The house really was haunted. One read about such things; sometimes a friend related an experience that had happened to a friend of his, but here was a rare phenomenon actually taking place in his garden and kitchen. He said: "Go on. What happened next?"

"I was frightened, of course. But it was only the natural fear that any woman would feel on finding a strange man in her house. Particularly when he refused to speak. But I never really believed... When we saw him in the garden, the thought did cross my mind... But I couldn't... I shouted at him again and he turned and walked back towards the door. His face! I saw it close up. Robert, it was like that of an animal. Dull, great, watery, expressionless eyes. A thing that would just follow its instincts. Then it walked through the closed door and I just lost my head. Thank God, the kids were upstairs. Robert, what are we going to do?"

"Get to the bottom of the matter." He smiled at her, feeling almost light-hearted, not really appreciating her deep-seated terror. "I've asked the estate agent chap to contact the last owner. If we can find out why, perhaps we shall know what must be done."

"But, Robert," her voice rose to a cry of protest, "we can't live in this house with that—that thing liable to walk in at any moment."

"I don't see why not," he said. "It can't do us any harm."

"Can't do us any harm!" She came up from her chair. "Do you realise what you are saying? Something unnatural that stalks round the garden, comes in through shut doors and has the face of a witless fiend—is harmless? Let me tell you this—stay here if you like, but I'm taking the children out of this damned place tonight."

"Now, don't be so bloody ridiculous." He was surprised to hear the note of harshness in his own voice, and actually rejoiced when he felt the wave of anger flood his being. "You will stay here and try to behave like a rational person. What you saw was a coloured shadow without substance or intelligence, and no reason for you to act like a hysterical school-girl."

He left her and went over to the fireplace where he stood looking down at the electric fire. The anger receded and he said calmly: "Go upstairs and lie down. We'll talk again when you are more yourself."

He heard her get up, and a little later the sound of her footsteps ascending the stairs, followed by the quiet closing of the bedroom door. Discord was coming into their lives, where before there had always been tranquillity. The house and that which pertained to it was responsible, and yet, try as he might, he could not dispel a feeling of deep satisfaction. The placid sea of his life was ruffled by exciting waves, and he was sailing a course that he knew instinctively was fraught with danger, yet he would not—even if it meant his eventual destruction—have missed a moment of it.

Robert went into the sitting-room and the two children turned speculative eyes in his direction, while Julia sat with lowered eyes in a chair by the fireplace. It was then that the truth unveiled her face and he knew himself.

He said: "Hullo, you with us again?" She looked up and his heart beat a little faster when he saw the look of undisguised pleasure in her eyes; the shy, tremulous smile that played around her lips. Then she lowered her head again and her voice came to him as a low, husky whisper.

"Yes. I am afraid I am a nuisance."

"What utter nonsense. You are always welcome. Always."

"Daddy," Joan too, perhaps found pleasure in discord, "what upset Mummy?"

"Nothing that need to concern." He frowned at her, and because this was unusual, she backed away. "I want to have a private word with Julia. You two push off somewhere. But don't disturb your mother."

They went with obvious reluctance, and Richard dared to look back with a questioning gleam in his eye. Robert got up and closed the door, then came back and sat opposite the girl.

"Julia, it's strange, but I've never asked you this before. Where do you live?"

"Round the corner," she said simply.

"How long ago was it, that you lived in this house?"

"Oh, a long time ago. I grew up here."

He began to marshal words with great care.

"This house has a reputation, hasn't it?"

He had reason to remember Edna's remark that this girl never looked you squarely in the eye. She was now staring at a point just over his right shoulder, while the now familiar smile played around her mouth.

"I don't know what you mean."

"Julia," his voice was reproachful, "you do. It is said to be haunted. A man in a brown coat wanders across the garden at sunset, and this afternoon he came into the kitchen. What do you know of him?"

A blast of terror twisted her face into a mask of pain, and she began to wring her hands and contort her shoulders. Her voice rose and became a wail of protest.

"I don't know. I can't remember."

"Try to," he pleaded, "it is so important. Don't you see, if this goes on, I will have to leave the house? I am not frightened, not any more, but my wife—the children. You do see? I must know who he is—was—and why he walks."

Her eyes met his now. Only for a second, but he was able to see the wild fear, the longing, the loneliness. Her words evoked a surge of protective tenderness, so that it took all his will-power not to cover the distance that separated them and take her in his arms.

"You can't go away. I'd be all alone. Something horrible happens to me when I am left alone."

"Then you must tell me who the man is. Why does he walk?"

"Because of something he did . . ." She creased her white brow into a frown of deep concentration. "Something awful. He did . . . did . . . did . . . something dreadful a long time ago."

"What? Julia, what did he do?"

She put a hand on either side of her head and stared, wide-eyed at the ceiling. Then, suddenly, she screamed. A terrifying, long drawn-out shriek that filled the room, then went echoing round the house. Even as Robert leaped to his feet and moved towards her, she ran to the door, jerked it open and raced into the hall. When Robert followed a few seconds later, he bumped into Richard, who clutched his father to avoid being overthrown.

"Dad, what's wrong?" he gasped. "Why did Julia scream like that?"

Robert pushed him roughly to one side and looked anxiously round the hall. "Where did she go? The state she's in, anything could happen."

Richard jerked his head towards the dining-room. "She went in there."

The girl was crouched on the floor near the fireplace; huddled together, with her arms clasped firmly round her legs and her face hidden beneath a screen of auburn hair. He went over to her and whispered: "Julia, please my dear, don't be frightened. I won't ask any more questions—not now. Please get up."

There was no movement, no sign that his words had been heard, and presently he reverted to his characteristic gesture of comfort: he patted her shoulder. She rolled over to one side, still in the grotesque position; an inanimate object that displayed no sign of life, seemingly in the throes of some kind of seizure. Robert ran back to the hall and bellowed up the stairs. "Edna, come down quickly."

It seemed an age before the bedroom door opened and Edna came walking slowly down the stairs. She seemed listless, displaying neither fear nor curiosity, and Robert's impatience flared into anger. "For God's sake get a move on. Didn't you hear that scream?"

"I heard," she said softly.

"Julia seems to be ill. She's rolled up on the floor and does not move. Look at her, see what you can do."

Edna came down into the hall and looked at him with a quiet smile. She was like a person who has gone beyond the frontiers of fear, and now exists in a limbo where emotion of any kind could not survive. "Don't you realise," she said simply, "it's this house? It's mad."

He seized her by the arm and pushed her roughly towards the dining-room door. "Get in there. What's the matter with you, for heaven's sake? The girl may be dying."

Once back in the dining-room, Robert looked around with helpless amazement. The room was empty and the French window was open, allowing the night breeze to sigh along the walls, playfully ruffling the curtains and causing a solitary dead leaf to dance across the carpet. He went to the open window and called out: "Julia . . . Julia . . ."

Edna laughed sardonically. "She won't come back. Not tonight. Don't you realise what she is? An unbalanced girl, who will play any number of hair-raising tricks to draw attention to herself. Particularly your attention. That scream. The stories she tells the children. Then laying herself out on the floor. But when she heard me coming, she knew here was someone who could see through her. So, wisely, she made a bolt for it."

Robert came up close to his wife and stared hard into her face. "She's different from anyone I have ever known. She has the soul of a butterfly. But you haven't the slightest idea what I am talking about, have you?"

Edna smiled grimly. "I should close the window if I were you. One never knows what might come walking in."

Robert took an early morning train to town the next day—just one hour after the post arrived—and on arriving at Waterloo, hired a cab which set him down at Emmwood Mansions, near Bryanston Square. A lift took him to the third floor and a door numbered 27. A middle-aged woman in a maid's uniform answered his knock.

"Yes. What is it?"

"I have an appointment with Mrs. Ames."

She moved to one side with apparent reluctance.

"You'd better come in. I will see if Mrs. Ames is disengaged."

He entered a small hall, to wait while the maid announced his arrival. In five minutes she returned and then led him down a narrow passage into a large room at the rear of the house. Mrs. Ames proved to be a little old lady with a mass of piled-up hair, clad in a plain black dress, relieved by a white *gorget*. She was seated by the window and gestured her guest to her chair by an imperious wave of her hand.

"Good morning, Mr. Erwin. Being of a retiring nature, I do not as a rule grant interviews. But as I believe I can be of service to you, I agreed that my identity should be revealed."

"I cannot thank you enough," Robert began, but the old lady interrupted him with another wave of her hand.

"I must express some surprise that you are still living in Ennerdale House. In the past, few prospective buyers have stayed more than three weeks, and one, in fact, was out within two days. What I had hoped to find was a nice matter-of-fact family who lacked what I believe today is called extra-sensory perception. Who, in other words, cannot see ghosts. You are clearly not such a person. Perhaps you can enlighten me as to why you did not take advantage of my probationary offer and leave by the end of the fourth week?"

"Mainly," Robert said, "because I liked the house, and also I suppose, I refused to believe in the existence of ghosts."

Mrs. Ames laughed shortly; a harsh little crackle that made Robert flinch.

"But I should imagine you were soon disillusioned. I am aware that the phenomenon is both fearful and possibly dangerous. You have a family?"

"Yes," Robert admitted, "a wife and two children."

"And they have seen the manifestation?"

"My wife has. Now you come to mention it, I am not certain about the children. But they know of it."

Mrs. Ames nodded. "With both parents so gifted, it is unlikely they are not also. I am, Mr. Erwin, a timid person and frankly, I was terrified at what I saw in that house. But I am also obstinate, and I refused, until my age weakened my resolve, to allow it to drive me out. I stuck to my guns for over twenty years and during that period, I never ceased to hope I could find a solution."

"You are a brave woman," Robert said with deep sincerity.

"I don't think so. Probably a silly one. Have you made enquiries as to the history of the house, Mr. Erwin?"

"No," he confessed, "it never occurred to me."

"Just as well. Such accounts are often coloured by imagination, and grossly inaccurate. Briefly, these are the facts. Tom Jenkins was what is broadly described as a tramp. One of those unfortunates who were unable to settle down after the First World War, and took to living, if that is the right word, on the casual charity dispensed by anyone who felt compassion for him. The owner of Ennerdale House in those days was a Mrs. Fortescue, a widow with a young daughter. She, I suppose you could say, encouraged him. She gave him food and allowed him to sleep in a small outhouse at the bottom of the garden. I had it demolished. You see, Jenkins first raped the daughter, then strangled her."

"How horrible." Robert shuddered and Mrs. Ames permitted herself another grim smile.

"You may well say so. The house has been—how shall I put it?—troubled ever since. But I must stress, Mr. Erwin, you are not just contending with a ghost. You are plagued with an entity. An intelligence, that if balked, will I am sure, prove malignant. Have you allowed it to enter the house?"

"I don't know about *allow*," Robert said, "but it certainly came into the kitchen."

"Then someone must have invited it," Mrs. Ames said sternly. "I would never allow it beyond the French windows. For heaven's sake, Mr. Erwin, drive it out. Treat it as you would an unwanted stray cat. Wave a pillow-case in its face, curse it, and do not be put out by its apparent distress. Better still, if you find it is firmly established, get out yourself."

"But," Robert frowned, "he does little harm. I grant you, the sight of a disembodied tramp walking round the garden, not to mention the kitchen, is not an experience I relish, but he has never even spoken. Surely he's in no condition to rape, let alone strangle anyone now?"

The silence lasted for a full minute then Mrs. Ames spoke.

"I think, Mr. Erwin, we have been speaking at cross-purposes. I was not referring to the shade of Jenkins, who walks the garden at sunset, and occasionally is seen in the house. I agree, he is completely harmless and will in time, no doubt fade away. No, it is the other one you have to fear. The girl in the white dress. Julia Fortescue. The victim. If she can be so-called, for it came out at the trial that she had so tormented the poor half-witted wretch, he went berserk."

It was some time before speech returned to Robert Erwin, and then he could only blurt out a torrent of words.

"But...but...she's a living person. Don't shake your head...She told me...told me...she lives round the corner."

Mrs. Ames' smile was positively sardonic.

"You are not very observant, Mr. Erwin. Round the corner from your house is the cemetery."

The exterior of the house was deceptively comforting.

The windows smiled out over the countryside, the red brickwork gleamed warmly in the sunlight, and the door was wide open, waiting for him to enter. The man who crossed the hall fully intended to order his family to pack a few essentials, then move out as soon as it was practicable. But when Robert came into the kitchen, he was already entertaining other thoughts. It was as though someone was whispering to him: *You are experiencing a unique situation—what have you to fear? The old woman lived here for twenty years, and she is still alive and well.*

There was also an urge to see the girl again, now that he *knew*. A fear-tinted curiosity clamoured more and more for satisfaction. Edna, who was going about her work in the kitchen, ignored his entrance. She slammed the dishes down on the Formica-topped table with a little more energy than was strictly necessary, and concentrated even more intensely on the task in hand. He said: "Hullo, I'm back," and he might have been an invisible ghost himself for all the heed she paid him. He fought down the rising wave of irritation, that he knew could soon flare up into a rage, before remarking casually: "I've been to see the late owner. A Mrs. Ames. A weird old body."

Edna broke the silence. "Oh, yes."

"She . . . she says, we should be careful. Look," he hesitated, the old self was warring with the new, "perhaps it would be better if you . . . "

Edna straightened up and stared at him with an expression he found it hard to analyse. It was half-expectant, half-fearful, as though she was afraid he would say something distasteful. She snapped abruptly: "What?"

They stood facing one another for several minutes, each trying to hide their intimate thoughts from the other, then Robert sighed and turned away. "Nothing," he said, "nothing at all."

The children were in the garden, cheerfully pulling up weeds from between the flowers, and greeted his arrival with a certain polite reserve that would have been unthinkable yesterday.

"We're busy," said Richard.

"Weeding," added Joan.

"Well done." He affected hearty approval, feeling like a stranger who must win their confidence. "Marvellous. Anything I can do to help?"

"No thank you," said Richard.

"We can manage," said Joan.

"I see," Robert put his hands in his pockets, shifted from one foot to another, then enquired with terrifying indifference: "Have you seen Julia? Has she been around today?"

"No," Richard answered briefly.

"We've gone off her." Joan stood up and rubbed her hands on the already stained skirt. "She's silly—and funny—all those stories. As if things called pimpkins could live behind the skirting board."

Robert caught his breath. Did they suspect? If so he would have to move out, empty the house and leave her to cry alone. Suddenly the prospect was completely unacceptable.

"I'm sorry to hear that. I thought she was..." He could not say *nice*, that would be stupid. "A rather imaginative girl who would be company for you."

Richard shrugged. "She was all right at first, but then... She's a wierdie... likes to make trouble... always crying."

"She's not our sort of person," Joan stated gravely.

Robert went back to the house and began looking for her. Questions, that up to now he had not bothered to consider, now presented themselves and demanded answers. Was she always here? Were there periods when she could not appear? Was she in fact a—he stumbled over the word—a person? Or something that was built out of atmosphere—terror—unrequited lust? He shuddered but continued to search.

Minutes passed and became hours; the sun sank down behind the tall trees, and shadows crept across the lawn and approached the house. Edna laid the table for the evening meal, then called the children, who had long since deserted the garden and were now romping in one of the upper rooms. When Robert entered the dining-room they were all seated at the table, and he took his seat without a word being said.

They ate in silence only broken by the rattle of cutlery on china, and the occasional hushed word that died almost before it was uttered. Now and again Edna would rise and go to the kitchen to fetch another course, or something she had forgotten and it was then that Robert's rage would bubble and threaten to erupt. Not until coffee was being served did he take a deep breath and attempt to break through the wall which surrounded him.

"Look here, let's . . . "

A sound came from the sitting-room. It could have been a door being softly closed, or the French windows protesting as they were slowly opened. But it might have been a thunder-clap, or even a trumpet-blast to announce the end of the world, for the effect it had on the four people seated round the table. Edna cried out: "Don't go. Please don't go," when Robert sprang up from his chair, and the two children whimpered and looked at him with terror-wide eyes.

Julia was seated on the sofa when he came into the room; her long-fingered hands clasped, her head lowered. She looked pitiful and rejected. Robert walked slowly towards her and lowered himself on to the sofa. He then leaned forward and whispered: "You've come back. I thought you had gone forever."

Her head came round and he saw her eyes gleam softly, possibly with pleasure—maybe even triumph. The smile was almost imperceptible. "You know?"

He nodded. "I know."

"And it makes no difference? You are not afraid?"

He moved nearer; sidled along the sofa until a bare two feet separated them. "I am afraid. Just a little. But it makes no difference. Perhaps, in my heart, I have always known."

The smile became more pronounced. "I have been looking for someone who would overcome his fear. You will have to travel a long way."

He sank down upon one knee and dared lay his hands on hers. They were cold. Death cold. "I will melt your coldness with my warmth, and take the burden of your sins—if sins there be—upon my shoulders."

Her eyes were brilliant and their fire set light to the dead desires that littered his brain. He felt the great *resolve* grow stronger with every heartbeat.

"Do what you must," she said, "and we will be together always."

Robert heard the gasp from the doorway and spinning round saw Edna standing there, her face a mask of disgust and terror.

"Get away from—from that thing," she said. "In the name of sanity, get away from *it*."

He got up and moved towards her, the great resolve was a voice; a mighty roar in his head that must be satisfied.

"She is lost, lonely, needing love and understanding."

He was still trying to convince Edna—and himself. As always endeavouring to evade his responsibilities, put off making the final decision. But Edna too could not change, had to blurt out the truth, no matter how distasteful it was.

"You *know* what she is. A monster... something that belongs to dark places, and you are giving it life. You have from the moment we set foot in this house. Lie to me if you must, but don't lie to yourself."

He was drawing nearer to her, smashing down the barriers, walking over ground he had hitherto only glimpsed in half-forgotten dreams. As he moved, words poured off his tongue. Thoughts that had festered in acid for fifteen years.

"Talk... talk, will nothing ever still that tongue, shut that mouth and give me peace? Soft words, maybe, wrapped in velvet and soaked in oil, but the sting was always there, while you waited for the unguarded flinch, the grimace of pain, who knows, the unexpected tear. Now it is my turn."

Edna shrieked. "Don't. You must understand. You are doing what she wants. Turn round, look at her face."

"I can see yours," he said gently.

A great joy exploded when he fastened his hands about her throat, and her slowly diminishing, gurgling screams were sweet music to his soul. Then it was over: a broken body lay at his feet, and he was a frightened man who had just murdered his wife. When he turned round, Julia was coming up from the sofa. Her white dress had slipped from one shoulder and she was giggling. An awful, immature giggling, such as a schoolgirl might make if she had played some silly practical joke on an unsuspecting friend. She began to back towards the window, and the giggles gradually merged and rose into a shrieking, ear-splitting laugh.

Somewhere near the window she vanished. Just sank to the floor and dissolved into a patch of coloured air, as though there was now no need for a pretence. Only the echo of that dreadful laugh lingered for a timeless second, then that too faded away, and Robert for a while, returned to full sanity.

The body at his feet stared up at him with bulging eyes; from somewhere came the sound of children crying, and far, far away a dog barked.

Then, Robert Erwin, like a drunkard being drawn back to the bottle against his will, walked over to the open French window and stood looking out at the night-shrouded garden. He raised his voice and sent out a cry that echoed along the avenues of space and time.

"Come back . . . come back . . ."

THE HUMGOO

GERALD MANSFIELD WAS lost, a not unusual occurrence, being the kind of person who has no sense of location. He knew that he was somewhere in Hampshire, that Portsmouth lay possibly thirty miles or so to the south, that he was driving through narrow lanes, having turned off the main road while suffering under the illusion that he would thus cut short his journey.

Suddenly he saw the sign. A long, white plaque with embossed black letters, which stated quite clearly—LOUGHVILLE. Gerald thought of a petrol station—the tank was nearly empty—a restaurant—his stomach being in like condition—and some intelligent person who could put him back on the shortest route to Portsmouth.

At first glance Loughville looked promising. A narrow main street, lined on either side by terraced houses, and what appeared to be a pub, backed by an old church at the far end. But when Gerald examined his surroundings more carefully, he found a general atmosphere of age and neglect. Cottages were not only old, but decrepit, with crumbling mortar and flaking paint, while the tiny front gardens displayed tall grass and wild flowers, which was in keeping with the tumbledown gates and reeling fences. He might have supposed the place to be deserted, were it not for the occasional plume of smoke that drifted up from almost every chimney and the thick and dirty net curtains that masked every window. As his car crept down the street, he had a suspicion that some curtains stirred as though a ripple of interest had roused the houses from an afternoon nap. And there was no doubt at all that one door opened very slightly, thus allowing a single, cold eye to peer round the edge.

Gerald drove into a narrow courtyard which lay before the inn and looked up at the building that could have been mistaken for another cottage, were it not for the dilapidated sign which hung over a solitary, green

painted door. This depicted a man in what appeared to be a white smock, and immediately below was the inscription: THE LOUGH INN. Gerald got out of his car, crossed the drive, and after some hesitation, opened the green door.

He entered a long, evil-smelling room and looked round with some surprise. A plain, unvarnished counter ran three-quarters of the length of the room, and terminated where a flight of stairs led to the upper regions. A large beer barrel stood at the right end of the bar, and the counter top was littered with a number of earthenware mugs. Two oak settles flanked an old-fashioned fireplace, and a long, backless bench stood against the wall on either side of the door. The floor was coated with filthy sawdust. There were no decorations of any kind, no advertisements which even the meanest of inns usually displays—nothing but bare essentials.

Gerald approached the bar, and as there was no one in attendance, rapped smartly on the stained counter. He waited for a full minute, then rapped again and looked expectantly at a ragged curtain which masked an open doorway set in the facing wall. Presently this stirred, a long-fingered and extremely dirty hand pulled it slowly to one side, and a tall, lean man emerged into view. He shuffled to the counter and stared at the visitor with mouth-gaping astonishment. Gerald decided here was an individual he would not care to meet on a dark night.

The face was naturally long and narrow; the eyelids were hooded and hung down over the watery eyes as clusters of wrinkled skin; excessively large ears stood up on either side of the completely bald head; a hooked nose jutted out over a mouth, which being open, revealed yellow, pointed teeth. He was dressed—if that was the right word—in what Gerald could only suppose to be a suit of filthy, striped pyjamas. The young man tried to veil his repulsion by a nervous smile and a polite voice.

"I wonder if you can help me? I seem to be lost. I was driving to Portsmouth and . . . "

"You cum by motor . . . car?"

The question was asked in a thick, slurred voice, which suggested its owner had either a vocal cord ailment or mucous-filled bronchial tubes. At the same time the watery eyes, in so far as they were capable of expression, gleamed with pleasurable surprise.

"You cum by motor . . . car from . . . outside?"

Gerald frowned and considered the possibility of backing towards the door. "Yes, I've driven down from London and intended to be in Portsmouth before nightfall. But, as I said, I seem to have lost my way. I was hoping you could direct me back to the main road."

The man nodded. A very slow jerking of his head, then, as though struck by a sudden thought, turned and shuffled back to the doorway. Gerald heard him mutter something in a low, growling voice, and almost at once a child dashed from behind the curtain, and after ducking under the bar, stood upright for a few moments, gazing at the visitor with the same open-mouthed astonishment that decorated the face of the innkeeper.

Gerald could not determine the child's sex, for the skinny body was attired in the remains of a little girl's nightgown, but there was certainly nothing feminine about the long, narrow head that was surmounted by a mass of tangled black hair. The innkeeper growled again and the child sped for the door, which Gerald had thoughtlessly left open.

"Sent for someone," the man intoned. "Someone who direct."

"Very kind," Gerald murmured, then added, "but I've no wish to cause trouble. I daresay if I keep going, I'll find a main road somewhere."

"Someone direct," the man repeated. "Have beer."

"Yes—well, that's an idea. I'll have half a pint."

The innkeeper, with the same slow movement which seemed to dominate all his actions, took up an earthenware mug, and after shuffling along the entire length of the bar, held it under the beer barrel and turned a spigot. When Gerald tasted the liquid, he found it to be both bitter and strong.

"Home brewed?" he enquired.

"Make it ourselves," the man growled.

"Then you are a free house?"

The question seemed to confuse the innkeeper, for he again assumed an expression of open-mouthed astonishment and did not answer. Gerald emptied the mug, then looked with pretended impatience at his watch.

"Look here, I don't think I'll bother to wait for your friend. I'll push along and hope for the best."

"They cum now," the man said.

And indeed, barely had Gerald time to note that singular had been transformed into multiple, when a large number of persons filed in through the doorway and formed a half-circle in front of the bar. The child, being the last to enter, slammed the door, then hastened to join its elders who were staring at the stranger with disconcerting interest.

They all bore an uncanny resemblance to the innkeeper. Same long, narrow heads, identical large ears and hooded eyes, but a few were endowed with a mop of tangled, greasy hair. Gerald could not avoid the impression that he had caused them all to rise from a loathsome and unsavoury bed. Filthy and torn pyjamas of every colour and design predominated; flannel nightgowns took second place, and one tall, lanky creature was wrapped in what appeared to be a badly stained bedsheet.

"Gentle... man lost," announced the innkeeper.

"Ah!" The tall lanky one ejaculated, and his Adam's apple went up and down as though it had been motivated by some intense excitement.

"Cum by motor... car," the innkeeper added and instantly two members of the assembly shuffled towards the door.

"Where's be 'e bound for?" enquired a short thing, in a spotted nightgown.

"Ports... mouth," the innkeeper answered.

Gerald, like a man lost in a particularly unpleasant nightmare, watched an awful nodding of heads. It was a slow nodding, which might have suggested that a very simple problem had been solved.

"I reckon that be a goodish way off," announced something in greenish pyjamas.

"Reckon 'e won't get there tonight," stated the man in the once white sheet.

"Or tomorrow," added the innkeeper.

They all tittered. A kind of low, gurgling giggle, such as a crowd of evil, backward children might make, while anticipating the result of an unpleasant practical joke. It was at this point that the door opened and the two persons who had gone out returned. Gerald gathered up his shattered courage and made a statement.

"Thank you all for your kind interest, but I must leave now. Don't worry, I'll find my way somehow."

"'E be leaving," said the tall lanky one with an expression of profound astonishment.

"Leav…ing?" enquired the innkeeper.

"Ah."

"Well," Gerald managed to grin. "I'll be on my way. Thanks again."

He strode purposefully towards the door and the half-circle obligingly parted in the centre and allowed him to pass. He reached the door, opened it and, feeling like a man who has against all expectations been released from prison, stepped out into the dying afternoon. He all but ran to his car, as though it were a refuge that would protect him from all danger, or a bastion from which he could fight off a hoard of grotesque attackers. But when he was safely inside, the door closed and the ignition switched on, he saw them clustered round the inn door watching him with amused interest. Before he pressed the self-starter, he actually waved to them, hoping that this would be accepted as a gesture of cheerful unconcern. No one bothered to wave back— neither did the self-starter respond to the urgent pressure of his foot. The continued silence, which should have been broken by the comforting roar of the engine, made his heart thump and he pressed his foot down until it seemed it must go through the floorboards—but to no avail. A sideways glance told him the line of night-attired figures was very slowly advancing, only now the hooded eyes were alight with malicious pleasure, and the child was dancing as though in anticipation of some unexpected treat.

Gerald had no alternative but to climb out and walk with assumed unconcern round to the front of the car. He raised the bonnet and the reason for the self-starter's non-co-operation became instantly apparent. The distributor had been smashed and every length of wiring pulled out. Uneasiness—active fear had not yet crossed the border— was temporarily swept away by a hot surge of rage.

"Who did this?" he bellowed at the now stationary, but interested audience.

"Be it broke?" asked the innkeeper.

"Of course it's bloody well broke. Who did it?"

One white face looked at another in a parody of helpless enquiry, then the tall, lanky one expressed an opinion.

"Be them vermin. I lay it be them vermin."

Then something in greenish pyjamas nodded with awful solemnity. "Real monsters, they be. Nothing be safe."

"Can anyone direct me to the nearest telephone?"

"No tele . . . phone . . . no tele . . . phone . . . no tele . . . phone . . . "

The tortured words rumbled mournfully along the line, then dropped down to the child, who lacking his elders histrionic powers, repeated them as a cry of triumph.

"*No tele . . . phone!*"

"How far is it to the nearest garage?"

The same enquiring looks were exchanged, but now heads were shaken and the innkeeper, who seemed to exercise some kind of authority, murmured: "Gar . . . age! No garage."

"The heavens sake!" Gerald looked anxiously from side to side. "Surely you can suggest something. What can I do?"

They all spoke in unison. "*Stay here.*"

"*Stay here!*" yelled the child.

"Soon be dark," said one.

"T'aint safe in the dark," said another.

"Be snug in pub," comforted yet another.

Dirty white fingers plucked at his coat sleeves, an elbow prodded his back and Gerald was half-led, half-forced back into the Lough Inn.

Gerald was given a room with an excellent view of the church-yard.

After a swift glance which evoked an involuntary shudder, he released the dust-grimed curtain and examined the room in which he was expected to spend the night. Like the bar, no effort had been wasted on non-essentials. A narrow wooden bedstead, on which lay a rumpled pile of bedclothes: a battered tallboy with tantalisingly familiar brass handles and a wooden chair. The floor was bare, faded wallpaper hung in drapes from crumbling plaster, while festoons of cobwebs decorated the cracked ceiling. Gerald decided that there would be no communication between himself and the bed and if he must spend the night in this room, a chair would be his only resting place. Even as he reached this decision, the door opened and a girl entered.

She was a diamond among pebbles. Or perhaps a better simile would be—a lamb among wolves. Her face was long, but not unnaturally so, her eyes, large and a deep cornflower blue, which contrasted with her shoulder-length black hair. She was dressed in a comparatively white nightgown and gave the impression that—unlike her associates—she was at least on nodding terms with soap and water. Gerald gaped at this beauty that had so unexpectedly emerged from the grotesque and watched her place a tray on the edge of the bed. She spoke with the same husky voice that seemed characteristic of the entire village, but it lacked that horrible gurgling quality.

"Dadda said you eat this."

He looked at the basin of brown stew from which lumps of meat jutted out like rocks in a calm sea, and wondered if his stomach would accept anything that had been cooked in this dirt-ridden place.

"What is it?" he enquired.

She smiled and her teeth were even and white.

"Stew rabbit. I cook."

He looked, sniffed, and after taking up a battered dessert spoon, finally tasted, "It's not bad." The stomach held a conference with appetite and decided to accept the rabbit stew. The girl watched him eat, then when the basin was empty, she timidly put out a hand and felt the soft texture of his camel hair suit.

"Good. Do all people on outside wear this?"

"Outside!" For a moment he thought that she had made some kind of obscure joke, or this was a clumsy attempt to start a flirtatious conversation, then he saw the wonderment in the blue eyes, and fear, which was never far away, came rushing back.

"Look, you are only a few miles from the main road. An hour's ride in my car would take you to a large town. This isn't the North Pole."

She shook her head. "I do not understand. Long ago the elders set gulf between them and us. Only once in many eatings has stranger from outside come through. No one but elders go out."

A theory formed from the mass of jumbled words that bedevilled his mind, giving a rational explanation for all he had seen and heard. A small community that had interbred for generations, and now was but a collection of semi-idiots who had lost track with reality. That must be the answer. And this girl was a throwback, a misfit who accepted superstitions and legends that had been passed down and elaborated on by crippled minds. He felt a twinge of pity.

"All people…" He paused, then tried again. "All people on the outside wear clothes like mine. But girls wear prettier ones—and you should too. Tell me, why are you all dressed in nightclothes? Surely you must be cold during the winter-time."

"These only clothes in boxes," she stated simply. "No clothes like yours. Only this," she pointed to her nightgown, "and others like Dadda's."

"Boxes!" He frowned and tried to understand. "You mean you found some boxes filled with nightgowns and pyjamas?"

She shook her head. "No. Only one clothes in each box. All comes from boxes." She nodded towards the chest of drawers with the brass handles. "Dickon, who work with hands, made that from boxes. Bed made from boxes. Chair made from boxes."

Gerald looked at the tallboy with renewed interest. It had been constructed from polished elm and was fitted with brass handles that were still tantalisingly familiar. The workmanship was crude, for he could see hammer marks where the craftsman had missed his aim and no attempt had been made to remove the numerous stains and scratches.

"Where did your people find these boxes?"

She nodded towards the window. "In ground. On gathering night. All come from boxes. Clothes, wood—food—for big eating."

Almost against his will, Gerald moved over to the window and looked down onto the churchyard. There was the church, grey, forlorn, with broken windows and gaping doorway, and there was a rugged crop of reeling tombstones that looked as if they had lost a long battle with a raging typhoon. But instead of graves were row after row of earth piles and yawning holes. The girl's voice came from behind his left shoulder.

"No more boxes left. All gone."

Gerald turned and for a thought-frozen moment, stood looking down at the white, beautiful face, then when understanding wriggled into his mind like a bad-intentioned snake, he sprang into violent and purposeful action. He reached the door in three running strides.

The innkeeper watched him pass with his habitual look of profound astonishment; three night-clad creatures who were propping up the inn wall raised their heads as he stood in the narrow courtyard and looked anxiously from side to side. The car had disappeared. There had been some wild notion of doing some running repairs, or at the very worst locking himself in—but now even these frail dreams evaporated and merged into the stream of cold despair. There was only one recourse: to keep running.

He ran down the road that skirted the church and disappeared under an archway of trees. He ran until it seemed his heart must burst and the most glorious pleasure would be to lie down in the tall grass and let his soul float away on a cool breeze. Eventually he stopped and looked back. No one had either been able or could be bothered to follow him. He remembered those slow-moving figures and gave a loud sigh of relief. He had now only to follow his nose and sooner or later he would reach the main road, or, at the very least, a telephone.

He walked for an hour. The road twisted, did a complete turn, ran between untilled fields, turned again, slid under an avenue of interlocking trees—and Gerald found himself back in the village street. He mastered a wave of near-panic and decided that if the road was not to be trusted, he would take to the open fields. He climbed a low bank, wended his way from tree to tree and presently came out into a large open space that rose gradually to a far-off crest. As he walked Gerald had the silly notion that he was getting nowhere, almost as if—and this was even more silly—the ground was moving and he was marking time. The notion appeared to have some substance when he crested the slope, for way down below lay the desecrated churchyard and the twin lines of huddled cottages, that at this distance looked like two long brown caterpillars on either side of a grey ribbon.

Gerald Mansfield wandered for the rest of the day. He walked away from the sun, he walked towards it. He crashed through overgrown hedges, jumped waterlogged ditches, waded through waist-high grass, crossed the road several times—and always came back to the village. The sun was setting when he reeled into the main—the only street— for the last time, and they were waiting for him.

"Had nice walk?" the tall, lanky one enquired.

"Been goodish distance?" asked the thing in greenish pyjamas.

"Eating time," announced the creature wrapped in a bedsheet.

"'Ot rabbit stew," promised the innkeeper.

He was escorted back to that awful bedroom, the door was shut and bolted on the outside and there followed the simple peace that follows a complete defeat. Gerald was so tired he actually flung himself down on the bed, but did not of course attempt to climb between the sheets. Apart from other considerations, there was an exciting suspicion that they had been made from a well-used shroud.

It was dark when the door opened and the girl, holding a candle in one hand and a tray in the other, entered the room. Gerald sat up and blinked at her. He had no idea how long he had been asleep, but his body was refreshed, if somewhat stiff, and his brain fully receptive. Horror rode in on the back of memory, but Gerald tried to ignore it. Fear would freeze his mind, paralyse his reasoning powers and therefore destroy any faint hope that this pretty young thing could be made to render assistance. He smiled with assumed cheerfulness as she laid the tray on the bed and pointed to the steaming basin.

"Rabbit stew again?" he enquired.

She shrugged. "Boxes empty. We have to make do."

He shuddered, although he could not really believe that the nightmare of mediaeval mythology could become stark reality. There must be another answer. The girl seated herself on the only chair and watched him eat and because curiosity would not be denied, he had to ask questions.

"You are different from the others. Do you know why?"

"My mother outsider. When I born...she got into the box. Then dug up for great eating. All happy."

Gerald put the half-empty basin down and did not wonder why his appetite had fled. He began to speak quickly, the words tumbling over one another in a vain effort to dislodge terror and re-establish reason.

"This is some kind of game, isn't it? People—cars—they must come through. It is impossible to think otherwise. If what you expect me to believe is true, then beauty, the commonplace—all—is only a brightly-coloured veil which hides the horrific. Why—God in Heaven—the entire world is but a pretty ball, pleasing on the outside a mass of seething maggots on the inner."

"Not understand." She shook her head. "Sometimes elders coming in on day of great eating and there is much dancing round fire. They bring in boxes."

A tiny spark of hope flickered across the darkness of his despair. "Then someone does come in! Tell me—please think carefully—when is day of—great eating?"

She was looking aimlessly out of the window and Gerald wondered if he were beginning to frighten her with all these questions. She answered him in a low voice. "When nightlight is big ball over big house."

"Big ball...nightlight?" His brain played with this imagery, tossed words to and fro and came up with the simple answer. "When the full moon is over the church! Tell me...what is your name?"

"Name?" She frowned and stirred uneasily and he knew that he would not retain her much longer. "You mean how am I called? Luna."

"Then, Luna, can you remember how these...what do you call them?...how these elders come. Do they walk?"

She giggled. It was the first natural girlish sound she had made and it seemed she was a little nearer to him because of it. "No. Elders come in motor-car. Big motor-car."

He leaned towards her and she did not shrink away. "One more question, Luna. I promise, just one more. You said your mother was an outsider. How did she get in? Did she come in . . . did she come with the elders?"

Again that childish shaking of head. "No. Dadda say she caught in trap. Like rabbit. Like you and motor-car. Trap not catch many. Last—ten great eatings ago."

"Luna, what will they do with me?

"You say . . . only one more question."

She got up and moved towards the door and it was then that the chords of reason snapped and he was clutching her arm, pouring out his terror-born words.

"Luna . . . tell me . . . in the name of mercy, tell me. What will they do with me?"

She was writhing in his grasp, struggling to break free, and her beautiful eyes were wild with alarm.

"Me not tell . . . Dadda beat me if I tell."

"He will never know. I promise. But I must know. Please tell me and I will let you go."

Luna became quieter, then she turned her head and whispered as though afraid the paper-draped walls might overhear the dreaded secret.

"You wear clothes like this," she pointed with her free hand at the nightgown, "then you go into box and bury in ground near big house . . . and when nightlight round they dig you up . . . and there will be great tearing and eating . . . "

Gerald's hand dropped away and Luna, finding she was free, slipped out through the half-open door and slowly bolted it behind her. Gerald paced the room, clasped his head between shaking hands and tried to come to terms with truth—as he saw it. One fact was certain, he was in the hands of imbeciles with a mania that included murder and—he might as well face the fact—eating their victims afterwards. Luna's last words raced across his brain: "And there will be great tearing and eating."

He went to the window and looked down. A drop of at least twenty feet and it would not be pleasant if he were to break a leg and be helpless to move when they came for him. But the bedclothes! He could make some sort of rope from them, and surely if he tried really hard, he must find a way back to the main road. It would be a great help if he knew where he was. Then he remembered the road map in his jacket pocket.

He spread it out on the bed and by the light cast by the guttering candle, anxiously studied the meandering lines that denoted roads and tried to pinpoint the position where he had turned off. "I passed that roundabout," he spoke aloud. "Yes, and that farm, so . . ." he jabbed his finger down, ". . . here is where I turned. It must be. The only side-road for miles. That being the case, where the devil is Loughville?"

His finger followed the line of the road and came to a space of open countryside and woodland. He widened the search area and muttered the names as they came within his line of vision. "Corhampton . . . Wickham . . . Tapnage . . . Farnham . . . but no Loughville." Then, desperate for a straw of hope, hungry for a crumb of reality, he grabbed at the improbable. Perhaps the map-makers had spelt the name wrongly. Or there was a misprint. Suppose there was a G where and L should be, or an O in place of a U. "Treat the name as an anagram and see what you come up with." Gerald thought hard. "HOUGL—ville? No. OUGHL—ville. Extremely unlikely." Then he exchanged one letter for another and stared with bulging eyes and gaping mouth at the result GHO—ville. Ghoulville. The place of the ghouls.

Had he been in any other situation Gerald would have laughed most heartily at this macabre joke. He would most likely have experi-mented with a few more place names and possibly have come up with one or more bizarre results. Good heavens—the anagram of Slough was ghouls. Was it possible . . . ? The arm of coincidence could not be that long. He was in the hands of ghouls.

The sheets—or shrouds—were made from tough, unbleached linen, and had it not been for his penknife, he would never have been able to tear them into long strips. The rest was easy. Five minutes later found him with a reasonably strong, knotted rope, which would more than reach to the ground. He pulled the bedstead up to the window, tied one end of his rope over the footboard and tossed the other out of the window. Then he prepared to climb down and found the task more difficult than he had supposed.

A bedstead made from coffin boards was not very heavy and the instant Gerald slid over the window-sill, the footboard left the floor and came crashing through the window-frame. This meant he was jerked out from the wall and was left hanging like a hooked fish over a patch of unkept, back garden. By a dint of sliding and going down hand over hand, he finally reached the ground and prepared to set up an all-time record for the hundred-yard sprint. It was then that he found that his labour and ingenuity had been completely wasted.

They moved in from both sides. Pyjamas, nightgowns, shrouds, faces faintly phosphorescent in the semi-darkness, two dozen or more nightmare figures shuffled in, bringing their gurgling voices with them.

"That was a goodish drop," Long and Lanky stated.

"'E made a fine old muck-up of your winder," observed Greenish Pyjamas.

"I reckon 'e be going for a walk again," Bedsheet suggested.

"What do you reckon we ought to do with 'im?" enquired the innkeeper.

"*Coffin 'im!*" shouted a shrill voice that was very near the ground.

The suggestion found favour with an overall majority—less one. Whatever courage Gerald still retained melted when cold, seemingly boneless hands grabbed his arms, caressed his neck, embraced his thighs and ankles and he was frog-marched round the inn and through the front door. His screams caused a certain amount of low, throaty laughter, and the child, whom he had come to dread more than the full-grown, slobbering adults, took full advantage of his helpless condition to poke him in the ribs, scream in his ear and bite his writhing fingers.

They passed him over the bar—and here there was a little ill-intentioned horseplay, pulling of arms, twisting of legs—through the curtained doorway and into a small room beyond. All had been prepared. The coffin was not one to be proud of. It was old, earth-caked, the wood cracked here and there, but for the lack of something better, still serviceable. Gerald was undressed with the greatest of care, for even he could appreciate that his wardrobe was of inestimable value, and when shared would replace worn out pyjamas, nightgown or shroud. When he was naked they all gathered round and drooled. He was the uncooked joint, the peeled potatoes and washed greens, the plum pudding or apple tart—and there was clearly a great hunger for food. Fingers clawed his bare leg, pointed teeth were bared, but Luna screamed out the merciful words: "*Don't tear…he not dead yet!*"

Like the coffin, the nightgown had seen better days; stained with unthinkable splodges, torn, smelly, but it fitted where it touched. They bound him with coffin-lowering ropes then, with surprising gentleness, laid him in the coffin. Dinner was now ready for the cold oven.

As the coffin lid was lowered he saw the circle of open-mouthed, hooded-eyed faces, and all were dribbling, gloating, lip-licking—save one. If hope still lived, it lay hidden in a pair of cornflower blue eyes that wept. Two large tears were creeping down the white cheeks, when the light was blotted out and he was shut in.

Age is sometimes ugly. It can also be spiteful, malicious or downright cruel. It can also, on occasion, be kind. Age had robbed the coffin of its former polished sheen, warped its wooden planks, tarnished its brass handles, but it had also given it some long, gaping cracks and these enabled Gerald to breathe. He could also hear, which was not quite so fortunate.

"Bury 'im now?"

"Aye. Then 'e be nice and ripe for great eating."

"I fancy's leg, meself. Rare and tender that be."

"Ah, but arm the tasty."

The voice of the innkeeper had an authoritative ring.

"Get 'im planted furst. Then when nightlight be big we tear and eat."

Gerald found himself being lifted up and there was a general swaying, which was occasionally disturbed by a violent bump, when the coffin made contact with doorpost or bar. Then the night breeze seeped in through the cracks and he knew he was on his way to the churchyard. There was no burial service and really he did not expect one; for what housewife says a prayer when she drops the steak into a pie dish? Just an ungentle lowering into a second-hand grave, then—and it was now that Gerald learned to pray—the hurried shovelling of loose earth, that crashed down on the coffin lid like rocks on a drum.

He tried to resign himself to death, but the body was young and healthy and it wanted to live, and the brain gave a great cry of terror when it saw the black, rolling plains that lay ahead. Gerald arched his bound legs, and his knees smashed up against the coffin's lid. Again age came to his assistance, for the wood was rotten and broke easily, rearing up through the loose earth in jagged splinters, so that his supply of air was reinforced by means of a narrow tunnel. Gerald held his breath, terrified lest the noise had attracted the attention of his grave-fillers, but it must have been masked by the sound of falling, for the shovelling continued without interruption and he increased his upward pressure when a trickle of earth seeped down into the coffin. Presently the, by now, faint thudding ceased, and after waiting for as long as he dared, Gerald pressed his head against the coffin lid and was rewarded by a soft popping sound as corroded screws flew from enlarged holes, plus the knowledge that the loose earth was giving way above him. Fortunately his burial had been more symbolic than actual, for those who put him down had every intention of shortly bringing him up again, and ghouls were not apparently addicted to hard work. Spluttering, sweating, with scratched face and soil-caked hair, Gerald Mansfield came up from his grave and looked anxiously round the deserted churchyard. The moon, which was but a nibble away from being full, lit up the Gothic scene, highlighted the grey stone church, the desecrated graves and reeling tombstones. The night breeze came rustling across the tall grass and made the young man shiver. By a miracle he was free from his coffin, but his position still bordered on the hopeless. Clad in a nightgown and trussed up like a roasting fowl, it would take all his strength and ingenuity to climb out of the grave, let alone put distance between himself and the sinister village.

His head was just above ground level, but by leaning against the grave-wall, he was able to draw his feet up and stand on one side of the coffin. Then followed ten minutes of wriggling, heaving and kicking the loose earth downwards, until he was able to at last roll over onto solid ground. He lay still for some time and gradually regained his breath and strength, then he looked up and all but slid back into the grave. A white figure was wending its way between the tombstones towards him.

Fear chased thoughts round into a mad circle and despair looked down from the night sky. One of them was coming back to finish the grave-filling operation, or perhaps the noise he had made when breaking out of the coffin had been heard and its implication only just realised. Gerald buried his face in the course grass, and, overcome by weakness, shock and cold terror, cried. He heard the slow footsteps draw nearer and waited for the clutch of flabby fingers and the harsh cry of a gurgling voice. The footsteps ceased when they had reached a spot but a few inches from his shaking head and a low voice said: "You get out! I afraid you not get out."

It was some time before Gerald dared to look up and when he did it was hard to believe that fortune still smiled upon him. Luna stood looking down at him, a gleaming carving knife in one hand, a spade in the other. When she bent over him with outstretched knife he shrank back with a little cry. She looked anxiously over one shoulder.

"No make noise. I cut loose."

She hacked at the confining ropes, and when they had fallen away, he still did not move, but lay staring up at her with wide eyes. Luna sat down beside him and looked sadly at the open graves.

"I could not let them do this to you. Others, old and fat and squeal like trapped rabbit. But you different. I feel sadness for you."

Gerald sat up and he felt pity, even tenderness for this lovely creature who belonged neither to monster world or human, but fear, the urgent demand for self-preservation left no room for gentle emotion. He could only ask the all-important question.

"Where can I hide?"

Luna pointed to the moonlit church. "In big house, they not go there. It is—not good. They fall down if going there."

The old grey building with its broken windows and sagging doors, was at once a place of sanctuary, a Mecca for the hunted, a resting place where hope could be reborn. He laid his hand on the girl's arm and she started as though his touch were a branding iron.

"Can you go in there?"

She nodded. "Yes. I am not as them. Dadda say I am humgoo. I have mother's blood. I too would go into ground, but Dadda chief and elders say I be left alone."

"How long must I stay there?" he asked.

"I not know. I bring you food when others not watch. But must be careful." She shuddered and again looked fearfully back at the inn. "They must not know or I suffer bad things."

"I'll go into the church now," he said. "And thank you. Thank you."

He rose and there was a fleeting thought that he should reward her bravery with a light kiss, but the shuddering suspicion of what food had passed those full, red lips, and what tasks had been performed by the long, white fingers, made him draw back. Without so much as a backward glance he ran towards the church and left her standing like a pathetic, white ghost among the dejected tombstones.

Time had breathed upon pews, floor and altar, and left behind a thick coating of dust, which sometimes stirred when a breeze slid in through the gaping windows, and rose up as nebulous spirals that drifted across deserted aisle and desolate chancel. Giant cobwebs hung from the roof and window-frames and Gerald occasionally heard the twitter of a sleeping bird that had nested high up among the shadowy beams. He walked slowly, not knowing, even here, what might be waiting for him, and his naked feet left their imprint in the thick carpet of dust—a giant among the pygmy trails that marked the passage of minute life. He went into the vestry and it was here that horror put on a new face and shot out a cold fist that hit him in the stomach.

The vestry was lit by a single, plain glass window—miraculously unbroken—and through this the moon sent a bright beam of light that illuminated a small oak table and a high-backed armchair. Seated at the table, dressed in a black, dust-coated cassock, was a grinning skeleton. In places the skin hung in wrinkled folds, and on the skull was a meagre mop of white hair, but otherwise it was a collection of white bones that glimmered softly through rents in the tattered cassock. It lent sideways and was only held in position by the chair arm; one bony hand lay on the table, but a few inches from a dust-covered book and an old-fashioned quill pen.

When the effects of shock died away, Gerald forced his legs to move across the vestry, and because—for no reason he could bring to mind—it seemed an important thing to do, he leaned over the table and pulled the book towards him. The skeleton appeared to nod, as though in approval, then, possibly disturbed even by this slight movement, slid sideways and fell with an awful clattering sound to the floor.

It was some while before Gerald was able to look for candles, but he finally found some in an unlocked cupboard, together with a number of moth-holed cassocks and a box of long, sulphur matches. When he had lit the candles and the most wearable cassock had given at least the illusion of warmth to his chilled body, he pulled a stool up to the now-vacated table and opened the book. Half the pages appeared to be filled with clerical engagements. Baptisms, weddings, funerals, they were all there, but Gerald turned the pages over impatiently and it was on that last, under the date 21 June 1872, that he found what he had been unconsciously looking for. The candles flickered as he read, casting shuddering shadows over the yellowed paper and the thick, faded writing:

Even as I write I can hear their howls. Almighty God, if you still live, listen to the prayer of your miserable servant and give him the power to set down the unthinkable evil I have witnessed. Although whether any eyes than mine will ever read these words is unlikely, for there seems no way to leave or enter this village. And I have tried... tried... tried. I must believe that we have been forsaken by God and man and handed over body and soul to the evil one.

Lord have mercy... mercy... for our sins are black and we have wandered from thy ways. Amen.

My flock was small, but fifty-five souls, and now they have gone and I, an old man, by virtue of this hallowed place, still live. We should have destroyed the first one. Crushed it underfoot, burnt its foul carcass and tossed the ashes to the winds. But, I—may I be forgiven—did implore mercy for the creature that bore a semblance to man when it squatted on a tombstone and did gibber upon us. I took it into my house and washed away the filth and clad it in clean raiment and laid it on a soft bed. All, as instructed by Holy Scripture. Where did I sin, merciful God? For should we not succour the afflicted, give good for evil?

Then one night when the moon was full, I saw it—cursed be

the eyes that see, the ears that hear—feeding *in the churchyard. Not on the hands, sitting on a pile of earth and gnawing . . . gnawing . . .*

We chased it away and sent to the constable, but he was a man of little sense and did not believe. For the one we drove away, twelve did return and they danced round the village bounds and since that day no mortal *soul has come in or gone out.*

I am weak, for I have not eaten these many days, so what I have to tell, must be written quickly. Others of their kind come in once a year when the moon is full and its light streams in through the north window. This I have noted. Should—by God's infinite mercy—one who has escaped them read these words—pay heed. Take the crucifix from the altar—for they fear it—and when the full moon paints a silver streak on the aisle beside the third pew from the chancel, then go you forth. Hold the crucifix on high and run . . . If you hold your soul dear . . . run . . . run . . . and if God be with you . . . the barrier may be crossed.

Their howls are louder and I hear screams . . . Lighten thou my darkness, I beseech you, oh Lord . . . for I am lost in a valley of darkness . . .

There was a blot after the last word, followed by a thick, straggling line, which suggested the pen had dropped from fingers too weak to hold it. Gerald got up and, leaving the book open upon the table, ran into the church and sat down in the third pew. He remained there for several hours, anxiously watching the yellow streak of moonlight as it crept slowly down the chancel and along the aisle. It came as far as the second pew, then began to fade as the moon moved gradually to the east. Tomorrow night—if the old man had not been mad, and if he had got his facts right—there were so many *ifs*—tomorrow night he would make his last—his very last bid for freedom.

The moonlight died, darkness closed in and despite the constant presence of terror, Gerald fell into a dreamless sleep.

He was awakened by sunlight and birdsong.

The church, flooded with golden light, looked even more desolate and sinister than it had the night before. The ever-moving spirals of dust whirled and leaped across the floor, like minute, restless ghosts.

The altar drapes twisted and flapped, the vestry door opened and closed, while its oil-starved hinges groaned a mournful protest. In striking contrast to all this gloom was the army of birds that swooped and dived among the roof-beams and sent out a chorus of twittering, whistling and early morning song, that under the circumstances was rather distracting. Gerald could not dismiss a ridiculous notion that they resented his intrusion and were loudly proclaiming his presence. A black starling alighted on a pew-back and examined him with bright, inquisitive eyes, then as though not at all reassured by what it saw, gave a startled cry and flew swiftly towards the altar. Gerald rose and stretched his aching limbs. He was stiff, cold, and now he came to consider the matter, very hungry, and wondered if and when Luna would bring him some food. He climbed up onto a pew-seat and peered cautiously out of an empty window-frame. His range of view included most of the churchyard and one side of the Lough Inn, and his morale was not improved when he saw his own freshly-turned grave. The ghouls—and he shuddered when this designation slipped uninvited across his brain—had not struck him as being particularly intelligent, but even the dimmest must surely soon realise, that that which had been put in, had unaccountably come out.

As though to substantiate this belief, the child suddenly ran out from beside the inn and went leaping across the churchyard, looking like a particularly unpleasant species of monkey on its way to a bone-picking session. It reached Gerald's one-time grave and after dancing round it with joyous anticipation, suddenly stopped and dropped down on all fours. The monkey image was now replaced by that of a vicious dog which has conceived the well-founded suspicion that it has been robbed of a succulent bone. This conception was dramatically enhanced when the child began to claw at the disturbed grave with both hands and toss up the earth in a frenzy of excitement. An agitated beaver could not have done a better job. Gerald watched the displaced earth grow higher and the head and shoulders of the burrowing child go lower, until all he could see was a skinny rump and a pair of jerking legs. Suddenly it sprang upright and after giving vent to a harsh and prolonged howl, went bounding across the churchyard towards the inn.

Gerald did not have to wait long. In no time at all a crowd of gesturing, prancing and clearly unhappy figures were congregating round his grave and appeared to be accusing the innkeeper of some misdemeanour. That personage apparently did not believe what he could not feel, for he flung himself down on the ground and plunged his arm into the loose soil. Gerald thought he looked like a plumber trying to remove an obstruction from a choked manhole. His probing efforts clearly confirmed everyone's worst suspicions, and when the innkeeper had regained his feet, the incriminating argument broke out all over again, and was only terminated by the child screaming some unintelligible words and pointing towards the church.

Gerald fled to the vestry, where he barricaded the door and prayed for nothing to happen. The ensuing silence was more nerve-wracking than a chorus of voices demanding—allegorically speaking—his blood and presently, finding his prayer appeared to have been answered, he unbarricaded the door and crept back into the church. Finding it empty he walked boldly down the aisle and peered out into the sunlit road.

There was absolutely no doubt that the ghouls entertained a respectable fear for the church and its immediate vicinity. Gerald counted seven of them leaning against the inn wall, and although his appearance caused an unwelcome stir of interest, not one attempted to approach the church. Dinner stood looking at prospective diners and for the time being there appeared to be no prospect of either making contact with the other. In consequence, Gerald felt a heartening revival of confidence and decided to try an interesting experiment. He walked swiftly to the altar and was delighted to find a tall, processional cross leaning against the left-hand wall. He wiped away the worst of the dust with his cassock sleeve, then held it on high and marched with due solemnity back to the front door. His reappearance was greeted with a prolonged howl and the ghouls hastily averted their faces and jog-trotted back into the inn. Gerald, whose, to date, only close-up view of a cross had been on a hot-cross bun, decided this one would never leave his side, and it had more protective value than a loaded bren-gun.

It was possibly an hour later when he heard a series of gasping screams and looking out he saw Luna suddenly emerge from the inn doorway, carrying a heavy iron saucepan in one hand and a tablespoon in the other. She ran towards the church, hotly pursued by the innkeeper who was brandishing a stout stick, while the remainder of the ghoulish crew remained clustered round the doorway, where they encouraged their leader with advisory howls. Gerald seized the processional cross and waved it wildly back and forth in an effort to assist the pursued and check the pursuer. He succeeded on both counts. The innkeeper stumbled and appeared to be in some distress, then shrieked when he saw the cross which Gerald was waving with more fervour than reverence. Luna passed through the doorway, while her terrified sire trotted back to the gesturing group of ghouls.

She placed the saucepan down on the front pew, then seated herself and raised tearful eyes to the young man who was more concerned with the steaming stew, than her distress.

"Dadda beat me because they say I cut you loose. So I take pot and come here. I not go back."

"Oh, dear," Gerald took a seat beside the saucepan and looked meaningfully at the battered spoon. "Sorry, if I got you into trouble. Is it—rabbit stew again?"

"No." She dabbed her eyes and sniffed. "Small animal and birds."

"Oh!"

"There will be much anger because I have taken it."

"Yes. I expect there will be." Gerald paused before allowing hunger to overcome restraint. "We mustn't let it grow cold. Are you hungry?"

Luna shook her head. "I eat this morning. For you."

Gerald seized the spoon and such is the nature of man, far from feeling any sense of gratitude for this act of devotion, he experienced a twinge of irritation because she had not brought something to drink. The girl sat and stared wistfully at the north window, in which a few fragments of stained glass still remained, and occasionally sighed deeply and loudly as though to draw attention to her distress. When his hunger had been appeased, Gerald laid down the spoon and looked at her with some concern.

"Look here, you mustn't give way, you know. Did . . . did he hurt you?"

Now tears seeped from the beautiful eyes and Gerald felt some surprise that a—what was she?—a humgoo, could cry like a normal human being. Despite the undoubted beauty, he could not forget her relationship to the things whose culinary designs on his person was still a matter of fearful concern. She poured a torrent of words, using the full extent of her limited vocabulary in an effort to make him understand.

"You no care if I be hurt or not. I only animal who cut ropes, bring food. If you go, Luna will be left behind and you not care if bad things be done to her."

This was so near the truth, conscience stirred and put a gentle tone in his voice. "Nonsense. I am very, very grateful for what you have done. And if—when—I escape, you must come with me. You must leave this place and live like a pretty girl should."

She stifled a sob and turned a face to him which was lit by a dawning smile of delight. "You take me outside? And I wear clothes like yours?"

"Better. You'll be able to have some nice dresses from Marks & Spencer's and wear shoes and stockings and watch television. You can't imagine what it will be like."

She jumped up and down on the hard seat in childish delight and Gerald wondered wryly how the monsters here would compare with those she would meet on the outside.

"You really take me outside? I do all the things you say and ride on tube?"

"Good heavens, what do you know about tube trains?"

Her smile was that of a beautiful, innocent child.

"Elders say, there much good eating on tube."

Whatever retort Gerald might have made to this statement, was cancelled by a whirling sound as a stone flew in through the open door and crashed against the chancel step. He jumped to his feet as Luna grasped his arm.

"Do not go near door. They use throwing sling and stone kill if it hit head. They kill many animals that way."

Another stone the size of a fist came in through a side window and chipped a fragment of wood from a pew back. Gerald grabbed the girl round the waist and half-dragged and half-carried her into the vestry, where he shut the door and retreated to a far corner. Then he turned to Luna.

"How long will this go on?"

She shrugged. "Not long. They not like long effort and will soon be tired. They wait for elders to come for great eating. Elders not like us. Have much wisdom."

"The . . ." Gerald swallowed and forced himself to ask the question. "The great . . . is that tonight?"

She nodded. "Elders bring in special . . . things and there be much dancing round fire in harvest place. We go before elders come. No escape when elders here. They have great magic and kill with a bang."

"Fine." Gerald nodded grimly. "That's all I need. A pack of gun-toting ghouls. Well, it seems the stone-throwing session is over for the time being, so I guess we had better try to get some sleep and get our strength up for a lot of running."

She giggled and looked at him shyly from under long lashes.

"You talk funny. Lots of words which I do not understand. But I do all things you say. You say sleep—Luna sleep. You say Luna wake up and run, I wake and run."

"Good girl. You do what I tell you and we'll get out of here somehow."

There was something terribly pathetic in the way she accepted his assurance with simple, unquestioning faith and obeyed his instructions with almost cheerful obedience. She sat down on the dust-covered floor in one corner of the room and was instantly asleep. Gerald sat watching her for some time and wondered how she would fare if they won free and reached his workaday world, where the only ghouls he knew were confined to property speculators' offices and "great eatings" to businessman's lunches. Then he heard another stone rattle across the church floor and fear flared up to drive all but the immediate future from his mind.

The day passed slowly and a fresh spectre came to haunt the little room. Suppose there was no moon tonight and he was unable to judge the exact time when it would be safe for them to run from the church? He looked anxiously out of the small window. So far as he could see there was no sign of cloud, but there were still eight or nine hours before the moon would be in position to advance a beam of light to a point in line with the third pew. One worry begat another. The ghouls—at least the adult ones—did not strike him as being fond of exercise, but how fast could they run when proposed nourishment was going all out for wide open spaces? Also—and Gerald experienced a new kind of shudder—a hail of well-aimed stones could bring him down before he had run two steps. He would have to run fast, weave from side to side and take advantage of every inch of cover, and all the time been hampered by the presence of the girl. Such was his fear, he even considered the possibility of leaving her behind, then he remembered that he would not be free now, but for her courageous act of cutting him loose, and knew, whatever the cost, they would leave together.

He too was asleep when the sun set, and awoke in total darkness, save for the reflection of dancing flames which flickered over the far wall. Gerald jumped to his feet and after climbing up on the bench, peered out of the vestry window. An immense fire was blazing away on the edge of the churchyard.

They—and this seemed to be a natural appellation—were feeding the fire with dead wood, which was being dragged from the nearby woods. Gerald watched the grotesque figures as they struggled with rotting branches, wrestled with young trees, saw the shower of sparks that rose up to the night sky as each offering was flung on to the flames. A motley collection of chairs and tables had been arranged in a rough circle round the fire, thus—and Gerald found he had the courage to face the fact squarely—creating an open-air dining hall, which must be a very necessary part of the forthcoming proceedings.

He looked anxiously up at the sky. Heavy cloud banks drifted like prowling ghost-hounds across the face of the moon, so at times its still light was shut off and the dancing flames of the bonfire took on a deeper, more sinister glow, while the moving figures threw long shadows that writhed and caracoled among the tombstones. Gerald climbed down from the bench, and after locating the shadowy figure of Luna, gently laid a hand on her shoulder. He whispered: "Luna, wake up. It's almost time to go."

Like a young animal, she was instantly awake and sat looking at him, her face a white blur in the semi-gloom. "We run now?"

The question was asked in her usual husky voice and he could detect no undertone of doubt or fear. He felt the now-familiar twinge of irritation when he realised the full extent of her complete faith in his ability to get them both through this time of intense and unthinkable danger. This was followed by a surge of unexpected pity as he took her outstretched hands and pulled her gently upright.

"I think so. Look, they have a fire burning out there and I saw lots of chairs and tables. Have you any idea how much longer it will be before anything happens?"

Luna climbed up onto the bench and stood looking out over the churchyard. Then she got down and put her head over to one side and he thought how young she looked.

"Not yet. They have to wash in river and put on clean clothes for great eating. The elders like us all to be clean. No stink."

Gerald nodded his approval and decided the unknown elders might be monsters, but at least they were fastidious monsters.

"We must go into church—big house," he said. "Then when time is ripe, we will go out."

She nodded and waited for him to open the door before walking out into the main body of the church, which was, to Gerald's horror, in complete darkness.

"When the moon—the big nightlight—shines through the window," he whispered, "and reaches here," he groped for the third pew, "then we must run. But the clouds are stopping the light from coming in."

"Then we go now."

"No," he shook his head violently. "If the road is not open, then they will catch up with us. But if the moon does not come out soon, then I will have to guess when the time is right and hope for the best."

They waited and listened to the chorus of howls that seemed to be part of the general air of festivity. Once a stone came hurling through the doorway, but Gerald thought it had been thrown as an act of bravado, or as a reminder that he had not been forgotten, rather than in aggression.

"I not worry," Luna"'s voice tried to comfort him. "We run fast and get through."

He choked back an outburst of fearful doubts and instead patted her shoulder approvingly. "That's the spirit. You must think of all the wonderful times you'll have when we get out of this place."

He heard her sigh of contentment and would have elaborated on the joys to come had not the moon chosen that moment to emerge from behind a drifting cloud. The beam of light glided down the chancel, flowed over the single step and did not stop until it reached the third pew. Gerald grasped, then shook his head in disbelief.

"Talk about a bloody miracle! Where's that damn cross?"

He stumbled around in the half-light looking for the mislaid cross and finally stumbled over it, measuring his length on the floor as though in retaliation for either irreverence or carelessness. He took a firm grip of the polished wood and whispered his final instructions.

"Keep close beside me and don't fall behind. Can you run fast?"

"As rabbit when chased by Dadda," she announced and Gerald groaned.

"I hope the hell *I* can. Ready?"

"You say run—I run."

He led her out into the church porch and caught his breath in dismay. Although the majority of the ghouls were occupied with preparing for the forthcoming feast, they had not neglected to post sentries on the church. Four of the sinister figures—now clad in clean white nightgowns—were lined up by the inn wall and came to instant, lively attention when Gerald and his companion appeared. Gerald took a deep breath and shouted: "*Run!*"

With cross held high, yelling at the top of his voice, and running as he had never run before, Gerald and the girl humgoo streaked out into the moonlight. The four sentries scattered before him like leaves buffeted by a mischievous wind, while screaming their alarm to the main pack around the bonfire. The inn was passed, the line of cottages became a menacing row of burrows from which disaster might emerge at any moment, then they too slipped into what-has-been and were replaced by low hedgerows and wide-open meadows that stretched out gently to rolling hills. Presently Gerald dared to look back and received an instant incentive to quicken his pace. The entire pack was less than a hundred yards behind. Running shoulder to shoulder, wedged so tightly together in the narrow lane, they resembled an avalanche of snow that must crush anything or anyone that stood in its path. Suddenly a stone went hissing by Gerald's head and he had time to marvel at the speed and velocity with which it travelled. His terror reached a new dimension when the missile crashed into a tree and became embedded in the smooth, grey trunk, so that his unprotected back became an expanse of quivering flesh, that anticipated a resounding thud and the ensuing agony, long before it arrived. When a stone glanced off his right shoulder, it came almost as a relief. Now he need no longer imagine; the pain was excruciating, but not unbearable and was followed by a merciful numbness that left his right arm limp and caused him to drop the processional cross. A loud howling from his rear announced the pack's displeasure at this sudden obstruction to progress, which resulted in a temporary respite from the hissing stones. But the girl who ran beside him with smooth, effortless strides gasped when he involuntarily cried out and said: "You hurt! Must not stop. Not very far now."

The lane gradually curved so that for a brief while they were hidden from the reassembled pack, but Gerald was not far from complete exhaustion and there was a feeling that surrender would be preferable to the agony of labouring lungs and tortured throat, not to mention sore, naked feet. His pace automatically slackened, but Luna grabbed his arm.

"No stop. We are there. Look."

Even before she had finished speaking, he saw the other road. The lane still continued to curve and if followed would have doubtlessly led back to the village, but running at right angles to it was a broader road that shimmered through a thin mist. Understanding came to Gerald and the words, "Mind conditioning", "Hypnotic blindness", flashed across his mind as with renewed energy he ran towards the bridge that spanned the gulf which separates fantastic from commonplace. When the full moon was in a certain position you were temporarily permitted to see.

The road to freedom was only a few steps away, when the grisly hunters came round the curve and their anger was expressed by a storm of hideous howls which could be likened to that of a pack of starving wolves who see their quarry escaping. The stones flew again, but now the aim was far from accurate, which suggested the hunters were as near exhaustion as the hunted. But one missile found its mark. Gerald heard a sickening thud and felt Luna's hand wrenched from his as the girl went hurling to the ground. Every instinct told him to leave her, to go on running until he was safely beyond the barrier of misty moonlight, but another emotion, that so far had not entered his pampered, sated life, made him stop and grip the back of the girl's gown. Regardless of menacing stones, howling monsters and protesting body, he dragged her onto the side road, through the mist, to finally collapse when he reached a spot some twenty yards beyond. There he lay and looked back down the road. Apart from a patch of silver mist there was nothing to distinguish it from a million other roads that interlaced rural England—nothing, that is to say, if the group of white-clad figures could be ignored. Gerald had time to wonder what superstition or taboo made it possible for them to advance through the mist barrier, before a groan from Luna made him forget all but the need to comfort.

With his one good arm he eased her onto the grass verge and smoothed the tangled hair from her pale forehead. She smiled up at him and pressed his hand against her cheek. Her voice was faint, but every word was distinct and became an arrow of remorse.

"I hurt bad. Feel nothing from waist down. Back broke like when Dadda hit rabbit."

He shook his head. "Nonsense. You will be all right. I'll go and fetch help."

She gripped his hand so tight he flinched.

"No. Do not leave me. Rabbit die soon when back broke. I soon die. Will never see outside and wear clothes like yours. Never wear clothes from . . . from . . ."

"Marks & Spencer's," he prompted gently and cursed himself for such stupid, unfeeling flippancy.

"It is better so. I would never be anything to you but an animal . . ."

"No!" He shouted the denial, but even as he did so, knew there was some truth in the accusation. "I never thought of you like that. I . . . I . . ."

She pulled his hand to her lips and caressed it softly. "Do you like—your little humgoo a little? Just . . . a little . . . little . . ."

"A lot. I like . . . love you, a lot."

For the last time her face was lit up by a joyful smile and she kissed his fingers, while the young man tried to suppress an involuntary shudder.

"Humgoo . . . half and half . . . but one half belong . . . to you . . ."

The last word ended in a sigh that drifted away on the night breeze and Gerald disengaged his hand from the now-limp grip, and closed the staring eyes. He sat and looked at the dead face for a little while and remembered that unfamiliar word. Humgoo. It sounded like a breed of horse, or maybe a pedigree dog. But a horse could neigh with pleasure when sighting its owner, and a dog could lick the hand of its master, and love—of a kind—could be transmitted through the barrier which divides king from subject. Such was the love he felt for the pathetic but still lovely corpse that lay before him. Then he remembered that danger still gibbered, gestured and howled but thirty yards away, and rising to his feet, walked quickly away.

Luna rested by the roadside, a sad reminder that oil should not flirt with flame.

Gerald walked for an hour, or at least so it seemed, for road crossed road, turnings met crossroads, and he might have been the last man on earth, wandering in a moonlit maze.

Then he heard the roar of traffic and his strength returned in a last strong flow, so that he was able to break into a stumbling, painful, but joyous run. He came out of a narrow lane into a wide motorway and the joy, the blessed relief, was such that he stood for a moment drinking in this glorious sight, while tears ran down his haggard face. He was free. He shouted the word several times. "Free! Free! Free!" And several youths on motorcycles whistled at him, being apparently under the impression that he was drunk. And so he was. Drunk on the wine of life, intoxicated on the heady spirit called—he jumbled a mass of words together and came up with the right ones—naked sight. He was seeing the world as if it really was for the first time. A place of beautiful motor roads, bright lights, wonderful petrol fumes, exquisite roaring cars—all of which were gloriously breaking the speed limit—and nowhere was there a sight or smell of a ghoul.

He ran, skipped, danced and sometimes walked along the road and presently his joy was crowned by the sight of two stationary vehicles. One was a very large, very shiny, and no doubt, very expensive Rolls-Royce—thrice blessed be that name—and the other was an equally large, plain van. When he drew nearer to this wonderful sight, he was able to count seven people clustered round the Rolls-Royce, all of whom appeared to be in a state of great agitation.

"Godfrey, how much longer are you going to be?" enquired a beautiful young woman in a fur coat. "We're late as it is."

A tall man in a black overcoat and a white muffler closed the bonnet and wiped his hands on a silk handkerchief.

"No longer at all. Finished. The old sparking plugs were playing up. If you'll pile in, we'll be on our way."

"You'll have to step on it," a short youth in a hideous green overcoat observed. "You know what happens..."

The man who had been addressed as Godfrey, smiled derisively. "My dear Tony, if you will get back to the goodies van and stop bleating like a demented sheep, no more time will be lost."

Gerald coughed and made his presence known.

"Excuse me. I wondered if you would be so kind as to give me a lift."

Godfrey swung round and took in the bedraggled cassock and bare feet of this petitioner for free transportation with an expression of comical surprise.

"Would you believe it? A tattered priest! Have you met with an accident or are you performing a penance?"

Gerald hastened to make the situation clear, particularly as certain members of the party were looking at him with some distaste.

"I'm not a priest. I've met with a...sort of accident, and I want to report it to the authorities as soon as possible."

Godfrey frowned. "Well, this is by way of being a club outing, and we are rather late for a bit of a do. But I daresay we can drop you at the end of the motorway."

"But we're over an hour late," Tony protested.

"Then ten minutes more won't make all that difference," Godfrey stated. "Right, in everyone. And you, sir, if you don't mind squeezing in between Daphne and myself on the front seat, we'll be away."

Three elegant gentleman seated themselves in the rear of the car, Tony and another man went back to the black van, and Gerald was sandwiched between Godfrey and Daphne on the front seat. Car and van glided away down the motorway. It is unfortunate that Gerald felt a great urge to communicate his recent experiences to a receptive ear.

"Look," his voice boomed out in the enclosed space and was perfectly audible to even the passengers on the back seat, "you won't believe this, but I haven't really been in an accident. I lost myself and landed up in a weird village."

For a while Gerald had wondered if anyone had heard or understood his announcement, for the silence was absolute, save for the gentle purr of the car engine. He decided to elaborate further.

"An awful place, inhabited by—I know you'll think I'm stark, raving mad—inhabited by ghouls."

Godfrey made utterance. "You don't say!"

"Yes. I don't blame you for doubting me. If a chap had told me yesterday that there was anywhere on earth where you could be buried alive, then dug up for what they call—this you won't believe—the great eating, I'd have called the nearest copper."

Godfrey nodded slowly, then as though coming to a sudden decision, swung the car into a side road. Gerald recognised it as the one from which he had recently emerged. He voiced his objection.

"I say, you've left the motorway."

Godfrey looked out of the side-window, then consulted the driving mirror. "You know, I do believe you're right."

A dreadful suspicion rummaged around among a host of newly-aroused fears and suddenly grew and became a certainty. His question was rather superfluous.

"You're not . . . ?"

Godfrey nodded. "Yes, we are. The jolly old elders taking in some goodies for the yokels. I say, this isn't your lucky night, is it?"

Gerald began to struggle and Godfrey smiled.

"Daphne, my love."

"Yes, Godfrey."

"Have you still got that shooting iron in your bag?"

"Yes, Godfrey."

"Then get it out, there's a good girl, and poke it into this blighter's ribs. He might break something."

Daphne obliged and Gerald surrendered his body and soul to the inevitable. He began to sob like a frightened child.

"Cheer up," Godfrey instructed, "after all, you are coming back in style. I can't wait to see their simple, honest faces, when you step out into the moonlight. I always find it pays to pamper the lower orders, just so long as you don't overdo it."

Daphne fingered Gerald's arm. "When he's had time to mature, he'll tear a treat."

The hedgerows flashed by and the full moon smiled benignly down on sleeping fields and murmuring trees. It also gently caressed the face of Luna as she lay, silent and still by the roadside, and painted a silver sheen on her wind-ruffled hair.

THE CRADLE DEMON

THEY BROUGHT HIM back from the christening, placed him with all the reverence that is due to the first-born in the blue-lined cot, then looked down upon him with moist, fond eyes.

"Isn't he sweet!" exclaimed the young mother, whose carefully prepared plans for no family before thirty had somehow gone awry. "Isn't he perfect?"

"He's all right," said the young father complacently. "I've seen worse."

The young mother slapped her spouse with playful coyness.

"Listen to you! Who was up all last night because he sneezed once? A teeny-weasy little sneeze."

"I was afraid he might keep me awake."

The young mother bent down and tucked the blue blanket more firmly round Adam Tom O'Malley Jones' minute body, then caressed his near-bald head.

"Look at his eyes! I ask you, have you *ever* seen the like? He looks so intelligent, one could swear he knows what I'm talking about. Yes, he does. Ickle didums-didums knows what Mummy is talking about. Yes, he does."

"Very unlikely," his father remarked with irritating common sense. "After all, he's only six weeks old."

"That's what you think, know-all. Anyone that's not blind can see he's very exceptional."

The young father put his head on to one side and surveyed his son and heir with thoughtful interest.

"Perhaps you're right," he agreed. "He does rather favour me."

Adam Paul Tom O'Malley Jones—for It had accepted the name which the creatures had bestowed upon It—gazed up at his adopted parents, but did not bother to probe their brains. He had already done so. Whatever knowledge they contained had been his since the second day after the birth of his flesh and blood vessel. He recognised that both the female and the male were important to his well-being during the formative years, but later he would be able to absorb them and discard their husks. In the meanwhile he must listen, watch, add to his growing fund of knowledge, and most important, adapt the flesh and blood vessel to his particular needs.

He had already begun work on his tiny brain. Under the pressure of his will, every minute cell was emerging into pulsating life and was in turn sending its stream of commands along every nerve link in the body. In a few weeks the vocal cords would be fully active, the eyes capable of long and short sight, the ears attuned to hear over large distances.

Others of his kind had drifted up from the lower planes and taken over flesh and blood vessels, but they had always been fully mature ones. In consequence, the brains had broken down under the sudden influx of power, or the hearts had not been able to cope with the changing body patterns, and the result had been disaster. But he was in on the ground floor. Soon he would be able to enjoy all fleshy appetites to the full.

Eating...drinking...and...

Mavis Thurlow was seventeen, healthy of body, pretty of face, and simple of mind. She lived in a world made up of circles and squares. The Jones' for example were square, otherwise why would they have green wallpaper and a collection of Bing Crosby records? She felt rather sorry for them. Mavis, of course, was distinctly round. She liked ugly boys, off-beat music, not wearing a bra, chamber-pots with plants in them, and work which required the smallest possible effort for the largest return. Babysitting seemed to fit under that category.

She was seated in the Jones' most comfortable armchair, aimlessly watching their colour television (with the sound turned off) and sipping from a cup of their tea, while a plate of their ham sandwiches sat on a conveniently nearby table awaiting her pleasure and inclination. The baby—the sole object of Mavis' comfortable sitting—was in its cot, which had been brought down to the lounge so that she would not be forced to ascend the stairs.

It was without doubt a round baby. It did not howl, demand a napkin change, insist on being rocked, cuddled or any other failing that square babies are heir to. On the other hand, it did not crow, gurgle, kick its legs up and down or toss its rattle on the floor, and therefore merited the added appellation of Weird-baby.

When Mavis had eaten the Jones' sandwiches, she decided that it might be as well if she at least took a brief look at her charge. She got up, ambled across the room and peered into the cot. As babies went, it did seem to be a reasonable enough looking specimen. Mavis was at an age when she appreciated the sowing, without being particularly enamoured over the harvest. It was lying flat on its back with wide-open eyes, and not a muscle twitched or a finger moved. For a moment Mavis wondered if it were dead.

"Hey!" she prodded the flat little stomach gingerly. "Are you all right?"

The head jerked round, a pair of dark and strangely intense eyes stared at her, then the lips parted and baby grinned. It could not under any circumstances be classified as a smile. It was a horrible, leering grin that bared a row of pink gums, from which sprouted one or two minute teeth. Neither could the accompanying expression be dismissed as an infantile beam of goodwill. Mavis had seen it only too often before. Only then it had been on the faces of middle-aged gentlemen with young ideas. She said, "Oh, my Gawd!" and retreated to her armchair with all the speed of a Red Riding Hood who has spotted a particularly well-toothed wolf.

After a while she gathered together her meagre stock of reasoning power and came to the conclusion she had been a "nit". After all, the little weirdie wasn't more than eighteen months old, and even if it were rounder than a blood-orange, it couldn't possibly be on the rampage at that age. After one or two anxious glances at the cot, she fumbled in her large and with-it bag and produced a copy of *Sex and How to Enjoy It* which entertained and instructed her for the next ten minutes.

Then she yawned, stretched, and was about to get up and switch the television over to another channel, when her bored glance alighted on the cot. Baby was sitting up and staring at her.

True, he no longer grinned. But there was a cold, calculating scrutiny; the dark little eyes glittered like chips of ice in yellow moonlight and the tiny pink-tipped hands opened and closed as they clawed at the rumpled bedclothes. Mavis made a funny little noise when the small figure swung its pudgy legs over the cot edge, then slid easily to the floor. It came trotting to her. Not crawling, not lurching from one leg to another, neither did it actually run—but came forward with an awful little jogging trot.

It reached her legs, which she kicked outwards in an automatic effort to push it away, and this made a kind of ramp for the diminutive arms to grasp, the legs to straddle; and up it came—gripping, wriggling, the face set in a frown of concentrated effort, the tiny throat contorting like an overworked concertina and sending out little, rasping cries.

Presently Baby was on Mavis' lap where, having reached this elevated platform, it immediately began a programme of investigation. One dimpled paw ripped her green shirt, and red-glass buttons flew across the room and landed on the carpet like a shower of blood-tinted hailstones. A petrified Mavis withdrew her allegiance to the Women's Liberation Movement when the shirt was pulled open and Baby took note of what lay therein. It was not until her limp hand was seized and her little finger pushed back by a grip of steel, that movement returned to her paralysed body.

She screamed very loudly, and flung the—once again—grinning infant from her. It seemed to bounce on the carpet, rolled over, then with one liquid movement, came up onto its feet. The round face was now a mask of naked, burning hate, and the rosebud mouth opened as a harsh, almost croaking voice said, "You bloody bitch! I'll make you sing."

It was then that Mavis remembered that legs could be useful as well as decorative, for she sprang up from her chair and ran for the door with even greater speed than on the memorable occasion when her mother's lodger had made known his intentions in the front parlour. Of course there was trouble with the door handle and she lost a few feet of essential lead, but the sound of a little croak of triumph soon enabled her to go all out for a second sprint once the door condescended to open.

The rapid patter of pursuing feet was within a hand's length of her nylon-clad legs when she saw the open dining-room door, and such are the brain-alerting results of terror, she was inside the room and had the door slammed before the infant hunter had time to change its direction.

There was no key in the lock but Mavis made good use of two chairs, reinforced by a heavy bookcase that normally she would not have been able to move.

The sounds that came from beyond the barricaded door were not at all reassuring. Kicking, pounding, scratching, interposed with shrieks of baffled rage, were answered by Mavis' terrified whimpers, and she might well have done something so square as to faint if the sound of the key being inserted in the front door had not come as a reprieve. Instantly Baby ceased its door pounding activities and a wonderful blessed silence temporarily descended on to the house. Mavis sank down on to the floor and had a good cry.

The united efforts of the young parents finally broke through the barricade, and voices that carried a tone of both anger and alarm brought Mavis to the stage of explanation.

"The baby!" she exclaimed. "It can walk—and talk."

"There," the young mother said, "didn't I say he was exceptional? Fifteen months, three weeks, two days, and five hours old, and he can walk and talk."

"He certainly shows promise," the young father admitted. "But that doesn't explain why our son was left all alone, while this stupid girl shuts herself up in the dining-room."

"Indeed it doesn't." The mother glared at the weeping Mavis. "We are waiting for an explanation."

"He got out of his cot...did awful things to me...swore at me...then chased me along the passage...and I did not dare come out." She raised an appealing face to the young father, who was not unmindful of her gaping shirt-front. "I am sure he meant to do something absolutely dreadful."

For a while shocked silence prevailed, then the young mother expressed an opinion.

"Drugs!" She's been taking some awful stuff. I really think it's too bad. I blame you, David, for not making more searching enquiries into her background."

The young father assumed an expression of hurt dignity.

"Now really, Doris, that is going too far. How was I to know the girl was on the hard stuff? She looked all right."

Anger was driving fear into the temporary retirement and Mavis loudly proclaimed her innocence.

"Who are you calling a druggie? I've never touched the stuff and I'll have my dad on you if you say I did. I tell you that kid attacked me. It can belt along like a bloody greyhound. It's a monster."

The young mother became an outraged manufacturer whose product had been slandered. "How dare you! My child is the sweetest, the most wonderful baby that's ever been. Don't stand there, David— say something."

The young father decided to be reasonable. He prided himself on this ability. "Now, Mavis, I'll tell you what we're going to do. You are coming with me—with us—into the lounge, and you're going to take a long look at our son..."

"Not on your nelly..."

"Look at our son and then ask yourself if he could possibly be— what you said he was. Okay?"

Mavis gave the matter some little thought.

"You will stand between me and him?"

"If you insist—yes."

Mavis nodded and wiped away the last lingering tear.

"All right. Then you'll see—and hear—for yourselves."

They went into the lounge and approached the cot. Fond parents looked down at that which they had produced. Mavis addressed her would-be ravisher. "Now, you little basket—did you, or did you not, chase me into the dining-room?"

Baby looked up at her with his innocent blue eyes, smiled a sweet, angelic smile and gave utterance.

"Glug…glug…glug…"

"Oh, he can't talk!" simpered the young mother.

"He's coming along," admitted the young father.

Baby decided to give them a bonus.

"Mum…ma. Mum…ma."

For a moment it seemed as if the young mother might be due for a severe attack of convulsions. She clasped her hands, wriggled her hips, gasped, all but choked, then managed to transform joy into a few words. "David, did you hear? He called me…mumma!"

"It certainly sounded like it," the young father agreed.

"Now what have you to say for yourself?" the young mother asked Mavis.

"He's having you on. He's evil, I tell you. When he grows up, he'll be a sex murderer—or something."

The baby said, "Glug…glug…", in a most agreeable manner.

"I wouldn't be at all surprised," Mavis went on, ignoring the young mother's shriek of rage, "if he doesn't take people over and make them do terrible things, like in the film *The Horror from Down Below*."

The baby's chortles grew into a croon of delight.

All this was too much for the young mother, for she broke down and had to be led over to a sofa by her husband, who did his best to console her by comforting words and rye whisky. Mavis, who dimly realised that square minds are not good receptacles for round truths, was about to explain what she meant and how she should have said it, when her attention was attracted by the baby. He raised his little head and whispered in a low, but perfectly audible croak: "You wait until I'm a little bigger. I'll come looking for you, and then…"

The sentences lapsed into a horrible gurgling chuckle, that excited an already overheated imagination, and created the suspicion that Baby was not a maker of empty promises. Without waiting to finish her scream, Mavis sped for the door and did not stop running until she was safely at home, explaining her adventures to an extremely incredulous mother.

The young parents did not speak for sometime after Mavis' abrupt departure, until the young father said: "I think you're right, dear. Dope without doubt."

"You can't deceive a mother," his wife commented complacently. "But never again must we trust our precious to a stranger."

"I suppose not," said the young father reflectively. "Pity, we have to go out sometime."

Suddenly the young mother sat up and assumed the expression of a Newton who had just remembered why the apple fell. "My young niece! Educated in a convent, never been out with a boy in her life, and hasn't taken so much as an aspirin. Let's invite her over. She can spend the summer with us."

Her husband tried to show enthusiasm. "Yep, it's an idea. Pretty enough. Certainly willing. Loves children. But she doesn't move very fast.

"She can't help that, darling," the young mother protested. "The psychiatrist explained she has a mental block that won't allow her to run."

"But she'd lose out even if a snail was chasing her."

"Never mind, all she will have to do is sit next to Baby and keep an eye on him."

The young father surrendered. He always did. He got up and moved towards the telephone. "I'll give her mother a ring."

In the cot Baby's eyes glittered like hot coals as he crushed his rattle between the thumb and forefinger of his left hand.

THE GIBBERING GHOUL
OF GOMERSHAL

FROM THE CASEBOOK OF THE WORLD'S ONLY PRACTISING PSYCHIC DETECTIVE

MR. REGINALD HAINES was a bald, ponderous man of some fifty-five years, who made a great business of smoking a pipe. He first rammed dark-brown tobacco into the bowl, then very slowly raised the stem to his mouth and inserted it between his large, white teeth. A few well-planned puffs, followed by three perfectly formed smoke rings, apparently informed him that the operation was proceeding satisfactorily, and he could now—after due thought and considera-tion—turn his attention to more pressing concerns.

"It gibbers," he said.

Francis St. Clare, the world's only practising psychic detective, leaned back in his chair and creased his handsome face into a thoughtful smile.

"Sounds interesting. Comes out of a graveyard, you say!"

Mr. Haines examined his pipe, cleared his throat, then nodded slowly.

"You must understand, Mr. St. Clare, when I retired last year, I bought an old cottage that stands on the edge of Gomershal Burying Ground. No one's been buried there since 1854 and the place is a proper mess. Anyroad, a week or two back when I was digging 'tator patch, I hears a sort of rustling and a scraping come from the old burial ground and I says to meself—hullo, a bit of hanky-panky going on in there. Know what I mean?"

"I can guess," Francis nodded. "Misbehaves among the graves. Sorry."

"Well, I climbs over the bit of wall, creeps through the trees—then I saw it. Down the pit—gibbering and when I tell you . . . "

St. Clare raised an elegant hand. "Don't. You've told me more than enough. It's a firm rule that I know nothing of the phenomenon, until I experience it for myself. Eye-witnesses rarely give an accurate account, and I prefer to take on a case with an open mind. Will it be possible for you to put us up?"

"Us?"

"Yes, my assistant and myself. I never go anywhere without Fred. She combs my hair."

The pipe had called it a day and gone out. Mr. Haines sighed deeply and thrust it into his pocket.

"Daresay, Jean—that's me daughter—could spend a few nights in the attic, then your assistant could have her room and you the spare. Yes, that'll be all right. I'll speak to the missus."

Francis stared thoughtfully at his blotting pad.

"There's just one little matter. My fee. I usually charge a hundred a day, plus expenses. The first hundred in advance."

Mr. Haines said, "Strewth!" and followed it up with an equally expressive, "Bloody hell!"

"However," Francis went on, "when a case promises to be of special interest, I have been known to ask for far less. Let's leave the question of my fee in abeyance for a while. Will it be convenient if we arrive at six o'clock precisely tomorrow evening?"

"Can't be too soon for me," his new client replied. "Anything particular you fancy for 'igh tea? A nice piece of smoked 'addock, maybe?"

"Great. And don't worry about Fred. She eats anything. Let me see if I got your address right—Woodbine Cottage, Copse Lane, Gomershal."

Both men rose as Mr. Haines said, "That's right. Turn off the M6 just after you pass through Clavering. My place is on the left. You can't miss it. Three parts surrounded by tombstones."

"Right. See you tomorrow evening then. Would you mind seeing yourself out? It's the housekeeper's day off."

The psychic detective waited until his new client had left the room, before sitting down and calling out:

"Okay, Fred—let's hear from you."

The thick blue curtains that masked the French windows parted and Frederica Masters stepped into the room. She was an extremely beautiful girl with ash-blonde hair and white skin, who wore a cynical expression as though her blue eyes had seen too much and forgotten too little in her short life. She wore a colourful costume that bordered on the bizarre. The bright red blouse had a dangerous split down the centre that revealed the valley between her breasts; the green mini-skirt was the stunted offspring of a broad belt, and her splendid nylon-clad legs would make any man's eyes widen with appreciation. Her voice was low and husky.

"Don't you think that one will be a complete waste of time? I ask you—a gibbering something!"

Francis fitted a cigarette into a long holder and lit it with a gold lighter.

"What about his atmosphere? Were you able to sort it out?"

Fred sank into a chair and crossed her legs.

"Suet pudding on the hoof. Not a spark of psychic awareness in his entire body. He wouldn't see a nasty if it came and sat on his lap. Don't I get a cigarette then?"

Francis pushed the box across the desk.

"That's why I think there's something 'orrible taking place down in darkest Gomershal. He's not the type to imagine a gibbering something."

"Oh, very bright. But you underestimate the effect of late-night horror films on TV. Everybody gets a free education these days."

Francis St. Clare nodded. "The child may be stupid, but she has moments of inspiration. Well, as the eunuch said to the actress—we shall have to wait and see."

Francis turned the car into Copse Lane and drove some hundred yards or more until he came within view of the picturesque cottage that was three-quarters surrounded by reeling tombstones and numerous skeletal trees. The psychic detective braked to a halt and, after switching off the engine, examined the scene with a professional eye.

Beyond the cottage rolling hills sloped down to open moorland that reached out green-and-russet-clad arms to embrace the low wall-surrounded burying ground. To the extreme right stood a ruined building that had probably been a memorial chapel, but was now only two jagged walls, rearing up from a mass of weed-infested masonry.

Francis asked: "Well?"

Fred sank back and stared thoughtfully out over the desolate countryside.

"There's the usual personality debris. I just had a glimpse of an earth-bound waif. Over there by that ruined building. An old woman in a long, tattered dress. I'd say she came to a bad end some—oh, I don't know—two hundred years ago? She's no problem. Wait a sec—there's a child—I think. The head is jutting up from that mound by the large broken tombstone. Probably buried alive. They often were a century or so ago. Poor thing's trying to get out."

Francis nodded. "But can you see anything out of the ordinary?"

"Not so far. But one rarely does in broad daylight. Hullo—there's a nifty-looking girl peering at us round the front doorway. Nothing ghostly about her. Don't you think it's about time we made ourselves known?"

"But it's only ten minutes to six."

"So, you'll be ten minutes early! Let's get in there—I want me 'igh tea."

The girl who stood in the open doorway was extremely pretty; an exquisite heart-shaped face that was enhanced by soft brown eyes and framed by long auburn hair. She smiled shyly and said:

"You must be Francis St. Clare and Miss Masters."

Fred ran a critical eye down the long out-of-date beige dress, then raised a slim eyebrow when she saw the cracked, down-at-heel shoes. "You can call me Fred. And this is the genius himself. He'd be happy if you curtsied and called him sir."

"It's one of her dafter days," Francis explained. "May we come in?"

The girl stood to one side and bobbed her head up and down. "Sorry...I wasn't thinking."

Francis—followed by Fred carrying two suitcases—entered a narrow passage, then without waiting for an invitation, turned left into what could only be the best-only-to-be-used-on-special-occasions front room. It had a faint damp smell and was equipped with fat, brocade-covered armchairs and matching sofa, a large glass-fronted cabinet that contained an assortment of china figurines, a bowl of waxed flowers, and a stuffed parrot in a brass cage. Fred exclaimed: "Knock me backwards, but never call me mother!" as Mr. Haines, preceded by a plump lady, entered the room.

He rubbed his hand on the seat of his trousers, then offered it for Francis' consideration. "Ah, Mr. St. Clare—so you're 'ere then? This is my lady wife—Doris."

Mrs. Haines had a pear-shaped figure, a full round face, thin lips and a pained expression that suggested she had recently eaten something very bitter and it was just beginning to play havoc with her digestion.

She nodded to Francis, and said, "Mr. St. Clare—delighted I'm sure," then shot Fred a glance of cold disapproval. "Good evening, Miss. I expect you'd like to freshen up."

"I feel fresh enough," Fred explained. "But if you mean do I want to go to the . . . "

"Thank you, we would," Francis raised his voice at the right moment. "Very kind."

"Jean will show you to your *rooms*," Mrs. Haines' voice emphasised the plural. "We'll be sitting down to table in twenty minutes."

The young girl led the way up a flight of narrow stairs, then first conducted Fred to a small room with a commanding view of the graveyard and Francis into a slightly larger one enhanced by a massive double-bed. He gazed upon it reflectively.

"This is the spare room," Jean explained. "It's usually used by my married sister and her husband when they visit us."

"And you've been turned out of your room to make room for Fred. I'm so sorry. But I don't suppose it'll be for long."

The girl shrugged. "I don't mind. I rather like the attic actually. Do you think—you'll be able to get rid of that—thing?"

Francis smiled gently and looked down into the troubled eyes.

"Is it so dreadful?"

She nodded. "I know we're not to tell you anything about it, but I seem to see more than either of my parents. Dad thinks it's a nuisance that someone like you can explain away and Mum—well—I don't think she really believes there's anything to explain. I made them send for you."

Francis said, "Ah!" and waited for her to continue.

"I've read about all of your cases. At least all that that writer has recorded. 'The Headless Footman of Hadleigh' and 'The Wailing Waif of Battersea'—it was wonderful how you solved those."

"The fellow dramatises dreadfully," Francis murmured.

"So—when I heard—and saw—what I did—I knew only you and—that beautiful girl could help us."

"I might," he declared airily, "but Fred is never much use. I only bring her along to carry the luggage."

Jean smiled shyly and fingered the flower-patterned bedspread.

"You only say that. You must love her really." She blushed and Francis experienced a pang of pity. "I'm sorry, I shouldn't have said that. What must you think of me?"

He tilted her head back until he was looking straight into her eyes. "Let's say, I tolerate her."

Her voice was just above a whisper. "And she must be in love with you. You're so—so handsome."

"Francis." Fred was leaning against the door-post. "Your smoked 'addock's getting cold."

Mrs. Haines watched Fred begin her third helping of baked rice-pudding, then made an utterance.

"You've got a healthy appetite, I'll say that for you. Don't pick at your food like some I could mention."

Fred pointed her spoon at Francis. "I need bags of grub. He wears me out. I mean to say, he might be a genius, but he's bone idle. Uses me as a packhorse."

Mrs. Haines' withering glance embraced both the psychic detective and her husband. "They're all bone idle and use us poor women as conveniences." She paused while Fred choked on a portion of rice-pudding. "Which brings me to the reason for your visit, Mr. St. Clare..."

"Please—call me Francis."

"In a short while there may well be some kind of disturbance. Frankly, Mr. St. Clare, I'm a plain, no-nonsense woman and have no time for ghosts, vampires and what-have-you. I think we're being pestered by some degenerate person that the local police should deal with."

"But I've had words with Sergeant Bilkins," Mr. Haines protested "and he more or less told me I was off my head."

"That's because you didn't insist that he come out here and see for himself. Well, since you're here, Mr. St. Clare, you might as well do what you can. Not that I've much faith..."

"Can I have a cup more tea?" Fred enquired, pushing her cup forward. "Francis, something funny has just come in."

St. Clare took a cigarette case from his breast pocket, saw Jean's warning glance and hastily replaced it.

"Funny giggle or funny peculiar?"

"Funny nasty. There's a horrid old man dressed in a grey, monkish robe..."

"Habit," Francis corrected. "I think."

"I don't know what his habits are, but he is certainly glaring at you."

"Probably a time-image. This old place must be packed with them."

Fred added two spoonfuls of sugar to her freshly filled cup.

"Oh, no he's not. I know a flaming time-image when I see one and this is an out and out nasty." She suddenly shivered and looked back over one shoulder. "Oh, no you don't! Francis, he's trying to materialise—draw power from me."

Francis St. Clare raised eyes that were suddenly alert, gleaming with interest.

"Shut down. Close your mind. Get shot of him."

Fred momentarily lowered her head and expelled her breath as one long sigh. Presently she relaxed and looked up.

"Okay. No panic. He's gone. But I had to blast him good and proper. And I'll tell you something else. He's not just an ordinary

housebound. I had a glimpse of trees—moon shining on purple hills."
She smiled appealingly at Mrs. Haines. "You don't suppose I could
have a slice of that chocolate cake?"

"How can you pack away all that nosh and remain reasonably slim,
is beyond me," Francis complained. "Mrs. Haines—Doris—you're not
to give her so much as a crumb. It's downright greediness."

"Don't take any notice of him. He denies himself nothing, but I'm
supposed to starve so as to keep the old psychic juices running.
Well..."

"Too true. And I want you at your best tonight. So, no cake."

"I will have some cake."

"You won't."

"Pig."

There was a loud crash as Mrs. Haines slammed a fork down on to
her dinner plate, thereby causing Mr. Haines to spill tea into his saucer.

"Stop it this instant. You both must be mad to behave like this in
someone else's house. I'm surprised and shocked."

Instantly she was confronted by two faces that wore repentant
smiles; was subjected to a combined barrage of charm that almost
succeeded in erasing her forbidding frown.

"You must forgive us, but we're not really quarrelling. It's just a way
of equating the fantastic with normality. Releasing the pressure if you
like."

"We have to strike sparks off each other. That makes us the perfect
team."

"That's all very well," Mrs. Haines protested. "But what about that
business of an old man in a robe?"

Francis dared to reach out and lay his hand on hers.

"I'm sorry—but you have a resident ghost. And a fully active, not
very nice ghost at that."

"Fiddlesticks!" Mrs. Haines retorted. "There is no such thing as a
ghost and if there was, I would have seen it."

I think I once caught a glimpse of it," Jean announced. "The edge of
a grey robe disappearing round a corner."

"Now you've got her going," her mother protested. "Heaven's above
knows, she's daft enough to believe anything."

Francis stared thoughtfully at the young girl, then enquired gently: "Well, Fred, has she got it?"

"Quite possibly, but still undeveloped. But she may well attract the attention of a powerful nasty. Even feed him."

Even while Mrs. Haines opened her mouth, prior to making yet another well-emphasised protest, there came an interruption that riveted everyone's attention and brought Jean up from her chair. Francis tried to identify the sound. A scream that came from a partially blocked throat? A screaming, bubbling howl that might have been made by a demented wolf? It rose to a high-pitched howl, then ceased.

"I say a semi-solid build-up," Fred stated, pulling the cake stand towards her. "Elemental structure activated by part-human agency. It's waddling round the house now."

"Malignant?" Francis enquired.

"As a rattlesnake. You'd better get ready for action."

There was a kind of squelching, shuffling sound, then a soft thud as though something flabby had bumped against the front door, before a nightmare face appeared in the window-frame. Small red eyes embedded in rolls of jutting fat, curved fangs that dimpled a receding chin, wrinkled ears that resembled miniature wings—and there was a corpse-like whiteness and an obscene sheen of moisture that made the bald head glisten like a seeping skin of lard. Francis jumped to his feet.

"Quick—someone fetch a bucket of water—several buckets of water. Fred—outside. This I must see."

"Gawd help us—must you?"

"Yes—move."

He ran out into the passage, pulled the front door open, then stumbled over the narrow step. His head jerked round and he rejoiced that he had been permitted to witness this rare phenomenon. He spoke to a very disturbed Fred who was still reluctant to leave the doorway.

"That, my angel is yer actual, no-nonsense common or graveyard ghoul. But damn your best frilly knickers if I ever expected to see one."

Fred made an interesting gurgling sound, but otherwise did not comment. She could only stare at the bowed shoulders, the hollow chest that surmounted the great bulging stomach, the bent, so terribly thin legs, the long arms that were equipped with two-taloned claws—and tried to disregard the sparse red hair that clung to the dead-white skin like streaks of strawberry jam. The mouth opened and closed, while a long black tongue ejected chattering—gibbering—sounds; and the thing was running forward, then retreating, like a monstrous over-grown rat that is gathering courage to take the first bite from a dying man. Francis shouted: "Where's that bloody water?" then swore loud and clear when Mr. Haines fell over the doorstep and sent the contents of a bucket flowing down the path.

The ghoul made another hair-raising shriek and leapt straight for the tall, young man who now stood with his head slightly forward, looking like a handsome leopard that is prepared to fight for its life. When the bloated face was a scarce twelve inches from Francis' own, he spat—sent a stream of saliva into one fat-embedded eye—then stepped back when the creature twisted its head round and shrieked with pain.

"Francis." Fred's voice came from behind his left shoulder. "Bucket."

"Kick it. Oh, I see what you mean. About time too. Right, chuck it over howling Harry."

"No way. I'm only the hired help."

"Give it to me. I get no co-operation."

He grabbed the bucket, waited until the monster had again advanced within spitting distance, then calmly poured its contents over the bald head. Water flowed down the grotesque face, over the hunched shoulders; cascaded onto the bulging stomach and formed a little pool round the claw-like feet. The immediate result was electrifying. Where water flowed, flesh bubbled—seethed—sent out spiral plumes of steam—and the ghoul began to disintegrate. The head collapsed like a deflated balloon, the stomach exploded with a muted popping sound; a taloned-claw parted company with a fast dissolving arm and landed on a clump of marigolds. Francis observed it with interest.

"Fred. Tongs and a plastic bag."

"God help us! All right."

Mr. Haines staggered out with another bucket of water, which he placed at Francis' feet and ran back into the house, after one quick glance at what remained of the ghoul. There was really no need for further action. The psychic detective watched a cloud of steam rising from a patch of damp earth, then greeted Fred with a tired smile when she reappeared carrying a transparent plastic bag and a pair of coal tongs.

"All over bar the screaming. But at least Howling Harry left us a souvenir."

Fred looked from left to right, then registered a request for information.

"Where the ruddy hell has it gone?"

"Back into the womb of Mother Earth, from whence it will, as sure as God makes little things grow, rise again when the invisible nasty-man has recovered from this little caper."

"But why hasn't that—that bit—gone as well?"

Francis sighed as he tested the tongs on a nearby stone, then shook his head in sad reproach.

"As I've had occasion to remark before, you have a brain the size of a split-pea. That dainty little mitt isn't in contact with Mother Earth—is it? It's bedded down on a bunch of marigolds—ain't it? There it remains for your delight and edification. So—you hold the bag open while I do the needful."

"It's wriggling," Fred protested.

"So it is. Who knows, with a bit of encouragement, it might stand up and dance the tango. Open the bag."

The tongs gripped a fragment of flesh, without doubt the two talons did wriggle in a most alarming fashion, then that which the ghoul had left behind dropped into the bag, the top of which Francis twisted into a rope and tied a knot.

"What are you going to do with it?" Fred enquired.

"Probably put it in a glass case and charge a discerning public a pound a go to have a look. Now let us join the happy family circle and talk of things both weird and wonderful."

Mr. Haines greeted the psychic detective with a worried frown and made an announcement.

"The wife's fainted."

Francis murmured, "You don't say!" and Fred said, "I don't blame her," then everyone turned their attention to the slumped figure in an armchair, which Jean was trying to revive with a burnt feather.

"Forgot all about her," Mr. Haines said, "what with all the excitement and all. Then when I came in here—there she was. Never thought Doris was the fainting type."

"Neither would I," Francis agreed, "although a common or graveyard ghoul on the rampage might well have a fainting effect on some people. Fred was once a leading light in the girl guides, so I should let her look the poor lady over. Fred."

Fred bent over the motionless Mrs. Haines, felt her pulse, raised one eyelid, then laid a hand on the moist forehead. She looked up and addressed the psychic detective.

"*Very* deep faint. I doubt if Mrs. Haynes will be herself for some time."

Francis nodded slowly. "But we can expect some action in a short while?"

"Pulse is getting stronger—I'd say in about fifteen minutes."

Mr. Haines displayed all the concern that is proper of a loving husband. "Is there anything serious? Should we call a doctor?"

Francis placed a hand on the man's bulky shoulder.

"You have my word your wife will be her old self in no time at all. Now, I think we should go into the other room. What she needs at the moment is rest."

"What? Leave Mum all by herself!" Jean exclaimed.

"Trust the young master, he knows what he's doing. We'll leave the door open."

With reluctance father and daughter led the way across the passage and into the dining-room, where Jean turned on the ceiling light, for the sun was setting and the room already shrouded with shadows. They sat round the long table, with Francis facing the open doorway.

"Reggie," he said quietly, "a few questions if you don't mind. How long have you lived in this house?"

"A mite over nine months. The sale went through on September the first of last year."

"And when did your—out of the ordinary trouble begin?"

Reginald Haines scratched his bald head. "Must be the best part of a month ago. After I'd cleared the garden."

"A bit of a mess, I expect. Apart from weeds, there'd be that usual collection of tins, discarded bedsteads and stuff like that?"

"Yes—there was. How'd you know that?"

Francis shrugged. "Clearly the house was unoccupied for some time before you bought it. The new window-frames and floorboards tell me that. And people have the unpleasant habit of dumping their rubbish in the unkempt gardens of empty houses. Tell me—where did you dump *your* rubbish?"

Mr. Haines blushed a deep red, then sent out his confession in a flurry of words. "I dug a hole between two graves in the graveyard. There was plenty of room—it wasn't as though I were disturbing—anything."

"Nice deep hole, presumably? The one in which you first saw the ghoul?"

After some hesitation Mr. Haines nodded. "Yes. But I filled it in at once. And put the grass back on."

Francis stared intently at the gaping doorway and the dimly lit room beyond. "Disturbed soil—iron that is such a good conductor for psychic power and the presence of... It's all becoming clear. Fred, how we doing?"

The girl looked dreamily up at the ceiling, then spoke with a low voice.

"He's been standing in the passage for some little while. Now he's gone into the living-room."

Jean half-rose from her chair and appealed to the psychic detective.

"How can you leave her in there? Knowing..."

Francis took her left hand in his and raised it to his lips. He radiated soothing, irresistible confidence.

"A while back I asked you to trust me. I do actually know what to do. This is the only way I can find out why—and most important—how."

Mr. Haines looked from his daughter to St. Clare, then pleaded for reassurance.

"Is Doris in some kind of danger?"

"Reggie," Fred explained gently, "your wife didn't faint—she's in a deep trance. This may come as a bit of a shock, but although she doesn't believe in ghosts—she's a natural medium. Not only has she been feeding old nasty with psychic essence, but helping to build-up the ghoul as well. When Francis dissolved it with water, her psycho was knocked into limbo and now..."

"She's an empty house waiting for a temporary tenant," Francis completed the explanation.

The sound of the body rising from a chair came from the room across the passage, followed almost immediately by a slow, heavy tread that gradually approached the open doorway. Francis raised his right hand and spoke with uncharacteristic seriousness.

"No one is to move or speak. I will do whatever talking that is necessary. Above all try not to show fear. Remember the thing which now inhabits Mrs. Haines' body can do you no harm, and I will ensure that its tenancy is of short duration. Fred, are you shut down?"

"Tighter than a miser's money box," she replied. "I've no intention of being taken over."

Mrs. Haines' body crossed the passage and slowly entered the room. The face might have been that of a corpse; white, without so much as a blinked eyelid to betray the existence of life or intelligence. One foot was raised very slowly, then lowered carefully, before the other was moved. The effect was a strange lumbering motion that created the impression that the body might fall over at any time. Francis was reminded of a novice trying to manipulate a pair of stilts.

The body came to a halt to the left of Mr. Haines' chair, where it stood and stared blankly at a picture over the fireplace. Francis crossed his left hand over his right.

"Fred."

"Present."

"What's going on?"

The girl closed her eyes and appeared to be listening.

"He's trying to make audible contact, which is not easy for a tired-out old wanderer. A matter of getting Mrs. H's brain to control the vocal cords. He's in a bit of a tizz-wazz too and is sending out hate-waves like nobody's business."

Mrs. Haines' mouth opened and Francis could see the tip of her tongue twisting as though it were trying to form words, and he nodded encouragingly when honest endeavour was rewarded by a long, drawn out croaking sound.

"Keep at it," he instructed. "Spit it out."

"Give him a chance," Fred protested. "I mean to say—it's not his body."

The mouth was wide open now, the tongue curled back and the eyes half-closed. Mangled words were manufactured by a harsh voice.

"I...a...m...c...m...b...l...l..l..."

"Who?"

"C...a...a...a...a...a...b...b...lllll..."

Francis expressed his impatience.

"For Pete's sake, we'll never get anywhere at this rate. Fred, give him a hand."

"Not on your nelly. I'm not parting with any of my essence."

"What are you saving it up for? Now, stop mucking about and get tuned in. I want this case settled by daybreak."

After some further hesitation Fred took Mrs. Haines' limp right hand into her own, then closed her eyes and appeared to fall into a deep sleep. Almost at once it seemed as if the lady had returned to normal life; with her free hand she pulled a chair back and sat down, then looked at the psychic detective with a faint smile.

"You are indeed a clever fellow," the voice was deep and not unpleasant, "and I'm obliged to you for this temporary return to flesh and blood life."

Francis shrugged. "I try to spread a little sunshine as I trot through life. I take it you are an earthbound?"

Mrs. Haines' head nodded. "For nigh on three hundred years I have wandered far and wide, looking for the miracle, that I could scarce believe would ever happen. Then that fool," there was a nod in Mr. Haines' direction, "dug into polluted ground and provided the iron which is essential—and that which can never die was once again able to obey my command."

"How were you able to raise a ghoul?"

"With blood—well shed. With words spoken in a certain way. For

I, Sir Charles Campbell, was well versed in such matters and found no difficulty in obtaining various members of the local peasantry, whose worthless bodies provided all that I needed. I fed the creature to excess and thus enabled it to take on a corporeal form and bring fear to those who would thwart my will."

"But alas," the psychic detective murmured, "I would imagine that the ill-bred peasantry did not appreciate the estimable use to which their worthless bodies were being put and demonstrated their ingratitude."

The voice spat out anger-tinted words.

"They came with the accursed priest at their head and put both me and my house to the flame. My ashes they buried in the graveyard, wrongly assuming that consecrated ground would ensure that my soul would not walk."

Francis sighed deeply and gave the unconscious Fred an anxious glance.

"And now—with your pet given a new lease of life—you doubtless intend to start up business again. Send the ghoul out to feed on the quick and the dead, then use it as a milking cow. Build yourself a secondary body. Become a buck-vampire."

Mrs. Haines' body jerked forward and her face was transformed by a menacing frown.

"Too much knowledge will choke the man of little wisdom. I will send my pet to see you again, but this time put not your faith in the cleansing power of water, for I will surround it by a black barricade."

"Will cost you a mighty lot of power," Francis stated. "Drain you drier than an anaemic girl at a vampire's picnic."

"It will be a worthwhile investment and I can recharge from this gifted girl afterwards. But hark you well. Before this night is done, the black hounds will chase your screaming soul across the mist-shrouded plains of Hades."

"And you will slither in the dark alley that runs between fire-tipped mountains," Francis countered. "And now," he raised his right hand with the first three fingers extended, "in the name of the Light Lords I command you to leave this woman and enter her no more."

Mrs. Haines jerked violently, swayed back and forth like a wind-swept tree, then looked round the room with an air of bewilderment. It was not long before she expressed indignation.

"What on earth is going on? Why are you all sitting here looking at me like that?"

"I haven't time to explain now," Francis said abruptly. "But I must ask you to follow my instructions to the letter. I want you, Mr. Haines and Jean to go upstairs and shut yourselves in the front bedroom and not come out until I say so. Form a circle and hold hands. Under no circumstances break the circle. Do you understand?"

"What I want to know…" Mrs. Haines began, but was quickly interrupted by her daughter.

"I will see that they do what you say," Jean promised. "But will you be all right?"

He gave her a reassuring smile. "Fred and I are the experts and it's our job to take risks. It will do no harm to pray for our success, for prayer is a certain way to concentrate mental energy into a desirable channel. Now, off with you."

"Here," Mr. Haines leant across the table, "is the missus all right now? I don't fancy being shut up with—what she was a while back."

"Doris is, without any possible doubt, her old self again."

Francis waited until he could hear the three pairs of feet ascending the stairs, before turning his attention to Fred. She was pale, but her eyes were still lit by the customary mischievous gleam.

"Well," he enquired, "all fit and ready for the fray?"

"No, I'm bloody well not. I gave my all so you could have a heart-to-heart with old nasty. What I fancy now is a nice underdone rump steak, surrounded by some roast potatoes, followed by a rum baba with bags of cream."

"When all this is over, you'll have just that."

"Promise?"

"Cross my heart and hope to live."

Fred released a sigh of intense pleasure.

"Okay. What shall I do?"

"Fetch the gear."

The dining-room had been cleared. All the furniture was piled against one wall, the carpet rolled back and what appeared to be a steel cage erected in the centre of the room. It was indeed an awesome contraption, being constructed of metal rods, each one slotting into the other, with a large opening facing the door and a smaller one in the rear. Long wires ran from various points to a control panel which lay on the mantleshelf.

"The phantocage," Francis announced, "has never been known to fail. Designed by me, how could it? My genius is a truly terrifying phenomenon."

"We've only used it once before," Fred pointed out. "And that was to trap a miserable old handel-monster. How do you know it will work with a ghoul?"

"Have you no faith in the young master?"

"No."

The psychic detective shook his head sadly. "You really must learn to use that under-developed organ you call a brain and try to think logically. Now, to lure any creature into a trap, we must have bait ... "

"No." Fred shook her head violently. "I won't do it. I'm not sitting in that thing waiting for a corpse-nibbler ... "

"Will you let me finish?"

"It's always the same. Whenever a thingy-goat is needed, it's me that has to bleat me heart out in some crazy contraption you've dreamt up."

"The hand," Francis shouted. "Nasty man seems unaware his pet is minus one little mitt. When he calls it up, the ruddy thing will do its nut and come looking for that which is lost. And where will it be? In the phantocage."

"Oh."

"Having said all that," Francis went on, "I will admit, it might be an added advantage if someone with a lot of lovely psychic energy were actually in the cage—sort of holding ... "

"Not a hope. Dismiss the idea from your great mind. You do it."

"I'd love to. You know that. But alas, I haven't got your natural attributes—apart from which I'd never be able to belt out of the cage in time."

"Good. Then just chuck that hand-thing in and we'll both watch from the sidelines."

"But, Angel, if ghoulie grabs it before I can get the power working . . ."

"For the last time—I won't do it."

Fred was standing in the phantocage with a taloned-claw on a dinner-plate, which she held out to the furthermost extent that her arms would allow. She groaned when a bubbling-shriek came from the direction of the graveyard.

"Not much longer now," Francis comforted her. "I've left the front door open."

"Oh, my Gawd! You would."

Horror that had been created from the debris of the human mind; a creature drawn up from the dark country where those that have never breathed slither in fire-tinted gloom, came howling across Mr. Haines' well-kept garden, round the house—and finally in through the open front-doorway. Once in the passage it paused, and emitted a rasping snort, then moved forward again, knocking a hall-stand to one side, brushing a picture from the wall, then making an unexplainable scratching sound.

With a dog-like bound it was in the doorway; bloated, slug-like, waving a white, ragged stump, where two jutting wrist bones glittered like moist ivory in the lamplight.

"Come and get your little mitty," Francis invited. "Held by a pretty lady who's got lots of lovely essence."

"I wish you'd shut up," Fred protested. "The damn thing's dribbling."

The ghoul blinked and seemed momentarily disconcerted by the bright light, then it went down upon its one hand—and raced towards the psychic detective. Francis ran to the far side of the phantocage and there watched the monster, which had crashed into the piled-up furniture and now was engaged in pulling a table out into the room.

"The light," Francis whispered. "It can't see well in this light. It probably thinks I'm hidden behind the furniture."

"Why the hell has it gone for you?" Fred demanded. "I've got its bloody hand."

"Nasty man is in the driving seat and has planted an auto-suggestion that I'm the answer to a ghoulish dream. Look out—here it comes again."

The ghoul moved slowly now, peering from left to right, then gave a howl of triumph when Francis darted round the phantocage and in through the front entrance. This action appeared to bewilder the creature, for it tugged at the bars and shrieked with frustrated rage. Fred voiced her disapproval.

"Fine old muck up. This thing is supposed to trap the ghoul, instead we're both inside. What happens if Howling Harry decides to join us?"

"That's the idea. Give me that plate."

"With pleasure."

"Now you get ready to bolt out through the back when it comes in through the front. Wait until I'm clear, then pull the switch. But you'll have to time it just right."

"Francis, I'm not at all that happy. Not really."

The ghoul was sidling round the cage, feeling its way from bar to bar; its red eyes watching the psychic detective with unblinking intensity.

"Get ready," Francis warned, holding the dinner-plate well out before him.

Suddenly, after a blur of movement, the ghoul was blocking the doorway, its one hand reaching out, the talons slightly curved, the mouth a gaping cavern, flanked by the fearsome, dripping fangs.

"Out," Francis breathed. "Down on your hands and knees and crawl to that fireplace and . . . "

The ghoul was in the phantocage and the psychic detective found himself face-to-face with a nightmare; staring into the red eyes, aware of the overwhelming stench—knowing he was a few seconds away from a terrible death and only a miracle could save him.

Then he dropped the plate.

The ensuing crash made the ghoul recoil, then look down as though to see what had caused the disturbance. Francis took full advantage of this moment of distraction; he was out through the back entrance, crouching on his haunches and shouting, "Fred—now!" before the monster had time to realise that its ordained victim had gone.

It bent down and was reaching out for its missing member, when the phantocage became a network of flashing light. Pencil thin streaks of white fire leapt across both entrances, and the cage resembled a set piece in a firework display. The ghoul screamed and for a moment— just before it disintegrated into a writhing mass of black mist—it changed into a lean old man with a long, grey beard, who glared his fear and rage at the psychic detective. Then the mist seeped down through the floorboards and there was only the stomach-heaving smell and a blob of grey jelly that fell from the cage roof on to Francis' lap.

He jumped up and shook himself violently. The viscous mess slipped to the floor with an obscene squelch, where it seethed for a few moments before disappearing.

"Ugh!" Fred had switched off the phantocage and was now standing by her employer's side. "What the hell was that?"

"All that remained of the hand," Francis replied with some regret. "Pity, I was hoping to keep it and possibly let you play with it sometimes. Never mind."

"You're revolting. Can I go to bed now?"

"After we've informed the Haines clan that all is well and the world's only practising psychic detective has scored again."

Fred made a rude noise.

Francis St. Clare was seated behind the steering wheel, with Frederica Masters by his side. The Haines family were clustered round the off-side window.

"I've definitely decided to move," Mr. Haines said. "I mean to say, if the missus is what you say she is—anything might come out of that graveyard."

"Very true," Francis agreed. "I should settle for a nice semi-detached in Wimbledon."

"A lot of poppy-cock," Mrs. Haines stated with deep conviction. "I didn't see anything, and I don't think anyone else did either. But I do know someone made a fine old mess of my dining-room table."

"I'm going to work in town," Jean announced shyly. "Share a flat with a friend. Perhaps we might run into one another sometime."

The car glided away to a chorus of goodbyes and presently was braked to a halt at the end of the lane. Francis waited until a stream of traffic passed and allowed him to turn onto the main road. Then he spoke.

"Why didn't you come out with some biting remark when the wench suggested we might get together?"

Fred nestled her head on his shoulder.

"I was too busy watching Old Nasty who was waving to us from the doorway. Or not so much waving as jerking two fingers in an upward direction."

Francis swore and changed gear.

"But I thought I'd cooked his goose. Good job they're moving."

"Yes, isn't it? Only, I wonder—do you suppose he'll move too? It might be wise to keep away from little Jeannie. Never know what she might have with her."

She had scarcely finished speaking when a suitcase which was laying on the back seat rose up and crashed against the roof. Fred glanced back over one shoulder, then proclaimed her concern.

"Francis . . . you've mucked it up again . . . we've got company . . ."

DOPPLEGÄNGER

MRS. FORTESCUE'S PARTY was in full swing when the Bayswaters arrived, which enabled her to greet Matthew in a loud voice and thus warn her guests that the time had come to stop whatever they were doing and pay homage to the long-awaited lion. She used Jennie as a sounding board.

"How nice of you to come, my dear." She raised her eyebrows and assumed an expression of arch surprise. "And you managed to bring your handsome and so brilliant husband! I was so afraid he just wouldn't find time to honour my little gathering."

Jennie gave her a dazzling smile and nudged Matthew, who was examining the running buffet with a critical eye.

"So sorry we are so late, but the car broke down and Matthew is hopeless with engines. He just raises the bonnet and swears."

Mrs. Fortescue's bosom quivered ominously and a fat, rumbling laugh gradually dissolved into her words.

"Genius is rarely practical. We've been discussing *Man on the Roof.* So original. Where does he get those wonderful ideas from?" She ventured to address Matthew, possibly a little disconcerted by his air of barely polite boredom. "Where *do* you get your ideas from, Mr. Bayswater?"

"My head."

Jennie slid a hand round his arm and nodded gently.

"He does. Get them from his head. He frightens himself sometimes. Particularly when he shaves. Says the sight of his head in the mirror is very unnerving first thing in the morning. Understandable in a way, isn't it?"

Mrs. Fortescue could be likened to a lady adrift in an open boat who is quite unable to read a compass.

"Yes . . . I mean no. Do help yourself to a drink or something."

"First sensible words I've heard yet," Matthew remarked. "What are those things on sticks?"

"Stuffed olives," Jennie edged him away from the temporarily speechless Mrs. Fortescue. "And that stuff on tiny biscuits is slivers of fried chicken."

"Good grief!"

A butler who had doubtlessly learnt his trade from P.G. Wodehouse, stood behind a long table and inclined his head when Matthew pointed to the whisky decanter, then poured a generous measure into a thick-based glass.

"Soda water or ginger ale, sir?" he asked.

"Ginger ale for the lady, more whisky for me."

A slight tightening of the man's lips might have been interpreted as an expression of disapproval, but he added the extra whisky, then removed a cap from the bottle of ginger ale with a quick flick of his wrist.

"Rudeness and booze act tonight?" Jennie enquired.

Matthew shrugged and took a tiny sip from his glass.

"Might as well. Give 'em something to talk about."

"So long as you don't drink all that whisky. You know alcohol upsets your stomach.

He raised a finger to his lips. "Hush, child. Do you want to spoil my image as the hard-drinking author? If anyone asks you, say my stomach is lined with asbestos."

Jennie giggled and smiled kindly at a tall, long-nosed young man who was gazing at her with gaping mouth and wide-open eyes.

"Well, you'd better take a good swig now, because here comes the real McCoy. Old Jeffrey Makepiece and I'd say he's pickled as a soused herring."

The short fat man with the bright-red face eased his way through the crowd, then laid a mottled hand on Jennie's bare arm. His watery eyes gleamed with tired lust.

"Jennie, me dear, I'd swear you're more beautiful than ever. Damn me eyes if you're not."

Jennie gently removed his hand, then performed a little curtsey. "Thank you, kind sir. And you're no less handsome than when I saw you last."

Makepiece pulled his stomach in, raised the discarded hand to his thinning hair, then stared unhappily at his empty glass.

"Why not apply for a refill?" Matthew suggested. "After all it's free."

"Damn me, I believe I will. The doctor's warned me off whisky, you know. Said it would kill me. So I've gone over to gin. No point in paying a doctor if you don't follow his advice."

Instantly Jennie was the epitome of solicitous concern; gripping Matthew's arm, trying to arouse his sympathy for someone held between claws of an irresistible vice.

"But you mustn't drink at all. That's what the doctor meant. Matthew, please—you tell him that. Surely he'll listen to you."

Makepiece watched his glass being replenished with gin, then chuckled with the satisfaction of a man who mistakes despair for bravery.

"Sweet child, how sweet of you to be concerned. But if I cease to drink, what on earth will I do?"

"Face reality," Matthew said softly.

"Good heavens, you're the last man to recommend that course of action. Matthew Bayswater, the weaver of fantasies! Daring to speak of reality! Maybe you have no need of that sadly neglected glass in your hand, but you have nevertheless built a bridge that spans the terrible gulf of what-is to what-might-be. Allow lesser men to seek a more mundane avenue of escape."

Matthew nodded slowly and took a rather longer sip from his glass. "You're so right. Drink what you will and God guide you through the mists."

"And now," Jeffrey Makepiece looked round the room, "I will perform at least one good deed. Unless I'm greatly mistaken our hostess has that young actor pinned against the wall and is about to introduce him to Maudie Perkins. Such an experience could well dry up the well of youth. Bless you, my children."

He ambled back into a forest of bodies and, so it seemed to Matthew, ceased to exist. Jennie sighed and slipped her hand into his.

"How sad, he used to be a fine actor—didn't he?"

Matthew grimaced. "He made a few ripples in a small pool. Frankly he terrifies me. There but for the grace of God... It only takes a few cosmic seconds to roll back down the hill."

"Matthew, you're being morbid."

"I know. These gatherings depress me. Why the hell did we come?"

"Because I made you. But we needn't stay long. Oh, Lord! Here comes Mr. What-can-you-do-for-me."

Leslie Mortimer still retained some vestige of the conventional good looks that had pulled in the bobby-sockers a generation ago, but now he wore the faintly desperate expression of a man who has retained his youth long past its grave-time. The suspiciously dark hair flopped down over a grotesquely unlined brow, the full lips were parted in a perpetual charming smile, thus revealing prettily capped teeth. But the fine eyes were hungry and raked Matthew's face.

"Matthew, my dear fellow! The veritable island of success in a vast sea of failure. A little bird informs me that *Grey Dawn* is about to be made into a film. And you've written the script."

"Such has been my fate," Matthew admitted.

"And," the actor went on, still maintaining his carefully adjusted faintly-interested expression, "I am also given to understand, you have formed a company to handle production."

"That little bird appears to have a long beak."

Leslie Mortimer released a peculiar rumbling laugh that had been waiting for some kind of humorous encouragement and now seemed reluctant to go back into retirement. A slim, white-face girl who clung to the actor's arm, as though it were the only available straw in a sea of uncertainty, giggled and jerked her head forward, looking rather like a pretty lizard that has spotted a particularly succulent fly.

"This is Lottie," Mortimer made a belated introduction. "I've promised her a part in my next film. She's got talent."

Matthew gave the girl a quick glance. "So I see. I understand the studios are rather quiet at the moment."

The laugh came again, only now it contained a rather strained quality. "There's always work for talent, dear boy. Of course if you have a part that would suit me, I might be able to spare a month or so."

Matthew looked thoughtfully at his half-empty glass and seemed to find it contents of enthralling interest.

"As a matter of fact I had thought of recommending you for the Harold Larkin role. Not the lead of course, but meaty for the right man. Has a few scene stealers."

The mask slipped. Matthew experienced an upsurge of pure happiness when he saw the gaping mouth, the expression of dawning delight, and wondered how he would have reacted, were he the suppliant and not the donor of cinematic crumbs. He waited for the gratitude explosion, the ego-boosting joy.

"You're not joking?"

"I never joke about the ridiculous."

"What can I say?" I'm most tremendously grateful. I promise—faithfully promise—you won't regret this."

Matthew sighed deeply and appeared to be rather bored with a matter of little concern.

"That's settled then. Pop along to Pinewood on Tuesday and I'll arrange for a few preliminary tests. Always supposing," he permitted himself a pale smile, "your busy programme allows you the time."

"I can manage it. Yes, indeed. It might mean cancelling one or two things, but I'll be there."

Lottie did a little dance and in consequence was in danger of revealing more that is considered acceptable in polite society.

"And what about me, Mr. Bayswater? I don't suppose you've anything at all that would fit me?"

Matthew was aware of the warning pressure of Jennie's hand and resisted the urge to make an obvious answer. Instead he raised an enquiring eyebrow and considered the distinct possibility of the casting office giving him hell on Tuesday morning.

"I don't know. Maybe a bit part with a few lines tacked on. Bring her along, Mortimer."

There was a moment of panic; a feeling that his generous hand had already given more than his credit allowed and at any moment he would be shown up as a worthless bankrupt. He heard Jennie's soft, lilting voice sending out an even flow of small talk, as always defending him from the slings and arrows of mediocrity. Possibly he had drank more of the whisky than he intended, because suddenly the room seemed to move slightly out of perspective, creating the impression he was standing on a slightly elevated position, looking down on a sea of white faces that elongated and pulsated rather like a television picture when the outside aerial has fallen down. Then a man with a completely bald head suddenly flashed into being and shouted:

"For God's sake, wake up, man!"

He vanished and all the faces took on their normal appearance, the room slid back into focus and all was as it had been, only he was left with an irrational fear, a strange notion that he had fallen into a deep pit and there was no guarantee that the experience would not occur again. There were more people round him now, all talking at once, their eyes devouring him and Jennie; and he suddenly wanted to be faraway, walking across a desolate moor, knowing that eternity slept under a benign sky.

The voice of James Fisher—agent, profit-seeking friend—rose up above the jungle of sound and told him what he always wanted to hear.

"Matthew, you're a damned lucky bastard. You sit on a throne and accept the homage of your worshippers and curse me liver if you've done all that much to deserve it. There's no democracy in life. Most of us are born with ugly bodies, no gifts worth talking about and have to spend our days crawling in the mud. Others like you have it made from cradle to grave. It's not fair."

Jennie of course gave a pretty demonstration of outraged indignation.

"He works very hard. And you've got a lot of room to talk. Ten percent of his earnings, just to re-type a contract and the cost of a postage stamp. It's the jackals who grow fat on the lion's . . . the lion's . . . "

"Kill," Matthew suggested.

She pushed back a lock of hair with her left hand.

"Well—the lion's something. And the jackals raise their young and keep wives and mistresses—all because Matthew sometimes sits up all night and uses his clever brain."

James winked at Matthew. "Oh come off it! He's only a high-paid liar."

"He's not a liar."

"Yes he is. He hasn't written a word of truth in his entire life. What is a novel but one long lie? An author creates a world of make-believe and expects everyone to share his illusion. When you come right down to it, the entire writing fraternity are nothing more than a crowd of psychopaths."

A roar of laughter greeted this definition and even Jennie was forced to smile.

"Anyway," she placed her two hands round Matthew's left arm, "he's a very nice psychopath."

"Let's settle for a thirsty psychopath and get me another drink. The one I had seems to have disappeared in one way or another."

"You drank it."

"I never did."

"Darling, I really do think it's about time we went home. You have to be up early tomorrow."

"Suppose I don't want to go home?" Matthew enquired.

"Then we stay here."

He smiled complacently. "That being the case we'll go."

James Fisher grinned and slowly shook his head.

"Oh, happy man who can spell the word freedom as he shakes his velvet chains. Are you permitted to come to my office tomorrow?"

"So long as I wear my woollen vest."

Mrs. Fortescue expressed deep regret when she found her star guest leaving early, although she had been heard to remark that his heavy drinking might prove an embarrassment.

"So soon, Mr. Bayswater! How sad. And there were so many interesting people I wanted you to meet."

Jennie put up a smoke screen and made a retreat sound like a victory. "We simply hate to go, but Matthew has a very early appointment tomorrow morning and he's not all that well."

"Indeed! Nothing serious, I hope?"

"No. Just been overdoing it. You understand?"

The lady nodded with due solemnity. "Indeed I do. He must take care of himself."

When they were in the car Jennie looked at him and smiled gently. "She's rather a duck and clearly thinks you're something that dropped from the sky."

Matthew swung the car round into the main road, then changed gear. "At this moment she's telling everyone who will listen that drink's my problem and how marvellously you cope."

"But isn't that what you want people to think?"

He shrugged. "It's a game I like to play. Does no one any harm."

"Yes, but why?"

"Because I'm terrified of ending up like Mortimer. Sucking up to someone like me and really hitting the bottle. Playing a game, having people think I'm already on the skids, is like pretending you're broke when there's a lot of money in the bank. Understand?"

Jennie's eyes glittered softly in the light cast by a passing car. "No. You have a lot of money in the bank and even if you never published another book, you'd never have to—well—act like Leslie Mortimer. These fits of depression worry me."

"Worry you! They murder my sleep."

He pulled up at the traffic lights and glanced out of the side window. People were passing along the pavement; each one a self-contained unit, but sharing a common fund of hopes and fears; looking forward to or dreading the birth of the next hour, day or month. Then he became aware of a particular face; thin, drawn, the eyes clouded by melancholy that was framed by a glass shop door. A hauntingly familiar face surmounted by untidy blond hair. A tall, bald-headed man came from behind a counter and apparently called out, for the face jerked round and looked back over one shoulder.

"Matthew," Jennie's voice came from beside him, "wake up, darling. The lights have changed."

Matthew was able to catch a glimpse of the shop fascia board before he drove off. He read:

L.W. SMITH, LTD. KITCHENWARE EQUIPMENT.

"What's bothering you now?" Jennie asked after a while.

"I don't know. Only… there's a man in that hardware shop by the traffic lights and I've a feeling I've seen him before, but for the life of me I can't think where."

"You'll remember," Jennie said consolingly. "When you least expect it, the memory will come back. But I know the feeling. It's damned irritating."

"Somehow I feel sorry for him. He looked damned miserable and I suppose that's no wonder. It must be a hell of a life selling pots and pans to bitchy women."

"Perhaps he owns the store and is making a bomb."

Matthew shook his head and turned into the drive.

"I don't think so. It looked as if the owner was choking him off for something. Come to think of it that old basket looked familiar as well."

But it was later that night when they were both in the king-size bed and Matthew was allowing his brain to dim down its awareness that the spark of memory flared up into a revealing flame.

"I remembered where I saw that man before."

Jennie turned on her bedside lamp and blinked at her husband with sleep-glazed eyes.

"What man? What on earth are you talking about?"

"The man in the shop. I see that face every morning in the shaving mirror. Take off a few pounds, add a generally unkempt appearance— and we might be twin brothers."

Jennie displayed mild interest. "That means you have a double! How extraordinary! You must invite him to tea."

"Good God! What a thought."

Presently Jennie turned out the light and Matthew lay back trying to come to terms with a situation that should have been both amusing and intriguing. Having a double that worked in a hardware shop was surely unique. But it was for some reason disturbing.

James Fisher emptied his glass, then replenished it from an adjacent bottle. He watched Matthew push his plate to one side and looked idly round the restaurant, then expressed his concern.

"You haven't eaten enough to keep a fly alive. You need a holiday."

Matthew shrugged and sipped from a glass of water.

"I'm all right. Jennie makes certain I eat a good breakfast and the old hag who rules our kitchen crams roast beef and Yorkshire pud down my throat come sunset. But lunch is a bad time for me. No appetite—no anything."

Fisher ran a forefinger round the rim of his glass.

"I often wonder—who shouldn't—why you don't pack it in for a bit. The stuff you've got in the pipeline will keep you in the super-tax bracket for quite sometime."

Matthew shook his head and spoke without really thinking.

"That would mean letting go and God knows where I would fall."

"You've lost me. Explain."

"I can't. Look, something happened last night which still bothers me. It's damned ridiculous really, but I'd be obliged if you would accompany me to a certain shop and supply moral support."

James Fisher lit a cigarette and blew out a nigh-perfect smoke ring.

"What kind of shop?"

"One that sells hardware—kitchen stuff. Last night I saw my double looking out of the doorway and damned if I can get the memory out of my mind."

Fisher assumed an expression of mock horror.

"For Chrissake! Don't tell me there's another face like yours floating around! This I must see."

Matthew beckoned to a waiter. "That's what I intend. The chances are on closer inspection the fellow will prove to have only a superficial resemblance. The place isn't far. By the traffic lights on the corner of Denby Street."

"Everything all right, sir?" the waiter enquired, as he accepted Matthew's luncheon card.

"Well, the steak tasted like burnt leather and the roast potatoes like underdone tennis balls. Otherwise I've no complaints."

"Thank you, sir. There's a ten percent cover charge."

The long shop-lined street looked so different in daylight; all the shops open and despite the bright sunshine, transformed into brilliantly lit grottos by overhead neon-strips. Matthew looked at the large, double-fronted shop on the corner and realised it presented a much fresher, glossy appearance than he remembered; was in fact a creation of chrome and glass with an illuminated sign on the fascia board that caused his heart to thud alarmingly. He braked the car to a halt and stared up at the blue, neon-letters and tried to understand.

KITCHEN KIT KAMP

This was far different for the L.W. SMITH, LTD. KITCHENWARE EQUIPMENT painted in large black letters on an off-white back-ground that he distinctly remembered seeing the night before. Neither did the interior of this ultra-modern establishment offer much comfort. In place of a long counter and rows of laden shelves were several modern kitchens, each one resplendent with stainless-steel and brightly plastic doors and drawer-fronts. He felt like someone who has come to view a cottage and is confronted by a palace.

"Well," James Fisher enquired, "are we going to meet your double or not?"

"It's all wrong," Matthew said in a low voice. "All terribly wrong."

"You don't have to tell me. The best part of seven hundred quid for a lot of plastic-covered chipboard. But that long-haired twit, who appears to be flogging his rubbish to an old lady, certainly doesn't look much like you."

Matthew looked up and down the street, took note of the chemist shop, the traffic lights and knew there was no possible doubt that he had driven to the correct location. Everything was as it should be—except the kitchen equipment shop.

"Let's go in," he said quietly, "but I've a feeling I'm just going to make a fool of myself."

He opened the door and stepped on to a gleaming, orange-coloured tiled floor, then walked boldly towards a large, imitation leather-covered desk where the young man with long hair, who, having bowed politely to the old lady, was now sorting through some papers. He looked up and bared his teeth in an engaging smile.

"How can I help you, gentlemen?"

Matthew found he was quite unable to speak, for it now seemed to be the height of absurdity to ask this callow youth if there was anyone employed on the premises who resembled him. But James suffered from no such reticence.

"We would like to settle a little argument. A friend of ours swears to God he's seen someone who is the spitting image of this gentleman in this shop..."

"Showrooms," the young man corrected.

"Pardon me. Well—have you anyone that looks like this guy?"

The young man shot Matthew one quick glance then shook his head.

"No. Anyway the only people employed here are my wife and myself."

"Perhaps a customer who was here late last night," James suggested.

"I was out last night. But Eileen was here. Hold on a sec and I'll fetch her."

He disappeared into an alcove that was hidden behind an eye-catching mauve curtain and presently returned accompanied by a very pretty girl with short auburn hair and the mien of a mature child. Matthew thought they might have been both manufactured in the same factory. She nodded vigorously.

"Oh, yes. I've seen him before."

James exclaimed: "Well, well, the mystery is about to be solved. Tell us, sweet one, where did you see this gentleman before?"

"On telly. When he was being interviewed about his last book. He's Matthew Bayswater."

James Fisher slapped him on the back. "May that teach you to keep your ugly mug off the box. Once seen it's never forgotten. However, it would appear that no one that looks like you works here."

"No such luck," the girl breathed.

"Daresay we can fit you in," her husband said quietly, possibly not at all that pleased by her unrestrained enthusiasm. "If you get a bit hard-up, there's worse jobs than selling kitchen furniture."

"Harold, really! What will Mr. Bayswater think?"

Matthew began to edge towards the door, anxious to terminate this ridiculous charade. "Thank you . . . Sorry to have taken up your time."

"Pleasure," the young man intoned, then added: "Pop in any time you're passing."

"I can't wait to tell my sister," his wife stared. "She'll never believe I've actually talked to Matthew Bayswater."

James Fisher nodded. "I know what you mean. Well, be good. Don't sell any wooden kitchens.

"There's a willing number there," he murmured, once they were back in Matthew's car. "Ready for a quick 'ow's yer father over the kitchen sink. Very nice too."

Matthew did not answer, but slid the gear lever into third, then drove the car over the traffic lights. He took careful note of the houses they passed, the TO BE SOLD sign that stood in front of one empty shop, and knew he had not mistaken the route taken the night before. There was no point in toying with such words as imagination, illusion, dined-well-but-not-wisely, or any other well-worn clichés that were apt to be used when the unusual raised its head. His eyes had relayed an accurate picture of an old-fashioned hardware shop, with a duplicate of himself standing behind a glass door to his fully-alert brain and no amount of self-deception could negate that fact. He swung the steering wheel round and began to head back to the office.

"Tell me, James," he said after a while, "who am I?"

The agent gave him a long, speculative look.

"You want me to treat that question seriously?"

"Of course. Otherwise I wouldn't have asked it."

"You're Matthew Bayswater, thirty-three years old, pretty as a picture and twice as smart. After leaving a secondary school at the age of fifteen you did all manner of dead-end jobs, which appear to have covered a wide variety of trades. At one time I believe you were an errand boy in a butcher's shop. But being a bright lad, you attended night school, wrote short stories and made a name for yourself when you won the Hickey Prize. Some rising young film producer made a film based on four of your stories, which by more luck than judgement turned out to be a blockbuster. You've never looked back since. Butcher's apron to riches. Oh yes—you married the lovely girl who is supposed to live next door, but never does. I think that sums up your distinguished career."

But I never worked in a kitchenware shop," Matthew said in a low voice.

Fisher nodded slowly as though he had spotted a glimmer of light in a dark room.

"This business of seeing your double in a shop doorway is getting you down, isn't it? Well, I'm no psychiatrist, but look at it this way. The chances are, if you had not had a lucky break, you might well have finished up in some such establishment. And you know it. The trouble is, success came to you too soon and too easily; and there just hasn't been time to dispel the feeling of insecurity that dominated your childhood. Last night the old sub-conscious flashed a picture of what-might-have-been. Now that theory might have as many holes as my grannie's drawers, but it's the best I can come up with at a moment's notice."

Matthew hooted the car horn when a thoughtless pedestrian suddenly stepped off the pavement.

"Sounds possible in an impossible sort of way. Very cut and dried. But there is much more to it. Much . . . much more."

Next day Matthew drove down to Camelot, where Henry Handel occasionally rested and pretended that his knighthood was something more than a romantic handle to put in front of his name. Originally the old house had been called Bottom Farm, but Sir Henry, after adding a few turrets and two flag poles, had boldly renamed it Camelot, possibly inspired by the role of Sir Lancelot, which he had once played in a joint Anglo-Italian film. He was a florid, well-padded man, still retaining the remnants of his former dashing good looks, who was now resigned to playing someone's father or benign uncle. Nevertheless, he had some claim to being regarded as a great actor.

This was something he could never forget and was apt to turn the most mundane conversation into well-delivered dialogue and a casual acquaintance into a captive audience. He greeted Matthew with a grave handshake, then exclaimed in a sonorous voice: "Young Bayswater, as I live and die!" then led him into a hall, that was enhanced by suits of armour, swords and some lethal-looking spears. From there they passed into what it pleased the worthy knight to call his "withdrawing room" which was equipped with pseudo-Tudor furniture and an equally fraudulent renaissance picture of Richard I trying to cut a cushion in half with a broadsword. Matthew seated himself in an extremely uncomfortable armchair and watched the actor pour sherry into two copper flagons.

"I don't think . . ." he began.

"Nonsense, dear boy. 'Tis but a goblet of dry sack which made our forbears the men they were. Besides it's whispered in the market place you are wont to gaze upon the grape when it is red. Take a little wine for thy stomach's sake, but for God's sake spare a thought for your liver." Sir Henry presented a full flagon to his guest, who estimated it must contain not less than half a pint of the rich brown wine. "Drink, drink and let us wash away dull care."

And he proceeded to follow his own advice with praise-worthy gusto and evident satisfaction. Then he wiped his lips on a towel-size handkerchief and waited until Matthew had taken an experimental sip.

"Well now! I learn you require me to saw the air before the camera. Tread the boards for the delectation of those who lurk in loathsome fleapits."

"You've received a copy of the script?" Matthew asked.

"Aye, that I have. I could wish the dialogue was more meaty—and more of it—but one must be thankful for what one gets these days. I am loath to sully your ears with mention of sordid monetary matters, but am I to understand that the remuneration will be . . ."

"Ten thousand for five days," Matthew stated with sordid briefness.

"'Tis a goodly round sum that will be welcomed by my depleted coffers. I could wish it were paid out in some discreet place, so that those who issue forth from the tax collector's lair know not of the transaction. I suppose thou wouldst not consider . . . ?"

Matthew shook his head. "I fear not. We have to make our returns."

Sir Henry sighed deeply and emptied his flagon.

"'Tis passing sad. Not only do they consume that which is to come, but demand that which hath passed away. Can you conceive?"

"I never have. According to our time table we will require your services during the first week in September."

"I will—God willing—be there. But now you must partake with us. Take nourishment with myself and that I am wont to call my good lady. We feast as one."

"The sole reason for my visit," Matthew confessed. "One of your lunches sets me up for the next month. What is it today? Baron of beef or roast peacock?"

"Only God and the woman knows. Wait—I will summon her." And Sir Henry raised his voice and bellowed: "Matilda—come forth, woman."

Matthew heard the patter of hurrying footsteps and rose when Matilda Handel entered the room. She was a slight, middle-aged woman; a fragile creature with a kindly fresh face and neat grey hair that was cut short in the current fashionable style. She said: "Matthew! What a nice surprise," and presented one cheek to be kissed. "If I'd known you were here I'd have rescued you sooner. I do hope Henry hasn't been too tiresome."

"The lad is to partake with us," Sir Henry announced.

Lady Handel waved an impatient hand. "Why you can't say he's staying for lunch like a normal person is beyond me. I'm delighted, Matthew, but it's rather pot luck today, I'm afraid."

"What, no bacon or beef?"

"Good heavens no! His digestion won't take that sort of thing these days. I've got some nice lamb chops with boiled potatoes and salad." She became suddenly aware of the two flagons and her hands flew to her mouth like two startled moths. "Henry, you haven't been making this poor young man drink all that awful sherry?"

"'Tis but a modicum of sack," the knight protested.

"Nonsense. And you well know the doctor said you were to confine yourself to a small glass of burgundy at dinner-time. Do you feel all right, Matthew?"

"I only drank a small amount. Besides, I have a reputation of being an accomplished drinker."

"That's as maybe. But a nice young actor who called the other day was incapable of speech or movement for several hours. No wonder we receive so few visitors." She turned to her husband and addressed him with maternal severity. "Henry, you will stop this period nonsense and show Matthew your knife collection."

"My armoury!" Sir Henry bellowed.

Well, show him whatever it is you've got up in there, while I give Cook a hand. The poor dear has back trouble and is quite unable to open the oven door."

She fluttered to the door and was soon heard pattering across the hall on her way to the afflicted cook. Sir Henry, after a few exasperated grunts, pulled in his not inconsiderable stomach and said: "Might as well see me collection. Unless you've seen it before."

"I have," Matthew admitted, "but I'm quite willing to see it again."

They crossed the hall, mounted a quite ordinary staircase and eventually came up into what, in a normal house, would have been the attic. But dormer windows now gave a commanding view of the surrounding countryside from both side walls, while on the long benches that ran the entire length of the room, were a miscellaneous collection of swords, daggers, spears, battle-axes and other instruments of mayhem. Matthew picked up an ornamental dagger.

"What period is this?"

"*Hamlet*—Oldfield Theatre 1928."

"And this sword?"

"*The Curse of the Seven Virgins*, Rome 1963."

After a few such answers Matthew remembered that Sir Henry's concept of history was strictly confined to either a theatre or a film set. He wandered round the room, ignoring the knight's rambling monologue, until he came to a small table set in front of one window. On it lay a pair of powerful binoculars.

"*The Harsh Sea*, 1951," Sir Henry volunteered.

Matthew clamped the binoculars to his eyes and moved his head from left to right so as to obtain a wide view of the panorama laid out before him. By adjusting the viewfinder he was able to make a distant house spring into close-up; every window, roof-tile, appeared but a few feet yards away. When the glasses were lowered he saw a child playing with a kitten in a hedge-rimmed garden; a young woman standing in an open doorway; a green car lurking on a gravelled drive. Then a clump of trees glided into the view, every leaf a silent tongue as they swayed gently in response to the prevailing wind. Further to the right was a cornfield, which gave way to an expanse of open meadow-land, where brown and white cows wandered with mindless contentment. By lowering the binoculars even further Matthew found he was looking at a man leaning against a gate.

The man was staring directly at the house—even possibly the very window…

"Sir Henry," Matthew spoke calmly. "I would like you to train these binoculars on that gate. The one immediately below the large oak tree."

Handel took the glasses and after squinting in the required direction, raised them to his eyes. Matthew waited.

"Got it," the knight announced. "Leads to old Jarvis' meadow. Fine example of an old gate. What wouldest thou I do now?"

"What do you think of the man leaning against the gate?"

"What man, dear boy? Apart from a few cows in the background, there's not a living body in sight."

Matthew took a deep breath and managed to subdue a pang of pure terror. "But I can still see him, even without the glasses. He hasn't moved."

Sir Henry gave him a quick glance, then again stared intently through the binoculars. "I suppose I'm looking at the right gate? For damn me soul if I can see anyone."

"There's only one gate," Matthew said quietly, "and you're looking at it. And if you can't see a man leaning against it and staring at this house, one of us is in a bad way."

The actor was now quite a different person to the rather ridiculous poser of a short time before; he handed the binoculars back to Matthew and said gently:

"Describe the fellow."

"Very well. But will you believe what I tell you?"

Sir Henry nodded very slowly. "I will—and I've no intention of questioning your sanity. All writers—and actors for that matter—are a bit cracked, but not enough to see a non-existent man."

Matthew again trained the glasses on the gate. His double's face came into focus, the eyes unblinking, the forehead creased by a troubled frown.

"I see a man who is a nigh-perfect duplicate of myself. If I start from the top and work my way down, this is a detailed description. Blond hair—like mine—but it needs cutting. My eyes, only they have a cowed expression. My height, but the shoulders seem to have acquired a stoop. My body, but I'd say a little thinner. For the rest—he's dressed in a wrinkled, serge suit, a dirty creased shirt, a lopsided spotted red tie. The trousers are a bit too short for him and I can see a pair of sagging socks and brown cracked shoes. That's about it. Unless I add he hasn't moved, blinked or given the slightest sign of life." Matthew lowered the binoculars and looked sideways at the actor. "And this is the second time I've seen him. The other night he was standing in a non-existent shop doorway."

Sir Henry drew him gently away from the window, then motioned him to a chair. When they were both seated he said: "I've read and heard about this kind of thing, but damn me if I ever believed there was anything to it. You must have guessed what. . . that thing out there is?"

"Someone who looks too like me for comfort," Matthew replied, "and apparently can't be seen by anyone else. Must be an illusion. That means I'm mad."

The knight looked uncomfortable. "If you're mad I'm a Dutchman. Look, as a writer you must have heard of this kind of thing. Remember the oldest curse in history? 'May you meet yourself coming downstairs'. My dear fellow, you've just described your doppelgänger."

"What the hell is that?"

"The ghost of yourself. Damn me, I played one once. Back in the thirties. A film called *The Curse of the Double-Man*. To get into the atmosphere I must have read every word printed on the subject. A lot of quite famous people have seen the damned things. Sir Walter Scott for one."

"With what result?"

If Sir Henry had appeared to be uncomfortable before, he now gave the impression he was sitting on a bed of hot nails.

"Well—pure coincidence of course—all getting on in years—but generally speaking they all died within a year. After seeing the doppelgänger that is."

Matthew digested this information, accepted the implication and was surprised to find that it did not cause him all that disquiet. There were worse fates than dying.

"As you appear to be an expert on this kind of thing," he said calmly, "perhaps you can tell me if these famous persons—did they always see an exact duplicate of themselves? Down to the smallest detail?"

The knight nodded. "Absolutely. Erasmus Aldbridge, the 17th-century philosopher, records he saw a mirror reflection. The doppelgänger was wearing his clothes, but buttoned on the opposite side. A hole that was in his right stocking was in the apparition's left."

"But this fellow isn't wearing my clothes," Matthew pointed out. "And there are other differences. Hair-style, weight, expression. That doesn't fit into your theory."

Sir Henry blew out his cheeks. "Beats me. Tell you what. I've got a book in the library. What's it called now? Hang on—it's coming back... *Unnatural Enmities* by Conrad Von Holstein. Hell of a family, you know. All of 'em dabbled in the black art for centuries. Old Conrad wrote this book around 1820, then disappeared shortly afterwards. And I'm damned sure there's a chapter on the doppelgänger. Look it out after lunch. Which reminds me, the woman will be screaming to high heaven if we don't get downstairs and play with her blasted lamb chops. Mind you there's a damned good rice pudding to follow."

Matthew got up and walked back to the window. After a while he said: "He's gone now."

Sir Henry"s voice came from behind him.

"Yes, well, maybe he was never there in the first place. Shouldn't take this too much to heart. Perhaps that sherry was a mite too strong and large. Fellow sees all sorts of things when he's had more than enough. Be best if we don't mention any of this to Matilda. Women never understand anything that's not connected with either the kitchen or bedroom. Let's go down."

They left the "armoury" and descended the stairs and were just in time to stop Lady Handel belabouring a large gong that was slung between two posts. She gave Matthew a sympathetic smile.

"You poor dear boy! I do hope that Henry hasn't bored you too dreadfully with the history of all those knives. I fear he has a weakness for the macabre."

Matthew allowed himself the luxury of a trite remark.

"It's all been most interesting. I've been admiring the view from the east window. It has some interesting features."

"Hasn't it?" Lady Handel agreed. "A visitor will always find something new."

Jennie had dusted everything that was available to be dusted, reluctantly refrained from doing something about Matthew's littered desk, then shot him an enquiring glance.

"Are you going to work all morning?"

"Read," he said.

"Oh! Anything nice?"

He looked down at the bulky, ancient book that Sir Henry had lent him and turned back the front cover. "Not very. *Unnatural Enmities*, by Baron Conrad Von Holstein."

"Ugh! Are you going to write about—what you said?"

"Maybe."

"I'll be across the hall if you need me. Coffee around eleven okay?"

He nodded and watched her perform that loin-warming walk that had to be seen from the rear to be really appreciated. It had something to do with the way her buttocks moved and the curve of her shoulders. Suddenly Matthew realised what a perfect partner she made; loving, but not clinging, always considering his welfare, the ideal bed companion, prepared to take part in any variation. In fact, had he created her as a character in one of his books, an editor might well be justified by saying: "Too perfect—lacks credibility."

She left the door open and presently he heard her humming a haunting tune while she cleared the dining-room table. Matthew turned his full attention to the book which now lay open before him.

UNNATURAL ENMITES

by

Baron Conrad Von Holstein: Count of Plön.

Translated by

Sir James Sinclair, Bart

1933

Matthew wondered who Sir James Sinclair was—or had been—and why he should have taken the trouble to translate such a book into English. Possibly Sir Henry could enlighten him on this point. The introduction was short, but gave him some information regarding the original author.

INTRODUCTION

Very little is known about the life of Baron Conrad Von Holstein, apart from his obsession with the occult and a profound knowledge of the various folk-tales and legends that the unlettered peasantry of central Europe have relayed from one generation to the next, since the dawn of history.

Certainly the Von Holstein family had a most sinister reputation since Baron Heinrich was burnt at the stake in 1556; having, according to contemporary records, not only mated his only daughter to the Primate Horrific (see page 272) but did call up the dreaded Holstein Horror as well. (See page 295).

It is interesting to learn that the baron—so far as I am aware—was the first man to coin the phrase 'Parallel-Universe'; believing apparently that there are innumerable planes of consciousness, the lowest being the habitat of the terrible life-forms that are recorded in this book.

Conrad was born on the 30th May 1786 and disappeared under mysterious circumstances on July 7th 1820, leaving behind this work which was long banned by the Catholic Church, although copies were circulating in certain countries as late as 1893.

Matthew turned the pages over until he arrived at number 95. He sat back and read.

THE DOPPLEGÄNGER

The doppelgänger or mirror-ghost is of great antiquity, it being recorded as the earliest known apparition that did bring fear and much despondency to primitive man. A drawing, both well executed and of exceedingly well-preserved colours, can be seen to this day in the Walbeck Cave, situated in the Neu-de-Mine district; depicting two men of same likeness, one of whom hath his hair standing on end.

The ancient Egyptians were also troubled with this affliction and it is recorded in the book of death that Rameses the third of that name, did see his other self come up from the river, thus causing the king to fall down into a great faint. In more recent time, when the great Elizabeth lay dying in her palace of Richmond, one lady in waiting whose duty it was to sit by the queen's side, having strayed into the long gallery, did see the queen's mirror-self approach towards her. She, fearing that Her Majesty had arisen and would rebuke her for leaving the place of vigil, cried out and said: "I did but answer a call of nature," but when the apparition was scarce two feet away, it vanished. When the lady returned to the bed chamber, the queen was still sleeping.

The ignorant do say that the doppelgänger is a harbinger of death, but I, being a grand master of the seventh circle, am of the opinion, nay of proven conviction, that the reason for its appearance is most complex and may well be the cause of our departure from this *place*. I speak not of the death of the material body.

On the dawn of St. Wilfred's day, I was being but newly awakened, saw my doppelgänger seated in a chair and displaying signs of deep distress. It wept and tore its hair and gazed upon me with great reproach, so that even I (who hath seen much that would cause a normal man to break his sanity) was much afraid and would have fled, had not the apparition been betwixt me and the door.

Presently it rose and walked (with resounding footsteps) to the left side of my bed and exclaimed in a loud voice:

"Why make you this hell for me?"

Then it departed, went I know not where, and I—being now somewhat recovered—rose and searched my chamber with great diligence, but found no evidence of an intruder. The thought came to me that we may well form a duplicate self, who has to

suffer in another place, for the sins committed here by its progen-
itor. Or conversely we have to endure the ills and misery of this
life, because of *that* which does evil under the alien sun.

Indeed cursed is he who thirsts after knowledge, for no man,
no matter how great his attainments, can entirely drain the cup
of truth. Little knowledge confuses the brain, leads us into dark
avenues of conjecture and awakens the gibbering ghosts of superstition. Three times more have I seen my doppelgänger, but I
pray to Almighty God that it come not again *within clutching
distance*, less that which I fear (but dare not commit to paper)
come about.

Matthew slammed the book closed and looked anxiously around
the room, aware of a suspicion that something—or someone—had
distracted his attention. Jennie had closed the door at some time while
he had been reading, but he could still hear her humming; a muted
sound that seemed to come from a long way off.

Then suddenly all sound was cut off. Was succeeded by an absolute
silence which made Matthew believe for one dreadful moment that he
had been struck deaf. The mantelpiece clock no longer sent out its
dignified loud tick, the gentle summer breeze continued to stir the
leaves of the old elm tree, but there was no muted, air-borne sigh.
Matthew pressed a typewriter key, it struck the white paper, formed a
small "e" and fell back when he released it—but made no sound of any
kind.

Then this awful, unnatural silence was shattered by a loud ranting
voice that came from just behind the closed door. The voice of a
woman whose spoonful of love had long since curdled and poisoned
her soul. It grew louder still as the speaker approached the door.

"...you sit there with your moon face and not a word to say for
yourself and I so hate your guts I'd like to take a coal hammer and bash
your head in until it bursts and stop you writing that muck that no
one wants to publish..."

She was by the door now, the handle was turning and Matthew was
whimpering, hands clasped over his ears, but the mad, bitter stream of
recrimination continued to sweep across his brain.

"...you think you're a bloody genius but you're nothing more than a gutless failure...bloody great fail...u...r...e...e."

The door opened and Jennie entered the room. She smiled sweetly and said, "Coffee on the boil darling."

Instantly normal sound returned. The clock resumed its dignified tick, the wind again wooed the restless leaves and far-far-away a dog barked. Matthew Bayswater pointed a quivering forefinger at his wife.

"What the hell are you playing at? Are you trying to drive me mad?"

The smile froze on Jennie's face, then gradually dissolved into an expression of horrified astonishment. She moved forward like a woman who has come face to face with a long-awaited and much dreaded spectre and is determined not to appear afraid. She spoke softly.

"What's wrong, Matthew? You're so white and your hands are shaking. Are you ill? Shall I ring for Dr. Waterman?"

His throat was choked with words and there was a need to abuse, to force her to provide a rational explanation.

"A damned silly joke—if that's what you meant it to be. Shouting and roaring away like that...telling me I'm a failure...I write rubbish...muck...that will never be published...and wanting to kill me..." He looked up at her. "Do you really hate and despise me?"

Jennie instantly put an arm around his shoulders, placed her face next to his, while her soft lilting voice spoke words of comfort, loving concern.

"Of course I don't despise or hate you. I love and respect you and always will. And as for being a failure...You're a terrific booming success. The great Matthew Bayswater. And don't you dare ever think otherwise!"

He repeated her words in a grotesquely loud whisper.

"I'm a terrific booming success and I must never think otherwise. Ever."

He began to feel better almost at once and decided to forget the entire episode. He was aware of a slow journey up the stairs, guided by a slender arm that encircled his waist; after a lapse of time that could have lasted from anything from ten minutes to an hour, he was between cool sheets that caressed his limbs like pleasure-seeking hands; and if the damnable logic-loving brain insisted that the problem would still be unsolved when he awoke, that, at the present moment in time, was of little importance.

Dr. Waterman put away his stethoscope and succeeded in looking very wise.

"Nothing wrong with you physically, but you certainly appear to be mixed-up mentally. Sounds like a job for one of those head-shrinkers. Probably got an anxiety complex, whatever that might mean."

"No psychiatrist for me," Matthew protested. "If I'm going nuts, I'll do it in privacy. No one is rummaging around in my brain."

The doctor shrugged. "That's up to you. But at least take a break and get away for a bit. No need to keep turning out that junk as you do. You must be worth a bomb. Now, if you were an over-worked, underpaid G.P. you'd have a good excuse for a nervous breakdown."

"Balls. A professional examiner of..."

"That's as maybe. But yours are nothing to get excited about." Waterman turned to Jennie. "As this exchange of scintillating wit will have informed you, he's down to his usual low form. Keep him off booze, work and how's-yer-father and he'll be all right."

"If necessary I'll tie him down to the bed," Jennie promised.

The doctor assumed an expression of shocked horror.

"Good God! Don't tell me you have to do that! No wonder he hears voices. I'll pop along tomorrow."

Scarcely had the door closed behind Jennie and the doctor than Matthew was out of bed and scrambling into his clothes. The bedroom was suddenly an evil place; the wardrobe might well conceal some as yet unthought-of-horror, that was only waiting for the unguarded moment to emerge into grotesque life. He also experienced a reluctance to look into the dressing-table mirror, being tormented by the ridiculous notion that his reflection might rebel and not faithfully reproduce either his appearance or his actions.

He was half-way down the stairs before Jennie realised that her patient was making a bid for freedom. She remonstrated, all but laid violent hands on him, but to no avail.

"I'll really go mad in that room and I'm not really ill. Nothing wrong that work won't cure."

"But you *are* ill. I know…know…"

He paused for a moment, then looked down into her eyes and thought for a moment he detected a gleam of—what? Derision? Contempt? Or loving concern? He pushed by her and made for the front door, smothering a feeling that blended fear with irritation. Her voice came to him just before he slammed the front door.

"Be careful. Don't do anything stupid."

Of course due to the excitement, the need to get out of the house, he had forgotten the car keys and lacking the courage to face Jennie again, there was no alternative but to travel on the Underground.

Grimy windows framed a view of undulating, dust-coated pipes: faces—mostly tired and drawn—stared either at the advertising cards or cast furtive glances at the graffiti that had been inscribed on the white enamel ceiling with chinagraph. Bodies swayed when the train roared round a curve, then went over to one side when it screeched to a halt at each station. Doors sighed, then slid open. A guard shouted something that sounded like: "Mindedaws", which was a signal for another drawn-out sigh, followed by a strange vibrating rattling noise.

The train was again swallowed by the pipe-infested tunnel and Matthew began to take a real interest in his fellow passengers, as indeed had been his practice for many years, having long ago come to the conclusion that a cross-section of the entire population of London must be packed into a medium-filled tube train compartment.

He counted sixty-nine bodies and estimated that at least forty were the rightful property of office workers. A man in blue overalls with a bulging leather bag was most certainly a plumber and a plump middle-aged woman with swollen ankles most likely worked in a store. One man who was strap-hanging by the door had a dead-white face and an almost completely bald head and defied definition. He stared at Matthew with unblinking eyes, then bared discoloured teeth in a mirthless grin. Matthew switched his gaze to the ceiling, but when he looked down again the man had gone. There was not the slightest sign of anyone even remotely like him anywhere.

This incident was a lesson well worth remembering. Never take anyone for granted—the dead—the misplaced—could well be moving from *here* to *there*, even as passengers are continually boarding and leaving a train.

Then he was out on the platform at Green Park Station, part of a shuffling crowd that made its way to the already-packed escalators. The majority took up positions on the right, but an energetic few—Matthew was among them—began to mount the steps on the left, thus ensuring they were borne up to the light of day in the shortest possible time.

Matthew looked up and felt his heart give one sickening thud. The doppelgänger was at the very top looking down.

There could be no doubt. His body—minus a few pounds—dressed in a cheap, shabby suit, was staring down at him with something akin to terror expressed in every line of its face. Once the initial shock had been absorbed, Matthew experienced a feeling of intense relief. Now he would be able to dispel his nightmare in the harsh light of reality. A close encounter; face to face, hear its voice, know why, explain how—pinpoint the exact location of where. He began to run up the moving stairs.

The doppelgänger turned and disappeared into the crowd which was pouring off the escalator. Gasping like a stranded fish, Matthew reached the upper region just in time to see his quarry making for the steps leading to Piccadilly. There were a lot of moving bodies between him and the steps, each one seemingly determined to retard his progress and a full three minutes had passed before he came up to street level.

He looked anxiously from left to right, then—with what relief—he saw the by-now familiar figure flanked by a tall man on one side and a short dumpy woman on the other, entering the colonnaded length of pavement which ran along the entire frontage of the Ritz Hotel. Matthew ran. To make better progress he left the pavement and sprinted along the gutter, thus earning a colourful rebuke from a taxi-driver who was forced to swerve out into the main stream of traffic. Heads were turned; someone called out: "Where's the fire?" as the young man raced towards what he hoped would be release from fear and doubt.

When he reached St. James' Street the tall man and the dumpy woman were standing on the kerb edge, waiting for the lights to change, before crossing the road. The short lady glared when he peered over her shoulder, then enquired in a breathless voice:

"The young man—who was walking between you and this gentleman—did you see where he went?"

The tall man provided an answer. "There never has been anyone between my wife and myself. I've been holding her arm since we came up from the station."

"But I saw him," Matthew insisted. "I saw him."

The traffic lights changed to green and the ill-assorted couple promptly crossed the road with heads held high and eyes staring resolutely to their front. Matthew allowed the crowd to flow round and past him, knowing there was little point in searching further, for if the creature had been anything more than a reflection cast out by his brain, it could have either entered a hotel or boarded one of the slow-moving buses. If he were not to go completely mad, he must try to accept the unusual and give it the appearance of normality.

He hailed a taxi and was driven to his London office.

When Matthew arrived home that night he was greeted by a very anxious Jennie, who clung to him as though he had just returned from a journey of a thousand miles.

"Have you been all right?" she asked.

"Fine," he said, then kissed her hard upon the lips. "I've been just fine. I said I would be. Don't worry."

It seemed as if she couldn't bear to lose contact with him and walked with an arm around his waist. "Sorry, darling, but we've got a visitor. I mean, she just turned up."

"Who?"

"Mrs. Fortescue. Just say hallo to her, then look at your watch."

"Oh Lord!"

"But it will be good for you to talk nicely to her. Strengthen your soul."

Mrs. Fortescue was seated in Matthew's favourite chair and extended a plump moist hand when he approached. He took it, bowed over it, then restored it to its owner. In a way he was not all that sorry to find the woman there. She would act as a source of minor annoyance and stop him thinking of more pressing concerns. Jennie poured tea from a silver pot into a blue cup, added milk and two lumps of sugar, before bringing the end result over to her husband.

"Mrs. Fortescue..."

"Lydia—please."

"Oh! I forgot. Lydia was saying just before you came in, that she thinks you should write an historical novel. One with a heroine that is captured by pirates and sold to a black magician and falls in love with a wandering minstrel. That's right, isn't it—eh—Lydia?"

Mrs. Fortescue nodded so violently, her hair—about which Matthew entertained grave suspicions—jerked back and forth like a woollen cosy on an agitated tea-pot. "That's so right, dear, it's all in my head, but I just haven't the ability to put it down on paper."

"I'm sure you've never tried," Matthew suggested with a tired smile.

"That's so true, but I have written some extraordinary fine letters. Everyone says so. But I do so love the past. Those days when men were men and women were..."

"Glad of it," Matthew prompted and was only saved from a poke in the ribs by the distance that separated him and his self-invited guest.

"You naughty man! But don't you just hunger for those days when castles were besieged and the defenders poured boiling oil on the attackers?"

"There are times when I think that such a practice had much to commend it."

"And Protestants or Catholics of the Spanish Inquisition or someone, used to rack priests and flatten thumbs with screw-things and burn people at stakes and—oh yes—there was that lovely Sir Walter Raleigh making a long speech before having his head chopped off. I mean to say, life is so tame these days."

"We've certainly gone to the dogs," Matthew agreed.

"And don't you think that lovely Henry VIII was simply wonderful? All those wives! And they all went to the block with such dignity."

"Only two. Anne Boleyn and Catherine Howard."

Mrs. Fortescue widened her eyes with surprise and gave the impression that she had not been misinformed, but cheated out of four heads into the bargain.

"Really! I could have sworn that Mary Queen of Scots lost her head as well."

"She did. But some fifty years later."

Conversation was hard to come by after that, until Jennie, who was trying with some success to subdue a giggling fit, said: "You have a daughter, I understand, eh—Lydia. It must be such a comfort to have children."

The lady frowned and sat upright before delivering a considered reply. "Daughters can be so sweet in the cradle, but so disappointing at the table. Such has been my experience. Susan was so cuddly when she was five—now at twenty-five—is a positive monster. I can think of no better word. A card at Christmas, a peck on my cheek at my birthday party—and three two-minute telephone calls since June." The slightly bovine eyes looked at Matthew sternly. "Do you realise I haven't seen or spoken to my daughter for six months?"

"Alas, I only read *The Times*."

Mrs. Fortescue's face had now assumed a deep red colour, as though she were either in constant and intimate contact with a whisky bottle or afflicted by high-blood pressure. Her voice was suddenly deeper and occasionally dispensed with the need for aspirates.

"It's no laughing matter. She's me daughter all said and done and it's not like 'er to disappear into the blue without so much as 'ow's yer father. She must have said where she was going."

Matthew looked helplessly round for Jennie, deciding it was about time she rescued him from this mad woman, but she had disappeared, so he was obliged to fend for himself. He scowled at the lady and wondered why she suddenly looked so shabby. For some reason he shivered.

"You forget, madam, I haven't the pleasure of your daughter's acquaintance. But I'm sure you'll hear from her soon. Daughters, like income-tax, always return."

Mrs. Fortescue pointed a fat forefinger at him and raised her voice until it had much in common with that of a bad-tempered cat.

"Don't come the old acid with me. You were never my idea of a 'usband for my Jennie and if she's given you the elbow, well and good, but I want to know where she's gone. Now, what 'ave you done with 'er?"

"Matthew," Jennie was back, seated a little to his left, her face expressing anxiety. "What's wrong, darling? You look so strange."

Matthew blinked and stared at Mrs. Fortescue with wide-eyed horror. The lady was again fashionably, if rather over-dressed; her large face pale, but expertly made-up, her bovine eyes lit by a gleam of gently enquiry. When she spoke her voice had little in common with the ranting deep tones of a few minutes before.

"I was explaining that I hadn't seen my daughter since Easter, when you—well—looked strange. Dear me, I do hope you're not unwell."

Matthew ran a moist hand over his forehead and tried to dismiss a feeling that he was on his way down a steep hill and his descent was getting out of control.

"I'm sorry, I thought . . . You really must excuse me, but I do rather feel off-colour."

Instantly Jennie was by his side, but he avoided her outstretched hand. He needed solitude where there would be no unanswerable questions posed by a lilting voice and a deep sleep that would blot out memory of all events that might have taken place in the past or the yet-to-be-born future.

"Please," he conjured up a smile, "I'll be all right. You stay here with Fortescue and try to atone for my rudeness." He turned to the lady who favoured him with a sympathetic smile. "It was so nice to see you again—forgive me."

Her smile became a simper. "I do understand. You talented people are so highly strung."

In fact solitude brought no relief and two pills little hope of sleep. Lying fully-dressed on the bed Matthew had no power to stop his brain from raising the wraiths of memory; the doppelgänger's terror-stricken face looking down at him from the top of the escalator and the recent transformation of Mrs. Fortescue.

If only these were the ingredients of a plot for a novel, what fun he would have finding the solution.

He closed his eyes and actually smiled. How would he set about it?

To start, the doppelgänger could be cast as a miserable failure with a nagging wife and a real-battle-axe of a mother-in-law. Good. Now rough in the background. Simple. Poor devil with literary aspirations, employed in a dead-end job (much like himself in the early years), who never gets the breaks, anxiety rides on his shoulders, perpetually tired, possibly impotent which would explain the wife's frustrated bitterness.

How about the wife? Imagine Jennie after being married for seven years to such a man. Not a cosseted, well-loved happy woman, but a poor miserable, deprived, ill-dressed creature who is probably forced to go out to work to maintain a reasonable standard of living. What would she be like now? A nagging harridan? A shrieking, fault-finding, unkempt, scraggy termagant? Good God, she'd probably hit the bottle!

Mother-in-law? Have to be careful here or you'll finish up with a Dickensian monster. But most certainly an unhappy, overweight, my-daughter– could-have-done-much-better-for-herself old bitch. A suitable parent for a perpetually dissatisfied wife to go home to—only of course she would always come back. A fairly basic situation that might well develop into something very nasty. Such as—and Matthew nodded gently—the possibility of the worm turning.

One day coming home and losing control...Dear God why have I been gifted with such an imagination?...striking that yapping mouth, fastening fingers around that scrawny throat until she can't nag anymore...no more insults...then take her down the stairs...dig-up the cellar...and hide...hide...and keep that old cow out...but above all escape...escape...into the world where one is rich and fabulously famous, with a beautiful loving wife who exists only to further one's happiness, and live there happily evermore.

Luke began to cry softly as the luxuriously-appointed bedroom shimmered and gradually changed into a place with filthy distempered walls, battered chest of drawers, scratched walnut wardrobe, faded linoleum and unsavoury bed. The room was saturated with the stench of dead hope.

Luke got up, slid his feet into a pair of slippers and shuffled towards the door. Out on the landing he paused and looked down over the banisters. The house was cold and empty; a mausoleum where loneliness and despair kept watch over illegal dead. He slowly descended the stairs and came down into the hall where a naked floor led into an evil-smelling kitchen on one side and almost empty lounge on the other. A little further on was a flight of steps that gave access to the cellar.

Luke sank to his knees, covered his eyes with shaking hands and screamed out the eternal prayer.

"Let me not face reality... I don't want reality. Freeze time here so that I can spend forever there. Please... please remove from me the curse *now*."

Gradually the house became warmer, the floor beneath his knees softer, and presently a soft lilting voice said:

"Matthew, what are you doing down there? Honestly you are the limit! I thought you were upstairs resting. Thank goodness Mrs. Fortescue has gone. What she would have said had she seen you kneeling on the floor I cannot imagine."

Matthew got up and slid his arm round Jennie's slim waist. The house was warm and comfortably furnished, outside was a world that revered Matthew Bayswater and all his works; by his side was a lovely adoring wife. He was a happy and successful man.

"Come, darling," he said, "come and help me do that which I cannot do by myself."

Together they mounted the stairs.

LES EDWARDS
A PORTFOLIO

Terror by Night (Universal-Tandem, 1974)

The Tenth Fontana Book of Great Horror Stories (Fontana Books, 1977)

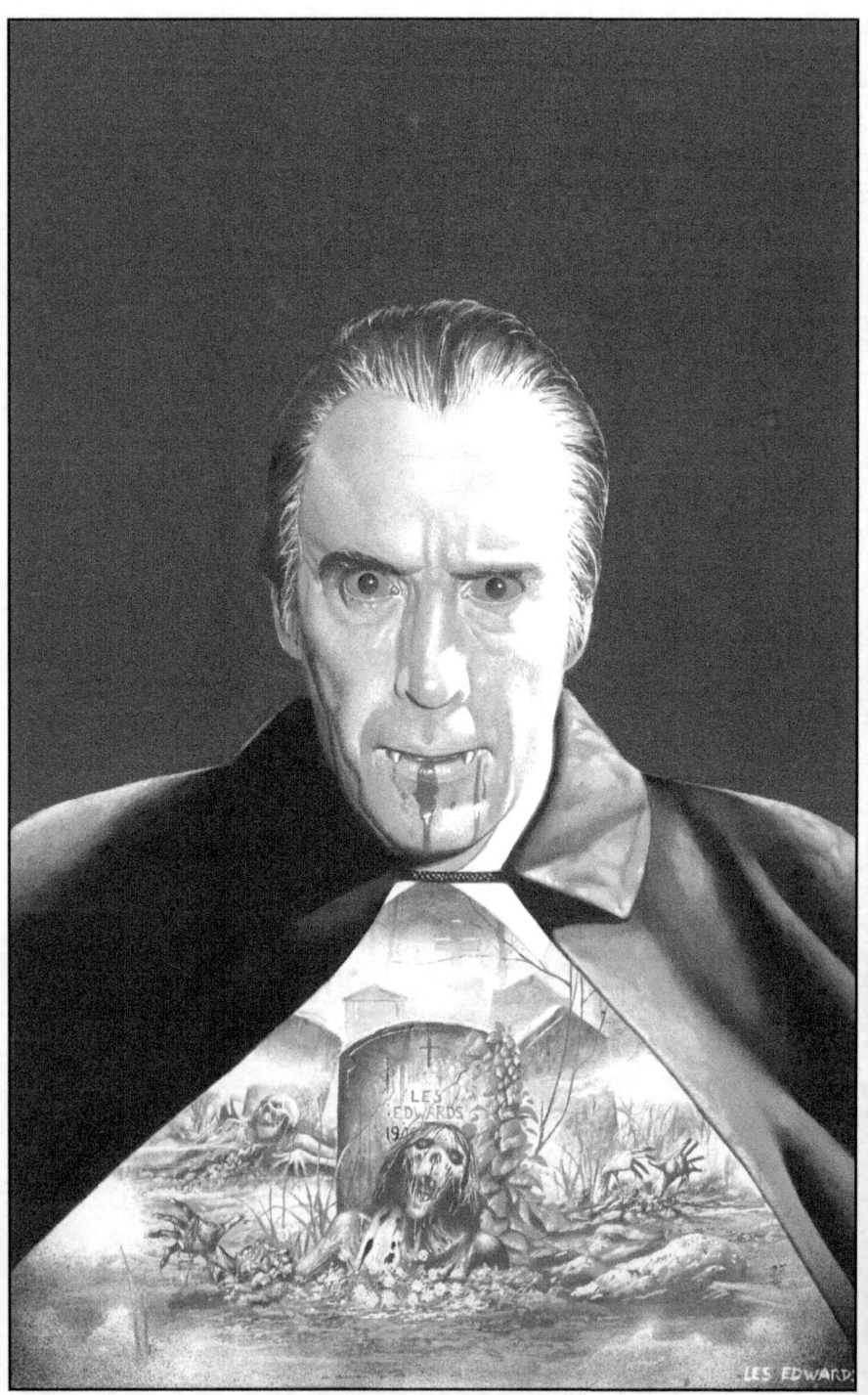

Horror-Zeit (Pabel, 1977)

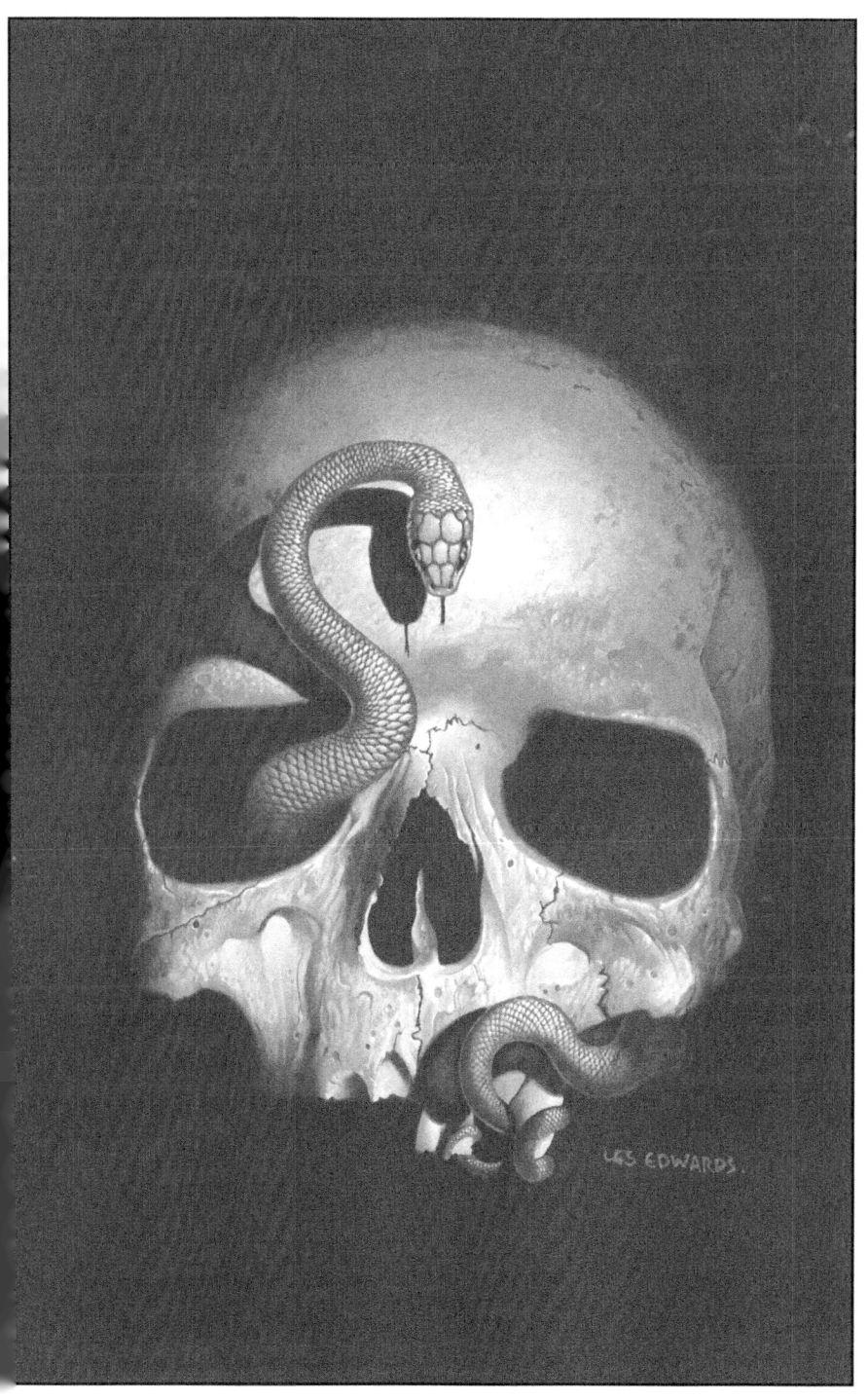

Zehn Teufelsküsse (Pabel, 1978)

Phantoms and Fiends (Robert Hale, 2000)

Great Ghost Stories: Tales of Mystery and Madness
(Cemetery Dance Publications, 2005)

Looking for Something to Suck: The Vampire Stories of R. Chetwynd-Hayes
(Valancourt Books, 2014)

Acquiring a Family

CELIA WATSON EXAMINED the front of her new house with a critical eye, but could detect nothing lacking. The five windows—three up and two down—gleamed as only freshly-cleaned glass can; the red brickwork looked as if it had been washed and sanded in the not-too-distant past, while frames, guttering and front door glittered with recently-applied green paint.

Celia had dreamed of such a house for a long time and it was only the event of an ancient uncle's demise, and the acquisition of his money, that had enabled her to buy this one. She was grateful for the late uncle's thoughtfulness in leaving her the wherewithal to enjoy not only this dream house, but sufficient funds to never again have to consider the dire prospect of gainful employment.

She took a large key from her handbag, fitted it into a keyhole, then flung the door open.

The pseudo-antique furniture suited the small house, ranging as it did from a credence table and umbrella-cum-hat-stand in the tiny hall, to the looming Tudor-style wardrobe and bed in what might be called the main bedroom. The last owner had decorated all the walls with light brown emulsion paint, and although this served as an excellent background for the furniture, it did have a rather depressing effect when viewed for the first time, but even this Celia managed to ignore.

She had seen the interior of the house before of course and agreed to take it as it stood, furniture, décor and all; she hoped she would live there for many years and die contented—if not happy—in the vast Tudor-style bed.

Such is one of the illusions that make up the foundation of that great fantasy we call life.

Celia Watson spoke aloud: "This is what I have always wanted. Thanks to God I am not too old to enjoy it."

She was fifty-three, an age that has escaped from the chains of youth, but has not yet slid into the iron cage of old age. At such a time of life one should be in a position to benefit from experience, while still enjoying clear mental powers and—hopefully—good health.

Celia enjoyed both.

But she was alone. A strange distaste for any form of close intimacy with persons of either sex resulted in her never marrying, or as for that matter encouraging anything more than superficial friendships, so that now—while still enjoying her own company—there was a fear-germ—a nagging thought—that she might have missed out on something essential to her well-being.

She swept, brushed, polished, arranged pictures and knick-knacks to her satisfaction, then manhandled heavy furniture from one place to another. But the time came when all that could be done was done and the bright hues of novelty died; then the fear-germ returned, a little larger, stronger than before.

Alien thoughts chased each other down the rarely explored avenues of the brain and eventually congregated into a ridiculous notion:

She should have had children.

Before moving into the cottage she would have laughed such an idea to scorn, for had she not ridiculed the premise that a woman's primary role was that of mother? "In this over-crowded planet," she often maintained, "I at least have not made the situation worse by brat production. Pity there's not a few more like me."

Now, while seated on a well-padded chair, she would splutter up from a shallow sleep, almost certain that she had been awakened by tiny fingers tugging at her skirt or the sound of laughing childish voices coming from the next room. Nonsense of course. The result of a wobbly tummy, plus the excitement of moving into her new home.

Perhaps it would be better to get out more, join a literary appreciation group or something. After all, she was now at that time of life when one wanted to be taken out of oneself—whatever that might mean—and it was most important not to pander to—well—fancies. She could remember one or two lukewarm friends who had gone distinctly funny after entering the fifties.

She joined the Ladies' Tuesday Afternoon Group, where the latest TV programme (if it were decent), the prime minister's latest misdemeanour, the prospect of an atomic war and other worthwhile subjects were discussed. As Celia prided herself on being an outspoken person who was not afraid of expressing her opinion, she had soon dethroned the current chairperson and made herself extremely unpopular, which as everyone knows, is the seal of success.

Then she took to attending evening classes, organised by the local county council, where she became proficient in basket-making, early Victorian letter writing, pottery and raising a garden in window boxes.

All this activity kept her as active as anyone could wish—or in many cases would want—and succeeded in taking her out of herself in no uncertain manner. There was no time for morbid *fancies* and hence no danger of her going distinctly funny.

For a while at any rate.

Basket-making became a boring pastime, early Victorian letter writers revealed themselves to be nothing more than persons with a penchant for not using one word when ten would do; pottery was a messy business, and as she already had an extensive garden, raising one in window boxes was a waste of time. Moreover, the Ladies' Tuesday Afternoon Group grew restless under her dictatorship, successfully organised a palace revolution, replaced her as chairperson by the wife of a coal merchant, which in effect meant she was sent into exile.

So it was that once again—as the time-honoured expression has it—time hung heavily on her hands, and she took to sitting in a comfortable armchair, trying to read a novel, which inevitably slipped from her hands, when she sank into a shallow sleep.

Almost every time she was awakened by tiny fingers tugging at her skirt, or the sound of laughing childish voices coming from the next room. But she could no longer say with hand on heart: "Nonsense of course."

Sometimes the tugging and the childish laughter took place when she was on the verge of awakening. She was in fact almost fully aware that four or five children were involved, possibly two by her knees and three in the next room. On occasion they made quite a clamour and it was this that rocketed her up from the pit of sleep, hurtled her into full awareness—then all sound and tugging stopped.

The phenomenon had an eerie effect, became more than a little disturbing, and Celia again began to wonder if she was indeed becoming distinctly funny and if the house, after all, was going to suit her.

Then she began to see. Only a glimpse at first.

After a particularly noisy session, shrill laughter, stamping of feet, the slamming of a door, plus violent tugging, Celia cried out, opened her eyes, then fell back in her chair.

She had a glimpse of a tiny figure attired in a white dress disappearing round a door-frame. A fleeting vision that might have been a vestige of a dream, or maybe an illusion created by the wakening brain (always supposing that organ ever sleeps), there were all manner of explanations, but when this last occurrence was matched up with the sounds, one's wondering invaded a new plane of conjecture.

A few days later she was permitted more than a glimpse. A good long look.

Sleeping again, but this time in her bed, with a bedside lamp sending a golden circle of light across the room, for the eerie, distinctly funny disturbances made total and even partial darkness unpleasant, to say the least. Lying on her left side, cheek nestled deeply in a plump pillow, her eyes sprang open, and she saw a child, a little girl, standing a few feet away, looking at her, attired in a white dress, with auburn hair groomed into tight ringlets, hanging down to her shoulders. Dark, limpid eyes gazed into her own and for a while it seemed as if time was frozen and Celia Watson would spend eternity staring at a child, while cold fear crept slowly up from her feet, like the soul-releasing chill that announces the approach of death.

Perhaps that good long look lasted two minutes—or five seconds—but it seemed as if time had stood still before the child vanished—ceased to be—became as never was.

But its image remained imprinted on Celia's brain, persisted in lurking behind her eyes, and when she closed the lids, there it was standing against a blazing red background.

Fearful to look upon, dreadful to consider—but—appealing.

When fear had unlocked it shackles, Celia leapt out of bed, ran out on the landing and raced into the bathroom, this being a sure place of refuge back in the innocent days of childhood, it being assumed that no one would dare invade its privacy once the engaged bolt had been slid into position. So far as she could remember, experience had never disproved this theory.

Seated on the lavatory pan she gave the matter her full attention and came to the conclusion that she might have over-reacted to the situation, fearsome though the experience had been. Had not her late, extremely wise Papa always maintained: "There is always a rational explanation for every extraordinary experience if only we take the trouble to look for it."

Therefore it stood to reason there was a rational explanation for all these sounds and visions, be they ghosts...

Celia shuddered on the lavatory seat and regurgitated that horrible little word:

"Ghosts!"

Her old new house was haunted!

She had never thought about ghosts before, save on the occasion when she read *The Turn of the Screw* by Henry James, and that did rather offer a rational explanation. The governess might have been distinctly funny. Had anyone asked her: "Do you believe in ghosts?" the answer undoubtedly would have been a head shaking "don't know," which might have been a cover-up for: "Maybe I do."

Now, sitting on the lavatory pan, she most certainly did.

She must leave the newly acquired house at the very break of day and never come back. Get the nice estate agent to put it on the market, then buy a well-appointed flat nearer town. That was what she must do.

Most certainly.

She shifted her behind into a more comfortable position and gave the matter some more thought.

"Why?"

Why give up this lovely new-old house, just because of some noisy ghost children?

After all, they only seemed to manifest when she was on the point of waking up and that surely could be borne. Repetition was already veneering the phenomenon with the gloss of familiarity, which in due course might well breed a kind of contempt.

Children? She should have had children if only their production had not necessitated a rather revolting physical function. Now she might acquire some without any effort on anyone's part: children that did not require feeding, clothing, cosseting, washing or any other beastly service.

Dream children. Ghostly waifs.

Celia rose from the lavatory pan, automatically pulled the chain, then bravely walked out of the bathroom. She crossed the landing and stood (for no particular reason) looking down over the bannisters. She cleared her throat three times, before calling out in a sing-song voice:

"Come on . . . children. Come to Mummy. Come to Mummy."

This language had always worked with a kitten she had once owned, but the ghost children seemed to be unimpressed. Not a sight or sound greeted eye or ear and presently Celia went back to bed, there surprisingly to fall into a deep sleep and not awake until the morning sun had turned the window into a golden square.

"Ghost children," Miss Broadfield-Blythe said gently, tapping Celia's knee with a pointed forefinger, "are the most harmless of wraiths. You see, my dear, they are seeking love."

Celia refilled her guest's cup and replaced a blue-woollen cosy on the tea-pot.

"Is that so?"

"Indeed it is. No doubt during their brief lives they never experienced that precious emotion and are now spending eternity looking for it."

"I've only seen one child," Celia pointed out, "although I've heard others. I think there's four or five."

Miss Broadfield-Blythe closed and opened her watery blue eyes, then rubbed her long nose.

"Bound to be more than one, but not more than six I'd say. Never in my long experience have I known there to be more than six ghost-children in one group. When I received your most interesting letter, I said to Mildred—we've worked on many a case together—I said, Mildred, a mass juvenile haunting, but not more than six, I'll be bound. Tell me, Miss Watson . . . It is Miss?"

Celia nodded.

"How sensible. Tell me, Miss Watson, how did you come to contact me? Did someone recommend me?"

"No, I saw your advertisement in the tobacconist's window. As I've made no progress myself, I thought an expert might be more successful."

Miss Broadfield-Blythe screwed up her face into an expression that might have denoted puzzlement and asked:

"Progress? Success? I'm not with you, dear. What kind of progress had you in mind?"

"Well, to bring the children out of hiding. I mean—I only hear or see them just before I wake up. Properly wake up, that is. I want to—well—make contact. See and hear them when wide-awake."

"For what reason, dear? Not to experiment I hope? Our spirit friends are not at all happy when experimented with."

Celia fluttered her hands. "No, indeed. I want . . . want . . . to sort of adopt them."

A wonderful smile spread slowly over Miss Broadfield-Blythe's face and for a while lent it a kind of beauty. "That's simply gorgeous, dear. Simply heart-stopping." She pulled forth an enormous handkerchief from a patch pocket. "Want to adopt poor, love-seeking spirit children! God bless you, my dear." She patted her eyes several times, then resolutely put the handkerchief away. "But let's get down to our muttons. What can I do to help you?"

Celia put on her little-I'm-lost-girl act, which had never been known to fail when dealing with masculine inclined middle-aged spinsters. "I rather hoped you'd be able to do something that will bring them out. Let me see and talk to them."

The lady medium looked thoughtful. "I will do my best, dear. Can't do more. No one can. I'll see what can be done with the atmosphere. Sort of taste it."

She pushed her tea cup to one side, laid her hands palms uppermost on the table, then closed her eyes. Presently she giggled. "One of them is tickling me. Right in the centre of my right hand. How charming." She called out in the same sing-song voice that Celia had used a few days before:

"Come to me, children dears. Come to your Auntie Ag, who you need not fear. Put your tweeny hands in mine and we'll say hullo to your mummy-to-be. Won't that be nice? Yes it will. Yes it will."

A loud crash came from above stairs, which sounded as if the cut-glass perfume container that resided on Celia's dressing table, had been knocked—or thrown—on to the floor. But that was all.

Miss Broadfield-Blythe intoned other inducements, but for all the response they received, she might as well have saved her breath. Presently she released a gentle sigh and said:

"Well, I'm sure I've stirred them up. Brought them to the surface, so to speak. You'll probably get results after I'm gone. Nothing startling at first. It takes time for this kind of thing to get really under way. But so far as I'm concerned there doesn't seem to be much more I can do. Not for today at any rate."

"I can't thank you enough," Celia replied. "If nothing else, you've put the entire business on a commonplace plane, which is truly remarkable. At least I won't be frightened now, no matter what I see or hear."

"Frightened! Why on earth should you be frightened? Those who have passed over, have no wish to frighten us. No wish at all. Just one little point, my dear. My fee is ten pounds."

For several days after Miss Broadfield-Blythe's visit, Celia saw and heard nothing, which was both a relief and a disappointment. A relief because she had by no means lost that inner dread which afflicts everyone who comes face to face with the unusual; disappointment, because she wanted to play the game of adopting dream children. One of those fantasies which it would be well if it never came to fulfilment.

Then one Sunday morning when the time-erupting sound of church bells was disturbing the dust of long-dead memories, a ripple of childish laughter came from the landing, followed by the thud of footsteps running down the stairs. Celia, who was about to open the front door, spun round, but there was nothing untoward to see. Nothing at all.

So she went out into the porch, double-locked the front door behind her, then went to church—a weekly social event she always enjoyed.

The old church with its stained-glass windows and lingering aroma that was comprised of burnt candles, prayer books and damp, made her for some reason think of crumbling tombs and deep underground vaults, where the noble dead have slept for centuries. Then the sunlight was filtered through the stained-glass and did something wonderful to a young girl's hair, even while it revealed the gaunt face of an old man, and caused a shadow-mask to form round his deep-sunken eyes.

Choirboys' high-pitched treble voices sent a melody of sound up to the ancient rafters, before crashing open doors in Celia Watson's brain, and an impression of long-long ago childhoods came drifting out on multi-coloured clouds, even as dust-motes drifted along light beams formed by sunlight and stained-glass.

The brain was quite unable to deal with this experience and closed down its awareness, so that Celia's next impression was that of shaking hands with the vicar who had hastened to the front porch for that purpose. She walked home in a not unpleasant bemused state, even though she knew—positively knew—something exciting was about to happen.

When she opened her front door, she could not be certain if three or four small shapes raced up the stairs and disappeared on the landing, but the brain suggested in an abstract sort of way that such may have been the case. She removed her hat and coat, went into the kitchen, there opened the gas-oven door and inspected the fillet-end of a leg of lamb, which had been sizzling gently on a low heat for two hours. Almost ready. The roast potatoes had also acquired a rich crisp brown-ness, and it only remained for her to ignite the gas ring under a saucepan of garden peas for Sunday lunch to be well on its way towards full preparation. She had long ago dispensed with apple pie and custard, which had been a permanent feature of childhood Sunday dinner, but those were the days when plumpness was considered to be a sign of good health.

She turned, reached out for a towel on which to wipe her hands—and saw them.

The little girl—the one she had seen before—and a slightly older boy dressed in a blue velvet suit—were standing in the kitchen doorway, watching her.

First the dread-chill which ran up from her feet and threatened to paralyse her heart; then the wonderment—the suggestion of joy—and the realisation she was viewing two ghosts (hateful word) in full daylight, while wide-awake and at close quarters. And it was no use trying to quell the racing heart and rub sweaty hands on the skirt of her dress, for the blend of emotions was sending some kind of current down through her nerve-grid and she was laughing and crying, both at the same time, and the two children continued to watch her, the hint of a smile on their angel faces.

With one hand she wiped tears from her streaming eyes and stretched out the other towards the two apparitions, half-hoping, half-dreading to make some kind of contact, but they continued to stare at her, the smile more pronounced, verging on derision. Then they started to drift away from her, back through the doorway, across the hall, until the two shapes were nothing more than splodges of coloured light on the far wall—the product of sunshine and glass.

Celia called out: "Come back . . . come back," and as though in derisive reply, the sound of childish laughter came from above stairs.

She slept hardly at all that night, the habit of trying to look in every direction at once, which she had acquired during the daylight hours, became even more pronounced once the sun had set. To lie in bed with the lights full on, jerking the head from side to side, straining the ears to catch every sound, became nerve-racking to say the least, particularly when fear became stronger than the desire to acquire ghost-dream children. To Celia it seemed nothing short of ridiculous that she should dread and desire. It was a state of being that surpassed being distinctly funny and verged on insanity.

Not until the sun sent its first infant shafts of light through the window curtains, did she relax on to her sweat-moist pillows and slip into an uneasy sleep. When she awoke much later in the morning, she was in time to see a small arm and shoulder disappear round the half-open door and experienced the by now familiar feeling of pleasure blended with fear.

No further phenomenon manifested for the next few weeks, and such was Celia's anxiety, she often forgot to eat, wash or change her clothes. In consequence people—particularly those who did not like her—began making half-pitying, half-scornful remarks and generally conjecture why this lapse from pride-in-appearance had taken place. The vicar decided it was his duty to investigate.

"The place is an awful mess," Celia objected.

The vicar, a tall handsome man with thick white hair, gave her a most charming smile and said: "But I've come to see you, dear lady, not your house. Please, I have walked a long way this morning and really would appreciate a cup of coffee."

This request—some might call it a command—for hospitality from a man of the cloth, could not be ignored, so Celia could do no less than stand to one side and allow the reverend gentleman to enter. He gave the living-room a quick glance and had to agree the place was indeed in an awful mess, for apart from an accumulation of dust, screwed-up balls of writing paper lay on the floor, table, chairs and mantelpiece; one half-sheet which seemed to have unrolled itself, caught his eye and he managed to decipher the words scrawled with a black ball point pen: *Come to me chi*

But if the room was in an awful mess, the woman could be aptly described as a wreck of her former self. Grey hair—strangely he could not remember seeing a single grey hair on her head before today—hung in rat-tails round and over a white-lined face; heavy blue pouches, drooped under watery eyes, which seemed to be in danger of running down sunken cheeks. A slight but persistent tic quivered at the right of her mouth, while there was a distinct tremor of the right hand.

This she raised and waved in the direction of a deep armchair. "Seat yourself, vicar, and I'll fetch you a cup of coffee."

The clergyman shook his head. "No, allow me to get you one. The kitchen is through there—" he in turn pointed to an open doorway "—as I remember. I used to visit this house in the days of Mrs. Fortescue."

"Really, I could not possibly allow you to..."

"Nonsense. You are clearly unwell and I'm quite capable of waiting on myself and you. Now you seat yourself. I'll find everything."

Celia did as she was bid, but watched the vicar disappear into the kitchen with great concern, and once called out: "It's in an awful mess... The coffee jar is on the shelf over the sink and there should be milk in the fridge..."

He returned after a lapse of ten minutes, carrying two mugs of steaming coffee and wearing an expression of deep anxiety.

"I found the coffee, but the milk in your refrigerator seems to have gone off, but fortunately I managed to unearth a tin of condensed. In fact your supply of fresh food seems to be—well—rather in the same state as the milk. Due no doubt to the sultry weather. But I do think someone should do something about clearing out—the debris—and re-stocking. I do really. But first drink this coffee. I did find some biscuits, but they were distinctly soggy."

"I'm so sorry, but I've been very busy lately, I've rather let things go..."

The vicar seated himself on the edge of the chair and took a tentative sip from his mug of coffee. "Please, no apologies are necessary. My job is to help and understand. Miss Watson—Celia—you are without doubt sorely troubled. Trouble shared is trouble halved. Please allow me to halve your trouble, then possibly discard the remainder."

This rather puzzling offer was accompanied by such a charming smile, Celia for the first time in a long while dared to hope that a male might have the necessary acumen to give sound advice and even understand what must be a unique situation. But still she hesitated.

"I'm not sure, Mr..."

"Rodney, Celia. Please."

"Yes, well yes, Mr... Rodney. I mean I'm not sure if you'll fully understand my problem. You see..."

"Yes, Celia?"

"The fact is this house is . . . well . . . "

"Rather lonely for one person?"

"No, far from it. No . . . It is haunted by the ghosts of at least five children."

The Reverend Rodney emptied his coffee cup and placed it gently on a nearby low table, and took one of Celia's hands in his.

"Dear Celia, let us take one point at time. Firstly we know that ghosts—as such—do not exist. When the body dies, the soul goes straight to Heaven, or—sadly—straight to the place of atonement. There can be no lingering."

Normally Celia would have accepted this dogma from a man of the cloth as literal truth, but now, having some first-hand evidence of ghosts, she was inclined to question the reverend gentleman's logic.

"But Mr . . . Rodney, cannot some souls, such as children's souls be not quite ready for such an extreme—grand place as Heaven—the other place being out of the question—and prefer to—well—stay where they were in life. Right here. It makes sense to me."

"What makes sense to us, Celia, need not make sense to the Almighty. This is the plane of sin and flesh. I need hardly point out how the two go together. Above is the world of light. Below the world of darkness. There are no age groups in eternity."

Celia took a deep breath and released a flow of words that revealed the truth as she saw it.

"But I have seen and heard the ghosts—disembodied souls of children. Here in this house—this room. First as dream figures—then as clearly as I see and hear you. And they need love. And I have so much to give, having sort of saved it up over the years. Please don't lie and tell me they don't exist."

The Reverend Rodney assumed a very grave expression and clearly thought deeply before answering. Then he cleared his throat and after regaining possession of Celia's right hand (which she displayed signs of wanting to withdraw), said in a deep attractive voice:

"Dear Celia, I am not going to dismiss what you have told me as the result of a fevered, even neurotic, imagination, brought about by loneliness and frustration—but I have heard stories about this house, which up to this time I never credited as being other than complete moonshine. But now..."

He paused for a while, then went on. "So far as I can gather this house—a long while ago—was inhabited by a couple called Ferguson—Jacob and Sarah Ferguson. And they did have five children—four boys and a girl. That must be admitted. There were five children. All ranging from five to thirteen years. The parents practised what they and some of their contemporaries called the old religion. In other words the black arts, devil-worship—witchcraft. The children were corrupted from birth and in time—for young minds are malleable—became even more evil than their parents. No one knows how the end came about, but it is assumed that the children killed their mother, then the father massacred them, before committing suicide himself. But there is one school of opinion that maintains it was the other way round. The children killed both parents, then themselves by some secret ritual, which ensured their souls would be withheld from torment and confined to the walls of this house. This I must disbelieve, but in view of your experience I am inclined to believe some personality residue, or manifestation of past evil, still lingers here. There can be no doubt you must leave this house at once. Leave it and never come back. It seems possible you have the kind of mind that can pick up impressions, time debris... I don't know. But you must leave this house."

Celia gazed upon the vicar with mounting anger, all her mistrust of the opposite sex revived. When he had finished speaking and given her hand a final squeeze, she remained silent for some while, before saying in a carefully controlled voice:

"First of all, vicar, I do not believe a single word of that horrid story. If there is a basis of truth in it, then the wicked parents left the poor little things to die of ill-treatment, and now their innocent souls are demanding—demanding, do you hear?—the love and protection that was never theirs in life. I intend to remain here and provide that love and protection."

"Celia..."

"My name is Miss Watson."

"Celia, you are dreadfully mistaken. This house is bad for you.

Believe me. I am convinced that is the truth. A hundred other people might be able to live here undisturbed. But not you. Come to the vicarage until ..."

"I would be obliged if you would leave now."

"You must allow me to convince you ..."

"I do not wish to be rude. Please leave now. And do not come back."

He conjured up a very wry smile. "I do hope I'm wrong and sincerely apologise if I have needlessly upset you. I should not have told you that ridiculous story, but if you can see and hear ..."

"Shut the door behind you as you go out."

"I hate ... simply hate ..."

"Pull the door sharply to or the Yale lock will not engage. I believe the wood is warped."

The slam of the front door was a prelude to an unnatural silence and the ensuing loneliness (a state she had never known before) possibly the reason for the sudden fit of crying. Her shoulders shook, tears poured down her cheeks, and it seemed as if the grief of a lifetime had suddenly found an outlet and was now smashing down all the carefully erected barricades of indifference.

But the fit passed, she wiped her eyes, gulped back one last sob and went into the sitting-room.

All five ghost children were waiting for her. The tallest one—blond hair, bright eyes, dressed in a green suit—standing by the window: the next—not so tall, auburn hair, dark eyes, in a long brown coat—to the left of the doorway. The little boy and girl she had seen before—to the left of the doorway: and another boy, of medium height, dressed in black, a long robe affair, his black eyes glittering in a rather alarming fashion if one looked at them too long. His black hair hung down to his shoulders.

Not one moved. Not so much as a blink or the merest movement of a finger. Motionless effigies. Three dimensional shadows of what had been. Images recreated from personality debris by her brain and projected by her eyes. Maybe the vicar had instinctively pinpointed the truth of the matter, but she could not believe these five shades had anything evil in their make-up. That must be impossible.

Now to give them life and make them her own.

She called softly. "Come, children. There's nothing to fear in this house now. I will be a mother to you all. Take from me the essence you need to live again. To be always with me, awake or asleep. So I can hear your voices, your footsteps—if possible feel your hands touching me."

The little boy and girl (they might have been twins) were the first to move. They glided to her and came to rest some two feet away, heads tilted, eyes looking up into hers. But she could not detect a glimmer of intelligence. Merely the glitter that might be reflected in the eyes of some animal. Then the tallest came to her and stood behind the twins (if such they were) and looked into her eyes (or so it seemed). Then came the lad in brown who took up a position to her right; finally the one in black—all save the dead-white face.

Her fearful-hopeful dream had been fulfilled. She was half-surrounded by the five ghost children.

Now what to do with them?

She turned and after saying: "Follow me, children," led the way into the kitchen. At least such was her intention, but when she looked back they had not moved. All stood in the same positions, staring at that spot she had just vacated, motionless again, and she giggled.

"Silly me. They will not be hungry. Food and kitchens mean nothing to them. It is love they need."

She went back to them and bending down whispered the wonderful message. "Children, I want you to know you are mine—I am yours from now on. Do you understand? We now belong to each other. Your loneliness is over. So is mine."

The boy in black moved slightly. His eyes gleamed like sparks floating in the dark.

"Can no one—not a single one of you, give me some sign that you understand?" Celia pleaded. "Don't let that awful clergyman be right. Please."

They all vanished. Were switched off. Were no more.

Celia spent the rest of the day looking for them.

The bed had come with the house and was very wide. Celia had always slept in a three-foot bed, never having had occasion to require anything larger. This might have been the reason she slept on the left side of this

giant and never parted upper from lower sheet on the right. Despite—
or maybe because of—the experience of that day, she slept soundly all
night; sank into a deep coma of unawareness that drugged every sense,
save for the one which had never been explained.

Then she awoke and lay quite still, knowing the unexpected had
happened, but unwilling at that moment to open her eyes and discover
what shape it had taken.

The senses returned to seventy-five percent normality, the brain
expelled the fog of sleep, but still Celia kept her eyes tight closed,
conjecture creating mental pictures that were without understanding.

Then hearing recorded a sound. Low childish laughter. Not far off,
but near—in this room—by—or on—her bed.

The demand to know would not be denied. Celia opened her eyes.

The window curtains were drawn apart and the room was flooded
with silver moonlight and revealed their slender forms in every detail.
All five children were seated on her bed. The two small ones, the twins,
on the spare pillows, the tall boy and he in brown way down at the
foot and he in black lying on his stomach, his head turned in her direction, the black eyes now glittering with an alien intelligence.

Joy came shuffling on reluctant feet, for had they not come to her,
sought her out of their own accord, and surely it was not their fault
they had so white faces, or that the lad in black should have rather
frightening eyes.

They had that death-beauty that rightfully belongs to some vivid
nightmare that has long been forgotten by the active mind, but still
can be recalled by the subconscious at that moment which separated
sleep from awakening. Celia thought briefly of sleeping castles where
mist formed strange shapes in ruined corridors.

She tried to sit up, but for some reason her body refused to obey the
dictates of her brain, although she was permitted to turn her head from
side to side, but that was hardly an asset, for some of the joy seeped
away every time she met the glittering-eyed gaze of the lad in black.

Then a giggle came from one or maybe all of them; a deep-throated
inane giggle that had the suggestion of a squeal, and undiluted fear
slid into her mind and she became as one who has encouraged the
presence of half-grown tigers. Instinct warned body and mind as she

succeeded in sitting up, but as freedom of movement returned to her, so, it would seem, it did to them. They all drifted off the bed and blanket and sheets went with them. Then the squealing inane giggle blending with the tearing of her nightdress, and they moved, danced, round the bed, while she called out in fear-joy ecstasy.

"No, children, you must not be so naughty. Please . . . please . . . you will hurt Mummy . . ."

The giggling became louder, the five moved faster until they became a whirling mass of coloured mist; a scratch appeared on Celia's right shoulder and seeped a thin trail of blood down her back. Her hair stood on end and she screamed when it was tugged abruptly. Invisible fingers poked at her naked flesh, pinched and punched, while a roaring darkness threatened to engulf her. Then all movement ceased as she was left trembling on the bed, as the dreadful five congregated in the doorway. All had dead-white faces now and everyone giggled, ejected the inane squealing sound from between lax lips.

Celia raised herself up onto her elbows and managed to speak reproachfully with a sob-racked voice.

"You naughty-naughty children. You've hurt and frightened Mummy who only wanted to love you."

The giggling took on a higher-pitched tone and the five turned and fled over the landing and running footsteps could be heard descending the stairs.

Then for a while silence—and loneliness.

For two days Celia dismissed the minor destruction as nothing more than infantile mischief with no sinister intent. All glass jars and bottles were smashed, the refrigerator door refused to stay shut, then ceased to function. "They don't understand," she told the empty house. "If they had been reared in a loving atmosphere, they wouldn't be like this. Never mind, patience and endurance will work the miracle. It must."

But on the morning of the third day, when she distinctly saw the lad in black dart from under her right elbow and deliberately upset the frying pan in which she was cooking some sausages, thus causing a roaring flame to soar up towards the ceiling and all but set her hair alight, then she very reluctantly accepted that the children were not just mischievous, but had at least some evil propensities.

But it made not the slightest difference.

Beauty can hide any number of imperfections and love can explain away any number of crimes. In an odd sort of way it was rather exciting having to keep one's wits alert as to what traps they had set overnight. The foot stool placed at the very top of the stairs, the bare patch of electric wiring, the turned-on gas taps that just needed a lighted match to send her hurtling into eternity. Probably join them in that dimension they inhabit. So far as was possible she experienced surprise at the ingenuity which resulted in the topmost cellar step being transformed into a death hazard by means of spirit of salts (transported from the loo) poured on the wooden supports. Had not her nose transmitted a warning, the undermined tread would have collapsed under her right foot.

"Artful monkeys," she murmured, after successfully smothering the blast of terror that threatened to destroy beyond repair the bastion of sanity. "I wonder what they'll think of next?"

If they were capable of thought, there was little for them to think of, from then on Celia rarely left a chair she had dragged into the hall, this being the place "her family" were most likely to materialise. She smiled indulgently when the twins removed her shoes and flung them across the room and laughed softly when the Reverend Rodney climbed in through the sitting-room window, then somehow finished up on the topmost cellar step. After the initial scream, he never bothered her again.

"I should have had children," she announced again and again. "I should have considered the possibility of having children, long ago. They are such a comfort."

In fact they gave her more than comfort. More likely satisfaction, fulfilment, a most gratifying understanding that she had not lived a solitary life in vain. For the children grew fatter, particularly the lad in black who became positively bloated. They never acquired the slightest hint of colour, for all their faces retained that rather disconcerting dead-white complexion, but Celia was certain it was a healthy pallor.

For herself—well—occasionally she became aware of her own alarming thinness, the fact that her hands were well-nigh transparent and she lacked the strength to do more than sit in her chair. But presently she took little interest in such mundane matters, for the antics of her family demanded all of her time. How they ran up and down stairs, in and out of those rooms she could see from her position in the hall, chasing each other, stopping now and again to plant a burning kiss on bare flesh, a reward out of all proportion to any slight discomfort she might suffer.

And they squealed with joyful excitement. Yes, really squealed with unrestrained joy. And Celia expressed joy with some such sound, for had she not at last managed to create a happy family?

They came in through the sitting-room window, the one the Reverend Rodney had inadvertently left open. Tall burly men in blue uniforms, followed by a more slender one in a neat grey suit.

He was the only one to be actually sick. One of the others exclaimed: "Oh, my God!" But generally speaking they were all fairly immune against being upset by the extremely unpleasant. Two made their way to the cellar steps, only to return a few minutes later, when the one with the three white chevrons on his right arm, stated briefly:

"The missing parson isn't missing any more. At the bottom of the steps, what's left of him. Oh, my Gawd! Look at them!"

Shouts that expressed horror, disgust and downright loathing, followed five bloated rats as they raced up the stairs.

A Walk on the Dark Side

A WIFE CAN play many roles. Cook, housekeeper, companion, bed-fellow, mother, gardener, interior and exterior decorator, window-cleaner and, on (hopefully) rare occasions, husband-killer. Of course, such a nice, beautiful, well-bred wife like Mary would not be so crude as to think of herself as a husband killer. And, as for murder, I very much doubt if such a word could be found in her entire vocabulary. Husband *removing* maybe. Putting down for his own good; necessary vaporising; erasure; helping into a better world; I rather like that, and I'm sure Mary does also. She is a kind person at heart and would try to convince herself she was doing me a favour.

I first became aware of my graveward journey when I trod on a bar of pink toilet soap that had been placed so conveniently on the top stair, so that when I went hurtling forward I hit that part of the banisters that had been skilfully weakened by an expert.

I recognised Leslie Bromley's work at once. He's very good with his hands and should have been a carpenter, but of course his snobbish mother insisted he work hard for little money so he could rise to the exalted height of Railway Executive.

My best friend and my ever-loving wife was a combination guaran-teed to loosen the most obstinate bowel and create nightmares in the most well-organised brain. My journey down the stairs and through the banisters did not fulfil their fondest hopes, but I landed on the hall carpet with a broken leg and several cracked ribs.

How Mary wept over me, kissed and fondled me so that I trembled like a sinful man on Judgement Day and begged to be told what I must do to make her really happy! She explained with a soft lilting voice and hands that were never still.

"Henry, I love you very much and will be very sad if—or when— something dreadful happens to you. But, you see, although I love you very much, I have come to love dear Leslie even more and he—well— he thinks I'm the most lovely, adorable person to walk the earth and that I'm very bedworthy into the bargain. He really is a most silly boy." She blushed and looked so young and innocent that I began to wonder if that bar of soap hadn't slid onto the top stair all by itself. But Mary was kind enough to explain even further. "Of course, being nice and conventional people we want to get married so as not to live in dreadful sin, but you are so against divorce."

"I might be talked into a change of heart," I suggested. Mary shook her lovely blonde head and bared her white even teeth in a dazzling smile.

"I doubt that. I honestly do. You've got such a conscience. My gosh! An awful active conscience. You'd change your mind in no time at all. Me—and darling Leslie—we've no conscience worth worrying about."

"But I . . . "

"Then there's the insurance. My word—an awful lot of money! I'm sorry, Henry, but you're worth so much more dead than alive."

Her glorious grey eyes told me she was enjoying this little exchange and, should I repeat it to a third party, those same eyes would widen with outraged astonishment and she would, furthermore, weep real tears for my insanity.

Next day, Leslie visited me all by himself and, on his knees, begged me to believe he had no wish to harm me, that he was still my best friend but that he could not help loving Mary, even while knowing she could never be his, unless—may the Good Lord forbid—some dreadful disaster removed me from the vineyard or whatever field of endeavour I happened to be toiling in when death went on the rampage.

My leg healed. I returned home. Mary insisted I spend the next week in a wheelchair. She took me for long trips along the riverbank. She pushed me—and the wheelchair—into the river. Not being able to swim, I drowned. As I went down for the third time, I could see Mary weeping piteously on the riverbank. I knew then she would make a beautiful widow.

When I returned to what could be described as consciousness, I was back in my own house and instantly became aware that Mary was explaining to two plain-clothes policemen that she was fully responsible for my untimely death and she would never—but never—forgive herself. "I should never," she explained tearfully, "have allowed him to talk me into wheeling him along the riverbank. I should have realised that my poor little arms lacked the strength to stop that heavy chair from sliding down the bank, particularly when dear Henry insisted on pushing the wheels forwards, saying he wanted to die, leaving me free to marry Leslie. As though I could ever love anyone but him!"

"Sort of 'assisted suicide'," one detective murmured and I could see that Mary thought he was coarse. The other one played his side of the record.

"Come off it, Charlie. There's no way she could hold that chair back once it had gone over the edge. The bank's steep thereabouts."

"Yeah. I know. But how did the chair come to be over the edge?"

"Charlie, you don't listen. The lady has explained. The dear departed pulled the right wheel over to the right, making it go over the edge. Could happen to anyone."

Mary clearly thought it was about time she made an at least token protest, but I could see she was half-scared out of her young life, seeing that authority seemed to be entertaining dire suspicions as to how I had come to my watery end. Well, an end to regular breathing, although otherwise I seemed to be alive—aware of my surroundings, gifted with sight and hearing. But not the slightest sign of a body. A mere speck of consciousness that floated some six feet above ground level. Life of a kind. Better than oblivion, which quite frankly was all I had ever expected.

The two men got up, Mary remained seated. The elder—the one who played the role of nasty policeman—said softly, "Opinions don't go very far with our superiors or the public prosecutor, so maybe we won't be back. But I tell you, young lady, your pretty face notwithstanding, there's a little man in my stomach who won't give me any peace. He will insist you pushed that poor bugger of a husband over the river bank, then sat back and watched while he choked his life away."

"You're an awful man," Mary stated tearfully, "and I'm going to complain."

"You do that. Yeah, I'd say you should complain about the awful copper who knows bloody well . . . "

"That's enough, Charlie," the nice policeman said. Then they both nodded to Mary and the nasty one said, "We'll let ourselves out. You sit there and have a good worry. Think, if your dear departed hubby still exists in some form or the other, he must hate your guts and if it's at all possible, he'll come back to do you dirt."

They left, and I came to rest a few feet above Mary and listened to her sobbing—not, I fear, from grief at my passing, but because the nasty policeman had upset her. Strange, but although my wife could commit murder and be completely untouched by the pangs of conscience, she was extremely sensitive. A harsh word, a frown, a hostile silence; any could reduce her to tears and rob her of sleep until peace had been restored. She spoke aloud.

"Henry, I know you've gone to a better world." Yes, that was her only comforting thought. She had sent me to a better world.

I tried to speak, too. "No, I'm not. I'm right here. And I intend to give you hell!" But although I could *think* the words, I seemed to lack the ability to *speak* them: in fact everything seemed to be one-sided. I could see and hear Mary, but I was invisible and silent to her. An atom of consciousness afloat in eternity.

I drifted very slowly downwards until I was a few inches from her face, gazing into those clear blue-grey eyes, trying to see the soul which must reside somewhere back in the brain. Alas, only eyes much magnified and awash with tears. I thought-shouted, "Murdering bitch!" before being hurtled back in a storm of impotent rage. Back and forth across the room, until I either willed myself to a halt or bumped into a particularly solid surface.

Rage faded; curiosity—always a besetting sin so far as I was concerned—demanded its due and I began to experiment, willing myself up to the ceiling, then down to the floor; sinking into thick carpet pile; shrinking to an atom of awareness in a vast red, blue and amber forest where minute insect life became visible to my special vision. Then I streaked up again and—by now greatly daring—slid into Mary's left eye: swam in a grey-blue lake until I reached a red shore and was permitted to float into the dimly lit interior of Mary's mind.

One might expect me to describe a fearsome place where the spectre of a red-handed monster shrieked over slime-coated rocks and roaring creatures raised sightless heads to a fire-tinted sky. Not a bit of it. A boring plain that seemingly stretched out to a far distant horizon; swirling dust-devils that danced a slow quadrille before collapsing into a rippling sea; a cold wind that consisted of gusty sighs and the occasional gasping cry. I made for the command post, the steps hewn out of pink rock—or some substance that looked very like it—and, after climbing them, eventually entered a small chamber with what looked like pork—or possibly veal—walls. They glistened with moisture (maybe water—diluted blood), and as the floor heaved slightly I was grateful for my disembodied state, for I am certain solid feet would have sunk into that dark brown morass.

I could see out of two blue-grey windows and looked upon the room where I had leapt from floor to ceiling but a few seconds before, prior to entering Mary's eyes. Was she aware, I wondered, that I possessed her? Presumably not, for the body was displaying no signs of panic; the white well-shaped hands were moving, fingers interlacing, the left thumb caressing the left palm—just under the fingers. But this had always been so. Hands that were never still, restless fingers, caressing thumbs.

But—and what a wonderful thought—I had not *really* taken possession yet. Not taken over completely. Making myself felt. I was still capable of emotion. *Rage* I had already experienced, now I basked in a warm glow of *joy*. I even performed a kind of astral dance, round and round that meat-walled chamber, springing up from the offal floor to bounce off a lamb-chop ceiling, before bursting out of the eyes and drifting across the room to a blind-shaded window.

Now there could be no doubt: Mary was alarmed. The lovely eyes were wide open, the full lips slightly parted as though in preparation for the release of a scream, and at that moment I love-hated her as never before in my flesh-and-blood life. Love and hate did not die with the flesh, but blended together, becoming one new created emotion that gave the soul a strange kind of life.

I watched the trembling shoulders, the startled eyes, the agitated hands, while the need for revenge forced a silent cry from my immortal being that streaked out across the vast emptiness of time space. Then she wept, cried actual tears, as indeed she had before when I first gazed into her eyes, but now they were tears of fear.

The doorbell sent its chimes through the house and I shrank down into the carpet, trying to blot out my awareness, but curiosity and the new emotion made from love-hate would not allow me to rest and I rose up in time to see Leslie enter the room. They kissed. Lord of love-hate-right-wrong-cursed-be-forever-damned—they kissed. A terrible embrace that pressed lips to lips, breasts to torso, thighs to thighs, lust to lust, until the burning need to penetrate, accept, take, give, rend, became one ...

I had never experienced the power which had made them commit and condone murder, made them risk their very existence so that they could be together, with no one—no ridiculous little demanding turd—getting in the way, demanding a share of a prize he could not possibly appreciate.

Merciful God, *pain* had not died with the flesh, either; I experienced that soul-searing agony that is usually reserved for those who have been fathered by the gods, and with it came a need to empty the cup of vengeance to its final, butter dregs. I followed them to the bed-room, watched Leslie denude that lovely body (much as a housewife removes the coarse leaves of a cabbage so as to get to the fresh tender substance beneath), then allowed her pleasure-seeking hands to expose his white skin, his rampant manhood—and suddenly I knew the road to vengeance ran between golden fields. It took me the best part of half an hour to learn—understand—but it proved to be time well spent.

Firstly, I took my one-time friend under full control and enjoyed to the utmost the glorious betrayer—murderess—who groaned and gasped beneath him-me; then I entered her, wandered in the feminine fields and came to realise they were not so different to those reserved for man. But Lord Satan, a lifetime of frustration burst its banks, and I do believe I could have killed them both with the one and only way of unendurable pleasure—but that was not my intention.

When both lay in a state of complete exhaustion I entered the female, took up my position in the meat-wall chamber and looked out of her blue-grey eyes. He, Leslie, false friend, murderer by intent, smiled weakly and said, "You look positively ferocious, love. I could liken your glorious eyes to those of a tigress."

Mary's essence knew I was there; I could feel her seething all around me, trying to regain control but not knowing how, while I used her vocal cords to good effect.

"Do I? Perhaps you are looking at a tiger that has gotten himself into the wrong cage."

His lips curved into an obscene smirk. "After the performance you have just put up, I'm inclined to think you might be right. Perhaps murder is the ultimate aphrodisiac."

In Mary's softest tone, I said, "You are a monster, aren't you?"

"But the kind of monster you like."

I made her lips perform a seductive smile. "How lovingly kind you are. Tell me, did you like Henry?"

I watched the cloud pass over his face, the brief flash in his eyes, and knew the cold wind of apprehension was sending its whimpering cry along the corridors of his brain. Still, his voice was calm. "I liked him well enough. A contemptuous liking maybe, but normally I would not have wished him harm."

"But you were willing to allow me—to remove him?"

He shrugged, and I wondered how long it would take for the cold wind of apprehension to reach gale force. "What's come over you? We got away with it, didn't we? An unfortunate accident. And hell, we did *warn* Henry. Fair's fair. We did warn him."

It was my turn to shrug. "The sickness called love blinds and deafens and strips the sufferer of all defence. The poor fool all but kissed the hands that pushed the wheelchair over the riverbank."

"Well," Leslie spoke with easy assurance, "he's gone to that land from which no one returns."

Mary's lips now assumed a grim smile. "I wouldn't swear to that. Not by any means."

"You are becoming morbid. Really, you worry me. Now is not the time for you to become all fanciful. You and I don't merely *love*, we *exist* for each other. The sins of one must be the sins of the other."

I again spoke with Mary's voice. "But suppose there is a law that demands retribution? The victim is guaranteed vengeance?"

He began to laugh. A prolonged, rumbling laugh. My anger grew so that I forgot my original intention to retain rigid control and not to reveal my continued existence until he had been carefully prepared. Mary's voice grew deeper—more masculine—and I forced it to shout.

"Laugh . . . laugh . . . but be assured the woman would scream to high Heaven if she were able! She's trying to break through meat-lined walls!"

He slid from the bed and backed to the door, his face slowly assuming an expression that portrayed horrified astonishment. Words dribbled from his lax lips. "You've cracked! My God! You're crawling up the wall!"

I sensed the germ of purpose that was coming into being—kill the woman lest her deranged brain make her tongue wag, and I could see his eyes moving from side to side looking for some object that could be used as an instrument of murder. But I was nearer to the heavy bedside lamp and I heard the plug leave the socket, the woman's screaming voice in her-my head, for she knew how this must end. Then I was transforming that hated face into blood-drenched ruin; splintering bone, snarling, kicking, truly alive as never before in my entire existence.

Then it was over, bloody vengeance complete and, after permitting the woman's body to move, forced it to take up the telephone receiver and dial the local police station. For the last time I spoke with her voice. "This is Mrs. Mary Smith of 23, Winslow Drive. You may be interested to know I have just killed my lover, Leslie George Bromley. This is my second murder. I'd be obliged if you would send along the two officers who investigated my husband's death."

Then I took her back to the bed and made her gaze upon the corpse that was looking more ugly by the second, and did not vacate her body until the doorbell rang.

Mary did not move, so the two men had to find their own way in—through a window, I believe—and presently ambled into the bedroom. The one called Charlie—the nasty one—shook his head as though in sad reproach. "Naughty. Trying to corner the market? I must say you did a good job."

Mary tried to explain, to tell the truth as she understood it. "It wasn't me. It was my husband, Henry. He got into my head and made me . . . my body do it."

Charlie looked at his companion. "You've got to hand it to her. I mean, having bumped off the husband, she then blames him for bumping off the boyfriend! That's class—real class."

The nice policeman shook his head even more sadly. "You don't get it, Charlie. She's trying to let us know she's round the bend, bonkers, up the pole."

"You don't say so!"

"Sure. I mean, if she can convince the Chief Super and a few head shrinkers, there'll be no trial. Just a nice comfy room in the loony-bin."

Charlie leaned down and looked into Mary's eyes. He spoke very softly: "Not on your proverbial nelly. Not a hope in Hell. Let's take her down to the station."

The nice policeman nodded agreement. "Yeah, let's do that."

At the doorway, Charlie stopped and looked back over one shoulder. Then he said, "You poor bugger, if you had anything to do with . . . But no—that's impossible. But if you *are* hanging about, relax. Call it a day. We'll take over from now on."

After they had gone I drifted out into the street and looked for the last time at the world I had known, then rose slowly up towards the cloudless sky.

I had started the long journey to the stars.

DAY SCHOOL

1

FEAR WAS A demon that rode on the shoulders of my elders and controlled their every action, word and thought. If a passer-by was seen to glance up at our house, lights were extinguished, curtains carefully parted and everyone peered out into the quiet, usually deserted street, while whispered questions came drifting through the gloom, like tiny winged ghosts fleeing from a grim pursuer.

I cannot remember hearing laughter in our house during my formative years, although Great Uncle Manfred did sometimes emit a kind of rumbling chuckle that was apt to taper off into a fearsome growl. Later, after Mother and Father had more or less explained the situation, I did realise my family had little to laugh about, and could only wonder why they were not in a perpetual state of tears. Of course at that early age I had to have the unpalatable facts camouflaged under a thick coating of pretence.

"Oh Monday," Mother said, creasing her beautiful face into an expression of anticipatory delight, "you will start school. Day school."

"The state insists," Father added as though determined to get his two cents worth in before Mother really got under way. "All kids have to go to a state school otherwise some interfering busybody comes . . ."

Mother cut him short with an impatient wave of her hand, a gesture he had learned never to ignore. Then she gave me a reassuring smile.

"Day school will be very nice. You will be able to learn lots of things it is important for you to know. There is really nothing for you to worry about—so long as you are very careful."

My reaction was terse and to the point.

"I will hate the meat-eaters' school."

Mother captured a sigh and turned it into a low laugh.

"Nonsense, just keep out of the sunlight. The principal has been given a certificate from Doctor Rosten that says you have a unique disease that will make you very ill should you be subjected to strong sunlight. Do you understand?"

I said yes, although the entire business was extremely confusing. I asked an intelligent question.

"Why should anyone go out into the sunlight? They will drip."

Father cleared his throat. "Meat-eaters do not drip. The sun cannot harm them at all. In fact they get out under the naked every moment they can. Nothing pleases them more than when they are baked brown."

Mother burst into tears and refused to be comforted by Father who kept saying: "He will be all right—he is very smart for his age," and I cried as well for by now I was scared silly. Then they both went into the next room and my primary education was postponed until the following evening, when the entire nest turned up to give moral support.

They poured into our small front room just after sunset and consisted of: Uncles Lucas, Kincaid, Balmoral and Gore, closely followed by aunts Matilda, Millicent, Rosealea and Tita, not to mention cousins Remi, Chandos, Aylward, Movita, Amber, Calota and a few whose names I could never remember. All were handsome or beautiful, and not one looked a day over twenty-five.

Great-Uncle Manfred, who arrived ten minutes after everyone else, was a different matter entirely. Tall, lean, black hair untouched by grey, he did not look old—but matured. We all stood up when he entered and did not move until he was seated in my father's favourite chair. His beautiful deep voice pronounced words as though each one were an intricate part of a prose poem, that once recited would never be heard again.

"The time has come," he said, "when our precious little one—the first cub to be born in this nest for two hundred years—must venture out into the cruel world of the meat-eaters.

"Would that by Beldaza's grace he could be spared this ordeal, for although we are a species set apart, we must bow down before certain laws ordained by those among who we live. This will not always be so, for although we are but a pitiful few, our nests wide apart, the day will surely come when our numbers will be as the sands of the desert."

Everyone nodded gravely and one or two murmured: "Be it so," but even I knew that no one really believed this miraculous multiplying would ever come about. Great-Uncle Manfred smiled gently and continued:

"And now must I address myself to the little one and arm him with the sword of knowledge, so that he will know how to act in the ranks of our enemies. Let him be brought forth."

I was—most reluctantly—'brought forth'. That is to say my father and mother all but dragged me towards the great partaker and seated me on a small stool at his feet. He looked down at me and never before or since have I seen such pity and love that lit his wonderful eyes.

"Carlos, you must listen carefully and do your best to understand what I am about to tell you. In an earlier age it would not have been necessary to burden your brain with such knowledge, until you had reached the time of fulfilment. But now we cannot hide you from official eyes and if we do not send you to their place of education many questions will be asked and that must not be. Nothing must endanger the existence of the nest. Should you succumb, fall by the wayside and in so doing so arouse curiosity, then will we decamp, disappear into the darkness and no hand will be raised to help you."

Mother cried out and was instantly hushed into silence by those standing around her. Great Uncle Manfred ignored the interruption and continued:

"We are the old ones. The Partakers. When meat-eaters cringed in caves we walked upright under the night sky. But immortality is a terrible burden for us to carry, even though Beldaza in his great mercy has drawn a veil over all that has taken place up to the last hundred years, save for one—like myself who can recall long dead centuries after long and arduous concentration."

He paused and I dared to ask a question. "What is im . . . mortality?"
Great-Uncle Manfred nodded his approval.

"A thirst for knowledge is a priceless gift. It means you-will-always-be so long as you walk the Earth along a devious path. For understand, my son, the few who know of our existence, hate us with a hatred that passeth all understanding. They have devised ways in which we can be destroyed and do not hesitate to use them. The stake driven through the heart—the head removed and the mouth stuffed with garlic—the all-consuming fire. So remember these instructions:

"Look upon all meat-eaters as your enemies.

"Guard your tongue and never let even one of them know you are a partaker.

"Worship Beldaza in your mind, but never mention his name aloud.

"Do not mistake caution for cowardice.

"Above all never let them know your intelligence is much higher than any meat-eater that has ever lived: you can blast their minds with a glance, kill with a light blow, out-run any creature on Earth, with practice change your shape. All these precious gifts has Beldaza bestowed upon you, but it is well if you do not over-use them."

Great-Uncle Manfred paused and sighed deeply. When he spoke again, his diction was less perfect.

"Alas, your path will not be an easy one. The urge to partake direct will hit you real soon, but you'll have to fight it or you're in dead trouble, seeing as how you're the first cub to be born for two hundred years."

Then he seemed to regret this lapse from conventional language and all but glared at me from my humble position at his feet. I could hear Mother's subdued sobbing, the ticking of the mantelpiece clock and the pounding of my own heart. The beautiful sonorous voice again claimed my full attention.

"The good doctor has provided certificates that will excuse you playing their barbaric games, eating their obnoxious food and going forth under the naked sun. Thus must you always appear sickly, refrain from running, jumping and indulging in pastimes that are natural to your age and over-brimming good health."

"What about their damnable crosses?" a female voice that I recognised as belonging to Aunt Matilda demanded. "Will he not have something called religious instruction to contend with?"

Great-Uncle Manfred frowned and waved a hand impatiently.

"Since when has anyone been seriously put out by two pieces of crossed wood? Close-up some of us may have experienced a slight uneasiness of the stomach, an urge to spit maybe, but nothing a swig of Grade A fluid cannot cure. A young cub can soon adjust.

"But now let us pray to Beldaza to protect this young cub."

Everyone made the X sign and lowered their heads, while Great-Uncle Manfred closed his eyes and sent down a prayer to He that reigns in dark places.

"Lord Beldaza, spread thy mighty hand over this little one who is about to set out along the thorny path, beset on either side by those who wield the sharpened stake, light the destroying fire, drive out into the terrible sunlight. Protect him great Beldaza. Bmen."

A little later I was sent to bed where I spent the entire night worrying about the future.

2

When I got up on Monday morning I dared not open the curtains for the sun shone from a clear sky and boded ill for my entrance into the dreaded day school. I naturally assumed I would not have to go, as Mother had always stressed the dangers of sunlight and to date never allowed me out of the house until well after moonrise. Of course there was my solar suit, a one-piece garment made of a double thickness of asbestos and padded with moist earth, but that was only meant to be used in an emergency, as it had the tendency to transform its wearer into the likeness of a pregnant bear. In fact Mother voiced her objection while I was drinking breakfast.

"He just cannot go. I would not send my worst enemy out in this."

Father stared unhappily at his empty glass and dared to express an opinion.

"But he will have to go, Virginia. Great-Uncle Manfred said he must no matter how hot it was. Otherwise they will send someone round. My fangs are dry with terror, but he must go."

At that moment Great-Uncle Manfred came in through the back doorway, not looking at all distressed, which made me wonder if there was any substance to the rumours he could walk about in sunlight for anything up to twenty minutes without any ill-effects. He glared at my parents, then pointed a quivering forefinger at me.

"Why is not the cub attired in his solar-suit and fully prepared for the great experiment?"

Mother drew herself upright and with amazing courage spoke back to the great partaker.

"I am not sending my son out into this weather, Great-Uncle. It is absolutely out of the question. Maybe later if it clouds over..."

The bellow of rage made the windows rattle and sent my poor mother reeling back until she collided with the table. I have never before—or since—seen such a diabolical expression on any face as that which now made my Great-Uncle look like something that escaped from a particularly unpleasant nightmare. His eyes blazed with fury, his fangs slid down over his lower lip—two immense, yellow curved tusks that to my knowledge he had never revealed before—and his cheeks were covered with a network of great black veins. He took one giant step forward and, reaching out a great claw of a hand, bunched up the front of my mother's dress and pulled her towards him. His voice became a loud harsh whisper:

"He will go to the meat-eater's school even if the sky is on fire...he will go every day until he adapts or drips out of existence. And if the Blood Squad get him...if but one meat-eater knows him for what he is...then we will not weep...but go up into the black hills of Dakota and pray to Beldaza that another will be born...one that will succeed and take his place among us and them, the highborn meat-eaters. Do you understand?"

Mother, after two unsuccessful attempts to speak, gasped:

"Yes, Great-Uncle," and then she was released, or rather pushed back over the table by a single, contemptuous jerk of that great hand. Then Great-Uncle Manfred looked down at me, his eyes still filled with rage, although the black veins on his face were beginning to fade and his tusks to retract.

"I will never forget. Mighty storms swept across this planet and those that are forever seeking the highway into corporal life gathered round your natal bed. Let there be no doubt in your mind—Beldaza loves you, even though you cannot always rely on his protecting hand poised above your head. Feed your ego with unreasoning hate for all meat-eaters. If it be Beldaza's will that we never meet again, then forget us—say I have no father, no mother, no nest. I am alone—unique."

He gradually calmed down, became once again the rather pompous, dignified elder that we had always known, and after peeping through a small parting in the curtains, ordered:

"Prepare him for full sun exposure. A cab will be here shortly."

I was bundled into my solar-suit that when buttoned up covered me completely save for a narrow slit in front of the eyes; and I could scarcely breathe, being all but suffocated by an overwhelming smell of damp earth. Mother thrust a nourishment bottle into the outside pocket and issued final instructions.

"Do not let them see you partaking. Shut yourself up in the john or somewhere private. And make certain you get a seat well away from the window. And..."

She was interrupted by a loud bang on the front door and Great-Uncle Manfred said quietly: "That must be the cab man. Go along, Carlos, he knows where to take you and has been well paid."

No one accompanied me to the door, possibly because Great-Uncle Manfred would not let them, and when I opened it—there stood a man dressed in a shabby grey suit and a peaked cap who looked down at my bulging solar-suit with glaring eyes and gaping mouth. It was a full minute before either of us spoke, then he exclaimed:

"Jesus Christ!"

I said: "You are to take me to school," in a loud voice for my mouth was covered and the cabman struck me—at least in his present state—as a person who might be hard of hearing. He looked from left to right as though to ensure there were no more like me in the vicinity, before answering:

"Yeah, well we'd better get moving," and all but ran to his cab which stood on the other side of the road.

I stepped out on to the pavement and the sunlight hit me like a ton of hot bricks. I had been out for a trial walk round the back garden once—and once only—and that had not been so terrible, for there had been the knowledge I could bolt back inside any time I wanted to. But this was a different matter entirely; I had to face up to eight hours of this among meat-eaters who apparently thought sunlight was something to get excited about. I scuttled across the road and clambered on to the back seat of the cab, while the driver watched me with something akin to horror.

I had never entered such a vehicle before and normally this would have been an excited occasion, but now I was only too aware the cab was sun-drenched and, solar-suit notwithstanding, I could not dismiss the notion my body was beginning to disintegrate. Then I spotted the blinds and promptly pulled them down, an action that in no way reassured my driver who slid back a glass partition and made a request for information.

"Eh, kid, what's the game then? How come you're done up like a bundle of garbage and pulled down the blinds in broad daylight. You nuts or summat?"

I gave the first answer that came into my head.

"I am suffering from a rare disease. The sun is bad for me."

The cab began to move slowly forward as though reluctant to move at all with such a strange passenger, while the driver made disturbing sounds under his breath. Then he asked:

"Is this disease catching? I mean I wouldn't want to go round looking like you."

"No it is a family illness."

He did not speak again but began to whistle a tuneless dirge, while doing his best to watch me in the rear mirror, a course of action that I frustrated by sliding off the seat and sitting on the floor. The cab went much faster from then on, until the moment arrived when it braked to a halt and I had now to venture out into the unknown. The cabman did not look back, but stared resolutely to his front.

"Out you get kid, and make it snappy. And let those blinds up before you go. Otherwise some wise guy will think something dodgy is going on back there."

I had been trained to do what I was told, but once the off-side blind was up, I felt a nigh-overwhelming urge to pull it down again. We were parked in front of a long line of spiked railings that bordered a rectangular expanse of concrete, while beyond stood a large red-bricked building that was not enhanced so far as I was concerned by six high windows that had been transformed into blazing mirrors by the sun.

But it was the mass of young meat-eaters that ran, fought, shouted and generally behaved like the embryo monsters they were, that claimed my full attention. I could almost taste the raw energy that poured out of every moving body, smell the ferocity, lust for cruelty—the animal stench.

And I, pampered cub of a minority species, had to go among them and gaze at close quarters upon their ugliness.

For they were ugly. Beauty of face and form is one of the many gifts Beldaza has bestowed upon all partakers and I have always taken for granted their pleasing features, graceful bodies and flawless white skins. Even Great-Uncle Manfred, who at times looked terrifying, still retained his share of the pack's good looks. But I can honestly say, after making due allowance for my fear and aversion, I never found one meat-eater cub that had the slightest pretension to beauty. Their complexions were either red or muddy white; many were blotched with unsightly eruptions, enlarged pores, fractured veins; flabby, wrinkled, pocked-marked and even scarred. Bodies were either bloated or grotesquely thin, hands pudgy with blunt fingers, limbs unnaturally long or conversely too short.

And their teeth! Irregular, often each crowding its neighbour like weather-stained tombstones in an overfull graveyard, some tainted with decay: If any partaker had been so cursed with essential equipment, he or she would have gone for a long walk under the noonday sun.

I climbed down from the cab and sprinted with all speed through the open gateway, through the suddenly stilled ranks of my enemies and into the red-bricked building. There I stopped and stood trembling, at that moment nothing more than a hunted animal that had taken refuge in the first dark hole available. From the playground (Beldaza! When did these monsters play?) came a sound that I could only liken to the ominous rumble of a rising storm, followed by the shuffle of many feet—and I knew that they were coming in to feed their curiosity, jeer at the unusual—perhaps offer physical violence to my unique person.

I was on the verge of blind unreasoning panic (with what results I dare not at that time consider) when a voice rang out from somewhere to my rear, and spinning round I saw a tall, lean male with a pale bitter face, surmounted by a mops of iron-grey hair.

"What in the saint's name have we got here?"

I shouted—for were they not crowded together in the doorway?

"I am Carlos Markland and . . . "

"Take that damn thing off. Unbutton for sweet Jesus' sake. Denude boy, reveal the carcass."

As I unbuttoned the head cowl and bared my face to the sunheated atmosphere, this terrifying deliverer glared at the pack that were now surging into the passage and raised his voice to a bellow of rage.

"Have you nothing better to do than gawk? By the Pope's great toenail, out . . . away . . . away . . . "

They vanished with the speed of rats confronted by a mad dog and the male was once again able to divert his attention to me, an action that appeared to cause him acute displeasure.

"Get that bloody thing off, boy. By St. Peter's great thumb, I've seen 'em come in here dressed in their Father's old reach-me-downs, football jerseys, flannel vests—but damn me hide if one had turned up wearing a padded coal sack. What in Muhammad's grandmother is it?"

I finally stepped out of my protective clothing and was able to supply a coherent answer.

"It is a solar suit. I am suffering from a rare disease and have to be protected from strong sunlight."

He nodded and eyed me with a shrewd, calculating look, that was not without an element of pity.

"Ah, yes, I have been warned. You'd better come into my room and bring that . . . that thing with you. Leave it in the cloakroom and that lot will have it ripped to bits in no time."

I followed him into a sparsely furnished room where I was motioned to a chair, before he took up a position behind a large battered desk. His manner was now less overbearing, his voice quieter, creating the impression that he was addressing another adult of his own station and attainments. I could only suppose he had sensed my exceptional intelligence.

"My name is Robert Haines and I am the principal of this school. I use the word school in a purely figurative sense, for in fact it's nothing more than a collection of cages in which we try to subdue, tame, and on rare occasion educate, the crowd of embryo delinquents that are now making the morning hideous with their raucous cries." He consulted a sheet of paper. "And you are Carlos Markland who mustn't go out or sit in the sun, eat school dinners, play games or be subjected to violence. In the name of St. Bridget's shawl, what's wrong with you?"

"It is something to do with my blood..."

"Sir. It's supposed to be a sign of respect if you call me sir."

"My blood, sir. It soon gets overheated."

He sighed deeply, then shook his head violently as though trying to dislodge some troublesome parasite.

"This is not a hospital, although it can be a short cut to one. I think it might be well if your parents came to see me. Are they in the phone book?"

"No, sir. And please, I do not think they could come out during the day, not unless it is cloudy."

"What! Do you mean this disease is a family affair?"

I nodded and wondered if I had told him too much.

"But not so bad as me, sir. You sort of grow out of it as you grow older."

"Well, I'll pop round and see them this evening. Tell your father I'll be round at eight o'clock if convenient."

The prospect made me shiver. A meat-eater crossing my mother's well-scrubbed doorstep! Alien eyes viewing the nest at close quarters and possibly noting much that could not be explained! Great-Uncle Manfred for example. But if I objected, yet another facet would be added to my already eccentric image and Mr. Haines might well consider it necessary to shift the problem on to more important shoulders.

I said, "Yes, sir. I will tell them you are coming."

He put his head on to one side and shot out an interrogatory finger.

"Your speech. It's been bothering me right from the start. No contractions. Are you foreign?"

"I beg your pardon, sir. I do not understand."

"You've done it again. Do not instead of don't. I've never come across anyone who did this before. Odd. Decidedly odd."

From outside came the sound of a shrill whistle and a voice shouting: "Come on, line up. We haven't got all day."

Mr. Haines rose and came round from behind his desk and waved an impatient hand when I clambered most reluctantly to my feet.

"Stay where you are. I'd better prepare Miss Pilbeam for what she is to expect. I'm putting you in grade one, although I have a feeling you ought to be way up. Blast me hide, you make me feel like a ten-year-old. Must be those damnable green eyes."

He left the room and I began to steel myself to meet those among whom I was to spend the next eight hours. A mighty tramping of feet came from behind the closed door, interposed by an occasional barked—or snarled—order which seemed to demand movement without so much noise, a requirement that I assumed bordered on the impossible.

Later I sprang to my feet in alarm as a chorus screamed a most terrible dirge that gradually emerged into a jumble of words, and only relaxed when I realised this was some kind of worship ritual, apparently appealing to a deity to bless America. Then Mr. Haines raised (so I assumed) his voice and addressed this god, beseeching it to look favourably on their activities and further more keep a watchful eye on the President and those set in authority under him.

The tramping sound and the shouting voices started all over again, but now they gradually dispersed, went thumping upstairs, receded along various corridors, gave birth to scraping of chair legs, dropping of books, yelps, and one harsh female voice demanding silence. I was impressed by this perpetual desire for silence which never seemed to be granted, due in no small measure to the appellant's need to make him or herself heard.

Mr. Haines re-entered the room and after wiping his forehead on an off-white handkerchief, jerked his head in the direction of the door.

"Come on, I'll get you settled in." He picked up my solar-suit with every sign of distaste and promptly dropped it over the nearest chair-back, "Great Christopher Columbus! It's damned heavy and wet. It stinks too! Am I to understand you're wearing this on doctor's orders?"

"Yes, sir, it keeps me cool."

"I should have thought it would have given you pneumonia or a broken back. You'd better leave it here—put it in that cupboard. I don't want the place smelling like a graveyard."

I followed him some five minutes later across a passage and into the room opposite, where I came face to face with pure undiluted horror. My solar-suit smelt of good clean earth, but the stench which greeted me like a hot foul blanket was born of dirt and corruption. Add this to the sight of forty or more ugly, vicious, cub meat-eaters, plus a yellow slab of sunlight that lay across the upper part of the room—and there was more than sufficient reason for me to cling to the doorpost and scream at the top of my voice. Mr. Haines stared at me with an almost comical expression of astonishment.

"Great Jehovah! What's wrong now?"

I managed to blurt out something about the sun, although that was when I noticed an iron-faced female who was glaring at me through immense horn-rimmed glasses.

"Miss Pilbeam, this is the one I mentioned at Assembly. It can't stand sunlight—excused games and school meals by doctor's orders. I suggest you lower the blinds."

Although Miss Pilbeam's face did not turn black, she did have a deep harsh voice and a strange resemblance to Great-Uncle Manfred when he was in a rage.

"With due respect, Mr. Haines, I cannot regulate my class to the whims of one pupil. If he's so sick that a spot of sunlight makes him shriek like a demented banshee, he ought to be in a hospital."

Mr. Haines put his mouth within a few inches of her ear and said in a loud whisper:

"For crying out aloud, pull the blind down and let both of us get a little peace."

She stumped across the room and pulled the cream-coloured blind down with such violence, I was alarmed lest it break free from its brackets and thus deprive me of even this slight protection. The result was a large oblong of shimmering gold, which was bearable so long as I did not stare at it.

"Better put him at the back," Mr. Haines advised. "In that far corner."

Two cub meat-eaters sat behind each desk. I was shepherded by the still irate Miss Pilbeam to the right furthermost corner and placed thigh to thigh, shoulder to shoulder, with a plump unwholesome monstrosity that exuded a strong odour of smoke and stale garbage. Needless to say all eyes were turned in my direction and I lowered my head trying to look as inconspicuous as possible. Then Miss Pilbeam barked:

"Face the front. The new boy has the same number of legs and arms as the rest of you. I'm now going to mark the register and you will ..."

She suddenly stiffened like a dog that has spotted a particularly succulent rabbit and pointed to a lean and hungry looking thing on my right. "Bret Norman—bring out whatever it is you are eating."

It was not until the thing had pulled a nauseating lump of something from its mouth (I am sure it was not meat) and had been made to deposit it into the trash basket, that I remembered I had left my nourishment bottle in the outer pocket of my solar suit. Partakers have to imbibe three times a day, plus a really big intake just after midnight, otherwise the saliva glands send out warning streams and I had no wish for the young meat-eaters to see me with froth-covered lips and dribbling chin. I would have to sneak into Mr. Haines' office while the creatures were consuming their meat and try to retrieve the bottle.

There was of course an alternative which I had not yet considered.

I cannot remember with anything like clarity what I was supposed to learn during the first hour—something to do with multiplication tables, I believe—but even in the midst of my misery, I could not help being impressed by the undoubted fact that meat-eaters can achieve little unless their endeavours are accompanied by a lot of noise. Much later I realised that this failing did much to assist the hunter in his quest for nourishment; who will hear the whisper when the entire world is screaming?

A bell rang and this was a signal for my companions (I spell the word with great reluctance) to charge from the room—despite Miss Pilbeam's loud protest—and take part in an activity that entailed running back and forth across the sun-drenched yard, yelling, fighting and generally behaving in the manner of creatures reared on a diet of dead animals.

Miss Pilbeam spoke with a surprisingly gentle tone.

"Carlos—that is your name?"

I said it was and waited for the inevitable questions.

"Carlos, am I to understand that your health forbids you to go out at all? That you cannot take part in any kind of recreation?"

"Only when the sky is covered by clouds."

She creased her forehead into a frown.

"Stand up, Carlos. It is not polite to remain seated when talking to a lady."

I at once jumped to my feet and performed a little bow and spoke in the way I had been trained.

"I do beg your pardon, gracious lady."

Miss Pilbeam raised her eyebrows and appeared to be considering me with deepened interest.

"You are singularly pale, but seem extremely healthy otherwise. In fact your clear eyes and gleaming hair suggest an abundance of good health. But there is something about you that—I find it difficult to put what I feel into words—something about you that is frightening. Your eyes . . . I cannot see you fitting into this school. They are a tough lot, but should you . . . "

She shook her head and hurried from the room which left me defenceless, a welcome prey to the giggling monsters who filed in through the doorway and sat on desks, leaned against walls and stared at me with lust-bright eyes. I saw the dust on their faces, the grime under their fingernails; all but tasted the stench which seemed to be an essential part of their being. Yet by meat-eater standards they were young, the oldest could not have existed for more than eight or nine winters, and surely there should not have been that air of bizarre self-confidence etched on each face.

One, a creature with red hair and a sprinkling of brown spots on its face, edged a little nearer and said:

"What was that gear you were wearing?"

Then another—straw-coloured hair and a snub nose—ventured to poke me with a stubby forefinger and pretend to be frightened when I twisted away and instinctively bared my teeth.

"How come you're afraid of the sun?"

I decided not to answer, calculating that silence would eventually send them in search of a more forthcoming victim. This proved to be an unwise decision.

"He's dumb!" Red-head exclaimed. "Stupid and dumb."

"Naw," Straw-hair shook his head. "He's just plain nuts. Anyone who's afraid of the sun must be nuts."

The tormenting words flowed over me and I tried to remember Great-Uncle Manfred's instruction to remain cool no matter the provocation, but I make no excuse for my lapse from that line of conduct that he had stated was essential if my own safety and that of the nest was to be preserved. It must be remembered I was in alien surroundings, terrified as never before in my short life and in imminent danger of being shamefully assaulted. When Red-head reached out a grubby paw and grabbed my tie, I acted from pure instinct, alive only to the need to protect myself. I unsheathed my fangs and sank them into the thin wrist.

I must give credit to where it is due and record that the creature did not scream or even cry out, but just snatched its hand away and took refuge among the group. They all stared at me with wide-open eyes, apparently fascinated by my bared fangs that I had not thought to retract, and the smear of essential fluid on my chin. I expected an outcry, a mad dash for the door, but they merely huddled together, fear reflected in their eyes, I sensed a feeling of excitement, a rising wave of awe. Presently one with a wart on his chin whispered:

"Say—are you—a vampire?"

I shouted: "No... no... no... " fearful aware that my fatal lapse had betrayed Great-Uncle Manfred, Mother and Father and the entire nest. "I am not... not... " then too late remembered to retract my fangs. A deep—dare I say?—a joyful sigh greeted this simple action and Red-head actually uttered an outrageous statement.

"He bit me! Now I'll be a vampire too."

And I made the second and without doubt the most fatal mistake; destroying any faint hope that might have remained of my staying at day school, or returning to the nest. I said: "No you will not. I only nipped."

Fortunately the rest of the class trooped in before anyone could say anything further and I was able to relax and try to decide what to do.

Miss Pilbeam must have been gratified by the unusual silence that permitted her to teach—if that is the right word—for an entire hour without once rebuking a pupil for talking. But I knew that another means of communication had replaced the spoken word, for I watched a slip of paper being passed from desk to desk, its contents quickly perused, before the reader's head was jerked in my direction. Every revealed face wore the same expression.

Fearful, joyous, burning and insatiable interest.

When this news bulletin reached my desk-mate, I gave it a quick, sideways glance, I read:

WHITE FACE IS A VAMPIRE. HE SUCKS BLOOD

3

The bell rang as the sun went out.

I can only suppose that Beldaza heard my repeated prayer for deliverance, as there would have been little hope of my escaping during that period when meat-eaters consume their nourishment, if the streets were still bathed in sunlight. The flight of a solar-suited partaker is as conspicuous as a black cat on a white wall.

They left the classroom with even more speed than at the morning break, for now there was an exciting topic to be discussed, a dire need to spread the news; evidence in the shape of two small punctures on Red-head's wrist that must be examined, exhibited as proof that a vampire was loose in the school.

I waited until the last one had passed through the doorway before moving, then once out in the passage, looked anxiously from left to right. A continuous roar told me they were congregated in their nourishment room and it was safe for me to sprint to Mr. Haines' office, there retrieve my solar suit, before fleeing into the city.

I opened the office door very carefully and peered into the room beyond, prepared to beat a hasty retreat should the room be occupied. But the principal had gone for his nourishment and I was able to run to the cupboard, pull out the solar suit, then as an after-thought—for it was a cumbersome article to carry over one's arm—stuff it into a carrier bag that I spotted on the desk.

Although several young meat-eaters were lounging around in the playground, not one tried to stop me as I walked through the gateway and for this sign of Beldaza's protection I was truly grateful. A thick covering of cloud hid the sun's face and my self-confidence increased as I progressed through several streets and gradually left that dreadful day school behind. But, after I had walked alone for the best part of an hour, reaction set in and I was forced to recognise the hopelessness of my position.

A cub without a nest. Doomed to wander the screaming streets, surrounded by aliens, with only one nourishment bottle between him and starvation; and possibly already a target for the blood squad. I was pushed and jostled by male and female meat-eaters, many of whom turned their heads and stared at me with undisguised curiosity. Cars and cabs roared on either side of the street and it seemed as if the entire planet was a terrifying monster that bellowed its rage because one cub-partaker was daring to walk under the daytime sky.

One elderly female stopped and bending over me asked:

"Are you lost, son?"

I said: "No, I am going to my place of residence," and subdued an urge to run for the nearest shadows.

"The reason I asked," she persisted, "is because you look so pale. Seal-white, if I may say so."

Great-Uncle Manfred had always stressed that we be polite at all times, particularly to meat-eaters, so I bowed and replied: "I am very well, thank you. I am going home."

She straightened up and nodded slowly.

"Well, I wouldn't hang around here if I was you. These streets are no place for a nice-looking boy like you to wander alone. Besides, I wouldn't be surprised if there isn't a storm later on."

I walked quickly away, but when I looked back she was still watching me with anxious eyes.

I wandered for a long time and eventually came to an area of green open space surrounded by tall railings. I went through an open gateway, resolutely ignored a male dressed in blue uniform who eyed me with some distaste, then ran across the close-clipped grass to a clump of trees that reared up against the grey sky like green-haired sentinels. To sink down in to the semi-gloom that lurked between mighty trunks, to smell raw earth, hear the murmuring protest of leaves that were teased by the gentle breeze—all combined to bring me a measure of peace.

I took out my nourishment bottle and drank deep, caring little that once it was empty I had no means of replenishing it. Below me the earth lived, breathed and sometimes groaned, for Beldaza had never intended that it maintain the teeming multitudes that wander across its scarred face. The trees also were; mourned the loss of long ago slaughtered brothers, whose domain was now covered by hideous structures created from bricks, concrete and steel.

But deep, deep down, cold rivers flowed serenely through total darkness; creatures that would never be tormented by the sense of sight, awake from a century long sleep, created a single thought, then slipped back into blessed oblivion. And all around me, invisible to ungifted eyes, were other beings that drifted around smooth tree trunks, merged into or from sap-moist wood and spoke through the voice of the sighing wind: "We...live...not...but...we...are."

Soothed by the presence of trees, wind and wood shades, I presently slipped into a dreamless sleep.

I was awoken by the sound of a bell and a voice shouting:

"Everyone out—closing time," and became aware that darkness was falling, spreading its protecting wings over the glowering sky and allowing twinkling lights to transform the grim city into a wonderland. I knew that the gleaming beauty would die at dawn; and once I had ventured back into those roaring streets, ugliness would be waiting in the lurking shadows.

I was surprised to find that the city was even more active than during the daylight hours. Great-Uncle Manfred had always maintained that meat-eaters wasted the darktime in sleep and thus made it more difficult for partakers to find suitable donators, but here were males and females pouring out of the subways, laughing and talking, staring into brilliantly lighted shop windows, some attired in strange costumes that gave them a slightly less grotesque appearance.

Most of the females exuded a mysterious odour that I began to associate with the perfume of flowers and this made me wonder if it could be the result of them supplementing their meat diet with murdered plant life. If so, I could not understand why the males did not also send out this far from unpleasant smell and came to the conclusion it might be considered unmasculine to consume flowers...

One grotesquely fat male, attired in a black suit and dazzling white shirt front, lurched unsteadily from a doorway and was positively saturated with a stench that made my stomach heave and forced me to break into a fast run. Only later did experience reveal that he must have partaken of some form of nourishment that contained a strong element of garlic. And not, as might be imagined, as a means of protection against us, but because he *actually liked it.*

Having taken shelter in a dark alley, I drained my nourishment bottle and faced the unpalatable truth that I would be in a sorry state by morning, unless I could locate another supply. I saw much that revolted me and little that was pleasing. Bleeding carcasses hung on hooks in shop windows, dead beings I recognised as fish, laying on white slabs and sending out a repulsive smell; and dangerous males that must have been possessed by malignant demons, for they staggered along pavements, shouting abuse at the very top of their voices. One, who might well have been the sire of Red-head, stood on a street corner and loudly proclaimed his desire to fight all and everyone who possessed the necessary courage to face him. Much of his unique language escaped my understanding, but now I can recall the actual words he used.

"You're a lot of yellow slobs," he informed the world at large, "and I can flatten the lot of you with one arm tied behind my back."

I can remember that large men in blue arrived and began blowing whistles and everyone fled in all directions, save me, who remained as an interested spectator, my thirst for knowledge completely overwhelming the need for caution, as I soon discovered when one blue male loomed over me.

"Haven't you a home to go to, kid?"

I said I had and began to back away, but he reached out a large hand and gripped my shoulder and attracted the attention of another blue-clad creature who had been engaged in dispersing the crowd.

"Harry, have you got the description of that kid who took off from that primary school today?"

Harry—for such appeared was his name—lumbered slowly in our direction, while removing a scrap of paper from a top pocket. He came within a few feet of me and began to read its contents with slow deliberation.

"About seven or eight years old, white face, black hair and good teeth. Dressed in a black suit, white shirt and probably carrying a bag." He looked me up and down, then slowly parted his lips, revealing the customary set of ill-matched teeth. "I'd say we've hit the jackpot, Charlie. There can't be two of 'em running around looking like that. Never seen such a white face, not outside a horror movie at any rate. It seems the other kids think he's a vampire and I can see why."

"Guess we'd better take him in, then,"

I broke free by jerking my shoulder from the big man's grip and was sprinting down the road before either of them realised what had happened. I turned into a dark alleyway, ran along its entire length, cleared a low fence with a single bound and landed in an extremely cluttered backyard.

A male who had just emerged from a narrow doorway and was engaged in buttoning up his fly buttons, yelped like a startled dog and peered at me through the deepening gloom.

"How in God's name did you do that? Came over the fence like a god-damned greyhound."

Being frightened I bared my fangs and snarled, which had the immediate effect of sending him towards a lighted doorway, shouting: "Mary, there's some nutty kid out here with bloody great teeth."

I leapt over a dividing wall, raced across another backyard, cleared a five-foot high gate with six inches to spare and found myself in a narrow road that was illuminated by widely-spaced street lamps. I settled down to a fairly fast jog-trot, determined to escape from the concrete jungle and find refuge in some solitary place where trees would grant some protection. Then I realised I had dropped the bag containing my solar suit in one or the other backyards and my predicament was now indeed desperate.

Moreover, all this activity was burning up my energy and unless I could soon find some liquid nourishment, there would be no need to worry about tomorrow's sunlight. I tried to remember how long a partaker could go unfed and still retain control of his faculties and seemed to recall Great-Uncle Manfred saying three missed intakes were the limit. A growing cub would in all probability succumb much sooner, and I was not eager to put such a conjecture to the test.

Those mean, unhappy streets seemed to go on forever and the inhabitants of the tall, glowering houses sat outside on flights of filthy steps, staring at me with malevolent eyes as I trotted by. And the hunger grew until it became an all-devouring passion; saliva seeped from my gaping mouth, fangs slid from moist sheaths and dimpled my chin, and a terrible, unfamiliar weakness rose slowly up from my pounding feet and made me stumble.

When I stopped running and rested for a while, a measure of strength returned and with it the relentless urge to live—to continue to be—which has enabled the pitiful remnants of my species to exist in a hostile world. I forced my body to go and presently came to an open square where a solitary tree stood with drooping branches and dust-covered leaves; a poor relation of those that had comforted me in the park.

The bark was rough and cracked, scored in many places by knives that had carved out initials, words which I did not understand, but suggested they had been formulated by minds unhinged by frustrated desire. I could sense the despair, the terrible loneliness that comes to every life-form when it is cut off from the pack-group and must continue-to-be in a tainted environment. I could not detect the presence of wood-shades, but there was one scrap of conscious life that sobbed a ceaseless lament from one of the lower branches and I received the impression it had deliberately ended its corporeal journey at the end of a rope. At that time this was beyond my comprehension, for surely every life-form from a blade of grass to a full-grown partaker recognised death as the common enemy and would never surrender to him.

From the far side of the square came a sound which I recognised as a possessed meat-eater singing and I momentarily forgot my hunger, fearfully aware that this creature would most probably be aggressive. I hid behind the tree and watched a short, lean figure lurch from side to side, pausing once in a while to kick a tin can—or whatever small object appeared in its path—all the while making the night hideous by a most untuneful refrain.

"Ne...l...l...y...oh...Ne...l...l...y...D...e...a...n...n.

"I'll take 'er knickers down...and...do 'er,

"Ne...l...l...y...D...e...a...n...an...n...n..."

It staggered into the shadows cast by my tree and stared up at the overwhelming branches with a look of outraged horror, apparently under the impression it was some kind of hungry monster.

"Don't stretch yer arms down to me, you bloody God-darn-bastard. I'm not going to stretch my neck like that other poor son-of-a-bitch..."

Then it fell flat on its face and lay perfectly still.

At first I thought it had ceased to be and its life force would now emerge, together with whatever demon shared the body. But a rasping snort, followed by a strange gurgling sound informed me it still breathed, but was apparently in a state of unconsciousness and I could now depart without fear of being molested. But when I came from behind the tree and looked upon the supine body, the terrible hunger that now racked my entire being rose up to an unprecedented level.

I stood still for a long time and allowed reason to take full control of my brain; transform fearful indecision into a cool logic. I had been mourning the loss of an empty nourishment bottle—here was one filled to overflowing. Instead of having to hunt, by Beldaza's great mercy, succulent prey had been delivered to my very feet. A thin scrawny neck was bared for my sustenance and I need only bend down and partake—drink my fill—extinguish the flame of hunger by a red flow of essence that would ensure me eternal life.

Fangs sank into flesh, a warm stream filled my mouth, poured down my contorting throat, filled my empty belly and flowed through my singing body. Bottle-feeding sates hunger, neck-partaking enriches the soul, lights a fire of ecstasy such as no meat-eater could ever experience—and renews strength in an instant.

I retracted my fangs, stood up and, after placing one foot on the motionless body, gave vent to the sated roar of a fully aroused buck-vampire.

I was weaned from the bottle.

I was blooded.

I was now a fully-fledged, alive and kicking hunter-partaker.

R. CHETWYND-HAYES:
A WORKING BIBLIOGRAPHY

(WITH COMMENTARY BY THE AUTHOR)

Compiled by Stephen Jones and Marc Damian Lawler

NOTE: With due acknowlegement to Scot D. Ryersson's interview with the author and Richard Dalby's anterior bibliography in *The Scream Factory* Issue #17 (Spring 1996), every effort has been made to physically inspect the items listed on the following pages. Ronald's comments ("R.C-H") are given in italics, while any additional parenthetic notes by the compilers are contained in the square brackets. As with any working bibliography, this is (and will remain) a work in progress. If anyone has any updates or corrections, we would be grateful to receive them c/o the publisher. Thank you.

—*Stephen Jones*

"*True courage is being able to see horror across a crowded room and still find it possible to ask for another cup of tea.*"

—R.C-H.

A. NOVELS

(INCLUDES AN ALPHABETICAL LISTING OF NOVELS WRITTEN BY R. CHETWYND-HAYES)

A1 **AND LOVE SURVIVED**
    a. _____, see The Dark Man [A5(c)].

A2 **THE AWAKENING**

a. _____, Magnum Books/Methuen Paperbacks, London, England, 1980 (pb)
Price: £1.25 / 224pp.
[Note: Film tie-in edition, credited to "Ronald Chetwynd-Hayes" on the cover. Based on the screenplay by Allan Scott, Chris Bryant and Clive Exton, which was itself based on *The Jewel of Seven Stars* (1903) by Bram Stoker.]
(*"How I came to be offered the contract to novelise* The Awakening, *I have not the slightest idea! I can remember sitting with a lady agent in a small West End cinema watching the film. Then, again armed with the script, I wrote the novel within two weeks. That was the time limit I was allowed."* R.C-H.)

A3 **THE BRATS: A NOVEL OF THE FUTURE**
a. _____, William Kimber & Co. Limited, London, England, 1979 (hc)
Price: £4.95 / 191pp / Cover art by David Jackson.
b. _____, The Science Fiction Book Club (UK)/ Readers Union, Newton Abbott, England, 1980 (hc)
(*"My novel* The Brats *I first wrote as a short story, then extended to full-length. It is not tinged with humour. I was given very stern instructions on that point. No sending up. The purists don't like it. Myabe the Duke of York was near the mark, but I tried so hard to keep to the straight and narrow path."* R.C-H.)

A4 **THE CURSE OF THE SNAKE GOD**

a. _____, Inner Circle Books, London, England. 1991 (hc)
Price: £11.95 / 191pp / Cover art by Chrissie Marks.
[Note: Although copyrighted 1989, this was the novel's first publication. The cover credits "Ronald Chetwynd-Hayes".]
(*"Well, I think that the current obsession with this stomach-turning horror will pass, but the ghost story or horror send-up is eternal. I will admit that some of my stories, like* The Curse of the Snake God, *are very grim."* R.C-H.)

A5 **THE DARK MAN**

a. _____, Sidgwick & Jackson, London, England, 1964 (hc)
Price: 21/- / 288pp.
b. _____, see The Dark Man [G1].
c. [as **AND LOVE SURVIVED**], Zebra Books/Kensington Publishing, New York, USA, 1990 (pb)
Price: $3.95 / 288pp.
[Note: A "Chronicles of Clavering Grange" novel. This novel was optioned three times by British producers Cyril Coke and Muriel Young as a four-part TV series.]
(*"The novel of my youth. The Man from the Bomb was my only publication until my first "real" novel* The Dark Man *was accepted by Sidgwick & Jackson. It was the story of a man who sets about solving his own murder. Should appeal to ladies with a romantic bent and both sexes who are interested in reincarnation. I don't much care for the book, but I will admit that the idea was good."* R.C-H.)

A6 **DOMINIQUE**

a. _____, Universal/W.H. Allen & Co. Ltd., London, England, 1978 (pb)
Price: £0.75p / 176pp
[Note: Film tie-in edition. Based on 'What Beckoning Ghost?' by Harold Lawlor (first published in the July 1948 issue of *Weird Tales*), which R.C-H included in *Gaslight Tales of Terror*. Cover photo of Dominique Ballard (Jean Simmons) in *Dominique* (1979)]

b. _____, Belmont Tower Books, New York, USA, 1979 (pb)
Price: $1.50 / 172pp.
[Note: Film tie-in edition.]
c. _____, Bucks Books/Horwitz, Australia, 1979 (pb).
d. _____, 5 Siglos, Spain, 1980 (pb).
[Note: Cover credits "R. Chetwind Hayes".]
(*"It was my first attempt at novelising a film and I found it very easy, so long as I was armed with the script."* R.C-H.)

A7 **THE GRANGE**

a. _____, see The King's Ghost [A11(b)].

A8 **THE HAUNTED GRANGE**

a. _____, William Kimber Limited/Thorsons Publishing Group, Northamptonshire, England, 1988 (hc)
Price: £9.95 / 184pp / Cover art by "Ionicus" [Joshua Charles Armitage].
[Note: A "Chronicles of Clavering Grange" novel. The working title was *Haunted Clavering*.]
(*"The real location of Clavering is Doddington, a small village on Kent. There my readers will recognise the Plough Inn, the Vicarage and, a little way back, a large ancient building that is the stand-in for Clavering Grange."* R.C-H.)

A9 **HELL IS WHAT YOU MAKE IT**

a. _____, Robert Hale, London, England, 1994 (hc)
Price: £15.99 / 160pp / Cover art by Barbara Walton.

A10 **KEPPLE**

a. _____, Robert Hale Limited, London, England, 1992 (hc)
Price: £13.95 / 191pp / Cover art by Barbara Walton.
[Note: Most copies have creases in the dust-jacket lamination.]

A11 **THE KING'S GHOST**

a. _____, William Kimber & Co. Limited, London, England, 1985 (hc)
Price: £7.95 / 220pp / Cover art by "Ionicus" [Joshua Charles Armitage].
b. [as **THE GRANGE**], Tor Books, New York, USA, 1988, (pb)
Price: $3.95 / 249pp / Cover art by David Mann.
[Note: A "Chronicles of Clavering Grange" novel.]
(*"The novel* The King's Ghost, *which relates what happ-ened when Queen Elizabeth I visited Clavering in 1590, was published as* The Grange *in America."* R.C-H.)

A12 **THE MAN FROM THE BOMB**

a. _____, Badger Books/John Spenser & Co., London, England, 1959 (pb)
Price: 2/- / 160pp / Cover art by Eddie Jones.
b. [as **DER EWIGE KREIS** (The Endless Circle)], Widukind/Gebrüder Zimmermann (Widukind Utopia-Spitzenklasse), Germany, 1961 (hc)
Price: DM 6.80 / 270pp / Translated by Walter Ernsting.
c. [as **DER EWIGE KREIS** (The Endless Circle)], edited by Günter M. Schelwokat, Moewig (Terra #244), Germany, 1962 (pb)
Price: DM 0.70 / 64pp / Cover art by Johnny Bruck.
[Note: Abridged version.]
d. [as **DER EWIGE KREIS** (The Endless Circle)], Moewig (Terra Nova #10), Germany, 1968 (pb)

Price: DM 0.80 / Illustrated by "Freytag" [H.J. Frey] / Cover art by Karl Stephan.
[Note: Reprint of the 1962 abridgement.]
(*"I did very little literary-wise until 1959, when a strange little publisher named John Spencer from Badger Books accepted my first book,* The Man from the Bomb. *They paid me £25 for it. The layout and printing were terrible! But, I was so delighted to see a book of mine in print I was inclined to overlook those defects."* R.C-H.)

A13 THE PARTAKER: A NOVEL OF FANTASY

a. _____, William Kimber & Co. Limited, London, England, 1980 (hc)
Price: £5.50 / 224pp / Cover art by Roger Garland.
(*"The truth about vampires. My first book written with an American background. Not a great success, but the idea is good. I would like to write it again with an English background. I used to get telephone calls from women who wanted to know if I was Carlos Markland."* R. C-H.)

A14 THE PSYCHIC DETECTIVE

a. _____, Robert Hale Limited, London, England, 1993 (hc)
Price: £14.99 / 208pp / Jacket illustrator: Barbara Walton.
[Note: A "Fred and Francis" novel. "Now to be a Hammer Film" on the dust-jacket. This book was re-optioned for filming by Hammer Film Productions Ltd. in 1998.]
(*"I completed a novel called* The Psychic Detective *which, I've heard, is to be made into a feature film by the new Hammer Productions. Then, using the same two characters, Freddie and Francis, from the book, they want to transform the entire thing into a television series for Warner Bros. and Hammer. This is something I have long hungered for."* R.C-H.)

A15 **WORLD OF THE IMPOSSIBLE**

a. _____, Robert Hale Limited, London, England, 1998 (hc)

Price: £16.99 / 224pp / Cover art by Barbara Walton.

[Note: This novel was assembled and edited by an uncredited Jo Fletcher from the author's original typescript.]

(*"I roughed out a story called* World of the Impossible *and gave it to Hammer Films. A long time afterwards a production manager for Hammer told me* W.O.T.I. *almost became a film. But sex was beginning to raise an ugly head at Hammer and, alas, I had not sexed it up."* R.C-H.)

B. COLLECTIONS

(INCLUDES AN ALPHABETICAL LISTING OF COLLECTIONS
CONTAINING SHORT STORIES WRITTEN BY R. CHETWYND-HAYES)

B1 COLD TERROR

Contents: *The Door, Neighbours, Never Take Drinks From a Strange Woman, Great-Grandad Walks Again, Who is Mr. Smith?, Birds of a Feather, The Ninth Removal, The Shadow, The Day Father Brought Something Home, In Media Res, The Fourth Side of the Triangle, Coming Home, An Act of Kindness, A Matter of Life and Death.*

a. _____, Universal-Tandem Publishing Co., Ltd., London, England, 1973 (pb)
Price: £0.30p / 240pp.

b. [as **LEICHENSCHMAUS** (Funeral Meal)], Pabel (Vampir Taschenbuch #20), Hamburg, Germany, 1975 (pb)
Price: DM 2.80 / 145pp / Translated by Thomas Schlück / Cover art by Les Edwards.
[Note: 'The Door' was re-titled 'Die blutende tür' (The Bleeding Door) and 'In Media Res' was re-titled 'Das alte baby' (The Old Baby).]

c. _____, Pyramid Books, New York, USA, 1975 (pb)
Price: $1.25 / 256pp / Cover art by George Ziel.

d. _____, Piccadilly Pubishing, UK, 2014 (e-book)

B2 THE CRADLE DEMON AND OTHER STORIES OF FANTASY AND TERROR

Contents: *The Pimpkins, A Walk In The Country, The Brats, Why?, The Chair, My Very Best Friend, The Cradle Demon, Reflections, My Mother Married A Vampire, Mildred And Edwina, Tomorrow At Nine, The Creator, The Sloathes.*

a. _____, William Kimber & Co. Limited, London, England, 1978 (hc)
Price: £3.95 / 205pp / Cover art by "Ionicus" [Joshua Charles Armitage].

[Note: This is titled *The Cradle Demon and Other Stories of Fantasy and Horror* on the cover.]

b. [as **DER DÄMON IN DER WIEGE** (The Demon in the Cradle)], Pabel (Vampir Taschenbuch #80), Hamburg, Germany, 1980 (pb)

Price: DM 3.80 / 161pp / Translated by Joachim Honnef / Cover art by George Smith.

[Note: 'The Pimpkins' was re-titled 'Die pünktchen' (The Dots).]

(*"I am of the opinion that* The Cradle Demon *is my best collection of short stories. An editor once said that it was the best collection of horror short stories she had ever read, but no, she couldn't get it reprinted in paperback because, she said, there was no demand for short stories!"* R.C-H.)

B3 DRACULA'S CHILDREN

Contents: Dracula's Genealogical Table, Prologue, Dracula's Wives from *Dracula* by Bram Stoker, Introduction, *Irma, Rudolph, Zena, Cuthbert, Marcus, Benjamin.*

a. _____, William Kimber & Co. Limited, London, England, 1987 (hc)

Price: £8.95 / 208pp / Cover art by "Ionicus" [Joshua Charles Armitage].

[Note: A contract from William Kimber & Co. Limited exists, dated February 3rd, 1987, for a book from R.C-H entitled *More Children of Dracula*, which could be the working title for this book.]

(*"Yes, the King of the Vampires did have children. Well, he had three wives and they had to serve some purpose."* R. C-H.)

B4 THE ELEMENTAL & OTHER STORIES

Contents: *The Elemental, A Time To Plant–a Time To Reap, Birth, The Labyrinth, Someone is Dead, The Jumpity-Jim, The Wanderer.*

a. _____, Fontana Books, London, England/ William Collins Sons & Co., Glasgow, Scotland, 1974 (pb)

Price: £0.35p / 187pp.

[Note: Cover photo of Madame Orloff (Margaret Leighton) in *From Beyond the Grave* (1974). The back cover blurb reads: "Fear has many faces. Here are eight of its more bizarre, more nerve-jangling aspects"—but the book includes only seven stories.]

b. _____, Fontana Books, London, England/William Collins Sons & Co., Glasgow, Scotland, 1975 (pb)
Price: £0.45p / 187pp.
c. [as **DAS LABYRINTH DES SCHRECKENS** (The Labyrinth of Dread)], Pabel (Vampir Taschenbuch #54), Hamburg, Germany, 1977 (pb)
Price: DM 3.00 / 145pp / Translated by Jürgen Saupe / Cover art by Nikolai Lutohin.
[Note: 'The Elemental' re-titled 'Der elementargeist' (The Elemental Spirit); 'The Wanderer' re-titled 'Die rastlose seele' (The Restless Soul).]
(*"There was a big fight between Tandem and Fontana about who was going to bring it out. Bertie Van Thal got me into that mess: 'Don't worry', he said, 'I'm your agent, I'll handle this for you'. Then he dropped me in it and said 'It's nothing to do with me'. The book finally came out from Fontana, and Tandem brought one out at the same time asby the author of* From Beyond the Grave*'—that's how they got over it."* R.C-H.)

B5 **THE FANTASTIC WORLD OF KAMTELLAR: A BOOK OF VAMPIRES AND GHOULS**

Contents: *Kamtellar, Birth, Looking for Something to Suck, The Gibbering Ghoul of Gomershal, Amelia.*
a. _____, William Kimber & Co. Limited, London, England, 1980 (hc)
Price: £5.50 / 192pp / Cover art by Roger Garland.

B6 **FRIGHTS AND FANCIES**

Contents: Foreword: The Final Curtain by Stephen Jones, *The Cat Room, The Mudadora, Ghoul at Large, The Third Eye, The Floaters, The Hoppity-Jump, Bongla, The Tele-Mon, Big-Feet, Package Holiday, Brownie, The Harpy, Walk in Darkness* (aka *One-Way Trip*), *The Wind-Billie, The Slippity-Slop, High World, Homemade Monster, The Great Indestructible, The Werewolf, The Gale-Wuggle,* Afterword: Time Travel and Me.

a. _____, Robert Hale, London, England, 2002 (hc)
Price: £17.99 / 270pp / Cover art by "Edward Miller" [Les Edwards].
[Note: "Edited by Stephen Jones".]

B7 GASLIGHT, GHOSTS, & GHOULS: A CENTENARY CELEBRATION

Contents: Introduction by Stephen Jones, A Writer in the Dark Lands: An Interview with R. Chetwynd-Hayes by Stephen Jones and Jo Fletcher, *Housebound, The Gatecrasher, The Day That Father Brought Something Home, The Door, The Elemental, The Jumpity-Jim, The Coloured Transmission,* R. Chetwynd-Hayes Photo Gallery, Bits and Pieces, *Something Comes in from the Garden, The Humgoo, The Cradle Demon, The Gibbering Ghoul of Gomershal, Doppelgänger,* Les Edwards: A Portfolio, *Acquiring a Family, A Walk on the Dark Side, Day School,* R. Chetwynd-Hayes: A Working Bibliography by Stephen Jones and Marc Damian Lawler, Obituary.

a. _____, PS Publishing Ltd., Hornsea, England, 2019 (hc)
There are three variants of this edition.
i. Description: trade edition
Price: £25.00 / 447pp / Cover art by Les Edwards.
ii. Description: 100-copy signed edition in slipcase
Price: £45.00 / 477pp / Cover art by Les Edwards.
iii. Description: 26-copy signed deluxe lettered traycased edition
Price: £125.00 / 477pp / Cover art by Les Edwards.
[Note: "Edited with an Introduction by Stephen Jones".]

B8 GHOSTS FROM THE MIST OF TIME

Contents: *Time Check, The Wanderer, Prometheus Chained, Doppelgänger, Cold Fingers, The Echo, Shona and the Water Horse.*
a. _____, William Kimber & Co. Limited, London, England, 1985 (hc)
Price: £7.50 / 205pp / Cover art by "Ionicus" [Joshua Charles Armitage].
[Note: Credited to "Ronald Chetwynd-Hayes" only on the dust-jacket.]

B9 THE HOUSE OF DRACULA

Contents: Draculain Genealogical Table, Introduction, *Caroline, Marikova, Karl, Gilbert, Louis.*

a. _____, William Kimber & Co. Limited, London, England, 1987 (hc)

Price: £9.50 / 206pp / Cover art by "Ionicus" [Joshua Charles Armitage].

[Note: A contract from William Kimber & Co. Limited exists, dated June 26th, 1986, for a book from R.C-H entitled *Stories of Dracula,* which could be the working title for this book.]

b. _____, Piccadilly Pubishing, UK, 2014 (e-book)

(*"I have always seen the funny side of the horror story. I mean, take* Dracula. *This faultlessly attired, pale-faced nobleman who climbs out of his coffin at every sunset—spotless white shirtfront—who does his laundry? We know he shaved, did he take a bath? We know he was a good cook. Did he wash up?"* R.C-H.)

B10 LOOKING FOR SOMETHING TO SUCK AND OTHER VAMPIRE STORIES

a. _____, see The Vampire Stories of R. Chetwynd-Hayes [B27(b)].

B11 THE MONSTER CLUB

Contents: The Basic Rules of Monsterdom, *Prologue, The Werewolf and the Vampire, Monster Club Interlude: 1, The Mock, Monster Club Interlude: 2, The Humgoo, Monster Club Interlude: 3, The Shadmock, Monster Club Interude: 4, The Fly-by-Night, Epilogue.*

a. _____, New English Library, London, England, 1976 (pb)

Price: £0.50p / 192pp.

b. [as **MONSTER-KLUBBEN**], Winther, Midnats-Gyseren #11 (Midnight Thriller #11), Copenhagen, Denmark, 1976, (pb)

Price: Kr. 9.50 / 155pp / Translated by Frits Remar / Cover art by Badia Camps.

c. [as **DER MONSTER CLUB**], Bastei Lübbe, West Berlin, Germany, 1979 (pb).

d. _____, see The Monster Club [G7].

e. _____, New English Library, London, England, 1981 (pb)
Price: £1.25 / 192pp.
[Note: Cover photo of Eramus (Vincent Price) in *The Monster Club* (1981).]
f. [as **HIRVIÖKLUBI: KERTOMUKSIA NYKYAJAN HIRVIÖISTÄ** (The Monster Club: Stories of Monsters of the Modern Age)], Kymppilehdet (Kyöpeli #1), Finland, 1983 (tpb)
221pp / Translator: Jorma-Veikko Sappinen,

g. [as **DER MONSTER CLUB**], in *Schock & Schreck: Horror, wie er im Buche steht* (Shock & Schreck: A Book of Horror), Autoren/Bastei Lübbe, Bergisch Gladbach, Germany, 1990 (pb). DM 8.00 / 366pp / Cover by Terry Oakes.
[Note: R. Chetwynd-Hayes is credited as "Robert Chetwynd-Hayes" on the cover and inside this international edition, that was printed in France, has prices for Italy, Austria, Netherlands and Spain, and also includes stories by Jason Dark, Stephen King, Charles Dickens and Robert Louis Stevenson. To apologise for the mistake, the German publisher sent R.C-H a crate of wine—for which he had to pay £10 import duty.]
h. _____, Severn House Publishers Ltd., Wallington, England, 1992 (hc)
Price: £13.00/$17.95 / 186pp.
[Note: First world hardcover edition.]
i. _____, Valancourt Books, Richmond, Virginia, USA, 2013 (tpb)
Price: $16.99 / 174pp / Cover art by John Bolton.
[Note: This edition adds 'Shadmocks Only Whistle: An Introduction to *The Monster Club*' by Stephen Jones.]
j. [as DER MONSTER-CLUB], in *Halloween-Kult: Romane und Erzählungen* (Halloween Cult: Novels and Stories) edited by Christian Dörge, Apex-Verlag, Munich, Germany, 2019 (hc).
/ 699pp.
k. [as DER MONSTER-CLUB], in Halloween-Kult: Romane und Erzählungen (Halloween Cult: Novels and Stories) edited by Christian Dörge, Apex-Verlag, Munich, Germany, 2019 (tpb).
/ 729pp.
[Note: Repeating the mistake from *Schock & Schreck: Horror, wie er im Buche steht* (1990), R. Chetwynd-Hayes is credited as

"Robert Chetwynd-Hayes" on the back cover and inside both the print-on-demand trade paperback and hardcover editions. When the publishers discovered they did not have the rights to reprint the book, they removed all copies from sale in early 2020.]

B12 THE NIGHT GHOULS AND OTHER GRISLY TALES

Contents: *The Ghouls, The Ghost Who Limped, Danger in Numbers, Something Comes in from the Garden, The Man Who Stayed Behind, Christmas Eve, Building Site Manuscript, No Need for Words, The Wailing Waif of Battersea, The Holstein Horror.*
a. _____, Fontana Books, London, England/William Collins Sons & Co., Glasgow, Scotland, 1975 (pb)
Price: £0.45p / 183pp / Cover art by Gordon Crabb.
b. [as **HORROR-ZEIT** (Horror-Time)], Pabel (Vampir Taschenbuch #50), Hamburg, Germany, 1977 (pb)
Price: DM 3.00 / 145pp / Translated by J. Saupe / Cover art by "C.A.M. Thole" [Les Edwards].
[Note: 'Christmas Eve' re-titled 'Heiliger abend' (Holy Evening); 'Building Site Manuscript' re-titled 'Berichte aus einer anderen zeit' (Reports from Another Time).]

B13 THE OTHER SIDE
a. _____, see Tales from the Other Side [B21(c)].

B14 PHANTOMS AND FIENDS

Contents: Foreword: Finding the Signal by Charles L. Grant, *Moving Day, She Walks on Dry Land, The Bodmin Terror, A Chill to the Sunlight, The Catomado, Regression, Matthew and Luke, Growth, Born This Night, The Sad Ghost, The Thing, The Underground, Shipwreck, Strange People, Fog Ghost, The Frankenstein Syndrome, My Dear Wife, A Sin of Omission, Feet of Clay, Non-Paying Passengers, It Came to Dinner,* Afterword: On Writing and Wraiths.
a. _____, Robert Hale Limited, London, England, 2000 (hc)
Price: £17.99 / 352pp / Cover art by "Edward Miller" [Les Edwards].
[Note: "Edited by Stephen Jones".]

B15 A QUIVER OF GHOSTS

Contents: *A Vindictive Woman, The House, Body and Soul, The Coloured Transmission, The Hanging Tree, The Ghost Who Limped, In Media Res, Dead Ghost, The Playmate, Calvunder, The Wanderer, Danger in Numbers, The Liberated Tiger, The Death of Me.*

a. _____, William Kimber & Co. Limited, London, England, 1984 (hc)
Price: £6.95 / 207pp / Cover art by "Ionicus" [Joshua Charles Armitage].
[Note: Credited to "Ronald Chetwynd-Hayes" only on the dust-jacket.]

b. _____, Piccadilly Pubishing, UK, 2014 (e-book)

B16 SHUDDERS AND SHIVERS

Contents: *Prologue, The Intruders, The Man in Black, Interlude #1, The Bed-Sitting Room, Interlude #2, The Cumberloo, Interlude #3, Twilight Song, Night on the Road, Interlude #4, Old Acquaintance, Epilogue.*

a. _____, Robert Hale Limited, London, England, 1995 (hc)
Price: £16.99 / 192pp / Cover art by Barbara Walton.

B17 6 x PANISCHE NÄCHTE [6 x Panic Nights]

Contents: *Manderville, The Resurrectionist, The Wanderer, The Ghost Who Limped, The Man Who Stayed Behind, Building Site Manuscript.*

a. _____, Pabel (Vampir Taschenbuch #57), Hamburg, Germany, 1978 (pb)
Price: DM 3.80 / 161pp / Translated by Dr. E. Malsch.
[Note: 'Manderville' re-titled 'Ein Ort namens Manderville' (A Place Called Manderville), 'The Resurrectionist' re-titled 'Salomes Töchter' (Salome's Daughter), 'The Wanderer' re-titled 'Die rastlose Seele' (The Restless Soul), 'The Ghost Who Limped' re-titled 'Herr Hinkebein' (Mr. Hinkebein), 'The Man Who Stayed Behind'

re-titled 'Der Mann, der nicht ins Jenseits wollte' (The Man Who Did Not Want to Die), 'Building Site Manuscript' re-titled 'Berichte aus einer anderen Zeit' (Reports from Another Time). Although this volume claims to be the German edition of *Tales of Fear and Fantasy* (by "Ronald Chetwynd-Hayes"), it also includes stories from *The Elemental & Other Stories* and *The Night Ghouls and Other Grisly Tales*, making it a unique collection.]

B18 TALES FROM BEYOND

Contents: *A Living Legend, Markland the Hunter, Shadow on the Wall, One Extra, The Painted Door, The Swing.*

a. _____ William Kimber & Co. Limited, London, England, 1982 (hc)

Price: £6.50 / 189pp / Cover art by "Ionicus" [Joshua Charles Armitage].

B19 TALES FROM THE DARK LANDS

Contents: *Mayfield, Something Comes in from the Garden, The Night Watch, The Astral Invasion, Someone in Mind, The Man Who Stayed Behind, Don't Know, Travelling Companion, The Switch-Back.*

a. _____, William Kimber & Co. Limited, London, England 1984 (hc)

Price: £7.50 / 205pp / Cover art by "Ionicus" [Joshua Charles Armitage].

B20 TALES FROM THE HAUNTED HOUSE

Contents: *Eight for Dinner, Alice in Bellington Lane, Great-Grandad is in the Attic, Next Door, The Phantom Axeman of Carleton Grange, The House on the Hill, A Clavering Chronicle.*

a. _____, William Kimber & Co. Limited, London, England, 1986 (hc)

Price: £8.95 / 176pp / Cover art by "Ionicus" [Joshua Charles Armitage].

b. _____, Piccadilly Pubishing, UK, 2014 (e-book)

B21 TALES FROM THE HIDDEN WORLD: FOUR EPISODES IN THE HISTORY OF CLAVERING GRANGE

Contents: Foreword, *Those That Serve, Life Everlasting, The Cringing Couple of Clavering, Home and Beauty.*
a. _____, William Kimber & Co. Limited, London, England, 1988 (hc)
Price: £9.50 / 206pp / Cover art by "Ionicus" [Joshua Charles Armitage].
[Note: A "Chronicles of Clavering Grange" collection. A contract from William Kimber & Co. Limited exists, dated July 28th, 1987, for a book from R.C-H entitled *Supernatural Tales*, which could be the working title for this book.]
(*"I first used it—both the village and Grange—in my novel* The Dark Man. *It has become even more evil over the years, ever since I discovered it was built on 'tainted ground'."* R.C-H.)

B22 TALES FROM THE OTHER SIDE

Contents: Introduction, *Woodwork–1850, Bricks and Mortar–1969, Loft Conversion–1980, Labour-Saving Devices–2000.*
a. _____, William Kimber & Co. Limited, London, England, 1983 (hc)
Price: £6.50 / 192pp / Cover art by "Ionicus" [Joshua Charles Armitage].
b. [as **KARTANON KIROUS** (Curse of the Manor)], Kymppilehdet, Finland, 1985 (pb)
Translated by Jorma-Veikko Sppinen.
c. [as **THE OTHER SIDE**], Tor Horror/A Tom Doherty Associates, Inc. Book, New York, USA, 1988 (pb)
Price: $3.95 / 273pp.
[Note: A "Chronicles of Clavering Grange" collection.]
(*"I have received many requests to write a full history of Clavering Grange, it being assumed that the twenty-odd years spent in unearthing records of that ill-fated establishment would enable me to do so."* R.C-H.)

B23 TALES FROM THE SHADOWS

Contents: *Run for the Tunnel, Night Sister, Acquiring a Family, Shades of Yesterday, The Passing of an Ordinary Man, The Carrier,*

Long Long Ago, *The Rational Explanation, Clavering Retreat, The Man on the Frame.*
a. _____, William Kimber & Co. Limited, London, England, 1986 (hc)
Price: £8.50 / 188pp / Cover art by "Ionicus" [Joshua Charles Armitage].

B24 TALES OF DARKNESS

Contents: *Darkness, Outside Interference, Tomorrow's Ghost, The Haunted Man, Which One?.*
a. _____, William Kimber & Co. Limited, London, England, 1981 (hc)
Price: £5.95 / 192pp / Cover art by "Ionicus" [Joshua Charles Armitage].
(*"Possibly my best collection of stories. Sold out and never remaindered."* R. C-H.)

B25 TALES OF FEAR AND FANTASY

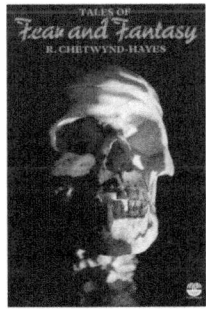

Contents: *Manderville, The Day of the Underdog, The Headless Footman of Hadleigh, The Cost of Dying, The Resurrectionist, The Sale of the Century, The Changeling.*
a. _____, Fontana Books/William Collins Sons & Co. Ltd., Glasgow, Scotland, 1977 (pb)
Price: £0.60p / 160pp.

B26 TERROR BY NIGHT

Contents: *The Throwback, The Ghostly Earl, Where Yesterday?: A Modern Fairy Tale, Lileas and the Waterhorse, Under the Skin, Lord Dunwilliam and the Cwn Annwn, The Echo, Bits and Pieces, The Monster, Housebound.*
a. _____, Universal-Tandem Publishing Co. Ltd., London, England, 1974 (pb)

Price: £0.35p / 186pp / Cover art by Les Edwards.
b. _____, Pyramid Books/Harcourt Brace Jovanovich, New York, USA, 1976 (pb)
Price: $1.25 / 207pp / Cover art by George Ziel.
[Note: This edition replaces 'Bits and Pieces' with 'The Colored [*sic*] Transmission' and the stories have been re-edited.]

B27 **THE UNBIDDEN**

Contents: *No One Lived There, Why Don't You Wash? Said the Girl with a Hundred Thousand Pounds and No Relatives, Don't Go Up Them Stairs, The Gatecrasher, A Family Welcome, Crowning Glory, The Devilet, Come To Me My Flower, The Playmate, Pussy Cat–Pussy Cat, A Penny for a Pound, The Head of the Firm, The Treasure Hunt, The Death of Me, Tomorrow is Judgement Day, The House.*
a. _____, Universal-Tandem Publishing Co. Ltd., London, England, 1971 (pb)
Price: £0.25p / 224pp / Cover art by Chris Achilleos.
b. [as **TEUFELSKRALLEN** (Devil Claws)], Pabel (Vampir Taschenbuch #14), Hamburg, Germany, 1974 (pb)
Price: DM 2.8 / 145pp / Translated by Thomas Schlück / Cover art by Josh Kirby.
[Note: 'The Gatecrasher' was re-titled 'Das ungebetene gast' (The Uninvited Guest); 'Crowning Glory' was re-titled 'Die perücke' (The Wig).]
c. _____, Pyramid Books, New York, USA, 1975 (pb)
Price: $1.25 / 190pp / Cover art by George Ziel.
d. [as **I ONDSKANS KLOR** (In the Claws of Evil)], Kalla Kårar, Ryslig Midnattsläsning #42 (Cold Cries, Awful Midnight Reading #42), B. Wahlström, Stockholm, Sweden, 1977 (pb)
Price: SEK 5.95 / 159pp / Cover art by Enric.
[Note: 'No One Lived There' re-titled 'I Ondskans Klor' (In the Claws of Evil); 'Why Don't You Wash? Said the Girl with a Hundred Thousand Pounds and No Relatives' re-titled 'En Ren Fasa' (A Pure Horror); 'The Gatecrasher' re-titled 'Seansen' (Seance); 'Come to Me My Flower' re-titled 'En Doft av Död' (A Scent of Death).]
e. _____, Piccadilly Pubishing, UK, 2014 (e-book)

B28 THE VAMPIRE STORIES OF R. CHETWYND-HAYES

Contents: Foreword: Never Had an Idea in His Life! by Brian Lumley, *My Mother Married a Vampire*, *A Family Welcome*, *Rudolph*, *The Labyrinth*, *The Sad Vampire*, *Amelia*, *Acquiring a Family*, *The Buck*, *Keep the Gaslight Burning*, *Birth*, *Louis*, *Looking for Something to Suck*, *Great-Grandad Walks Again*, *The Fundemental Elemental*, *The Werewolf and the Vampire*, Afterword: Never Beastly to Vampires by Stephen Jones. Illustrated by Jim Pitts.

a. _____, Fedogan & Bremer, Minneapolis, USA, 1997 (hc)

There are two variants of this edition.

i. Description: trade edition
Price: $27.00 / 253pp / Cover art by Les Edwards.
ii. Description: 100-copy signed edition in slipcase
Price: $95.00 / 267pp / Cover art by Les Edwards.
[Note: "Edited by Stephen Jones"]

b. [as **LOOKING FOR SOMETHING TO SUCK AND OTHER VAMPIRE STORIES**], Robert Hale, London, England, 1998 (hc)
Price: £16.99 / 265pp / Illustrated by Jim Pitts / Cover art by Barbara Walton.
[Note: "Edited by Stephen Jones"]

c. [as **LOOKING FOR SOMETHING TO SUCK: THE VAMPIRE STORIES OF R. CHETWYND-HAYES**], Valancourt Books, Richmond, Virginia 2014 (tpb)
Price: $17.99 / 296pp / Illustrated by Jim Pitts / Cover art by Les Edwards.

[Note: "Edited by Stephen Jones". This print-on-demand edition drops the original Foreword by Brian Lumley and replaces it with a revised and updated piece by the Editor. It also adds an additional story, 'The Great Indestructible', and additional interior illustrations by Jim Pitts.]

C1 THE FIRST ARMADA MONSTER BOOK

Contents: Introduction by R. Chetwynd-Hayes, *The Sad Vampire* by "Angus Campbell" [R. Chetwynd-Hayes], *The Last of the Dragons* by E. Nesbit, *Dimblebee's Dinosaur* by "Howard Peters" [Sydney J. Bounds], *A Ride to Hell* by Ruth Manning-Sanders, *Inside the Monster* by Lucian of Samothrace, *The Chimaera* by Nathaniel Hawthorne, *The Guardian at Hell's Mouth* by Sydney J. Bounds, *Something in the Cellar* by Rosemary Timperly, *Theseus and the Minotaur* by Charles Kingsley, *The Sea Serpent* by Gerard James, *The Thing in the Pond* by Paul Ernst, *Big-Feet* by R. Chetwynd-Hayes.

a. _____, Armada/Fontana Paperbacks, London, England, 1975 (pb)
Price: £0.35p / 125pp

b. _____, Armada/Fontana Paperbacks, London, England, Scotland, 1977 (pb)
Price: £0.40p / 125pp

c. _____, Armada/Fontana Paperbacks, London, England, Scotland, 1981 (pb)
Price: £0.85p / 125pp

(*"What exactly is a monster? According to my dictionary it is—I quote—'Something out of the usual course. A misshapened man or animal. Any legendary, fabulous creature, such as a vampire, dragon, dinosaur, chimaera, sea-serpent, minotaur or centaur. Well, I managed to find stories about all these monsters except the centaur. In any case, I cannot believe there is anything particularly monstrous about a creature which is part man, part horse. Certainly those portrayed in Walt Disney's* Fantasia *looked rather nice."* R.C-H.)

C2 THE SECOND ARMADA MONSTER BOOK

Contents: Introduction by R. Chetwynd-Hayes, *The Giant Who Sucked His Thumb* by Adrien Stoutenbury, *The Lambton Worm* by Winifred Finlay, *The Prince and the Trolls* by John Hampden, *The Wyvern* by Bernard Henderson and Stephen Jones, *The Dragon Tamers* by E. Nesbit, *The Aliens* by Roger Malisson, *The Giant of Grabbist* by Dinah Starkey, *The Well at Worm's End* by Sydney J. Bounds, *Morag and the Water Horse* by Barbara Ker Wilson, *The Green Thing* by Rosemary Timperly, *Homemade Monster* by R. Chetwynd-Hayes. Illustrated by Gary Rees.

a. _____, Armada/Fontana Paperbacks, London, England, 1976 (pb)
Price: £0.40p / 127pp / Cover art by Gary Rees.
b. _____, Armada/Fontana Paperbacks, London, England, 1980 (pb)
Price: £0.40p / 127pp / Cover art by Gary Rees.
(*"In this collection I have tried to introduce some new monsters, while at the same time not completely neglecting the old."* R.C-H.)

C3 THE THIRD ARMADA MONSTER BOOK

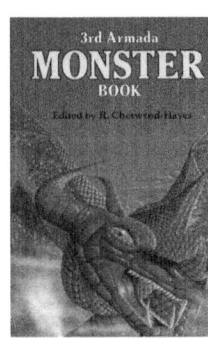

Contents: Introduction by R. Chetwynd-Hayes, *The Story of the Three Young Shepherds* by Ruth Manning-Sanders, *The Gargoyle* by Roger Malisson, *The Story of the Giant Dumpling and How He Became a Hero* by John Cunliffe, *The Machine Monster* by Daphne Froome, *The Three Golden Apples* by Nathaniel Hawthorne, *The Serpent and the Cockatrice* by Pamela Cleaver, *Twelve Great Black Cats and the Red One* by Sorche Nic Leodhas, *Valley of the Monsters* by Sydney J. Bounds, *Visitor in the Night* by Rosemary Timperley, *Prince Prigio and the Firedrake* by Andrew Lang, *The Harpy* by R. Chetwynd-Hayes. Illustrated by Peter Archer.

a. _____, Armada/Fontana Paperbacks, London, England, 1977 (pb)
Price: £0.40p / 125pp / Cover art by Peter Archer.
(*"Welcome to the third book of monsters. Once again I have managed*

to find some unusual monsters; strange and wonderful creatures that I am certain you have never met before." R.C-H.)

C4 THE FOURTH ARMADA MONSTER BOOK

Contents: Introduction by R. Chetwynd-Hayes, *The Werewolf* by "Angus Campbell" [R. Chetwynd-Hayes], *The Bungling Bunyip* by Pamela Vincent, *The Four Big Trolls and Little Peter Pastureman* by Cyrus Graner, *Movie Monster* by Samantha Lee, *The Miller and the Orge* by Barbara Leonie Picard, *The Tardigrotifer* by Daphne Froome, *The Treasure Castle* by Dinah Starkey, *The Miser-Mon* by Terry Tapp, *The Hoppity-Jump* by R. Chetwynd-Hayes. Illustrated by Peter Archer.

a. _____, Armada/Fontana Paperbacks, London, England, 1978 (pb)
Price: £0.50p / 125pp / Cover art by Peter Archer.
(*"I have come to the conclusion that there are three kinds of monsters. Nasty. Sad. Funny. Some are all three."* R.C-H.)

C5 THE FIFTH ARMADA MONSTER BOOK

Contents: Introduction by R. Chetwynd-Hayes, *The Wind-Billie* by "Angus Campbell" [R. Chetwynd-Hayes], *The Stone Monster* by Guy Weiner, *Satan* by Sydney J. Bounds, *A Touch of Sinbad* by Glenn Chandler, *The Water Monster* by Jacynth Hope-Simpson, *King Arthur and the Dragon* by Dinah Starkey, *The Terror of Tottercombe-on-Sea* by Daphne Froome, *Sludge* by Terry Tapp, *The Giant of St. Michael's Mount* by Eileen Molony, *The Tele-Mon* by R. Chetwynd-Hayes. Illustrated by Sarah McCready.

a. _____, Armada/Fontana Paperbacks, London, England, 1979 (pb)
Price: £0.60p / 127pp / Cover art by Sarah McCready.
(*"Well, there we are. Ten stories—ten different monsters. I do hope you enjoy reading this little book and will let me know which story you liked best."* R.C-H.)

C6 THE SIXTH ARMADA MONSTER BOOK

Contents: Introduction by R. Chetwynd-Hayes, *The Mudadora* by "Angus Campbell" [R. Chetwynd-Hayes], *The Slippity-Slop* by "Henry Glynn" [R. Chetwynd-Hayes], *Legend of the Spiders* by Keith Timson, *The Prince and the Dragon* by Andrew Lang, *The Bean Rock Monster* by Terry Tapp, *Monster in Distress* by Patricia Moynehan, *Captain Castleton's Biscuit Beetle* by Daphne Froome, *The Gale-Wuggle* by R. Chetwynd-Hayes. Illustrated by Eric Kincaid.

a. _____, Armada/Fontana Paperbacks, London, England, 1981 (pb)
Price: £0.85p / 128pp / Cover art by Eric Kincaid.
(*"My interest in monsters began on the day I first saw the film* King Kong, *having convinced the lady in the ticket office that I was over sixteen years of age. I still regard the stand-up fight between Kong and a dinosaur as one of the most exciting action scenes ever filmed. But, alas, we have all grown too sophisticated in recent years and have had a surfeit of giant apes, and dinosaurs, pterodactyls, golems, things from outer space, and nameless horrible wriggly things. For that reason I have again tried to gather together a collection of quite remarkably horrible monsters in this book."* R.C-H.)

C7 CORNISH TALES OF TERROR

Contents: Introduction by R. Chetwynd-Hayes, *The Limp Corpse* by Robert Hunt, *The Roll-Call of the Reef* by by Sir Arthur Quiller-Couch, *The Hooting Cairn* by Robert Hunt, *The Misanthrope* by J.D. Beresford, *Arise, Tucker* by Robert Hunt, *The Botathen Ghost* by R.S. Hawks, *The Phantom Ship* by Robert Hunt, *All Souls' Night* by A.L. Rowse, *Calling of the Dead* by Robert Hunt, *The Narrow Way* R. Ellis Roberts, *The Hour Has Come . . .* by Robert Hunt, *The Phantom Hare* by M.H., *Was it 'The Flying Dutchman'?* by Robert Hunt, *The Iron Pineapple* by Eden Phillpotts, *Give Me My Teeth–Give Me My Teeth* by Robert Hunt, *Wish Me Luck* by H.A. Manhood, *The Hell-Hounds* by T.Q. Couch, *Mrs. Lunt* by Sir Hugh Walpole, *The Suicide's Spearman* by Robert Hunt, *The Birds* by Daphne du Maurier, *The*

Bargest by "R.C.H." [R. Chetwynd-Hayes], *The Spectre Bridegroom* by Robert Hunt, *The Kenidzhek Witch* by Robert Hunt, *The Bodmin Terror* by R. Chetwynd-Hayes.

a. _____, Fontana Books, London, England/William Collins Sons & Co., Glasgow, Scotland, 1970 (pb)
Price: £0.25p / 190pp

b. _____, Fontana Books, London, England/William Collins Sons & Co., Glasgow, Scotland, 1971 (pb)
190pp

c. _____, Fontana Books, London, England/William Collins Sons & Co. Ltd., Glasgow, Scotland, 1974 (pb)
Price: £0.35p / 190pp

c. _____, Fontana Books, London, England/William Collins Sons & Co. Ltd., Glasgow, Scotland, 1976 (pb)
Price: £0.50p / 190pp / Cover art by Justin Todd

(*"Cornall is the ideal setting for a tale of terror. Wreckers luring ships on to rocks, Piskies that gallop a farmer's horse half to death on a moonlit night, Giants who hurl great boulders at each other, Mermaids who: 'Comb their hair, yellow as gold, by the noontide sun, at the water's edge', the fairy miners known as 'Knockers', phantom ships that sail over the moors—Cornwall has them all."* R.C-H.)

C8 **DOOMED TO THE NIGHT**

Contents: Introduction by R. Chetwynd-Hayes, *A Man from Glasgow* by W. Somerset Maugham, *A Visit to Amelia Pride* by Barbara Joan Eyre, *Browdean Farm* by A.M. Burrage, *Strange Happenings at Canalaps* by Daphne Froome, *The Cold Embrace* by Miss Braddon, *An Authentic Narrative of a Haunted House* by J. Sheridan Le Fanu, *The Double-Bedded Room* by The Marquess of Lorne, *In the Dark* by Mary E. Penn, *And Not One Penny to the Innkeeper* by Margaret Chilvers Cooper, *At Ravenholme Junction* by Anonymous, *The Conjurer* by Richard Middleton, *How the Third Floor Knew the Potteries* by Amelia Edwards, *The Pipe Smoker* by Martin Armstrong, *A Jug of Syrup* by Ambrose Bierce, *The Legend of Gorie Grange* by Anonymous, *The Man Who Died* by Eric Ambrose, *The Day That Father Brought Something Home* by R. Chetwynd-Hayes.

a. _____, William Kimber & Co. Limited, London,

England, 1978 (hc)
Price: £4.25 / 207pp / Cover art by "Ionicus" [Joshua Charles Armitage].
(*"I have come to the conclusion that the world is hungry for ghosts and there just aren't enough of them to go round. Take me for example. I have written nine collections of stories that deal mainly with the habits, occupations and hobbies of ghosts: edited nine anthologies – and never a sight or sign of a disembodied spirit has disturbed the night of my discontent. And I am prepared to wager my best shroud that ninety-nine per cent of the population of this planet is phantom-bereft—or if you prefer—ghost-starved, and moreover could spend a month of Hallowe'en nights in Borley Rectory without seeing anything more alarming than a marauding mouse. Fortunately for a horror-monger like myself, a favoured few seem to have better luck and are not afraid to narrate their experiences. So there we are. Seventeen stories. Some chilling, some humorous, a few down-right terrifying. May you never hear invisible footsteps following you down the stairs."* R.C-H.)

C9 THE NINTH FONTANA BOOK OF GREAT GHOST STORIES

Contents: Introduction by R. Chetwynd-Hayes, *Death Cannot Wither* by Judith Merril, *The Lady's Maid's Bell* by Edith Wharton, *Keeping His Promise* by Algernon Blackwood, *The Coat* by A.E.D. Smith, *The Four-Fifteen Express* by Amelia B. Edwards, *Sally* by Patrick Davis, *The Song in the House* by Ann Bridge, *The Sweeper* by "Ex-Private X" [A.M. Burrage], *The Glove* by Roger Hicks, *The Return of Imray* by Rudyard Kipling, *The Liberated Tiger* by R. Chetwynd-Hayes.

a. _____, Fontana Books, London, England/William Collins Sons & Co. Ltd., Glasgow, Scotland, 1973 (pb)
Price: £0.30p / 190pp / Cover art by Alan Lee.
b. _____, Fontana Books, London, England/William Collins Sons & Co. Ltd., Glasgow, Scotland, 1974 (pb)
190pp / Cover art by Alan Lee.
c. _____, Fontana Books, London, England/William Collins Sons & Co. Ltd., Glasgow, Scotland, 1975 (pb)
Price: £0.45p / 190pp / Cover art by Alan Lee.

d. _____, Fontana Books, London, England/William Collins Sons & Co. Ltd., Glasgow, Scotland, 1978 (pb)
Price: £0.70p / 190pp / Cover art by Alan Lee.
(*"I wish I could say truthfully that I had seen a ghost. I have read about reputedly haunted houses, listened to friends who knew someone who had experienced some kind of psychic phenomena, but as a professional horror-monger I really am ashamed to say that the dim world of the hereafter has, to date, given me the go-by. This I feel, is nothing short of a tragedy, because I would dearly like proof that some form of life exists beyond the grave."* R.C-H.)

C10 THE TENTH FONTANA BOOK OF GREAT GHOST STORIES

Contents: Introduction by R. Chetwynd-Hayes, *The House in the Wood* by John Hastings Turner, *Fear* by P.C. Wren, *The Furnished Room* by O. Henry, *To Keep Him Company* by Rosemary Timperley, *In the Mist* by Elizabeth Walter, *On the Brighton Road* by Richard Middleton, *Smee* by "Ex-Private X" [A.M. Burrage], *Master Ghost and I* by Barbara Softly, *The Moonlit Road* by Ambrose Bierce, *Two Trifles* by Oliver Onion, *Wicked Captain Walshawe* by Joseph Sheridan Le Fanu, *Monkshood Manor* by L.P. Hartley, *The Chapel Men* by A.E. Ellis, *The Birthright* by Hilda Hughes, *Non-Paying Passengers* by R. Chetwynd-Hayes.

a. _____, Fontana Books, London, England/William Collins Sons & Co. Ltd., Glasgow, Scotland, 1974 (pb)
Price: £0.35p / 190pp / Cover art by Alan Lee.
b. _____, Fontana Books, London, England/William Collins Sons & Co. Ltd., Glasgow, Scotland, 1975 (pb)
Price: £0.45p / 190pp / Cover art by Alan Lee.
c. _____, Fontana Books, London, England/William Collins Sons & Co. Ltd., Glasgow, Scotland, 1977 (pb)
Price: £0.60p / 190pp / Cover art by Alan Lee.
(*"Experience has taught me that people like three ingredients in a collection of ghost stories. Fear, to make them shudder, pathos to make them shed the occasional tear, and humour to dilute the other two. But, of course, the greatest of these must be fear."* R.C-H.)

C11 THE ELEVENTH FONTANA BOOK OF GREAT GHOST STORIES

Contents: Introduction by R. Chetwynd-Hayes, *Justice* by The Gibsons, *Aunt Cassie* by Virginia Swain, *The Woman's Ghost Story* by Algernon Blackwood, *The Ghost of U65* by G.A. Minto, *Footsteps Invisible* by Robert Arthur, *Night Doings at Deadman's* by Ambrose Bierce, *The Earlier Service* by Margaret Irwin, *Scots Wha Ha'e* by Dorothy K. Haynes, *The Whittaker's Ghost* by George Bernard Shaw, *Lady Celia's Mirror* by "Roger Malisson" [Catherine Gleason and Rita Morris], *The Lonely Inn* by Thomas Burke, *The Green Scarf* by A.M. Burrage, *The House of Desolation* by "Alan Griff" [Donald Suddaby], *The Man in the Mirror* by Sydney J. Bounds, *The Attic* by Pamela Vincent, *The Woman in Black* by Peter Hackett, *Haunted Ground* by Oliver La Farge, *The Man Who Sold Ghosts* by Roger F. Dunkley, *Matthew and Luke* by R. Chetwynd-Hayes, Acklowledgements *[sic]*.

a. _____, Fontana Books, London, England/William Collins Sons & Co. Ltd., Glasgow, Scotland, 1975 (pb) Price: £0.45p / 183pp / Cover art by Alan Lee.

b. _____, Fontana Books, London, England/William Collins Sons & Co. Ltd., Glasgow, Scotland, 1978 (pb) 183pp (*"It would seem that ghosts haunt the most unlikely places and objects. Houses I will accept. After all what are old houses for, but the perambulations of restless spirits, who moan, shriek, rattle chains and generally behave in the traditional manner? So—having read about ghosts that lurk in houses, submarines, streets, holes-in-the-floor, churches, time, gardens, inns, mirrors, scarfs, chess-sets, brains, trains, ground, and egos—don't bother to climb under the bed. There's bound to be one there too."* R.C-H.)

C12 THE TWELFTH FONTANA BOOK OF GREAT GHOST STORIES

Contents: Introduction by R. Chetwynd-Hayes, *Escort* by Daphne du Maurier, Elaina by Elizabeth Fancett, *Twisted Shadow* by Roger F. Dunkley, *First-Foot* by Clodagh Gibson-Jarvie, *The Leaden Ring* by S. Baring-Gould, *That Summer* by Barbara Joan Eyre, *The Tapestried Chamber* by Sir Walter Scott, *The Tunnel* by Patrick Davis, *Ghost Stories of the Tiled House* by Joseph Sheridan

Le Fanu, *The Matinee* by William Abney, *The Travelling Companion* by Elizabeth Walter, *Summer and Miss Swanson* by Rick Ferreira, *January Ides* by Margaret Chilvers Cooper, *Barleyriggs* by Dorothy K. Haynes, *From Another World* by Rosemary Timperley, *A Little Night Fishing* by Sydney J. Bounds, *A Fairly Great Reckoning* by "Roger Malisson" [Catherine Gleason and Rita Morris], *Brooding Dark* by Pamela Vincent, *Cold Fingers* by R. Chetwynd-Hayes.

a. _____, Fontana Books, London, England/William Collins Sons & Co. Ltd., Glasgow, Scotland, 1976 (pb)
Price: £0.50p / 190pp / Cover art by Alan Lee.
b. _____, Fontana Books, London, England/William Collins Sons & Co. Ltd., Glasgow, Scotland, 1977 (pb)
Price: £0.60p / 190pp
c. _____, Fontana Books, London, England/William Collins Sons & Co. Ltd., Glasgow, Scotland, 1981 (pb)
Price: £1.00 / 190pp

(*"I have often thought that there ought to be more ghosts—of one kind or another—on the sea than the land. After all, there is more of it and water could be a perfect conductor for the peculiar vibrations that appear to be necessary for psychic phenomena. Ships are but floating houses, that over a period of time must become saturated with emotional atmosphere which—under certain circumstances—may be able to crystallize as a time-image. This could be an explanation for the countless stories of so-called phantom-ships; ghosts that float over the water and other like disturbances."* R.C-H.)

C13 THE THIRTEENTH FONTANA BOOK OF GREAT GHOST STORIES

Contents: Introduction by R. Chetwynd-Hayes, *The Case of the Long Dead Lord* by Dennis Wheatley, *The Lonely Apparition* by Charles Thornton, *The Dead Smile* by F. Marion Crawford, *Crimson Lake* by Daphne Froome, *Old Shadows* by Ken Alden, *The Man with the Flute* by Rosemary Timperley, *The Taipan* by W. Somerset Maugham, *Not Yet Solved* by Anonymous, *Into the Mad, Mad World* by Terry Tapp, *The Hostelry* by Guy de

Maupassant, *Disappearance* by "Roger Malisson" [Catherine Gleason and Rita Morris*]*, *The Ghost Machine* by Roger F. Dunkley, *The Rocker* by Oliver Onions, *The Cape-Cod Poltergeist* by Margaret Chilvers Cooper, *28 Tower Street* by Duncan Forbes, *The Grey Cottage* by Mrs. Claxton, *Mother Love* by Pamela Cleaver, *My Dear Wife* by R. Chetwynd-Hayes.

a. _____, Fontana Books, London, England/William Collins Sons & Co. Ltd., Glasgow, Scotland, 1977 (pb)
Price: £0.60p / 189pp / Cover art by Alan Lee.
(*"I wonder why we all—and I do mean all—are so interested in ghosts? Maybe it is a subconscious need to have some confirmation that there is an afterlife; that we continue to exist, in no matter what form, once this brief earthly journey comes to an end. Undoubtedly there would be certain advantages to being a ghost. One could—given freedom of movement—sit in on Cabinet meetings, take a free trip round the world, and scare the living daylights out of anyone one did not like."* R.C-H.)

C14 **THE FOURTEENTH FONTANA BOOK OF GREAT GHOST STORIES**

Contents: Introduction by R. Chetwynd-Hayes, *Fall in at the Double* by L.P. Hartley, *The Man on the Ground* by Robert E. Howard, *Round the Fire* by Mrs. Crowe, *The St. Christopher Medallion* by James Turner, *Melody in a Minor Key* by Mary Williams, *One Who Saw* by A.M. Burrage, *Never, Never Leave Me* by Terry Tapp, *Thirteen at Table* by Lord Dunsany, *The Ghost of Dorothy Dingley* by Daniel Defoe, *Masks and Voices* by Rosemary Timperley, *The Late Arrivals* by K.B. Hill, *The Doll's Ghost* by F. Marion Crawford, *The Sutor of Selkirk* by Anonymous, *The Three Sisters* by William Wymark Jacobs, *Siren Song* by Barbara Joan Eyre, *Madam Crowl's Ghost* by Joseph Sheridan Le Fanu, *The Sad Ghost* by R. Chetwynd-Hayes.

a. _____, Fontana Books, London, England/William Collins Sons & Co. Ltd., Glasgow, Scotland, 1978 (pb)
Price: £0.70p / 190pp / Cover art by Alan Lee.
(*"Another year has passed since I wrote the last introduction to a Fontana Book of ghost stories and tried to make up my mind what to include and —often regretfully—what to reject. Many authors*

confuse horror with pleasurable fear and I find that some editors are in a like quandary. How many times has 'The Monkey's Paw' been served up as a ghost story? It is a wonderful tale—but without sight or sound of a ghost from the first page to the last. So there you are. Seventeen stories, umpteen ghosts and—I hope—a multitude of shudders. May black demons watch around your bed." R.C-H.)

C15 THE FIFTEENTH FONTANA BOOK OF GREAT GHOST STORIES

Contents: Introduction by R. Chetwynd-Hayes, *The Man from Glasgow* by W. Somerset Maugham, *Master of Hounds* by Peter A. Hough, *The Dead Man of Varley Grange* by Anonymous, *Christmas Entertainment* by Daphne Froome, *John Charrington's Wedding* by E. Nesbit, *The Primrose Connection* by Margaret Chilvers Cooper, *The Saving of a Soul* by by Sir Richard Burton, *No Living Man So Tall* by Rosemary Timperley, *The House by the Headland* by "Sapper" [Herman Cyril McNeile], *Drury Lane Ghost* by W. MacQueen-Pope, *The Night Walkers* by Sydney J. Bounds, *The Business of Madame Jahn* by Vincent O'Sullivan, *Here Today* by James Fisher, *White Christmas* by David E. Rose, *Only Child* by Frances Stephens, *The Bearer of the Message* by Fritz Hopman, *The Herb Garden* by Meg Buxton, *The Hanging Tree* by R. Chetwynd-Hayes.

a. _____, Fontana Books, London, England/William Collins Sons & Co. Ltd., Glasgow, Scotland, 1979 (pb)
Price: £0.75p / 191pp / Cover art by Alan Lee.
b. _____, Fontana Books, London, England/William Collins Sons & Co. Ltd., Glasgow, Scotland, 1981 (pb)
Price: £0.95p / 191pp / Cover art by Alan Lee.
(*"I am of the opinion that to write a successful ghost story, the author must believe in the existence of ghosts. I do—although I have yet to experience any form of psychic phenomenon myself. I cannot understand why anyone should harbour doubts. Surely it is inconceivable that such a complicated being as an intelligent man or woman ceases to be once the chains of corporeal life have fallen away. And if we are granted a state of continuous memory, then it must follow that regrets, awareness of incompleted tasks, a burden of guilt that may well be the result of misdeeds spread over several lifetimes, might compel*

certain of us to linger in this vale of tears." R.C-H.)

C16 THE SIXTEENTH FONTANA BOOK OF GREAT GHOST STORIES

Contents: Introduction by R. Chetwynd-Hayes, *Canon Alberic's Scrapbook* by M.R. James, *Mariners* by Terry Tapp, *Beyond the Red Door* by Kenneth Hill, *The Story of Medhans Lea* by "E. Heron and H. Heron" [Kate Prichard and Hesketh Prichard], *Just for the Record* by Patricia Moynehan, *The Cook's Room* by Pansy Pakenham, *Norton Camp* by William Charlton, *The Prescription* by Marjorie Bowen, *The Rock Garden* by Heather Vineham, *Brickett Bottom* by Amyas Northcote, *The Swan* by Pamela Hansford Johnson, *The Children and the Apple Tree* by Meg Buxton, *The Water Ghost of Harrowby Hall* by John Kendrick Bangs, *Destination Glen Doll* by A. Scupham, *She Walks On Dry Land* by R. Chetwynd-Hayes.

a. _____, Fontana Books, London, England/William Collins Sons & Co. Ltd., Glasgow, Scotland, 1980 (pb)
Price: £0.95p / 192pp.
(*"To have a full chilling effect a ghost should be heard and not seen. Possibly this is the reason that radio is such a perfect medium for the ghost story, because the listener is only permitted to hear approaching footsteps, creaking doors, a disembodied sigh—and his imagination does the rest. To actually meet a ghost face-to-face must be an anti-climax; merely confronting a man or woman who might be a little transparent round the edges."* R. C-H.)

C17 THE SEVENTEENTH FONTANA BOOK OF GREAT GHOST STORIES

Contents: Introduction by R. Chetwynd-Hayes, *The Reaper's Image* by Stephen King, *Help the Railway Mission* by Dorothy K. Haynes, *The Cupboard* by Jeffery Farnol, *The Shot-Tower Ghost* by Mary Elizabeth Counselman, *After Dark* by Tony Richards, *Dead Man's Barn* by A.E. Ellis, *The Passing of Edward* by Richard Middleton, *The Last Innings* by Daphne Frome, *Christmas Eve in the Blue Chamber* by Jerome K. Jerome, *Catherine's*

Angel by Heather Vineham, *The Lamp* by Agatha Christie, *Welcombe Manor* by "Roger Malisson" [Catherine Gleason and Rita Morris], *The Bed* by Terry Tapp, *An Unsolved Mystery* by E. Owens Blackburne, *Which One?* by R. Chetwynd-Hayes, *The Horrors of Sleep* by Emily Brontë.

a. _____, Fontana Books, London, England/William Collins Sons & Co. Ltd., Glasgow, Scotland, 1981 (pb)
Price: £1.00 / 190pp.

(*"So—sixteen chilling stories and one mystic poem, the work of seventeen authors, a few long in their graves, others but recently departed, the rest still with us and eagerly awaiting the reception of their latest efforts. Remember today's modern story is tomorrow's classic. Happy Shuddering."* R.C-H.)

C18 THE EIGHTEENTH FONTANA BOOK OF GREAT GHOST STORIES

Contents: Introduction by R. Chetwynd-Hayes, *Eye to Eye* by Roger F. Dunkley, *Housewarming* by Steve Rasnic Tem, *Kindred Spirits* by Rick Kennett, *The Ankardyne Pew* by W.F. Harvey, *Outside Agency* by Daphne Froome, *The Empty Schoolroom* by Pamela Hansford Johnson, *Off the Deep End* by Phillip C. Heath, *The Summer House* by Heather Vineham, *The Ferries* by Ramsey Campbell, *The New Old House* by Robert Solomon, *Bad Company* by Walter de la Mare, *The Old Rectory Well* by Patricia Moynehan, *Streets of the City* by Tony Richards, *Kecksies* by Marjorie Bowen, *Above and Beyond* by Charles Brameld, *The Chair* by R. Chetwynd-Hayes.

a. _____, Fontana Books, London, England/William Collins Sons & Co. Ltd., Glasgow, Scotland, 1982 (pb)
Price: £1.25 / 192pp.

(*"So—sixteen stories, every one written by a well established and in some cases world famous author. All written with the deliberate intention of scaring the living daylights out of the reader. I sincerely hope and pray this intention is realised. May black angels keep watch around your bed."* R.C-H.)

C19 THE NINETEENTH FONTANA BOOK OF GREAT GHOST STORIES

Contents: Introduction by R. Chetwynd-Hayes, *Situation Vacant* by Meg Buxton, *Drake's Drum* by Rick Kennett, *In the Dark* by Mary E. Penn, *A Day Out* by Richard Davis, *The Fetch* by Tina Rath, *Shadows on the Grass* by Steve Rasnic Tem, *Guests from Gibbet Island* by Washington Irving, *Safety Zone* by Alan W. Lear, *The Way Shadows Fall* by James Turner, *The Tryst* by Garry Kilworth, *An Apparition* by Guy de Maupassant, *Lost Eden* by Heather Vineham, *Still Life* by Daphne Froome, *They Walk At Evening* by Mary Williams, *Tomorrow's Ghost* by R. Chetwynd-Hayes.

a. _____, Fontana Books, London, England/William Collins Sons & Co. Ltd., Glasgow, Scotland, 1983 (pb) Price: £1.50 / 191pp.

(*"It does not seem possible that almost twelve years have passed since I first agreed to take on the chore of editing the* Fontana Books of Great Ghost Stories. *All ten of my previous collections are (thankfully) still selling, as indeed are the earlier eight selected by my predecessor Robert Aickman. Ghost-story addicts still demand the same mixture: a preponderance of modern plots where recognizable characters find themselves in bizarre circumstances, blended with a few oldies that have not been too over-exposed. But I find that my main problem is attracting authors who—to coin a phrase—can hide time-bleached skulls behind new faces."* R.C-H.)

C20 THE TWENTIETH FONTANA BOOK OF GREAT GHOST STORIES

Contents: Introduction by R. Chetwynd-Hayes, *Aunt Hester* by Brian Lumly, *Skin Deep* by "Roger Malisson" [Catherine Gleason and Rita Morris], *How Fear Departed from the Long Gallery* by E.F. Benson, *Carrie Liddicoat's Cottage* by Meg Buxton, *The Diary of William Carpenter* by John Atkins, *The Roads of Donnington* by Rick Kennett, *The Running Tide* by "Ex-Private X" [A.M. Burrage], *A Lady in the Night* by Dorothy K. Haynes, *The Villa Désirée* by May Sinclair, *Graveyard Lodge* by Heather Vineham,

Ordeal by Fire by Gladys Law, *Our Lady of the Shadows* by Tony Richards, *The Rip Current* by Daphne Froome, *My Very Best Friend* by R. Chetwynd-Hayes.

a. _____, Fontana Books, London, England/William Collins Sons & Co. Ltd., Glasgow, Scotland, 1984 (pb)

Price: £1.50 / 190pp / Cover art by Les Edwards.

(*"I sometimes like to think that long after I am dead and gone, these Fontana Books of Great Ghost Stories will become collector's items. Not impossible. If so—which stories will still be readable—and reprintable—in that, hopefully, far off age? Obviously those that do not date, continue to entertain and scare. Make the reader say: 'They don't write 'em like that anymore.' I do not write for posterity, but I always have it in mind. We all haunt the future and are of the stuff from which ghosts are made; often fit subjects for our own imaginative creations. Planting fantasy seedlings that, perhaps, will not be out of place in the literary landscape of a hundred years hence. Always supposing there is anyone left who can read."* R.C-H.)

C21 **GASLIGHT TALES OF TERROR**

Contents: Introduction by R. Chetwynd-Hayes, *The Last Victim* by "Roger Malisson" [Catherine Gleason and Rita Morris], *A Tale of a Gaslight Ghost* by Anonymous, *The Paupers' Feast* by Sydney J. Bounds, *Number 13* by M.R. James, *Up, Like a Good Girl* by Dorothy K. Haynes, *An Authentic Narrative of a Haunted House* by J. Sheridan LeFanu, *The Glass Staircase* by R. Thurston Hopkins, *The Maid, The Madman and the Knife* by Rosemary Timperley, *What Was It?* by Fitz-James O'Brien, *The Veritable Verasco* by James Jauncey, *The Silver Highway* by Harold Lawlor, *Mrs. Raeburn's Waxwork* by Lady Eleanor Smith, *The Phantom of the Lake* by Edmund Mitchell M.A., *Keep the Gaslight Burning* by R. Chetwynd-Hayes.

a. _____, Fontana Books, London, England/William Collins Sons & Co. Ltd., Glasgow, Scotland, 1976 (pb)

Price: £0.50p / 191pp / Cover art by Justin Todd.

(*"Here are fourteen* Gaslight Tales of Terror, *including one or two oil-lamps and a few guttering candles. With one exception all the stories have either a Victorian or Edwardian background, although this was not strictly necessary, as I can remember houses lit by gas in 1950. But although—if newspaper reports are to be believed—ghosts and other horrors have not been exorcised by the advent of space travel and colour television, one feels they were more at home during the reign of Queen Victoria. And I do mean* at home*: in pea-souper fogs, on gloomy streets where the lamp-lighter with his long pole trudged wearily from post to post, and a potential Jack the Ripper lurked in dark alleyways. Make certain you keep the gaslight burning while reading this book."* R.C-H.)

C22 **GREAT GHOST STORIES**

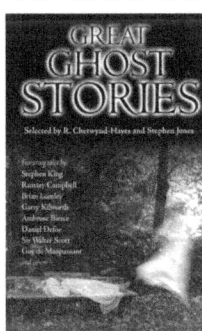

Contents: Foreword by Stephen Jones, Introduction by R. Chetwynd-Hayes, *The Four-Fifteen Express* by Amelia B. Edwards, *On the Brighton Road* by Richard Middleton, *The Moonlit Road* by Ambrose Bierce, *The Whittaker's Ghost* by "G.B.S." [George Bernard Shaw], *The Leaden Ring* by S. Baring-Gould, *The Tapestried Chamber* by Sir Walter Scott, *Ghost Stories of the Tiled House* by Joseph Sheridan Le Fanu, *The Dead Smile* by F. Marion Crawford, *The Ghost of Dorothy Dingley* by Daniel Defoe, *The Dead Man of Varley Grange* by Anonymous, *John Charrington's Wedding* by E. Nesbit, *The Night Walkers* by Sydney J. Bounds, *Brickett Bottom* by Amyas Northcote, *The Water Ghost of Harrowby Hall* by John Kendrick Bangs, *The Reaper's Image* by Stephen King, *Christmas Eve in the Blue Chamber* by Jerome K. Jerome, *House-warming* by Steve Rasnic Tem, *The Ferries* by Ramsey Campbell, *The Fetch* by Tina Rath, *Guests from Gibbet Island* by Washington Irving, *The Tryst* by Garry Kilworth, *An Apparition* by Guy de Maupassant, *Aunt Hester* by Brian Lumley, *Our Lady of the Shadows* by Tony Richards, *She Walks on Dry Land* by R. Chetwynd-Hayes.
a. _____, Carroll & Graf, New York, USA, 2004 (tpb) Price: $13.00 / 326pp / Cover photo: Michael Gesinger.
[Note: "Selected by R. Chetwynd-Hayes and Stephen Jones".]
b. _____, Carroll & Graf, New York, USA, 2004 (tpb) Price: $14.00 / 326pp / Cover photo: Michael Gesinger.
[Note: "Selected by R. Chetwynd-Hayes and Stephen Jones".]
c. [as **GREAT GHOST STORIES: TALES OF MYSTERY AND MADNESS**], Cemetery Dance Publications, Maryland, USA, 2005 (hc)

There are two variants of this edition.

i. Description: trade edition
Price: $40.00 / 356pp / Cover art by Les Edwards.
ii. Description: 52-copy signed, lettered edition in traycase
Price: $500.00 / 356pp / Cover art by Les Edwards.
[Note: Sold out before publication.]
[Note: "Selected by R. Chetwynd-Hayes and Stephen Jones".]
d. _____, Carroll & Graf, New York, USA, 2007 (tpb)
Price: $14.95 / 326pp / Cover photograph by Michael Gesinger.
[Note: "Selected by R. Chetwynd-Hayes and Stephen Jones".]

C23 SCOTTISH TALES OF TERROR

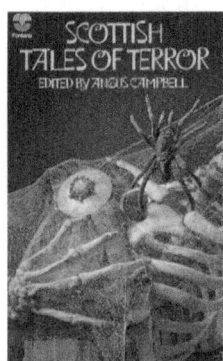

Contents: Introduction by "Angus Campbell" [R. Chetwynd-Hayes], *Brown God in the Beginning* by Angus Stewart, *The Mad Son of Queensbury* by Francis Bamford and Sacheverell Sitwell, *The Body-Snatcher* by Robert Louis Stevenson, *A Story of Loch Skipport* by John L. Campbell and Trevor H. Hall, *The Ghost of Sergeant Davis* by Sir Walter Scott, *The Inheritance* by Simon Pilkington, *Shona and the Water Horse* by R. Chetwynd-Hayes, *The Fisherman's Tale* by R. Macdonald Robertson, *The Phantom Chief* by Sir Walter Scott, *The Silver Mirror* by Sir Arthur Conan Doyle, *The Haunting of St. Giles* by Elliott O'Donnell, *The Horns of the Bull* by W.S. Morrison, *The Dog of Roslin* by R. Macdonald Robertson, *Wandering Willie's Tale* by Sir Walter Scott, *The Old Manse of Lairg* by R. Macdonald Robertson, *Consanguinity* by Ronald Duncan, *Loch Sin* by Arthur Waugh and Gwen Benwell, *The House in the Glen* by John Connell, *The Nuckelavee* by K.M. Briggs, *The Lovers* by John Keir Cross, *The Standing Stones* by Otta F. Swire, *The Head* by Dorothy K. Haynes, *The Witches of Auldearne* by Sir Walter Scott, *The Lass with the Delicate Air* by Eileen Bigland, *The Walking Dead* by Otta F. Swire, *Sawney Beane and his Family* by John Nicholson, *The Brownie of the Black Hags* by James Hogg, *My Grandfather is Rising* by John L. Campbell and Trevor H. Hall.
a. _____, Fontana Books, London, England/William Collins Sons & Co. Ltd., Glasgow, Scotland, 1972 (pb)
Price: £0.25p / 190pp.

[Note: "Edited by Angus Campbell".]
b. _____, Fontana Books, London, England/William Collins Sons & Co. Ltd., Glasgow, Scotland, 1974 (pb)
Price: £0.35p / 190pp.
[Note: "Edited by Angus Campbell".]
c. _____, Fontana Books, London, England/William Collins Sons & Co. Ltd., Glasgow, Scotland, 1975 (pb)
190pp.
[Note: "Edited by Angus Campbell".]
d. _____, Fontana Books, London, England/William Collins Sons & Co. Ltd., Glasgow, Scotland, 1979 (pb)
Price: £0.80p / 190pp / Cover art by Justin Todd.
[Note: "Edited by Angus Campbell".]
(*"For, let it be understood, this was my intention when compiling this anthology—to murder sleep. To draw you gradually into a morass of unquiet thoughts that, once the light is out, should blossom forth into a white-petalled flower of doubt—as to whether the dressing-gown hanging on the bedroom door is, indeed, what it should be."* R.C-H.]

C24 TALES OF TERROR FROM OUTER SPACE

Contents: Introduction by R. Chetwynd-Hayes, *I, Mars* by Ray Bradbury, *Eight O'Clock in the Morning* by Ray Nelson, *Girl from Mars* by Robert Bloch, *Heresies of the Huge God* by Brian W. Aldiss, *The Head-Hunters* by Ralph Williams, *The Animators* by Sydney J. Bounds, *The Night of the Seventh Finger* by Robert Presslie, *No More for Mary* by Charles Birkin, *Invasion of Privacy* by Bob Shaw, *The Ruum* by Arthur Porges, *The First Days of May* by Claude Veillot, *Specialist* by Robert Sheckley, *No Morning After* by Arthur C. Clarke, *Shipwreck* by R. Chetwynd-Hayes.
a. _____, Fontana Books, London, England / William Collins Sons & Co. Ltd., Glasgow, Scotland, 1975 (pb)
Price: £0.45p / 190pp / Cover art by Justin Todd.
(*"Although in the course of compiling this collection I have read an average of fifty science-fiction anthologies, none of the stories I selected have much to do with science. With one exception, they deal with invaders that either menace or disconcert the inhabitants of this*

already, agitated planet. Having—I sincerely trust—read this book from cover to cover, you will have some idea of what to expect in the near future. You could be crushed by a giant insect from outer space, eaten by a blonde from Mars, lose your head to a celestial hunter, become an animated corpse in an empty house, come second in a race with a Ruum, be turned into an egg-laying machine by a Shrill, or have a one-sided conversation with a lump of jelly. It doesn't leave much time to worry about the rising cost of living." R.C-H.)

C25 TALES TO FREEZE THE BLOOD: MORE GREAT GHOST STORIES

Contents: Foreword by Stephen Jones, Introduction by R. Chetwynd-Hayes, *The Furnished Room* by O. Henry, *The Night-Doings at "Deadman's"* by Ambrose Bierce, *A Little Night Fishing* by Sydney J. Bounds, *Not Yet Solved* by Anonymous, *The Hostelry* by Guy de Maupassant, *The Grey Cottage* by Mrs. Claxton, *Round the Fire* by Catherine Crowe, *The Doll's Ghost* by F. Marion Crawford, *Madam Crowl's Ghost* by J. Sheridan Le Fanu, *The Cold Embrace* by Mary Elizabeth Braddon, *At Ravenholme Junction* by "Anonymous" [Mary E. Penn], *How the Third Floor Knew the Potteries* by Amelia B. Edwards, *The Saving of a Soul* by Sir Richard Burton, *The Bearer of the Message* by Fritz Hopman, *Canon Alberic's Scrapbook* by M.R. James, *The Story of Medhans Lea* by "E. Heron and H. Heron" [Kate Prichard and Hesketh Prichard], *The Passing of Edward* by Richard Middleton, *An Unsolved Mystery* by E. Owens Blackburne, *The Horrors of Sleep* by Emily Brontë, *Streets of the City* by Tony Richards, *In the Dark* by Mary E. Penn, *Shadows on the Grass* by Steve Rasnic Tem, *The Roads of Donnington* by Rick Kennett, *The Day That Father Brought Something Home* by R. Chetwynd-Hayes.

a. _____, Carroll & Graf, Maryland, USA, 2006 (tpb) Price: $15.95 / 270pp / Cover photograph by Simon Marsden [Note: "Selected by R. Chetwynd-Hayes and Stephen Jones".]

C26 WELSH TALES OF TERROR

Contents: Introduction by R. Chetwynd-Hayes, *Jordan* by Glyn Jones, *Old Ben* by Hazel F. Looker, *A Cry of Children* by John

Christopher, *The Cyoeraeth* by W. Howells, *The Shining Pyramid* by Arthur Machen, *The Brown Hobgoblin of Bedd Gelert* by D.E. Jenkins, *Animals or Human Beings* by Angus Wilson, *The Man on a Bike* by Hazel F. Looker, *The Morgan Trust* by Richard Bridgeman, *Dead Man's Candle* by Marie Trevelyan, *Water Horses and Spirits of the Mist* by Marie Trevelyan, *Be This Her Memorial* by Caradoc Evans, *The Tolling Bell* by Marie Trevelyan, *The Black Lady of Boverton* by Marie Trevelyan, *The Lost Gold Mine* by Hazel F. Looker, *Satan and a Load of Bibles* by Rev. Elias Owen, *Mrs. Jones* by Dorothy K. Haynes, *The Ghost of Pont Cnnca Bach* by W. Howells, *The Reverend John Jones and the Ghostly Horseman* by Ronald Seth, *Corpse Candles* by W. Howells, *Cadi Hughes* by Glyn Jones, *The White Lady of Aberglaslyn Pass* by D.E. Jenkins, *Black Goddess* by Jack Griffith, *The Devil's Tree* by Rev. Elias Owen, *The Stranger* by Richard Hughes, *A Perilous Struggle* by D.E. Jenkins, *Lord Dunwilliam and the Cwn Annwn* by R. Chetwynd-Hayes.

a. _____, Fontana Books, London, England/William Collins Sons & Co. Ltd., Glasgow, Scotland, 1973 (pb) Price: £0.30p / 188pp.

b. _____, Fontana Books, London, England/William Collins Sons & Co. Ltd., Glasgow, Scotland, 1975 (pb) Price: £0.45p / 188pp / Cover art by Justin Todd.

c. [as **GESPENSTERGESCHICHTEN AUS WALES** (Ghost Stories from Wales)], S. Fischer Verlag, Frankfurt, Germany, 1978 (pb) 139pp / Translated by Karl H. Kosmehl.

(*"I had a good deal of fun when compiling this anthology of Welsh Tales of Terror, although the task was not an easy one. The Principality is rich in folk-lore and has more than its fair share of ghosts—in fact, so far as I can see, one cannot walk down a country lane after sunset without encountering a headless horseman or a pack of hell-hounds on the rampage. My difficulty lay in selecting from a mass of material an assorted collection that dealt with the many aspects of Welsh supernatural life."* R.C-H.)

D. OTHER PUBLICATIONS

(INCLUDES AN ALPHABETICAL LISTING OF OTHER PUBLICATIONS
WRITTEN, EDITED OR BASED ON THE WORK OF R. CHETWYND-HAYES)

D1 GHOUL 1

Contents: Beyond Terror, *I Met the Great Indestructible: Exclusive Interview with Count Dracula* by "Hans Clutcher" [R. Chetwynd-Hayes], Things Aren't What They Used to Be by Denis Gifford, Horror-Scope, Christopher Lee, *Ghoul at Large* by R. Chetwynd-Hayes, On the Prowl: Chilling News from the Scream Scene, Kiss Me Quick, Vampire Kite Competition, Ghoul Gazette by R. Chetwynd-Hayes, Master of Horror 1: Edgar Allan Poe by Walter Gillings, *Some New Pleasures Prove* by Charles Birkin, Celluloid Screams, Preymate of the Month.

a. _____, New English Library, London, England, 1976 (magazine)
Price: £0.40p / 48pp / Cover art by Bruce Pennington.
[Note: Edited by an uncredited R. Chetwynd-Hayes, who also most probably wrote many of the unsigned features.]

D2 THE MONSTER CLUB

a. _____, Pioneer Press/Studio System, London, England, 1980 (magazine)
30pp / Cover art by John Bolton.
[Note: Film tie-in comic commissioned by producer Milton Subotsky to promote the film at the Cannes Film Festival. Limited to 1,000 copies. Edited and adapted by Dez Skinn, from the novel by Ronald Chetwynd-Hayes. Illustrated by John Bolton and an uncredited David Lloyd.]

b. _____, in *Halls of Horror* Vol.3, No.1 [Issue 25], Quality Communications Ltd., London, England 1983 (magazine).

c. _____, in *John Bolton's Halls of Horror* No.1, Eclipse Comics, USA, 1985 (comic book).

d. _____, in *John Bolton's Halls of Horror* No.2, Eclipse Comics, USA, 1985 (comic book).

[Note: Reprinted over two-issue "Micro-Series" with artwork colourised by Tim Smith, the title was changed to 'The Monster Cabaret'.]

e. _____, Dez Skinn Publishing, England 2018 (magazine) 30pp / Cover art by John Bolton.

[Note: Signed and numbered edition limited to 100 copies.]

D3 **SHOCKS**

Contents: Introduction by David J. Howe, *Christmas Eve, The Fly-by-Night, Head of the Firm, The Day of the Underdog.*

a. _____, The British Fantasy Society, Stockport, England, 1997 (chapbook)

Price: £6.00 / 60pp / Cover art by David J. Howe.

E. NON-FICTION

(Includes an alphabetical listing of non-fiction
written by R. Chetwynd-Hayes)

E1 AFTERWORD: ON WRITING AND WRAITHS
a. _____, Phantoms and Fiends [B13].

E2 AFTERWORD: TIME TRAVEL AND ME
a. _____, Frights and Fancies [B6].

E3 AUTHOR'S NOTE
a. _____, see The Monster Club [B10].

E4 THE BARGEST
a. _____, see Cornish Tales of Terror [C7].

E5 GHOUL GAZETTE
a. _____, see *Ghoul* 1 [D1].

E6 INTRODUCTION [as by "Angus Campbell"]
a. _____, see Scottish Tales of Terror [C23].

E7 INTRODUCTION
a. _____, see The Ninth Fontana Book of Great Ghost Stories [C9].

E8 INTRODUCTION
a. _____, see Welsh Tales of Terror [C26].

E9 INTRODUCTION
a. _____, see The Tenth Fontana Book of Great Ghost Stories [C10].

E10 INTRODUCTION
a. _____, see The First Armada Monster Book [C1].

E11 INTRODUCTION
   a. _____, see The Eleventh Fontana Book of Great Ghost Stories [C11].

E12 INTRODUCTION
   a. _____, see Tales of Terror from Outer Space [C24].

E13 INTRODUCTION
   a. _____, see The Second Armada Monster Book [C2].

E14 INTRODUCTION
   a. _____, see The Twelfth Fontana Book of Great Ghost Stories [C12].

E15 INTRODUCTION
   a. _____, see Gaslight Tales of Terror [C21].

E16 INTRODUCTION
   a. _____, see The Third Armada Monster Book [C3].

E17 INTRODUCTION
   a. _____, see The Thirteenth Fontana Book of Great Ghost Stories [C13].

E18 INTRODUCTION
   a. _____, see The Fourth Armada Monster Book [C4].

E19 INTRODUCTION
   a. _____, see Doomed to the Night: An Anthology of Ghost Stories [C8].

E20 INTRODUCTION
   a. _____, see The Fourteenth Fontana Book of Great Ghost Stories [C14].

E21 INTRODUCTION
   a. _____, see The Fifth Armada Monster Book [C5].

E22 INTRODUCTION
   a. _____, see The Fifteenth Fontana Book of Great Ghost Stories [C15].

E23 **INTRODUCTION**

    a. _____, see The Fantastic World of Kamtellar: A Book of Vampires and Ghouls, William Kimber & Co. Ltd., London, England [B5].

E24 **INTRODUCTION**

    a. _____, see The Sixteenth Fontana Book of Great Ghost Stories [C16].

E25 **INTRODUCTION**

    a. _____, see The Sixth Armada Monster Book [C6].

E26 **INTRODUCTION**

    a. _____, see The Seventeenth Fontana Book of Great Ghost Stories [C17].

E27 **INTRODUCTION**

    a. _____, see The Eighteenth Fontana Book of Great Ghost Stories [C18].

E28 **INTRODUCTION**

    a. _____, see The Nineteenth Fontana Book of Great Ghost Stories [C19].

E29 **INTRODUCTION**

    a. _____, see Tales from the Other Side [B21].

E30 **INTRODUCTION**

    a. _____, see The Twentieth Fontana Book of Great Ghost Stories [C20].

E31 **INTRODUCTION**

    a. _____, see Great Ghost Stories [C22].

E32 **INTRODUCTION**

    a. _____, see Tales to Freeze the Blood: More Great Ghost Stories [C25].

E33 ONE-WAY TRIP

a. _____, in *Dancing with the Dark: True Encounters with the Paranormal by Masters of the Macabre* edited by Stephen Jones, Vista/Cassell Group, London, England, 1997 (pb).

b. [as **NEOPAKOVATELNÝ VÝLET** (Unique Exchange)], in *Valcík s Temnotou: Mistri Hororu Vypráveji o Svých Setkáních se Záhadným a Nevysvetlitelným* (Dancing with the Dark: True Encounters with the Paranormal by Masters of the Macabre) edited by Stephen Jones, Apsida/Kniziní Klub, Prague, Czech Republic, 1998 (hc).

c. _____, in Dancing with the Dark: *True Encounters with the Paranormal by Masters of the Macabre* edited by Stephen Jones, Carroll & Graf Publishers, Inc., New York, USA, 1999 (tpb).

d. [as (**VIAGGIO DI SOLA ANDATA** (One-Way Journey)], in *La Danza delle tenebre* (Dancing with the Dark) edited by Stephen Jones, Bompiani, Milan, Italy, 1999 (tpb).

e. [as **WALK IN DARKNESS**], see Frights and Fancies [B6]. [Note: This version is significantly different.]

f. _____, in *A Ghostly Cry: True Encounters with the Paranormal* by Stephen Jones, Fall River Press/Barnes & Noble, New York, USA, 2009 (hc).

E34 THE TURN OF THE SCREW

a. _____, in *Horror 100 Best Books*, edited by Stephen Jones and Kim Newman, Xanadu Publications Limited, London, England, 1988 (hc).

There are two variants of this edition.

i. Description: trade edition
Price: £11.99 / 256pp.
ii. Description: 300-copy signed
Price: £100.00 / 256pp.

b. _____, in *Horror 100 Best Books*, edited by Stephen Jones and Kim Newman, Carroll & Graf Publishers, Inc., New York, USA, 1988 (hc).

c. _____, in *Horror 100 Best Books*, edited by Stephen Jones and Kim Newman, Carroll & Graf Publishers, Inc., New York, USA, 1990 (tpb).

d. _____, in *Horror: 100 Best Books*, edited by Stephen Jones and Kim Newman, New English Library/Hodder and Stoughton Ltd., London, England, 1992 (tpb).

e. _____, in *Horror: 100 Best Books*, edited by Stephen Jones and Kim Newman, Carroll & Graf Publishers, Inc., New York, USA, 1998 (tpb).

E35 WALK IN DARKNESS

a. _____, see 'One-Way Trip' [E33(e)].

F. SHORT STORIES

(INCLUDES AN ALPHABETICAL LISTING OF SHORT STORIES WRITTEN BY R. CHETWYND-HAYES AND PUBLISHED IN BOOKS AND MAGAZINES)

F1 **ACQUIRING A FAMILY**

a. _____, see Tales from the Shadows [B22].

b. _____, in *The Years Best Horror Stories XV* edited by Karl Edward Wagner, DAW Books, New York, USA, 1987 (pb).

c. _____, in *Horrorstory Volume Five* edited by Karl Edward Wagner, Underwood-Miller, San Francisco, USA, 1989 (hc).

d. _____, see The Vampire Stories of R. Chetwynd-Hayes [B27].

e. _____, see Gaslight, Ghosts, & Ghouls [B27].

F2 **ALICE IN BELLINGTON LANE**

a. _____, see Tales from the Haunted House [B19].

F3 **THE AMAZING PINK CAR**

a. _____, in *Fun on Wheels* compiled by Mary Danby, Armada/William Collins Sons & Co. Ltd., London, England, 1973 (pb).

F4 **AMELIA**

a. _____, see The Fantastic World of Kamtellar and Other Stories of Fear and Horror [B5].

b. _____, see The Vampire Stories of R. Chetwynd-Hayes [B27]

(*"'Amelia' was written quite recently and is very nasty. The lovely lady came slithering up from the stew-pot uninvited, a daughter of Satan who invades the so-called normal, world, that I can never imagine to be other than a horror-surrounded island, situated off the southern coast of Hell. Read your newspapers before you dare to disagree with me."* R.C-H.)

F5 **AN ACT OF KINDNESS**
    a. _____, see Cold Terror [B1].
    b. _____, see From Beyond the Grave [G2].

F6 **THE ASTRAL INVASION**
    a. _____, see Tales from the Dark Lands [B18].
    [Note: A "Fred and Francis" story.]

F7 **THE BED-SITTING ROOM**
    a. _____, see Shudders and Shivers [B15].

F8 **BENJAMIN**
    a. _____, see Dracula's Children [B3].

F9 **BIG-FEET**
    a. _____, see The First Armada Monster Book [C1].
    b. _____, see Frights and Fancies [B6].
("*I could not be bothered with the common or garden monster, so I invented one of my own:* Big-Feet. *If you should be walking down the Ashford-Canterbury road, and you happen to be in the right place, at the right time, and in the right mood, who knows...?*" R.C-H.)

F10 **BIRDS OF A FEATHER**
    a. _____, see Cold Terror [B1].

F11 **BIRTH**
    a. _____, see The Elemental & Other Stories [B4].
    b. _____, see The Fantastic World of Kamtellar: A Book of Vampires [B5].
    c. [as **NAISSANCE** (Birth)], in *Antarès: Science Fiction & Fantastque sans frontièrs* Volume 33 edited by Jean-Pierre Moumon and Martine Blond, les Editions Antarès, La Valette, France, 1989 (magazine).
    d. _____, see The Vampire Stories of R. Chetwynd-Hayes [B27].
("*When I wrote 'Birth', I am certain it was prompted by my curiosity regarding what takes place after death—if anything. Should continuity of thought survive, then surely there must be an intense urge to get back into a physical body in the quickest possible time. Or—as in the case of my hero—make another one.*" R.C-H.)

F12 **BITS AND PIECES**
    a. _____, see Terror by Night [B25(a)].
    b. _____, see Gaslight, Ghosts, & Ghouls [B27].

F13 **THE BODMIN TERROR**
    a. _____, see Cornish Tales of Terror [C7].
    b. _____, see Phantoms and Fiends [B13].
(*"This is the result of taking people I know, casting them in bizarre roles, then allowing imagination to do the rest."* R.C-H.)

F14 **BODY AND SOUL**
    a. _____, see A Quiver of Ghosts [B14].

F15 **BONGLA**
    a. _____, see Phantoms and Fiends [B13].
[Note: This was originally started as a novel in 1990.]

F16 **BORN THIS NIGHT**
    a. _____, see Phantoms and Fiends [B13].
[Note: The working title for this story was 'The Party'.]

F17 **THE BRATS**
    a. _____, see The Cradle Demon and Other Stories of Fantasy and Terror [B2].

F18 **BRICKS AND MORTAR–1969**
    a. _____, see Tales from the Other Side [B21].
[Note: A "Chronicles of Clavering Grange" story.]

F19 **BROWNIE**

    a. _____, in *The Third Armada Ghost Book* edited by Mary Danby, Armada/May Fair Books Ltd., London, England, 1970 (pb).
    b. _____, in *Spooky Stories 1* edited by Barbara Ireson, Carousel, London, England, 1975 (pb).
    c. _____, in *Ghosts That Haunt You* edited by Aidan Chambers, Viking, New York, USA, 1980 (hc).
    d. _____, in *Ghosts that Haunt You* edited by Aidan Chambers, Puffin Books Ltd., London, England, 1983 (pb).

e. _____, in *The Bumper Book of Ghost Stories 2: School Book Fairs Special* edited by Anonymous (Mary Danby), HarperCollins, London,
England, 1991 (pb).

f. _____, in *Dread and Delight: A Century of Children's Ghost Stories* edited by Philippa Pearce, Oxford University Press, USA, 1995 (pb).

g. _____, in *A Century of Children's Ghost Stories: Tales of Dread and Delight* edited by Philippa Pearce, Oxford University Press, USA, 1996 (pb).

h. _____, in *Favorite Ghost Stories* edited by Aidan Chambers, Kingfisher Books/Macmillan, New York, USA, 2002 (pb).

i. _____, in *Favourite Ghost Stories* edited by Aidan Chambers, Kingfisher Books/Macmillan, London, England, 2002 (pb).

j. _____, see Frights and Fancies [B6].

k. _____, in *More Ghost Stories* edited by Aidan Chambers, Kingfisher Books/Macmillan, New York, USA, 2004 (tpb).

F20 **THE BUCK**

a. _____, see The Vampire Stories of R. Chetwynd-Hayes [B27].

F21 **BUILDING SITE MANUSCRIPT**

a. _____, see The Night Ghouls and Other Grisly Tales [B11].
b. [as **BERICHTE AUS EINER ANDEREN ZEIT**], see 6 x Panische nächte [B16].

F22 **CALVUNDER**

a. _____, in *The Twelfth Ghost Book* edited by Anonymous [Polly Parkin], Barrie & Jenkins, London, England, 1976 (hc).
b. _____, in *The Second Bumper Book of Ghost Stories* edited by Polly Parkin and James Hale, Pan Books, London, England, 1978 (pb).
c. _____, see A Quiver of Ghosts [B14].

F23 **CAROLINE**

a. _____, see The House of Dracula [B8].

F24 **THE CARRIER**
    a. _____, see Tales from the Shadows [B22].

F25 **THE CATOMADO**
    a. _____, in *Frighteners* edited by Mary Danby, Fontana Books, London, England/William Collins Sons & Co. Ltd., Glasgow, Scotland, 1974 (pb).
    a. _____, in *Frighteners* edited by Mary Danby, Fontana Books, London, England/William Collins Sons & Co. Ltd., Glasgow, Scotland, 1976 (pb).
    c. _____, see Phantoms and Fiends [B13].

F26 **THE CAT ROOM**

    a. _____, in *The Twelfth Armada Ghost Book* edited by Mary Danby, Armada/Fontana Paperbacks, London, England, 1980 (pb).
    b. _____, in *Ghost Stories* edited by Anonymous, St. Michael, London, England, 1982 (hc).
    c. _____, in *Ghost Stories* edited by Anonymous, Cathay Books, New York, USA, 1984 (hc).
    d. _____, see Frights and Fancies [B6].

F27 **THE CHAIR**
    a. _____, see The Cradle Demon and Other Stories of Fantasy and Terror [B2].
    b. _____, see The Eighteenth Fontana Book of Great Ghost Stories [C18].
    c. _____, in *Worlds of Fantasy & Horror* Vol.1, No.4, Winter 1996-7 edited by Darrell Schweitzer, Terminus Publishing Co., Inc., King of Prussia, Pennsylvania, USA, 1996 (magazine).
    d. _____, in *Weird Tales Summer 1994–Summer 1996* edited by Darrell Schweitzer, Wildside Press, Rockville, Maryland, USA, 2003 (tpb).
(*"What can I say about it? It is true? Could be. Someone is almost certain to write in and say they have such a chair and would like to dispose of it. My advice will be—hang on to it. Haunted chairs will soon be the vogue and worth their weight in postage stamps."* R.C-H.)

F28 THE CHANGELING
a. _____, see Tales of Fear and Fantasy [B24].

F29 A CHILL TO THE SUNLIGHT
a. _____, in *A Chill to the Sunlight: Tropical Stories of the Macabre* edited by Rick Ferreira, William Kimber & Co., London, England, 1978 (hc).
b. _____, see Phantoms and Fiends [B13].

F30 CHRISTMAS EVE
a. _____, see The Night Ghouls and Other Grisly Tales [B11].
b. _____, in *Horror for Christmas* edited by Richard Dalby, Michael O'Mara Books, London, England, 1992 (hc).
c. _____, in *Horror for Christmas* edited by Richard Dalby, Headline, London, England, 1993 (tpb).
d. _____, in *Mistletoe & Mayhem: Tales for the Holidays* edited by Richard Dalby, Castle Books, USA, 1993 (hc).
e. _____, in *Horror for Christmas* edited by Richard Dalby, Brockhampton Press, Leicester, England, 1995 (hc).
f. _____, see Shocks [D3].
[Note: This story was transcribed into Braille by the Royal National Institute for the Blind in 1997.]
g. _____, in *Christmas Under the Covers* edited by Marc Damian Lawler, Amazon, England, 2021 (tpb).

F31 A CLAVERING CHRONICLE
a. _____, see Tales from the Haunted House [B19].
[A "Chronicles of Clavering Grange" story.]

F32 CLAVERING RETREAT
a. _____, see Tales from the Shadows [B22].
[A "Chronicles of Clavering Grange" story.]

F33 COLD FINGERS
a. _____, see The Twelfth Fontana Book of Great Ghost Stories [C12].
b. _____, see Ghosts from the Mist of Time [B7].
(*"My ghosts are always nasty. Sometimes in fact really vile, and the thing which materializes in Miss Partridge's third-floor back, is no*

exception... Which only demonstrates what an awful mind I must have." R.C.-H.)

F34 THE COLOURED TRANSMISSION

a. _____, in *The Tenth Ghost Book* edited by Aidan Chambers, Barrie & Jenkins, London, England, 1974 (hc).
b. _____, in *The Bumper Book of Ghost Stories* edited by Aidan Chambers, Pan Books, London, England, 1976 (pb).
c. [as **THE COLORED TRANSMISSION**] see: Terror by Night [B25(b)].
d. _____, see A Quiver of Ghosts [B14].
e. _____, in *After Midnight* edited by Charles L. Grant, Tor Books, New York, USA, 1986 (pb)
f. _____, see Gaslight, Ghosts, & Ghouls [B27].

F35 COME TO ME MY FLOWER

a. _____, see The Unbidden [B26].

F36 COMING HOME

a. _____, see Cold Terror [B1].
b. _____, in *Ghosts in Country Villages* edited by Denys Val Baker, William Kimber & Co., London, England, 1983 (hc).

F37 THE COST OF DYING

a. _____, see Tales of Fear and Fantasy [B24].

F38 THE CRADLE DEMON

a. _____, see The Cradle Demon and Other Stories of Fantasy and Terror [B2].
b. [as **LE DÉMON AU BERCEAU** (The Devil in the Cradle)], in *Les Masques de la peur* (The Masks of Fear) Fiction spécial No.33, October 1983 edited by Richard D. Nolane, OPTA, Paris, France, 1983 (magazine).
c. _____, in *Chamber of Horrors* edited by Anonymous [Emma Blackley], Octopus Books, London, England, 1984 (hc).
d. _____, see Gaslight, Ghosts, & Ghouls [B27].

F39 THE CREATOR

a. _____, see The Cradle Demon and Other Stories of

Fantasy and Terror [B2].

b. _____, in *The Mammoth Book of Frankenstein* edited by Stephen Jones, Robinson Publishing, London, England, 1994 (tpb).

c. _____, in *The Mammoth Book of Frankenstein* edited by Stephen Jones, Carroll & Graf, New York, USA, 1994 (tpb).

d. _____, in *The Mammoth Book of Frankenstein* edited by Stephen Jones, Justsystem, Japan, 1995 (hc).

e. _____, in *The Giant Book of Frankenstein* edited by Stephen Jones, Magpie Books, London, England, 1995 (tpb).

f. _____, in *The Giant Book of Frankenstein* edited by Stephen Jones, The Book Company International, Australia, 1995 (tpb).

g. _____, in *Tutte le storie di frankenstein* (All the Stories of Frankenstein) edited by Stephen Jones, Newton Compton, Italy, 1996 (tpb).

h. _____, in *Франкенштейн* (Frankenstein) edited by Stephen Jones, Azbooka-Atticus Publishing Group, Russia, 2012 (hc).

i. _____, in *The Mammoth Book of Frankenstein* edited by Stephen Jones, Robinson Publishing, London, England, 2015 (tpb).

j. _____, in *In the Shadow of Frankenstein: Tales of the Modern Prometheus*, Pegasus Books, USA, 2016 (hc).
[Note: A softcover Adavance Reading Copy also exists.]

k. _____, in *In the Shadow of Frankenstein: Tales of the Modern Prometheus*, Pegasus Books, USA, 2017 (tpb).

F40 THE CRINGING COUPLE OF CLAVERING

a. _____, see Tales from the Hidden World: Four Episodes in the History of Clavering Grange [B20].[A "Chronicles of Clavering Grange" and a "Fred and Francis" story.]

F41 CROWNING GLORY

a. _____, see The Unbidden [B26].

b. _____, in *World of Horror* No.3 edited by "Gent Shaw" [Jim Shier], Dallruth Publishing Group, London, England, 1974 (magazine).

F42 THE CUMBERLOO
a. _____, see Shudders and Shivers [B15].

F43 CUTHBERT
a. _____, see Dracula's Children [B3].

F44 DANGER IN NUMBERS
a. _____, see The Night Ghouls and Other Grisly Tales [B11].
b. _____, see A Quiver of Ghosts [B14].
c. [as **TROP Ç'EST TROP** (Enough is Enough)], in *Show Effori* (Show Dread) No.1, May 1996 edited by Daniel Conrad, France, 1996 (magazine).

F45 DARKNESS
a. _____, see Tales of Darkness [B23].

F46 THE DAY FATHER BROUGHT SOMETHING HOME
a. _____, see Cold Terror [B1].
b. [as **THE DAY THAT FATHER BROUGHT SOMETHING HOME**], see Doomed to the Night: An Anthology of Ghost Stories [C8].
c. [as **LE JOUR OÙ PAPA RAMENA QUELQUE CHOSE À LA MAISON** (The Day Father Brought Something Home)], in *Antarès: Science Fiction & Fantastque sans frontièrs* Volume 36 edited by Jean-Pierre Moumon and Martine Blond, les Editions Antarès, La Valette, France, 1990 (magazine).
d. [as **THE DAY THAT FATHER BROUGHT SOMETHING HOME**], see Tales to Freeze the Blood: More Great Ghost Stories [C25].
e. _____, see Gaslight, Ghosts, & Ghouls [B27].
(*"This first appeared in a collection of my stories which as published by Tandem Books under the title* Cold Terror. *Since then the book has been published in the United States, Germany and Sweden and quite a few people have been kind enough to write to me and state how much they enjoyed this particular story and request that I explain how it came to be written. So far I have been able to supply only one answer. I just don't know. I write all my stories blind. That is to say I sit down behind a typewriter and hope to hell that fingers and brain will come up with something readable. Believe it or not, usually this slap-dash procedure works, although the end result varies considerably. It is possible that the excitement of not knowing what is going to happen next, keeps me going. With regard to this particular*

specimen—having re-read it after a long period of time, made allowances for what I should have put in, what I should have left out, I have to admit it's not at all a bad story." R.C-H.)

F47 **THE DAY THAT FATHER BROUGHT SOMETHING HOME**
a. _____, see 'The Day Father Brought Something Home' [F46(b)(d)]

F48 **THE DAY OF THE UNDERDOG**
a. _____, see Tales of Fear and Fantasy [B24].
b. _____, in *Tales of Witchcraft* edited by Richard Dalby, Michael O'Mara, London, England, 1991 (hc). [Note: The working title for this anthology was *Witches and Wizards*.]
c. _____, in *Tales of Witchcraft* edited by Richard Dalby, Dorset House Publishing Co., New York, USA, 1991 (hc).
d. _____, in *Tales of Witchcraft* edited by Richard Dalby, Book Sales, New York, USA, 1994 (hc).
e. _____, in *Suuri noitakirja* (Great Witch Book), edited by Richard Dalby, Book Studio, Helsinki, Finland, 1994 (pb).
f. _____, in *Tales of Witchcraft* edited by Richard Dalby, Brockhampton Press, Leicester, England, 1995 (hc).
g. _____, see Shocks [D3].
h. _____, in *Tales of Witchcraft* edited by Richard Dalby, Barnes & Noble, New York, USA, 1998 (hc).

F49 **DAY SCHOOL**
a. _____, see Gaslight, Ghosts, & Ghouls [B27].
[Note: Originally written circa 1989, this was subitted to *Fear* magazine, where the editor considered running it over two issues.]

F50 **DEAD GHOST**
a. _____, in *Ghost After Ghost* edited by Aidan Chambers, Viking Children's Books, New York, USA, 1982 (hc).
b. _____, in *Ghost After Ghost* edited by Aidan Chambers, Puffin, London England, 1984 (pb).
c. _____, see A Quiver of Ghosts [B14].

F51 **THE DEATH OF ME**
    a. _____, see The Unbidden [B26].
    b. _____, see A Quiver of Ghosts [B14].

F52 **THE DEVILET**
    a. _____, see The Unbidden [B26].
    b. _____, in *100 Fiendish Little Frightmares* edited by Stefan Dziemianowicz, Martin H. Greenberg and Robert Weinberg, Barnes & Noble, New York, USA, 1997 (hc).

F53 **DON'T GO UP THE STAIRS**
    a. _____, see 'Don't Go Up the Stairs' [F53(b)].

F54 **DON'T GO UP THEM STAIRS**
    a. _____, see The Unbidden [B26].

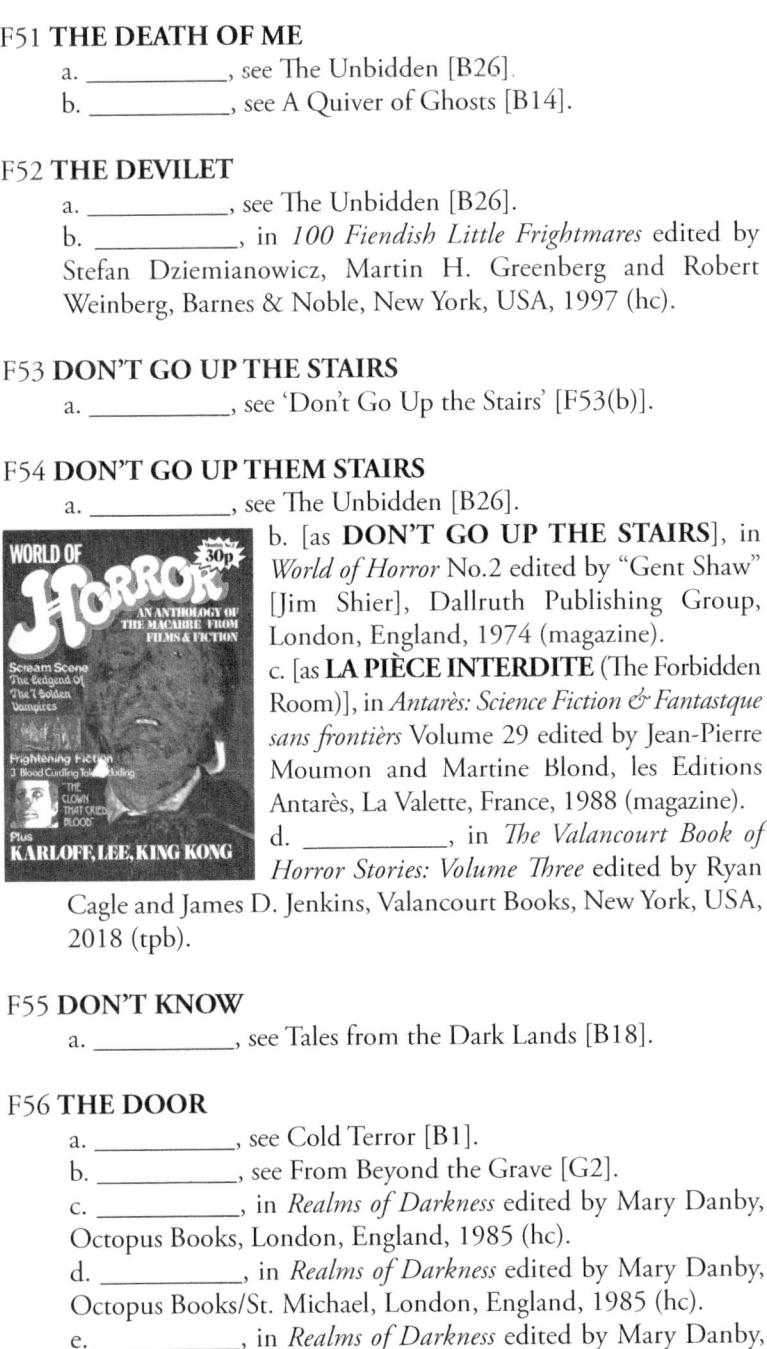

    b. [as **DON'T GO UP THE STAIRS**], in *World of Horror* No.2 edited by "Gent Shaw" [Jim Shier], Dallruth Publishing Group, London, England, 1974 (magazine).
    c. [as **LA PIÈCE INTERDITE** (The Forbidden Room)], in *Antarès: Science Fiction & Fantastque sans frontièrs* Volume 29 edited by Jean-Pierre Moumon and Martine Blond, les Editions Antarès, La Valette, France, 1988 (magazine).
    d. _____, in *The Valancourt Book of Horror Stories: Volume Three* edited by Ryan Cagle and James D. Jenkins, Valancourt Books, New York, USA, 2018 (tpb).

F55 **DON'T KNOW**
    a. _____, see Tales from the Dark Lands [B18].

F56 **THE DOOR**
    a. _____, see Cold Terror [B1].
    b. _____, see From Beyond the Grave [G2].
    c. _____, in *Realms of Darkness* edited by Mary Danby, Octopus Books, London, England, 1985 (hc).
    d. _____, in *Realms of Darkness* edited by Mary Danby, Octopus Books/St. Michael, London, England, 1985 (hc).
    e. _____, in *Realms of Darkness* edited by Mary Danby,

Chartwell Books Inc., New Jersey, USA, 1988 (hc).
f. _____, in *Haunts: Reliquaries of the Dead* edited by Stephen
Jones, Ulysses Press, Berkeley, California, USA, 2011 (tpb).
[Note: A "Chronicles of Clavering Grange" story.]
g. _____, see Gaslight, Ghosts, & Ghouls [B27].

F57 DOPPLEGÄNGER
a. _____, see Ghosts from the Mist of Time [B7].
b. _____, in *Masters of Darkness III* edited by Dennis
Etchison, Tor Books, New York, USA, 1991 (pb).
c. _____, in *The Complete Masters of Darkness* edited by Dennis
Etchison, Underwood-Miller, San Francisco , USA, 1991 (hc).
d. _____, in *The Complete Masters of Darkness* edited by Dennis
Etchison, Underwood-Miller, San Francisco , USA, 1991 (tpb).
g. _____, see Gaslight, Ghosts, & Ghouls [B27].

F58 THE ECHO
a. _____, see Terror by Night [B25].
b. _____, see Ghosts from the Mist of Time [B7].

F59 EIGHT FOR DINNER
a. _____, see Tales from the Haunted House [B19].

F60 THE ELEMENTAL
a. _____, see The Elemental & Other Stories [B4].
b. _____, see From Beyond the Grave [G2].
c. _____, in *Uncanny Tales of Unearthly and Unexpected
Horrors* edited by Helen Hoke, Lodestar Books/Dutton, New
York, USA, 1983 (hc).
d. _____, in *The Mammoth Book of Ghost Stories 2* edited
by Richard Dalby, Carroll & Graf, New York, USA, 1991 (tpb).
e. _____, in *The Mammoth Book of Ghost Stories 2* edited
by Richard Dalby, Robinson Publishing, London, England, 1991
(tpb).
f. _____, see Scary Stories [G9].
g. _____, see Gaslight, Ghosts, & Ghouls [B27].

F61 EPILOGUE
a. _____, see The Monster Club [B10].
b. _____, in *Flotsam Fantastique: The Souvenir Book of the World*

Fantasy Convention 2013 edited by Stephen Jones, World Fantasy Convention 2013/PS Publishing, Hornsea, England, 2013 (hc).

F62 EPILOGUE
a. _____, see Shudders and Shivers [B15].

F63 A FAMILY WELCOME
a. _____, see The Unbidden [B26].
b. _____, see The Vampire Stories of R. Chetwynd-Hayes [B27].

F64 FEET OF CLAY
a. _____, see Phantoms and Fiends [B13].

F65 THE FLOATERS
a. _____, in *After Hours* #25, Winter 1995 edited by William G. Raley, Sunset Beach, California, USA, 1995 (magazine).
b. _____, see Frights and Fancies [B6].

F66 THE FLY-BY-NIGHT
a. _____, see The Monster Club [B10].

b. _____, in *More Devil's Kisses* edited by " Linda Lovecraft" [Michel Parry], Corgi Books, London, England, 1977 (pb).
[Note: The series came to an abrupt end when Scotland Yard seized copies of this second book, and Corgi was threatened with prosecution under the Obscene Publications Act.]
c. [as **NACHTFLIEGER** (Nightflie)], in *Zehn Teufelsküsse* (Ten Devil's Kisses) edited by Michel Parry, Pabel, Horror Taschenbuch #68, Hamburg, Germany, 1978 (pb).
d. _____, in *Midnight* edited by Charles L. Grant, Tor Books, New York, USA, 1985 (pb).
e. _____, see Shocks [D3].

F67 FOG GHOST
a. _____, in *Gaslight & Ghosts* edited by Stephen Jones and Jo Fletcher, World Fantasy Convention 1988/Robinson Publishing, London, England, 1988 (hc).
b. _____, see Phantoms and Fiends [B13].

F68 THE FOURTH SIDE OF THE TRIANGLE
a. _____, see Cold Terror [B1].

F69 THE FRANKENSTEIN SYNDROME
a. _____, in *Dark Voices 4: The Pan Book of Horror* edited by David Sutton and Stephen Jones, Pan Books, London, England, 1992 (pb).
b. _____, see Phantoms and Fiends [B13].

F70 THE FUNDEMENTAL ELEMENTAL
a. _____, see The Vampire Stories of R. Chetwynd-Hayes [B27].

F71 THE GALE-WUGGLE
a. _____, see The Sixth Armada Monster Book [C6].
b. _____, see Frights and Fancies [B6].
(*"What can I say? Well—firstly, it is completely true. Honestly. Go out on a very windy day and look up at the sky. Sooner or later the clouds will assume the shape of a creature with large pointed ears, a grotesque head and two blazing eyes. That will be* The Gale-Wuggle. *And what is more, if you look very carefully, you may discover that what at first appeared to be rooks are, in fact, little old ladies wearing top-hats and black cloaks. Never take anything for granted. My hero is a sick boy who attracts the attention of the Gale-Wuggle—and other strange beings as well."* R.C-H.)

F72 THE GATECRASHER
a. _____, see The Unbidden [B26].
b. _____, see From Beyond the Grave [G2].
c. _____, in *Jack the Knife: Tales of Jack the Ripper* edited by Michel Parry, Mayflower, London, England, 1975 (pb).
d. _____, in *Psycho-Mania!* edited by Stephen Jones, Robinson Publishing, London, England, 2013 (tpb).
e. _____, in *The Big Book of Jack the Ripper* edited by Otto Penzler, Vintage Crime/Black Lizard, New York, USA, 2016 (tpb).
f. _____, see Gaslight, Ghosts, & Ghouls [B27].

F73 THE GHOSTLY EARL
a. _____, see Terror by Night [B25].

b. _____, in *Haunting Tales* edited by Barbara Ireson, Faber & Faber, London, England, 1973 (hc).

c. _____, in *Haunting Tales* edited by Barbara Ireson, E.P. Dutton, Boston, USA, 1974 (hc).

d. _____, in *Haunting Tales* edited by Barbara Ireison, Puffin Books, London, England, 1978 (pb).

e. _____, in *Haunting Tales* edited by Barbara Ireison, Puffin Books, London, England, 1979 (pb).

f. _____, see Dramarama: Spooky [G3].

g. _____, in *Spooky* edited by Pamela Lonsdale, Thames/Methuen, London, England, 1983 (hc).
[Note: TV tie in.]

h. _____, in *Spooky* edited by Pamela Lonsdale, Thames/Magnet, London, England, 1984 (pb).

i. _____, in *Spooky* edited by Pamela Lonsdale, Prentice-Hall, New Jersey, USA, 1985 (hc).

j. _____, in *Haunting Tales* edited by Barbara Ireison, Puffin Books, London, England, 1986 (pb).

F74 THE GHOST WHO LIMPED

a. _____, see The Night Ghouls and Other Grisly Tales [B11].

b. [as **HERR HINKEBEIN**], see 6 x Panische nächte [B16].

c. _____, in *Shadows 3* edited by Charles L. Grant, Doubleday Books, New York, USA, 1980 (hc).

d. _____, see A Quiver of Ghosts [B14].

e. _____, in *Shadows 3* edited by Charles L. Grant, Berkley Books, New York, USA, 1985 (pb).

f. _____, in *Shadows 3* edited by Charles L. Grant, Berkley Books, New York, USA, 1986 (pb).

g. [as **THE LIMPING GHOST**], in *The Mammoth Book of Ghost Stories* edited by Richard Dalby, Robinson Publishing, London, England, 1990 (tpb).

h. [as **THE LIMPING GHOST**], in *The Mammoth Book of Ghost Stories* edited by Richard Dalby, Carroll & Graf, New York, USA, 1990 (tpb).

i. [as **THE LIMPING GHOST**], in *The Anthology of Ghost Stories* edited by Richard Dalby, Tiger Books International, London, England, 1994 (hc).

j. [as **THE LIMPING GHOST**], in *Phantastic Book of Ghost Stories* edited by Richard Dalby, Barnes & Noble, New York, USA, 1996 (tpb).

k. _____, see My So-Called Life and Death [G7].

l. [as **THE LIMPING GHOST**], in *Phantastic Book of Ghost Stories* edited by Richard Dalby, Metro Books, New York, USA, 2002 (hc).

m. [as **THE LIMPING GHOST**], in *The World's Greatest Ghost Stories* edited by Richard Dalby, Barnes & Noble, New York, USA, 2004 (tpb).

n. [as **THE LIMPING GHOST**], in *The World's Greatest Ghost Stories* edited by Richard Dalby, Magpie Books, New York, USA, 2004 (tpb).

F75 **GHOUL AT LARGE**

a. _____, see Ghoul 1 [D1].

b. _____, see Frights and Fancies [B6].

F76 **THE GHOULS**

a. _____, see The Night Ghouls and Other Grisly Tales [B11].

b. _____, in *Nightmares* edited by Charles L. Grant, Playboy Press, California, USA, 1979 (pb).

c. _____, in *Nightmares* edited by Charles L. Grant, Playboy Press, California, USA, 1979 (pb). [Note: Second printing.]

d. _____, in *Nightmares* edited by Charles L. Grant, Playboy Press, California, USA, 1980 (pb).

e. _____, in *Nightmares* edited by Charles L. Grant, Berkley Books, New York City, USA, 1982 (pb).

f. [as **MORTS-VIVANTS & CIE** (Undead & Co.)], in *Antarès: Science Fiction et Fantastque sans frontièrs* Volume 11 edited by Jean-Pierre Moumon and Martine Blond, les Editions Antarès, La Valette, France, 1983 (magazine).

[Note: This issue also contains an interview with R. Chetwynd-Hayes by Martine Blond and Jean-Pierre Moumon.]

g. _____, in *Nightmares* edited by Charles L. Grant, Berkley Books, New York City, USA, 1984 (pb).

h. [as **LA CRIATURA** (The Creature)], in *Las Mejores Historias De Terror III* edited by Charles L. Grant, editorial Martínez Roca, Spain, 1984 (tpb).

i. _____, in *The Mammoth Book of Zombies* edited by Stephen Jones, Robinson Publishing, London, England, 1993 (tpb).

j. _____, in *The Mammoth Book of Zombies* edited by Stephen Jones, Carroll & Graf, New York, USA, 1993 (tpb).

k. _____, in *The Giant Book of Zombies* edited by Stephen Jones, Magpie Books, London, England, 1995 (tpb).

l. _____, in *The Giant Book of Zombies* edited by Stephen Jones, The Book Company International, Australia, 1995 (tpb)

m. _____, in *The Giant Book of Zombies* edited by Stephen Jones, Parragon Book Service, London, England, 1995 (tpb)

n. _____, in *The Monster Book of Zombies: Tales of the Walking Dead* edited by Stephen Jones, Metro Books/Barnes & Noble, New York, USA, 2009 (hc).

o. [as УПЫРИ], in Зомби (Zombie)] edited by Stephen Jones, Azbooka-Atticus, Russia, 2010 (hc).

p. _____, in *Zombies! Zombies! Zombies!* edited by Otto Penzler, Vintage Crime/Black Lizard, New York, USA, 2011 (tpb).

q. _____, in *Zombies: A Compendium of the Living Dead* edited by Otto Penzler, Corvus Grove Press/Atlantic Books, London, England, 2012 (tpb).

r. _____ in *The Mammoth Book of Zombies!* edited by Stephen Jones, Robinson Publishing, London, England, 2013 (tpb).

s. _____, in *Zombies! Tales of the Walking Dead* edited by Stephen Jones, Skyhorse Publishing/A Herman Graf Book, New York, USA, 2013 (tpb).

F77 **THE GIBBERING GHOUL OF GOMERSHAL**

a. _____, see The Fantastic World of Kamtellar and Other Stories of Fear and Horror [B5].

b. _____, in *Shadmocks & Shivers: New Tales Inspired by the*

Stories of R. Chetwynd-Hayes edited by Dave Brzeski, Shadow Publishing, Birmingham, UK, 2019 (tpb).
[Note: A "Fred and Francis" story.]
c. _____, see Gaslight, Ghosts, & Ghouls [B27].
(*"'The Gibbering Ghoul of Gomershall' is a previously unpublished account taken from the casebook of the world's only practising psychic detective, Francis St. Clare. But he and his glamorous assistant Frederica Masters (Fred for short) have made three earlier appearances, and for a long time there has been talk of a television series, which has still to materialise as something more concrete. In contrast to what has gone before, their escapade is light-hearted, written more for giggles than shudders, but, I hope, none the less entertaining. I like this pair, no matter where they came from, and would hate to see them buried in an unmarked grave."* R.C-H.)

F78 **GILBERT**
a. _____, see The House of Dracula [B8].

F79 **GREAT-GRANDAD IS IN THE ATTIC**
a. _____, see Tales from the Haunted House [B19].

F80 **GREAT-GRANDAD WALKS AGAIN**
a. _____, see Cold Terror [B1].
b. [as **LES DENTS D'ARRIÈRE-GRAND-PAPA** (Great-Grandad Walks Again)], in *Antarès: Science Fiction & Fantastque sans frontièrs* Volume 22 edited by Jean-Pierre Moumon and Martine Blond, les Editions Antarès, La Valette, France, 1986 (magazine).
c. [as **LA RÉSURRECTION DE GRAND-GRAND-PAPA** (Grandpa's Resurrection)], in *Trois saigneurs de la nuit/3: Ghoules, Vampires, Loups-garous* (Three Tanners of the Night/3: Ghouls, Vampires, Werewolves)], edited by Jacques Finné, NéO Livres/ Nouvelles Éditions Oswald, France, 1988 (tpb).
a. _____, see The Vampire Stories of R. Chetwynd-Hayes [B27].

F81 **THE GREAT INDESTRUCTIBLE**
a. _____, see 'I Met the Great Indestructible: Exclusive Interview with Count Dracula' [F97(b–c)].
b. _____, see The Vampire Stories of R. Chetwynd-Hayes [B28(c)].

F82 **GROWTH**

    a. _____, in *The Fifteenth Fontana Book of Great Horror Stories* edited by Mary Danby, Fontana Books, London, England/ William Collins Sons & Co., Glasgow, Scotland, 1982 (pb).

    b. [as **CROISSANCE** (Growth)], in *Revue Phénix* No.23, August 1990 edited by Marc Bailly, Racour, France, 1990 (tpb).

    c. _____, see Phantoms and Fiends [B13].

F83 **THE HANGING TREE**

    a. _____, see The Fifteenth Fontana Book of Great Ghost Stories [C15].

    b. _____, see A Quiver of Ghosts [B14].

    c. _____, in *Winter Chills 1* (BFS Booklet No.9) edited by Peter Coleborn, The British Fantasy Society, Birmingham, England, 1987 (chapbook).

    d. _____, in *Chillers for Christmas* edited by Richard Dalby, Michael O'Mara, London, England, 1989 (hc).

    e. _____, in *Chillers for Christmas* edited by Richard Dalby, Guild Publishing, London, England, 1989 (hc).

    f. _____, in *Chillers for Christmas* edited by Richard Dalby, Popular Culture Ink, USA, 1990 (hc).

    g. _____, in *Chillers for Christmas* edited by Richard Dalby, Headline Publishing, London, England, 1990 (pb).

    h. _____, in *Chillers for Christmas* edited by Richard Dalby, Gallery Books, New York, USA, 1990 (hc).

    i. [as **DER GALGENBAUM** (The Gallows Tree)], in *Eiskalte Weihnachten* (Ice Cold Christmas)] edited by Richard Dalby, Droemer Knaur, Munich, Germany, 1993 (pb).

    j. [as **DER GALGENBAUM** (The Gallows Tree)], in *Eiskalte Weihnachten* (Ice Cold Christmas)] edited by Richard Dalby, Droemer Knaur, Munich, Germany, 2002 (hc).

    K. [as **DER GALGENBAUM** (The Gallows Tree)], in *Eiskalte Weihnachten: Geschichten Von Mord Und Totschlag* (Ice Cold Christmas: Stories of Murder and Death), edited by Richard Dalby, Droemer Knaur, Munich, Germany, 2004 (hc).

(*"Yes, I wrote that. A few people may recognise the setting, but I hasten to add that this is the only authentic part about it. I am always seeking new names for my characters that will in some way fit into their personalities. Movita slid into my brain, and yes, it did undoubtedly belong to the sad, rather sweet girl who saw the walker of the haunting path from her bedroom window. But where on earth did the name come from? I have never known a girl called Movita and so far as I can ascertain no one else has either. So maybe I have invented a new name, which I venture to suggest is no mean achievement."* R.C-H.)

F84 **THE HARPY**
a. _____, see The Third Armada Monster Book [C3].
b. _____, see Frights and Fancies [B6].
(*"Well, now—what can I say? It's true of course. Every single word. You must believe that."* R.C-H.)

F85 **THE HAUNTED MAN**
a. _____, see Tales of Darkness [B23].

F86 **THE HEADLESS FOOTMAN OF HADLEIGH**
a. _____, see Tales of Fear and Fantasy [B24].

F87 **THE HEAD OF THE FIRM**

a. _____, see The Unbidden [B26].
b. _____, in *World of Horror* No.4 edited by "Gent Shaw" [Jim Shier], Dallruth Publishing Group, London, England, 1974 (magazine).
c. _____, see Shocks [D3].

F88 **HIGH WORLD**
a. _____, see Frights and Fancies [B6].

F89 **THE HOLSTEIN HORROR**
a. _____, see The Night Ghouls and Other Grisly Tales [B11].

b. [as **UNE PINTE DE BON SANG** (A Pint of Blood)], in *Weird: Fantastique, Epouvante, Heroic-fantasy* No.6, September 1986 edited by C.E. [Claude-Éric] Devaux, Weird, Genlis, France, 1986 (magazine).

F90 HOME AND BEAUTY

a. _____, see Tales from the Hidden World: Four Episodes in the History of Clavering Grange [B20].
[A "Chronicles of Clavering Grange" story.]

F91 HOMEMADE MONSTER

a. _____, see The Second Armada Monster Book [C2].
b. _____, see Frights and Fancies [B6].
c. _____, in *Terrifying Tales to Tell at Night: 10 Scary Stories to Give You Nightmares!* edited by Stephen Jones, Sky Pony Press/Skyhorse Publishing, New York, USA, 2019 (tpb).
d. _____, in *Histórias Assustadoras Para Contar à Noite: Dez Narrativas Tenebrosas Que Lhe Darão Pesadelos!* edited by Stephen Jones, Pipoca & Nanquim, São Paulo, Brazil, 2021 (hc).
e. _____, in *Storie terrificanti da [non] legger di notte: 10 racconti spaventosi che vi faranno venire gli incubi!* edited by Stephen Jones, Cut-Up Publishing, La Spezia, Italy, 2021 (hc).
(*"About the descendant of Doctor Frankenstein, who tries his hand at a spot of monster-making."* R.C-H.)

F92 THE HOPPITY-JUMP

a. _____, see The Fourth Armada Monster Book [C4].
b. _____, see Frights and Fancies [B6].
(*"Yes, another new monster. A very nasty creature, which has the unfortunate habit of swallowing cabinet ministers…"* R.C-H.)

F93 THE HOUSE

a. _____, see The Unbidden [B26].
b. _____, see A Quiver of Ghosts [B14].

F94 HOUSEBOUND

a. _____, in *The Third Fontana Book of Great Horror Stories* edited by Christine Bernard, Fontana Books, London, England/William Collins Sons & Co. Ltd., Glasgow, Scotland, 1968 (pb).

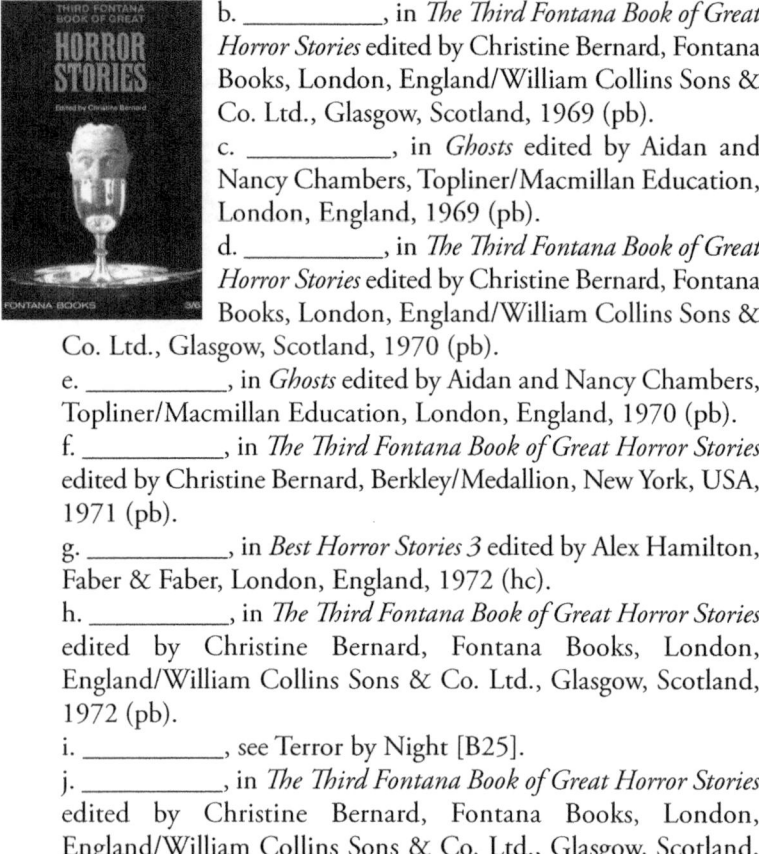

b. _____, in *The Third Fontana Book of Great Horror Stories* edited by Christine Bernard, Fontana Books, London, England/William Collins Sons & Co. Ltd., Glasgow, Scotland, 1969 (pb).

c. _____, in *Ghosts* edited by Aidan and Nancy Chambers, Topliner/Macmillan Education, London, England, 1969 (pb).

d. _____, in *The Third Fontana Book of Great Horror Stories* edited by Christine Bernard, Fontana Books, London, England/William Collins Sons & Co. Ltd., Glasgow, Scotland, 1970 (pb).

e. _____, in *Ghosts* edited by Aidan and Nancy Chambers, Topliner/Macmillan Education, London, England, 1970 (pb).

f. _____, in *The Third Fontana Book of Great Horror Stories* edited by Christine Bernard, Berkley/Medallion, New York, USA, 1971 (pb).

g. _____, in *Best Horror Stories 3* edited by Alex Hamilton, Faber & Faber, London, England, 1972 (hc).

h. _____, in *The Third Fontana Book of Great Horror Stories* edited by Christine Bernard, Fontana Books, London, England/William Collins Sons & Co. Ltd., Glasgow, Scotland, 1972 (pb).

i. _____, see Terror by Night [B25].

j. _____, in *The Third Fontana Book of Great Horror Stories* edited by Christine Bernard, Fontana Books, London, England/William Collins Sons & Co. Ltd., Glasgow, Scotland, 1974 (pb).

k. _____, in *The Third Fontana Book of Great Horror Stories* edited by Christine Bernard, Fontana Books, London, England/William Collins Sons & Co. Ltd., Glasgow, Scotland, 1977 (pb).

l. _____, in *Ghosts* edited by Aidan and Nancy Chambers, Topliner/Macmillan Education, London, England, 1978 (pb).

m. _____, in *Sinister, Strange, and Supernatural* edited by "Helen Hoke" [Helen Jeanne Lamb Watts], Elsevier/Nelson, New York, USA, 1980 (hc).

n. _____, in *Ghosts* edited by Aidan and Nancy Chambers, M Books [Macmillan Education], London, England, 1990 (hc).

o. _____, see Gaslight, Ghosts, & Ghouls [B27].

F95 **THE HOUSE ON THE HILL**
   a. _____, see Tales from the Haunted House [B19].

F96 **THE HUMGOO**
   a. _____, see The Monster Club [B10].
   b. _____, see The Monster Club [G6].
   c. _____, see Gaslight, Ghosts, & Ghouls [B27].

F97 **IN MEDIA RES**
   a. _____, see Cold Terror [B1].
   b. _____, in *The Australian Women's Weekly*, Vol.46, No.18, Wednesday, October 4 1978, Sydney, Australia (magazine).
   c. _____, see A Quiver of Ghosts [B14].

F98 **I MET THE GREAT INDESTRUCTIBLE: EXCLUSIVE INTERVIEW WITH COUNT DRACULA** [as originally by "Hans Clutcher"]
   a. _____, see Ghoul 1 [D1].
   b. [as **THE GREAT INDESTRUCTIBLE**], see Frights and Fancies [B6].
   c. [as **THE GREAT INDESTRUCTIBLE**], see Looking for Something to Suck: The Vampire Stories of R. Chetwynd-Hayes [B27(c)].

F99 **INTERLUDE NUMBER 1**
   a. _____, see Shudders and Shivers [B15].

F100 **INTERLUDE NUMBER 2**
   a. _____, see Shudders and Shivers [B15].

F101 **INTERLUDE NUMBER 3**
   a. _____, see Shudders and Shivers [B15].

F102 **INTERLUDE NUMBER 4**
   a. _____, see Shudders and Shivers [B15].

F103 **THE INTRUDERS**
   a. _____, see Shudders and Shivers [B15].

F104 **IRMA**
   a. _____, see Dracula's Children [B3].

F105 **IT CAME TO DINNER**

a. _____, in *The Fourteenth Pan Book of Horror Stories* edited by Herbert van Thal, Pan Books, London, England, 1973 (pb).

b. _____, in *The Fourteenth Pan Book of Horror Stories* edited by Herbert van Thal, Pan Books, London, England, 1974 (pb).
[Note: Second printing.]

c. _____, in *The Fourteenth Pan Book of Horror Stories* edited by Herbert van Thal, Pan Books, London, England, 1976 (pb).

[Note: Third printing.]

d. _____, in *The Fourteenth Pan Book of Horror Stories* edited by Herbert van Thal, Pan Books, London, England, 1977 (pb).
[Note: Fourth printing.]

e. _____, in *The Fourteenth Pan Book of Horror Stories* edited by Herbert van Thal, Pan Books, London, England (pb).
[Note: Fifth printing.]

f. _____, in *The Fourteenth Pan Book of Horror Stories* edited by Herbert van Thal, Pan Books, London, England, 1980 (pb).
[Note: Sixth printing.]

g. _____, see Phantoms and Fiends [B13].

F106 **THE JUMPITY-JIM**

a. _____, see The Elemental & Other Stories [B4].

b. _____, in *The Mammoth Book of Terror* edited by Stephen Jones, Robinson Publishing, London, England, 1991 (tpb).

c. _____, in *The Mammoth Book of Terror* edited by Stephen Jones Carroll & Graf, New York, USA, 1991 (tpb).

d. _____, in *The Anthology of Horror Stories* edited by Stephen Jones, Tiger Books International, London, England, 1994 (hc).

e. _____, in *The Giant Book of Horror* edited by Stephen Jones, Magpie Books, London, England, 1996 (tpb).

f. _____, in *The Giant Book of Horror* edited by Stephen Jones, Parragon Books, Bath, England, 1996 (tpb).

g. [as **IL SALTAPICCHIO** (The Saltapychio)], in *Terrore!* edited by Stephen Jones, Newton & Compton editori, Italy, 1996 (tpb).

h. _____, see Gaslight, Ghosts, & Ghouls [B27].

(*"I am greatly affected by a beast of my own invention called the 'Jumpity-Jim'. He is a very nasty one indeed, who would alight on any naked virginal back if there was one nearby. This creature first made an appearance in my collection,* The Elemental, *published by Fontana Books in 1974. I later used him again in the Clavering Grange story, 'Loft Conversion–1980', which can be found in* Tales of the Other Side." *R.C-H.)*

F107 **KAMTELLAR**

a. _____, see The Fantastic World of Kamtellar and Other Stories of Fear and Horror [B5].

[Note: This was originally entitled 'Hell, Dear Boy, is Where You Find It'.]

(*"'Kamtellar' was originally a novel that did not quite come off and is here presented as a 40,000-word novella. Undoubtedly the idea originated from an incident recorded in Ambrose Bierce's* Mysterious Disappearances." *R.C-H.)*

F108 **KARL**

a. _____, see The House of Dracula [B8].

F109 **KEEP THE GASLIGHT BURNING**

a. _____, see Gaslight Tales of Terror [C21].

b. _____, see The Vampire Stories of R. Chetwynd-Hayes [B27].

c. _____, see Keep the Gaslight Burning [G4].

(*"I have been accused of having an obsession for moors. Too true: I passed through a period when I fell in love with the Brontë sisters, particularly Emily. I still think that* Wuthering Heights *is one of the greatest novels in the English language. I read and re-read all their works; gathered all the information I could find about their lives— and finally paid a visit to Haworth Parsonage. I defy anyone who has heard the wind that perpetually howls across those bleak moors not to think of hell-hounds, or see nebulous shapes that drift across the rippling heather, forever condemned to roam the limitless plains of time and space. Here is yet another story that was germinated from a seed planted during that visit." *R.C-H.)*

F110 LABOUR-SAVING DEVICES–2000
a. _____, see Tales from the Other Side [B21].
[Note: A "Chronicles of Clavering Grange" story.]

F111 THE LABYRINTH
a. _____, see The Elemental & Other Stories [B4].
b. [as **LE LABYRINTHE** (The Labyrinth)], in *Antarès: Science Fiction et Fantastque sans frontièrs* Volume 14 edited by Jean-Pierre Moumon and Martine Blond, les Editions Antarès, La Valette, France, 1984 (magazine).
c. _____, in *Haunted Travellers* edited by Denys Val Baker, William Kimber & Co., London, England, 1985 (hc).
d. _____, see The Mammoth Book of Vampires [D63].
e. _____, see The Vampire Stories of R. Chetwynd-Hayes [B28].

F112 THE LIBERATED TIGER
a. _____, see The Ninth Fontana Book of Great Ghost Stories [C9].
b. _____, see A Quiver of Ghosts [B14].
c. _____, see Haunted [G5].
(*"The Liberated Tiger', was, as indeed are all my stories, written blind. In other words, I took up my ballpoint pen and began to write. I had no idea how it would end until the last page but one."* R.C-H.)

F113 LIFE EVERLASTING
a. _____, see Tales from the Hidden World: Four Episodes in the History of Clavering Grange [B20].
[A "Chronicles of Clavering Grange" story.]

F114 LILEAS AND THE WATER-HORSE
a. _____, see 'Shona and the Water-Horse' [F183(b)].

F115 THE LIMPING GHOST
a. _____, see 'The Ghost Who Limped' [F73(g–m)].

F116 A LIVING LEGEND
a. _____, see Tales from Beyond [B17].
b. _____, in *The Mammoth Book of New Terror* edited by

Stephen Jones, Robinson Publishing, London, England, 2004 (tpb).

c. _____, see *The Mammoth Book of New Terror* edited by Stephen Jones, Carroll & Graf, New York, USA, 2004 (tpb).

d. _____, see *The Mammoth Book of New Terror* edited by Stephen Jones, Carroll & Graf, New York, USA, 2006 (tpb).

e. _____, see *The Mammoth Book of New Terror* edited by Stephen Jones, Carroll & Graf, New York, USA, 2007 (tpb).

F117 LOFT CONVERSION–1980

a. _____, see Tales from the Other Side [B21].
[Note: A "Chronicles of Clavering Grange" story.]

F118 LONG, LONG AGO

a. _____, see Tales from the Shadows [B22].

b. _____, see in *The Year's Best Fantasy Stories 13* edited by Arthur W. Saha, Daw Books, New York, USA, 1987 (pb).

c. [as **SOUVENIR LOINTAIN** (Faraway)], in *Antarès: Science Fiction & Fantastque sans frontièrs* Volume 27 edited by Jean-Pierre Moumon and Martine Blond, les Éditions Antarès, La Valette, France, 1987 (magazine).

d. _____, in *The Year's Best Fantasy Stories 13* edited by Arthur W. Saha, DAW Books, New York, USA, 1988 (hc).

e. [as **TANTO, TANTO TEMPO FA** (Long, Long Ago)], in *Il Meglio della Fantasy 1987* (The Best of Fantasy 1987)] edited by Arthur W. Saha, Armenia Editore, Milan, Italy, 1988 (tpb).

F119 LOOKING FOR SOMETHING TO SUCK

a. _____, in *The Fourth Fontana Book of Great Horror Stories* edited by Christine Bernard, Fontana Books, London, England/William Collins Sons & Co., Glasgow, Scotland, 1969 (pb).

b. [as **EN QUÊTE DE QUELQUE CHOSE À SUCER** (In Search of Something to Suck)], in *Histoires anglo-saxonnes de vampires* edited by Jean Marigny, Libraire des Champs-Élysées, Paris, France, 1978 (tpb).

c. _____, see The Fantastic World of Kamtellar and Other Stories of Fear and Horror [B5].

d. _____, in *The Monster Book of Monsters* edited by Michael O'Shaughnessy, Xanadu Books, London, England, 1988 (hc).

e. _____, in *The Monster Book of Monsters* edited by Michael O'Shaughnessy, Bonaza Books, USA, 1988 (hc).

f. _____, in *After Hours* #8, Autumn 1990 edited by William G. Raley, Mission Viejo, California, USA, 1990 (magazine).

g. _____, see The Vampire Stories of R. Chetwynd-Hayes [B27].

(*"Looking for Something to Suck' is not perhaps a wise title in this age when people are apt to allow their minds to stray into erotic side-roads, but I never even considered such an implication when I wrote the story. But a word or warning. If you have a nervous disposition for heaven's sake give this one a miss. I still get the occasional LETTER! One gentleman who lives in Devon maintains he lay trembling in his bed for four hours, until he realised that the thin streak of shadow that kept wriggling across the floor, was the result of a tree branch swaying back and forth in the moonlight. A lady who resides in Surrey states that seven years after first reading the story she still is unable to enter a dark room, and is of the opinion that people like me should not be allowed to write such things. Maybe she's right at that."* R.C-H.)

F120 LORD DUNWILLIAM AND CWN ANNWN

a. _____, see Welsh Tales of Terror [C26].

b. _____, see Terror by Night [B25].

c. _____, in *Spectre 3* edited by Richard Davis, Abelard-Schuman, London, England, 1976 (pb).

d. _____, in *Phantom Lovers* edited by Denys Val Baker, William Kimber & Co., London, England, 1984 (hc).

e. [as **LORD DUNWILLIAM ET LES CWNNANNWN** (Lord Dunwilliam and the CwnnAnnwn)], in *Antarès: Science Fiction & Fantastique sans frontièrs* Volume 45 edited by Jean-Pierre Moumon and Martine Blond, les Editions Antarès, La Valette, France, 1994 (magazine).

(*"Lord Dunwilliam and the Cwn Annwn' grew out of the legend of King Arawn and the Hell-Hounds."* R.C-H.]

F121 **LOUIS**
    a. _____, see The House of Dracula [B8].
    b. _____, see The Vampire Stories of R. Chetwynd-Hayes [B27].

F122 **MANDERVILLE**
    a. _____, see Tales of Fear and Fantasy [B24].
    b. [as **EIN ORT NAMENS MANDERVILLE**], see 6 x Panische nächte [B16].

F123 **THE MAN IN BLACK**
    a. _____, see Shudders and Shivers [B15].

F124 **THE MAN ON THE FRAME**
    a. _____, see Tales from the Shadows [B22].

F125 **THE MAN WHO STAYED BEHIND**
    a. _____, see The Night Ghouls and Other Grisly Tales [B11].
    b. [as **DER MANN, DER NICHT INS JENSEITS WOLLTE**], see 6 x Panische nächte [B16].
    c. _____, see Tales from the Dark Lands [B18].

F126 **MARCUS**
    a. _____, see Dracula's Children [B3].

F127 **MARIKOVA**
    a. _____, see The House of Dracula [B8].

F128 **MARKLAND THE HUNTER**
    a. _____, in *Sea Tales of Terror* edited by J. [Jozeph] J. [Jacob] Strating, Fontana Books, London, England/William Collins Sons & Co., Glasgow, Scotland, 1974 (pb).
    b. _____, in *Sea Tales of Terror* edited by J. [Jozeph] J. [Jacob] Strating, Fontana Books, London, England/William Collins Sons & Co., Glasgow, Scotland, 1975 (pb).
    c. _____, see Tales from Beyond [B17].
    d. [as **MARKLAND, LE CHASSEUR** (Markland

the Hunter)], in *Histoires d'océans maléfiques* (Stories of Evil Oceans) edited by Jacques Finné, Librairie des Champs-Élysées, Paris, France, 1978 (tpb).

e. _____, in *Brighton Shock! The Souvenir Book of the World Horror Convention 2010* edited by Stephen Jones, World Horror Convention 2010/PS Publishing, Hornsea, England, 2010 (hc).

There are two variants of this edition.

    i. Description: trade edition.

    ii. Description: 100-copy signed and numbered edition.

[Note: A limited-run of 100 black or red slipcases were produced to hold this volume and a companion hardcover *Pocket Programme*, and a limited number of single-volume blue slipcases were produced by PS Publishing.]

F129 A MATTER OF LIFE AND DEATH
    a. _____, see Cold Terror [B1].

F130 MATTHEW AND LUKE

    a. _____, see The Eleventh Fontana Book of Great Ghost Stories [C11].

    b. _____, see Phantoms and Fiends [B13].

    c. _____, see Tales from the Dark Lands [B18].

(*"All about a haunted ego. Well—why not? It makes a change."* R.C-H.)

F131 MILDRED AND EDWINA
    a. _____, see The Cradle Demon and Other Stories of Fantasy and Terror [B2].

F132 THE MOCK
    a. _____, see The Monster Club [B10].

F133 THE MONSTER
    a. _____, in *The Fifth Fontana Book of Great Horror Stories* edited by Mary Danby, Fontana Books, London, England/William

Collins Sons & Co., Glasgow, Scotland, 1970 (pb).

b. _____ , in *The Fifth Fontana Book of Great Horror Stories* edited by Mary Danby, Beagle Horror, New York, USA, 1971 (pb).

c. _____, in *The Fifth Fontana Book of Great Horror Stories* edited by Mary Danby, Fontana Books, London, England/William Collins Sons & Co., Glasgow, Scotland, 1971 (pb).

d. _____, in *The Fifth Fontana Book of Great Horror Stories* edited by Mary Danby, Fontana Books, London, England/William Collins Sons & Co., Glasgow, Scotland, 1974 (pb).

e. _____, see Terror by Night [B25].

f. _____, in *65 Great Tales of Horror* edited by Mary Danby, Sundial Publications/Octopus Books, London, England, 1982 (hc).

g. _____, in *65 Great Tales of Horror* edited by Mary Danby, Random House, New York, USA, 1984 (hc).

h. _____, in *Fantasy Tales* Vol.12, Issue No.6, Spring 1991 edited by Stephen Jones and David Sutton, Robinson Publishing, London, England, 1991 (tpb).

i. _____, in *Fantasy Tales* Vol.2, Issue No.3, Spring 1991 edited by Stephen Jones and David Sutton, Carroll & Graf, New York, USA, 1991 (tpb).

[Note: This volume is erroniously numbered "6" on the spine.]

j. _____, in *The Giant Book of Fantasy Tales* edited by Stephen Jones and David Sutton, The Book Company, Sydney, Australia, 1996 (tpb)

F134 MONSTER CLUB INTERLUDE: 1
a. _____, see The Monster Club [B10].

F135 MONSTER CLUB INTERLUDE: 2
a. _____, see The Monster Club [B10].

F136 MONSTER CLUB INTERLUDE: 3
a. _____, see The Monster Club [B10].

F137 MONSTER CLUB INTERLUDE: 4
a. _____, see The Monster Club [B10].

F138 MOVING DAY

a. _____, in *The Third Book of After Midnight Stories: A Kimber Ghost Book*, edited by Amy Myers, William Kimber & Co., London, England, 1987 (hc).

b. _____, in *The Year's Best Horror Stories XVI*, ed. Karl Edward Wagner, DAW Books, New York, USA, 1988 (pb).

c. [as **VERHUISDAG** (Moving Day)], in *De Beste Horror verhalen van het Jaar* (The Best Horror Stories of the Year)] edited by Karl Edward Wagner, Loeb, Netherlands, 1988 (tpb).

d. [as **STĚHOVÁNÍ** (Migration)], in *Nejlepší horory roku I* (Best Horror Stories 1)] edited by Karl Edward Wagner, Gabi, Czech Republic, 1994 (hc).

e. _____, see Phantoms and Fiends [B13].

F139 THE MUDADORA [as originally by "Angus Campbell"]

a. _____, see The Sixth Armada Monster Book [C6].

b. _____, see Frights and Fancies [B6].

(*"This creature is a very nasty specimen and not one I would like to meet in a dark wood. Imagine a skeleton that over a long period gradually becomes coated with mud, then acquires a hideous kind of life. How Mr. Campbell came to learn about this particular monster, I have not the slightest idea, but I am extremely grateful to him for this graphic, if hair-raising story. I am certain that every monster-lover will find it shudderingly good."* R.C-H.)

F140 MY DEAR WIFE

a. _____, see The Thirteenth Fontana Book of Great Ghost Stories [C13].

b. _____, see Phantoms and Fiends [B13].

(*"I like to think that 'My Dear Wife' is a story with a moral: always make sure you have got rid of one before taking on a new one. Otherwise life—and death—can become very complicated."* R.C-H.)

F141 MY MOTHER MARRIED A VAMPIRE

a. _____, see The Cradle Demon and Other Stories of Fantasy and Terror [B2].

b. _____, see The Monster Club [G6].

c. _____, see The Vampire Stories of R. Chetwynd-Hayes [B27].

F142 MY VERY BEST FRIEND

a. _____, see The Cradle Demon and Other Stories of Fantasy and Terror [B2].

b. _____, see The Twentieth Fontana Book of Great Ghost Stories [C20].

(*"Based loosely on incidents that took place in my own childhood, which did not however include the supernatural parts. They are the result of an active imagination and wishful thinking. Wouldn't we all like a beauti-ful, ghostly guardian who smoothed the path through life for us? The Tabernacle of the Lord's Wrestlers did exist, although not under that name, and not a few of its members did behave in the manner I have described."* R.C-H.)

F143 NEIGHBOURS

a. _____, see Cold Terror [B1].

F144 NEVER TAKE DRINKS FROM A STRANGE WOMAN

a. _____, see Cold Terror [B1].

F145 NEXT DOOR

a. _____, see Tales from the Haunted House [B19].

F146 NIGHT OF THE ROAD

a. _____, see Shudders and Shivers [B15].

F147 NIGHT SISTER

a. _____, see Tales from the Shadows [B22].

F148 THE NIGHT WATCH

a. _____, see Tales from the Dark Lands [B18].

F149 THE NINTH REMOVAL

a. _____, see Cold Terror [B1].

b. _____, see The Price of Fear [G8].

F150 NO NEED FOR WORDS

a. _____, see The Night Ghouls and Other Grisly Tales [B11].

b. [as **PAS BESOIN DE MOTS** (No Need for Words)], in *Antarès: Science Fiction & Fantastque sans frontièrs* Volume 34 edited by Jean-Pierre Moumon and Martine Blond, les Editions Antarès, La Valette, France, 1989 (magazine).

c. _____, in *100 Fiendish Little Frightmares* edited by Stefan Dziemianowicz, Robert Weinberg and Martin H. Greenberg, Barnes & Noble, New York, USA, 1997 (hc).

F151 NON-PAYING PASSENGERS

a. _____, see The Tenth Fontana Book of Great Ghost Stories [C10].

b. _____, in *The Phantom Coach: Thirteen Journeys Into the Unknown* edited by Peter C. Smith, William Kimber & Co., London, England, 1979 (hc).

c. [as **PASSEGGERI NON PAGANTI** (Non-Paying Passengers)], in *Horror Story No.17* edited by Sergio Bissoli, Garden Editoriale, Italy, 1998 (pb).

d. _____, see Phantoms and Fiends [B13].

(*"What can I say? It's true—every word of it. Honestly. If you don't believe me, stand on Platform 16 at Waterloo Station during the evening rush hour and look out for the—more than one—odd passenger that climbs aboard the five-forty train for Shepperton. You'll be surprised—to say the least."* R.C-H.)

F152 NO ONE LIVED THERE

a. _____, see The Unbidden [B26].

b. [as **DAS LEERE HAUS** (The Empty House)], in *Ratten: 18 Horror-Stories* edited by Joachim Körber, Wilhelm Heyne Verlag, Munich Germany, 1993 (tpb).

F153 OLD ACQUAINTANCE

a. _____, see Shudders and Shivers [B15].

F154 ONE EXTRA

a. _____, see Tales from Beyond [B17].

F155 THE ORATOR

a. _____, in *The Lady*, London, England, 1953 (magazine).

F156 OUTSIDE INTERFERENCE

a. _____, see Tales of Darkness [B23].

F157 **PACKAGE HOLIDAY**
a. _____, see Frights and Fancies [B6].

F158 **THE PAINTED DOOR**
a. _____, see Tales from Beyond [B17].
[Note: This is a slightly revised version of the story originally published as 'The Ressurrectionist' (F171).]

F159 **THE PASSING OF AN ORDINARY MAN**
a. _____, see Tales from the Shadows [B22].

b. [as **DISPARITION D'UN PETIT HOMME ORDINAIRE** (The Passing of an Ordinary Man)], in *Revue Phénix* No.34, March 1993 edited by Marc Bailly, Racour, France, 1993 (tpb).
[Note: Credited on the cover and inside as "Ronald-Chetwynd Hayes".]

F160 **A PENNY FOR A POUND**
a. _____, see The Unbidden [B26].

F161 **THE PHANTOM AXEMAN OF CARLETON GRANGE**
a. _____, see Tales from the Haunted House [B19].
[Note: A "Fred and Francis" story.]

F162 **THE PIMPKINS**
a. _____, see The Cradle Demon and Other Stories of Fantasy and Terror [B2].

F163 **THE PLAYMATE**
a. _____, see The Unbidden [B26].
b. _____, see A Quiver of Ghosts [B14].
c. _____, in *100 Twisted Little Tales of Torment* edited by Stefan Dziemianowicz, Robert Weinberg and Martin H. Greenberg, Barnes & Noble, New York, USA, 1998 (hc).

F164 **PROLOGUE**
a. _____, see The Monster Club [B10].

b. _____, in *Flotsam Fantastique: The Souvenir Book of the World Fantasy Convention 2013* edited by Stephen Jones, World Fantasy Convention 2013/PS Publishing, Hornsea, England, 2013 (hc).

F165 PROLOGUE
a. _____, see Dracula's Children [B3].

F166 PROLOGUE
a. _____, see Shudders and Shivers [B15].

F167 PROMETHEUS CHAINED
a. _____, see Ghosts from the Mist of Time [B7].
(*"The story that is read in Chapel in 'Prometheus Chained'—'Why Don't You Wash? Said the Girl with a Hundred Thousand Pounds and No Relatives'—by the Immortal S, was first published in my collection The Unbidden [Tandem Books] in 1971. I was at that time ghosting for Stephen Markham."* R.C-H.)

F168 PUSSY CAT–PUSSY CAT
a. _____, see The Unbidden [B26].

F169 THE RATIONAL EXPLANATION
a. _____, see Tales from the Shadows [B22].

F170 REFLECTIONS
a. _____, see The Cradle Demon and Other Stories of Fantasy and Terror [B2].

F171 REGRESSION

a. _____, in *The Fourth Book of After Midnight Stories* edited by Amy Myers, William Kimber & Co., London, England, 1988 (hc).
b. _____, in *The Year's Best Horror Stories XVII* edited by Karl Edward Wagner, DAW Books, New York, USA, 1989 (pb).
c. [as **TERUGKEER** (Return)], in *De Beste Horror verhalen van het Jaar* (The Best Horror Stories of the Year)] edited by Karl Edward Wagner, Loeb, Netherlands, 1989 (tpb).
d. _____, see Phantoms and Fiends [B13].

F172 **THE RESURRECTIONIST**
a. _____, see Tales of Fear and Fantasy [B24].
b. [as **SALOMES TÖCHTER**], see 6 x Panische nächte [B16].
[Note: A slightly revised version of this story was published as 'The Painted Door' (F157). This story was optioned for filming in 1999.]

F173 **RUDOLPH**

a. _____, see Dracula's Children [B3].
b. _____, in *The Mammoth Book of Dracula: Vampire Tales for the New Millennium* edited Stephen Jones, Robinson Publishing, London, England, 1997 (tpb).
c. _____, in *The Mammoth Book of Dracula: Vampire Tales for the New Millennium* edited by Stephen Jones, Carroll & Graf, New York, USA, 1997 (tpb).
d. _____, see The Vampire Stories of R. Chetwynd-Hayes [B27].
e. _____, in *Il grande libro di Dracula* (The Great Book of Dracula)] edited by Stephen Jones, Newton & Compton Editori, Italy, 2000 (tpb).
f. _____, in *Il grande libro di Dracula* (The Great Book of Dracula)] edited by Stephen Jones, Newton & Compton Editori, Italy, 2004 (tpb).
g. _____, in *Il grande libro di Dracula* (The Great Book of Dracula)] edited by Stephen Jones, Newton & Compton Editori, Italy, 2008 (tpb).
h. _____, in *The Mammoth Book of Dracula* edited Stephen Jones, Robinson Publishing, London, England, 2011 (tpb).
i. _____, in *The Mammoth Book of Dracula* edited by Stephen Jones, Running Press, New York, USA, 2011 (tpb).
j. [as *РУДОЛФ* (Rudolph)], in *Дракула* [Dracula], edited by Stephen Jones, Azbooka-Atticus, Russia, 2012 (hc).
k. _____, in *In the Footsteps of Dracula: Tales of the Undead Count*, edited by Stephen Jones, Pegasus Books, New York, USA, 2017 (hc).

F174 **RUN FOR THE TUNNEL**
a. _____, see Tales from the Shadows [B22].

F175 THE SAD GHOST

    a. _____, see The Fourteenth Fontana Book of Great Ghost Stories [C14].

    b. _____, in *When Graveyards Yawn* edited by Denys Val Baker, William Kimber & Co., London, England, 1982 (hc).

    c. _____, see Phantoms and Fiends [B13].

(*"I have to thank Miss Rosemary Timperley for the name Sorel that I lifted from her novel* The Passionate Marriage *and which she kindly gave me permission to use. On re-reading the story, I have formed the opinion that Sorel is sweet, her parents dull, Grandma an interfering old busy-body—and the ghost a gormless idiot who only comes to his senses on the last page."* R.C-H.)

F176 THE SAD VAMPIRE [as originally by "Angus Campbell"]

    a. _____, see The First Armada Monster Book [C1].

    b. _____, see The Vampire Stories of R. Chetwynd-Hayes [B27].

(*"The vampire is considered to be a nasty piece of work. You know— fangs, all that blood, climbing in and out of coffins and generally behaving in an irresponsible fashion. But wait until you have read 'The Sad Vampire' by Angus Campbell. Have you thought how awful it must be to never see the sun? To run when someone shows you a crucifix? To say nothing of a continuous diet of blood . . .!"* R.C-H.)

F177 THE SALE OF THE CENTURY

    a. _____, see Tales of Fear and Fantasy [B24].

F178 SHADES OF YESTERDAY

    a. _____, see Tales from the Shadows [B22].

F179 THE SHADMOCK

    a. _____, see The Monster Club [B10].

    b. _____, see The Monster Club [G6].

    c. _____, in *The Mammoth Book of Monsters* edited by Stephen Jones, Robinson Publishing, London, England, 2007 (tpb).

    d. _____, in *The Mammoth Book of Monsters* edited Stephen Jones, Carroll & Graf, New York, USA, 2007 (tpb).

    e. [as ШЕДМОК (Shadmock) in Монстры (Monsters)] edited by Stephen Jones, Azbooka-Klassika, Russia, 2009 (hc).

f. [as **SHADMOCK**], in *Wielka Księga Potworów Tom 1* (The Great Book of Monsters Volume 1), Fabryka Słów, Poland, 2010 (tpb).

F180 THE SHADOW
a. _____, see Cold Terror [B1].

F181 SHADOW ON THE WALL
a. _____, see Tales from Beyond [B17].

F182 SHE WALKS ON DRY LAND
a. _____, in *Haunted Shores: Thirteen Tales of the Supernatural* edited by Peter C. Smith, William Kimber & Co., London, England, 1980 (hc).
b. _____, see The Sixteenth Fontana Book of Great Ghost Stories [C16].
c. _____, in *Tales from Beyond the Grave* edited by Anonymous [Emma Blackley], Octopus Books, London, England, 1982 (hc).
d. _____, in *Tales from Beyond the Grave* edited by Anonymous [Emma Blackley], Gallery Books, New York, USA, 1989 (hc).
e. _____, see Phantoms and Fiends [B14].
f. _____, see Great Ghost Stories [C22].
g. _____, in *Stories to Make You Shudder Book 1* edited by Cornelius Clarke, Shudder Books, London, UK, 2019 (tpb).
(*"Lastly there is my own 'She Walks on Dry Land' which for a change I have set in the Regency period. Well—why not? I like to write about arrogant earls that ride into lonely villages and get their deserts after hitting the innkeeper over the head with a riding crop. It must have been fun being an arrogant earl back in 1812."* R.C-H.)

F183 SHIPWRECK
a. _____, see Tales of Terror from Outer Space [C24].
b. _____, in *Space 8* edited by Richard Davis, Hutchinson Books, London, England, 1983 (hc).
c. _____, see Phantoms and Fiends [B13].
(*"Not satisfied with the unholy league that is either on its way, or already in our midst, I have imported a lump of intelligent jelly. Well—why not? It will make a nasty change."* R.C-H.)

F184 **SHONA AND THE WATER-HORSE**

    a. _____, see Scottish Tales of Terror [C23].

    b. [as **LILEAS AND THE WATER-HORSE**], see Terror by Night [B25].

    c. _____, in *65 Great Spine Chillers* edited by Mary Danby, Octopus Books/St. Michael, London, England, 1982 (hc).

    d. _____, in *65 Great Spine Chillers* edited by Mary Danby, Octopus Books/St. Michael, London, England, 1983 (hc).

    e. _____, in *65 Great Spine Chillers* edited by Mary Danby, Reed Dump, Winconsin, USA, 1985 (hc).

    f. _____, see Ghosts from the Mist of Time [B7].

    g. [as **SHONA ET LE CHEVAL-DES-EAUX** (Shona and the Water-Horse)] in *Antarès: Science Fiction & Fantastque sans frontièrs* Volume 25 edited by Jean-Pierre Moumon and Martine Blond, les Editions Antarès, La Valette, France, 1987 (magazine).

    h. _____, in *65 Great Spine Chillers* edited by Mary Danby, Chartwell Books, London, England, 1988 (hc).

(*"When I was editing* Scottish Tales of Terror—*under the pseudonym Angus Campbell, I might add—I came upon several accounts of this dreaded Water Horse. I used that as a basis for one of my own stories. I certainly hope that my readers will recognise it as being a prose poem."* R.C-H.)

F185 **A SIN OF OMISSION**

    a. _____, in *The Tenth Fontana Book of Great Horror Stories* edited by Mary Danby, Fontana Books, London, England/William Collins Sons & Co. Ltd., Glasgow, Scotland, 1977 (pb).

    b. _____, in *The Tenth Fontana Book of Great Horror Stories* edited by Mary Danby, Fontana Books, London, England/William Collins Sons & Co. Ltd., Glasgow, Scotland, 1980 (pb).

    c. [as **THE SIN OF OMISSION**], see Spine Chillers [G12].

    d. _____, see Phantoms and Fiends [B13].

F186 **THE SIN OF OMISSION**

    a. _____, see 'A Sin of Omission' [F184(c)].

F187 **THE SLIPPITY-SLOP** [as originally by "Henry Glynn"]

a. _____, see The Sixth Armada Monster Book [C6].
b. _____, see Frights and Fancies [B6].
(*"'The Slippity-Slop', by Henry Glynn, contains a dire warning. Do not dig deep holes in the garden—there's no way of knowing what you may find, until it is too late. Should you stumble across a large egg with roots, throw it over the fence into the next-door garden and let someone else do whatever is necessary. But under no circumstances put it in the loft—that's the way to finish up with something that slips and slops... slips and slops..."* R.C-H.)

F188 THE SLOATHES
a. _____, see The Cradle Demon and Other Stories of Fantasy and Terror [B2].

F189 SOMEONE IN MIND
a. _____, see Tales from the Dark Lands [B18].

F190 SOMEONE IS DEAD
a. _____, see *The Elemental & Other Stories* [B4].
b. [as **DIS-MOI QUI TU HANTES...**(Tell Me Who You Hate...)], in *Antarès: Science Fiction & Fantastque sans frontièrs* Volume 20 edited by Jean-Pierre Moumon and Martine Blond, les Editions Antarès, La Valette, France, 1985 (magazine).
c. _____, in *Dark Detectives: Adventures of the Supernatural Sleuths* edited Stephen Jones, Fedogan & Bremer, Minneapolis, Minnesota, USA, 1999 (hc).
There are two variants of this edition.
i. Description: trade edition.
ii. Description: 100-copy signed edition in slipcase.
d. [as *КТО-ТО МЕРТВЫЙ* (Someone is Dead)], in *Мистика* (Mystic)] edited by Stephen Jones, Azbooka-klassika, Russia 2010 (hc).
e. _____, in *Dark Detectives: An Anthology of Supernatural Mysteries* edited by Stephen Jones, Titan Books, UK/USA, 2015 (tpb).
f. _____, in *Dark Detectives: An Anthology of Supernatural Mysteries* edited by Stephen Jones, Titan Books, UK/USA, 2016 (pb).
g. _____, in *Phantasmagoria Special Edition Series #1: R.*

Chetwynd-Hayes Centenary Collector's Edition edited by Trevor Kennedy, Phantasmagoria Publishing/TK Pulp, UK, 2019 (magazine). [Note: A "Fred and Francis" story.]

F191 SOMETHING COMES IN FROM THE GARDEN
a. _____, see The Night Ghouls and Other Grisly Tales [B11].
b. _____, see Tales from the Dark Lands [B18].
c. _____, see Gaslight, Ghosts, & Ghouls [B27].

F192 STRANGE PEOPLE

a. _____, in *The Fifth Book of After Midnight Stories* edited by Amy Myers, Robert Hale, London, England, 1991 (hc).
b. _____, see Phantoms and Fiends [B13].
[Note: Written in 1988, R.C-H considered calling this story 'The Unfortunates'.]
(*"I wrote it for Amy Myers'* Fifth After Midnight Stories *which folded when Collins took Thorsons over and cancelled the contract. I also sent a copy to Karl Edward Wagner, who promptly accepted it for his* Year's Best Horror *series, only to have to put it to one side when I had to explain it had not been published anywhere last year. But he is still prepared to include it in one of his collections when it has appeared."* R.C-H.)

F193 THE SWING
a. _____, see Tales from Beyond [B17].

F194 THE SWITCH-BACK

a. _____, see Tales from the Dark Lands [B18].
b. _____, in *Weird Tales* No.306, edited by Darrell Schweitzer, Terminus Publishing Co., Inc., Philadelphia, Pennsylvania, USA, 1993 (pb). [Note: This version was slightly revised.]

F195 **THE TELE-MON**
a. _____, see The Fifth Armada Monster Book [C5].
b. _____, see Frights and Fancies [B6].
(*"Now, as I have stated before, all my stories are true. Honestly. And it is a fact that if you watch television too long and too often something very nasty does start to grow in the cathode tube . . ."* R.C-H.)

F196 **THE THING**

a. _____, in *The Seventh Pan Book of Horror Stories* edited by Herbert van Thal, Pan Books, London, England, 1966 (pb).

b. _____, in *The Seventh Pan Book of Horror Stories* edited by Herbert van Thal, Pan Books, London, England, 1967 (pb).

c. _____, in *The Seventh Pan Book of Horror Stories* edited by Herbert van Thal, Pan Books, London, England, 1968 (pb).

d. _____, in *The Seventh Pan Book of Horror Stories* edited by Herbert van Thal, Pan Books, London, England, 1968 (pb).

e. _____, in *The Seventh Pan Book of Horror Stories* edited by Herbert van Thal, Pan Books, London, England, 1970 (pb).

f. _____, in *The Seventh Pan Book of Horror Stories* edited by Herbert van Thal, Pan Books, London, England, 1971 (pb).

g. _____, in *The Seventh Pan Book of Horror Stories* edited by Herbert van Thal, Pan Books, London, England, 1972 (pb).

h. _____, in *The Seventh Pan Book of Horror Stories* edited by Herbert van Thal, Pan Books, London, England, 1973 (pb).

i. _____, in *The Seventh Pan Book of Horror Stories* edited by Herbert van Thal, Pan Books, London, England, 1973 (pb).

j. _____, in *The Seventh Pan Book of Horror Stories* edited by Herbert van Thal, Pan Books, London, England, 1974 (pb).

k. _____, in *The Seventh Pan Book of Horror Stories* edited by Herbert van Thal, Pan Books, London, England, (pb).

l. _____, in *The Seventh Pan Book of Horror Stories* edited by Herbert van Thal, Pan Books, London, England, (pb).

m. _____, in *The Seventh Pan Book of Horror Stories* edited by Herbert van Thal, Pan Books, London, England, 1980 (pb).

n. _____, in *Secret City: Strange Tales of London* edited by Stephen Jones and Jo Fletcher, The 1997 World Fantasy

Convention/Titan Books, London, England, 1997.
There are two variants of this edition.
    i. Description: trade paperback edition.
    ii. Description: 300-copy special hardcover edition.
  o. _____, see Phantoms and Fiends [B13].

F197 THE THIRD EYE

a. _____, in *The Fourteenth Armada Ghost Book* edited by Mary Danby, Armada/Fontana Paperbacks, London, England, 1982 (pb).
b. _____, in *The Green Ghost and Other Stories* edited by Mary Danby, Armada/William Collins Sons & Co., Glasgow, Scotland, 1989 (pb).
c. _____, see Frights and Fancies [B6].

F198 THOSE THAT SERVE

a. _____, see Tales from the Hidden World: Four Episodes in the History of Clavering Grange [B20].
[Note: A "Chronicles of Clavering Grange" story.]

F199 THE THROWBACK

a. _____, see Terror by Night [B25].

F200 TIME CHECK

a. _____, see Ghosts from the Mist of Time [B7].

F201 A TIME TO PLANT–A TIME TO REAP

a. _____, see The Elemental & Other Stories [B4].

F202 TOMORROW AT NINE

a. _____, see The Cradle Demon and Other Stories of Fantasy and Terror [B2].

F203 TOMORROW IS JUDGEMENT DAY

a. _____, see The Unbidden [B26].

F204 **TOMORROW'S GHOST**
a. _____, see Tales of Darkness [B23].
b._____, see The Nineteenth Fontana Book of Great Ghost Stories [C19].
[Note: A "Chronicles of Clavering Grange" story.]
(*"This first appeared in my hardcover collection* Tales of Darkness *published by William Kimber, and is—maybe—for what it is worth—the best ghost story I have so far written. It is also in keeping with the overall theme of this collection—old houses and the link that connects one time period to another. As a matter of interest, Clavering Grange was the setting for my first novel,* The Dark Man, *and is used again in my collection of four long stories,* Tales from the Other Side, *which was published by Kimber in May 1983. The ghost of Cynthia Sinclair still walks the deserted corridors of the old mansion."* R.C-H.)

F205 **TRAVELLING COMPANION**
a. _____, see Tales from the Dark Lands [B18].

F206 **THE TREASURE HUNT**
a. _____, see The Unbidden [B26].

F207 **TWILIGHT SONG**
a. _____, see Shudders and Shivers [B15].

F208 **THE UNDERGROUND**
a. _____, in *After Midnight Stories* edited by Amy Myers, William Kimber & Co., London, England, 1985 (hc).
b. _____, see Phantoms and Fiends [B13].
e. _____, in *The Platform Edge: Uncanny Tales of the Railways* edited by Mike Ashley, British Library Publications, London, England, 2019 (tpb).

F209 **UNDER THE SKIN**
a. _____, see Terror by Night [B25].
b. _____, in *The Scream Factory* Issue #17, Spring 1996

edited by Bob Morrish, Peter Enfantino and John Scoleri, Deadline Press, Arizona, USA, 1996 (magazine).

[Note: This issue also contains an interview with R. Chetwynd-Hayes by Scot D. Ryerson and 'R. Chetwynd-Hayes: A Bibliography' by Richard Dalby.]

F210 **A VINDICTIVE WOMAN**

a. _____, in *65 Great Tales of the Supernatural* edited by Mary Danby, Octopus Books, London, England, 1979 (hc).

b. _____, in *65 Great Tales of the Supernatural* editedby Mary Danby, Octopus Books/St. Michael, London, England, 1980 (hc).

c. _____, in *65 Great Tales of the Supernatural* editedby Mary Danby, Octopus Books/St. Michael, London, England, 1982 (hc).

d. _____, see A Quiver of Ghosts [B14].

e. _____, in *Great Vampires & Other Horrors*, Chancellor Press, London, England, 1992 (hc).

f. _____, in *Great Vampire Stories*, Chancellor Press, London, England, 2002 (tpb).

F211 **THE WAILING WAIF OF BATTERSEA**

a. _____, see The Night Ghouls and Other Grisly Tales [B11].

F212 **A WALK IN THE COUNTRY**

a. _____, see The Cradle Demon and Other Stories of Fantasy and Terror [B2].

F213 **A WALK ON THE DARK SIDE**

a. _____, in *Skeleton Crew: Portraits of Horror*, Vol. 2, Issue 3, September 1990, Argus, Hemel Hempstead, England (magazine).

[Note: This issue also contains an interview with R. Chetwynd-Hayes by Stephen Jones and Jo Fletcher.]

b. _____, see Gaslight, Ghosts, & Ghouls [B27].

F214 **THE WANDERER**
    a. _____. see The Elemental & Other Stories [B4].
    b. [as **DIE RASTLOSE SEELE**], see 6 x Panische nächte [B16].
    c. _____, see A Quiver of Ghosts [B14].
    d. _____, see Ghosts from the Mist of Time [B7].
    [Note: A "Chronicles of Clavering Grange" story.]

F215 **THE WEREWOLF** [as originally by "Angus Campbell"]
    a. _____, see The Fourth Armada Monster Book [C4].

    b. _____, in *The Mammoth Book of Werewolves* edited by Stephen Jones, Robinson Publishing, London, England, 1994 (tpb).
    c. _____, in *The Mammoth Book of Werewolves* edited by Stephen Jones, Carroll & Graf, New York, USA, 1994 (tpb).
    d. _____, in *The Giant Book of Werewolves* edited by Stephen Jones, Magpie Books, London, England, 1995 (tpb).
    e. _____, in *The Giant Book of Werewolves* edited by Stephen Jones, The Book Company International, Australia, 1995 (tpb).
    f. _____, in *The Giant Book of Werewolves* edited by Stephen Jones, Parragon Book Service, Bath, England, 1995 (tpb).
    g. [as **IL LICANTROPO** (The Werewolf)], in *Lupi mannari!* (Werewolves!)], Newton & Compton Editori, Italy, 1997 (tpb).
    h. _____, see Frights and Fancies [B6].
    i. [as *ОБОРОТЕНЬ* (Werewolf)], in *Оборотни* (Werewolves) edited by Stephen Jones, Azbooka-klassika, Russia, 2008 (hc).
    j. _____, in *The Mammoth Book of Wolf Men: The Ultimate Werewolf Anthology* edited by Stephen Jones, Robinson Publishing, London, England, 2009 (tpb).
    k. _____, in *The Mammoth Book of Wolf Men: The Ultimate Werewolf Anthology* edited by Stephen Jones, Running Press, New York, USA, 2009 (tpb).
    (*"Angus Campbell has come up with a monster which—although a most terrifying creature to meet on a dark night—also appears to be rather unhappy and is not all that fearful, if only you can pluck up courage to pat its head."* R.C-H.)

F216 **THE WEREWOLF AND THE VAMPIRE**

a. _____, see The Monster Club [B10].

b. [as **LUNE DE MIEL LYCANTHROPIQUE** (Lycanthropic Honeymoon)] in _Antarès: Science Fiction et Fantastque sans frontièrs_ Volume 7 edited by Jean-Pierre Moumon and Martine Blond, les Editions Antarès, La Valette, France, 1982 (magazine).

c. _____, in _Vampires: Two Centuries of Great Vampire Stories_ edited by Alan Ryan, Doubleday & Co., Inc./SFBC, New York, USA, 1987 (hc).

d. _____, in _Vampires: Two Centuries of Great Vampire Stories_ edited by Alan Ryan, Doubleday & Co., Inc., New York, USA, 1987 (hc).

e. _____, in _The Penguin Book of Vampire Stories: Two Centuries of Great Stories with a Bite_ edited by Alan Ryan, Penguin Books, London, England, 1988 (tpb).

f. _____, in _The Penguin Book of Vampire Stories_ edited by Alan Ryan, Guild Publishing, London, England, 1988 (hc).

g. _____, in _The Penguin Book of Vampire Stories_ edited by Alan Ryan, Penguin Books, London, England, 1989 (tpb).

h. _____, in _The Penguin Book of Vampire Stories_ edited by Alan Ryan, Bloomsbury Publishing, London, England, 1991 (hc).

i. _____, in _The Penguin Book of Vampire Stories_ edited by Alan Ryan, Claremont Books/Godfrey Cave Associates Ltd./Penguin Group, London, England, 1995 (hc).

j. _____, see The Vampire Stories of R. Chetwynd-Hayes [B27].

k. _____, in _The Vampire Archives: The Most Complete Volume of Vampire Tales Ever Published_ edited by Otto Penzler, Vintage Crime/Black Lizard/Vintage Books, New York, USA, 2009 (tpb).

l. _____, in _The Vampire Archive_ edited by Otto Penzler, Quercus, London, England, 2009 (tpb).

m. _____, in _The Vampire Archives: The Most Complete Volume of Vampire Tales Ever Published_ edited by Otto Penzler, Vintage Crime/Black Lizard/SFBC, New York, USA, 2010 (tpb).

n. _____, in _Fangs: The Vampire Archives Volume 2_ edited by Otto Penzler, Vintage Crime/Black Lizard/Vintage Books, New York, USA, 2010 (pb).

o. _____, in *The Penguin Book of Vampire Stories* edited by Alan Ryan, Penguin Books, London, England, 2011 (tpb).

F217 WHERE YESTERDAY?

a. _____, see 'Where Yesterday? A Modern Fairy Story' [F217(b)].

F218 WHERE YESTERDAY? A MODERN FAIRY STORY

a. _____, see Terror by Night [B25].

b. [as **WHERE YESTERDAY?**], in *Dark Horizons* Issue No.33 edited by Phil Williams, The British Fantasy Society, Shrewsbury, England, 1992 (magazine).

[Note: This version was edited for publication.]

F219 WHICH ONE?

a. _____, see Tales of Darkness [B23].

b. _____, see The Seventeenth Fontana Book of Great Ghost Stories [C17].

c. [as **LEQUEL?** (Which?)], in *Antarès: Science Fiction & Fantastque sans frontièrs* Volume 15 edited by Jean-Pierre Moumon and Martine Blond, les Editions Antarès, La Valette, France, 1984 (magazine).

d. _____. in *Black Cat Tales of the Unexpected Vol.3* edited by Neil A. Miller, Black Cat Books/Neil Miller Publications, Kent, UK, 1996 (chapbook).

e. _____, see Haunted [G14].

(*"I ask you to accept there is life after death and that one can hold a very lengthy conversation with a ghost. Where this plot came from I have not the slightest idea, as I write blind, never knowing what my characters will get up to, and pound happily away on my typewriter, hoping the combination of fingers and brain will come up with something readable. Believe it or not, usually this slap-dash procedure works, although the end result varies considerably. It is possible the excitement of not knowing what is going to happen next keeps me going."* R.C-H.)

F220 WHO IS MR. SMITH?

a. _____, see Cold Terror [B1].

b. [as **MR. SMITH**], in *Antarès: Science Fiction & Fantastque sans frontièrs* Volume 31 edited by Jean-Pierre Moumon and Martine Blond, les Editions Antarès, La Valette, France, 1988 (magazine).

F221 **WHY?**

    a. _____, see The Cradle Demon and Other Stories of Fantasy and Terror [B2].

    b. [as **LA PETITE FILLE DU CIMETIÈRE** (The Girl of the Cemetery)], in *Antarès: Science Fiction & Fantastque sans frontièrs* Volume 3 edited by Jean-Pierre Moumon and Martine Blond, les Editions Antarès, La Valette, France, 1981 (magazine).

    c. [as **LA PETITE FILLE DU CIMETIÈRE** (The Girl of the Cemetery)], in *Carfax* No.12, February 1986 edited by Pierre D. (jada) Lacroix, Canada, 1986 (magazine).

F222 **WHY DON'T YOU WASH? SAID THE GIRL WITH £100,000 AND NO RELATIVES**

    a. _____, see The Unbidden [B26].

[Note: This story was later incorporated into 'Prometheus Chained' (F165)]

F223 **THE WIND-BILLIE** [as originally by "Angus Campbell"]

    a. _____, see The Fifth Armada Monster Book [C5].

    b. _____, see Frights and Fancies [B6].

(*"I'm sure you've never heard of a Wind-Billie, for example. In the days when roaring coal fires were the only means of heating a house and the north wind happened to be in a contrary direction, smoke often poured out into the room and made everyone cough. Now, they might have believed that the flue was choked with soot, but Angus Campbell, in 'The Wind-Billie', has uncovered the murky truth. A most peculiar monster had set up home in the chimney-pot."* R.C-H.)

F224 **WOODWORK–1850**

    a. _____, see Tales from the Other Side [B21].

[Note: A "Chronicles of Clavering Grange" story.]

F225 **WOODWORK–1969**

    a. _____, see Tales from the Other Side [B21].

[Note: A "Chronicles of Clavering Grange" story.]

F226 **ZENA**

    a. _____, see Dracula's Children [B3].

G. MEDIA ADAPTATIONS

(INCLUDES AN ALPHABETICAL LISTING OF ADAPTATIONS IN OTHER MEDIA BASED ON WORK BY R. CHETWYND-HAYES)

(*"I often dream of a television series called* The Clavering Chronicles, *which would relate the dreadful fates that befall various people who live in that accursed place over the centuries."* R.C-H.)

G1 **THE DARK MAN**

[Note: This novel was apparently serialised on the South African Broadcasting Corporation (SABC) circa 1979.]

G2 **FROM BEYOND THE GRAVE**

a. _____, Amicus Productions/Columbia-Warner Distributors, UK, 1974, Colour.

Director: Kevin Connor. Producers: Max J. Rosenberg and Milton Subotsky. Screenplay: Robin Clarke and Raymond Christodoulou [based on stories by R. Chet-wynd-Hayes]. With: Ian Bannen (Christopher Lowe), Ian Carmichael (Reginald Warren), Peter Cushing (The Proprietor), Diana Dors (Mabel Lowe), Margaret Leighton (Madame Orloff), Donald Pleasence (Jim Underwood), Nyree Dawn Porter (Susan Warren), David Warner (Edward Charlton), Ian Ogilvy (William Seaton), Lesley-Ann Down (Rosemary Seaton).

[Note: The working title was *The Unbidden*, and this includes the stories 'An Act of Kindness' scripted by Kevin Connor, 'The Door' and 'The Gatecrasher' scripted by Robin Clarke and 'The Elemental' scripted by Raymond Cristoudolou. Unused scripts for 'Don't Go Up Them Stairs' by Kevin Connor, and 'It Came to Dinner' and 'The Ninth Removal' by Robin Clarke were never used and are held as part of the R. Chetwynd-Hayes Archive at The University of Liverpool Library. This film was first shown on

UK TV on July 26, 1980.]
(*"Needless to say, I was delighted with the all-star cast, and could scarcely believe that such famous names were actually going to give life to characters I had created, in the most part, in the small hours that separate midnight from sunrise."* R.C-H.)

G3 **THE GHOSTLY EARL**
a. _____, *Dramarama: Spooky*, Thames Television, May 16, 1983, UK Colour.
Director: Richard Handford. Producer: Vic Hughes. Teleplay: Alan Seymour, based on a story by R. Chetwynd-Hayes. With: Robert McBain (The Earl), Caroline Dudley (Clare), Geoffrey Beevers (Lord Rillington), Suzanne Neve (Lady Rillington), Terence Rigby (Wilkinson), Nigel Hughes (Jeweller).

G4 **KEEP THE GASLIGHT BURNING**

a. _____, Igor Studios/White Room Entertainment, USA, 2018, Colour.
Directors: Lou Elsey and Dave Elsey. Producers: Don Bies and Anna Bies. Screenplay: Dave Elsey, based on a story by R. Chetwynd-Hayes. With: Markie Post (Mrs. Maxwell), Kate Armstrong Ross (Maya Griffiths), Maureen Studer (Mrs. Duncan), Rick Baker (Mr. Maxwell).

G5 **THE LIBERATED TIGER**
a. _____, *Haunted*, BBC Radio 4 Extra, England, February 26, 2013.
With: Rosemary Leach, Leslie Sands.
[Note: "Rosemary Leach and Leslie Sands star in R. Chetwynd-Hayes' 1972 ghost story 'The Liberated Tiger'. Roland is dying. But could he possibly be haunting his wife while he is still alive?" Written by Patricia Mays, this was apparently recorded in July 1984 to be used in the BBC World Service series *Thirty-Minute Theatre* "*Haunted 84*", but there is no record of an original transmission date and may never have previously been broadcast.]

G6 THE MONSTER CLUB

a. _____, Chips Productions/Sword & Sorcery/ITC Entertainment, UK, 1980, Colour. Director: Roy Ward Baker. Producer: Milton Subotsky. Screenplay: Edward and Valerie Abraham, from the novel by Ronald Chetwynd-Hayes. With: Vincent Price (Eramus), Donald Pleasence (Pickering), John Carradine (R. Chetwynd-Hayes), Stuart Whitman (Sam), Richard Johnson (Father), Barbara Kellermann (Angela), Brit Ekland (Mother), Anthony Valentine (Mooney), Simon Ward (George), Patrick Magee (Innkeeper).

(*"When I saw Carradine he was seventy-four years old and crippled with arthritis. At the preview, a lady came up to me and said, 'I'm so sorry you suffer from arthritis.' I said, 'I don't, that's John Carradine!'"* R.C-H.)

G7 MY SO-CALLED LIFE AND DEATH

a. _____, *Night Visions*, Angel Brown Productions/Warner Bros. Television/Fox Network, Canada/USA, August 23, 2001, Colour.

Director: Ernest Dickerson. Producers: Erin Maher, Kay Reindl and Drew Matich. Teleplay: Naren Shankar, based on a short story by R. Chetwynd-Hayes. With: Maria Sokoloff (Julia), Steve Bacic (Handyman), William Pavey (Brian), Wanda Cannon (Mother), Kurt Max Runte (Father), Henry Rollins (Host).

[Note: "A girl's first crush can be magical, but as Julia is about to learn, magic is a short step from horror . . ." Based on R.C-H's story 'The Ghost Who Limped' (F72).]

G8 THE NINTH REMOVAL

a. _____, *The Price of Fear*, BBC World Service, UK, November 11, 1973.

Producer: John Dyas. Writer: Barry Campbell, from the story by R. Chetwynd-Hayes. With: Vincent Price (Price), Freda Jackson (Amelia Sidgwick), Richard Pearson (Brigadier/Jarvis), Clare Sutcliffe (Anne Franklin/Miss Davis), Michael Segal (Parsons), Alan Rowe (Man (in train)/Drunken Scot),

b. _____, *The Price of Fear*, BBC World Service, UK, April 20, 1974.

c. _____, *The Price of Fear: Four Dramatisations with Master of the Macabre, Vincent Price*, BBC Radio Collection/BBC Enterprises Ltd., UK, 1990 (double cassette).

d. _____, *The Price of Fear*, BBC Radio 7, UK, June 7, 2003.

d. _____, *The Price of Fear*, BBC Radio 7, UK, June 8, 2003.

d. _____, *The Price of Fear*, BBC Radio 7, UK, May 7, 2005.

e. _____, *The Price of Fear*, BBC Radio 7, UK, April 11, 2010.

[Note: "The death of a promiscuous young girl provides all the ingredients for a classic murder mystery . . . or does it?"]

(*"I couldn't find anyone who had it, so I had to go into the bowels of the BBC in London and get someone to play it to me. I'm hoping it will stimulate some interest in me too."* R.C-H.]

G10 THE PSYCHIC DETECTIVE

[Note: R.C-H's 1993 novel was twice optioned for filming by the revived Hammer Films—before publication and again in 1997—but nothing ever became of it.]

G11 SCARY STORIES

[Note: Stage production of 'Subsoil' by Nicholson Baker and 'The Elemental' by R. Chetwynd Hayes as part of the 1998–1999 Season of Book-It Repertory Theatre, Seattle, Washington, USA.]

G12 THE SIN OF OMISSION

a. _____, *Spine Chillers*, A Jackanory Unit Production/BBC One, December 9, 1980, UK, Colour.

With: John Woodvine.

b. _____, *Spine Chillers*, A Jackanory Unit Production/ BBC Two, February 9, 1982, UK, Colour.

[Note: "A flat head rose up, and small, watery-blue eyes glittered with malevolent intent, while jaws opened to their fullest extent, and Mr. Faversham was permitted to view a pink-lined cavern that was equipped with two yellow, pointed fangs . . ."]

G13 **SOMETHING IN THE WOODWORK**

a. _____, *Rod Serling's Night Gallery*, Universal Studios/NBC, January 14, 1973, USA, Colour.

Director: Edward M. Abroms. Producer: Jack Laird. Teleplay: Rod Serling, from a short story by R. Chetwynd-Hayes. With: Geraldine Page (Molly Wheatland), Leif Erikson (Charlie Wheatland), Paul Jenkins (Joe Wilson), John McMurtry (Jamie Dilman), Barbara Rhoades (Julie), Rod Serling (Host).

(*"I was thrilled when I saw it. Someone, I cannot recall who, had done an excellent job."* R.C-H.]

G14 **WHICH ONE?**

a. _____, *Haunted*, BBC Radio 4 Extra, England, February 27, 2013.

With: Reginald Marsh.

[Note: "Reginald Marsh stars in R. Chetwynd-Hayes' 1981 tale, set in 1940, when a fire warden team is put to the toughest test during a bombing raid. Will they all survive?" Written by Patricia Mays, this was apparently recorded in July 1984 to be used in the BBC World Service series *Thirty-Minute Theatre "Haunted 84"*, but there is no record of an original transmission date and may never have previously been broadcast.]

H. UNPUBLISHED WORKS

(INCLUDES AN ALPHABETICAL LISTING OF UNPUBLISHED WORKS
BY R. CHETWYND-HAYES)

H1 AFTERWORD

[Note: In 1989 R.CH-H wrote a fictional 'Afterword' for a proposed book entitled *Shadow Plays: The Dark Fiction of Charles L. Grant* edited by Thomas Liam McDonald.]

H2 AN ACT OF KINDNESS

[Note: A 37pp script treatment written circa 1971 by R.C-H is held as part of the R. Chetwynd-Hayes Archive at The University of Liverpool Library.]

H3 BROTHER IN DARKNESS

[Note: A one-page typescript and one-page carbon are held as part of the R. Chetwynd-Hayes Archive at The University of Liverpool Library.]

H4 THE DOPPLEGÄNGER

[Note: R.C-H apparently wrote a synopsis, Prologue and first chapter for this proposed novel in 1978 based on his short story 'Matthew and Luke' (F128) and sent them to various publishers and his American agent at the time. It finally ended up as a short story in *Ghosts from the Mist of Time* (B7).]

(*"Already the storyline has changed. Matthew was electrocuted in his bath, but has a brief experience of drowning—because at that moment Luke was trying to drown himself in the river. I've started on chapter one. A party given by Mrs. Fortesque who has an enormous appetite for celebrities. She is also afflicted with artistic pretentions... '... and had developed the habit of discussing music with actors, writing with artists and painting with authors, maintaining that this disconcerting turnabout of professions made certain that the poor dears did not talk shop. Like most ladies endowed with a large bosom, she gushed; poured out a flow of complimentary words, all delivered with a loud, sonerous voice.' Get the idea? This is of course only a bare outline and the plot will doubtlessly change as I write the book. The style? Pathos and humour—plus a feeling of mouting terror. Imagine living in a world that is slowly disintergrating around you."* R.C-H.)

H5 GHOST AT SUNSET
[Note: A complete 22pp typescript and carbon are held as part of the R. Chetwynd-Hayes Archive at The University of Liverpool Library.]

H6 THE GHOST CAT
[Note: Mentioned in a letter from London Management literary agency dated June 27, 1977, held as part of the R. Chetwynd-Hayes Archive at The University of Liverpool Library.]

H7 THE GHOUL OF LOUGHVILLE
[Note: A complete 10pp carbon typescript is held as part of the R. Chetwynd-Hayes Archive at The University of Liverpool Library.]

H8 THE HIDDEN ROAD
[Note: A one-page carbon typescript is held as part of the R. Chetwynd-Hayes Archive at The University of Liverpool Library.]

H9 THE HOUSE GUEST
[Note: An incomplete 5pp typescript is held as part of the R. Chetwynd-Hayes Archive at The University of Liverpool Library.]

H10 THE INVADERS
[Note: A complete 36pp carbon and photocopied typescript is held as part of the R. Chetwynd-Hayes Archive at The University of Liverpool Library.]

H11 KEPPLE
[Note: A complete 72pp script is held as part of the R. Chetwynd-Hayes Archive at The University of Liverpool Library. There is no indication of who wrote it.]

H12 **LOFT CONVERSION**

[Note: A 12pp script treatment by R.C-H is held as part of the R. Chetwynd-Hayes Archive at The University of Liverpool Library.]

H13 **LONDON WALL**

[Note: A one-page carbon typescript and fragment are held as part of the R. Chetwynd-Hayes Archive at The University of Liverpool Library.]

H14 **THE MAN WHO FLOATED IN SPACE**

[Note: A complete 6pp carbon typescript is held as part of the R. Chetwynd-Hayes Archive at The University of Liverpool Library.]

H15 **MEANIES AND MONSTERS**

[Note: A proposed collection of short stories sent to Robinson Publishing circa late 1990s.]

H16 **MURDER AT CHRISTMAS**

[Note: Apparently a novel R.C-H was working on circa February 1990.]
(*"Well, I must get back to writing my first Who-Dun-It*—Murder at Christmas.*"* R.C-H.]

H17 **THE SECOND FRONT DOOR**

[Note: A 10pp incomplete typescript is held as part of the R. Chet-wynd-Hayes Archive at The University of Liverpool Library.]

H18 **SEPTILIUM**

[Note: Proposed novel in 1988 based on R.C-H's short story 'Crowning Glory' (F41).]
(*"Don't you agree that* Septilium *is catching, particularly if you are bitten. You are aware—are you not?—that* they *start as boils, then erupt into thin white worm-things that coil round the hair. So what the Countess is suffering from is revealed quite early in the book; it is the slow revealment (my new word) of what is happening to Gore that builds up to a climax. I think Greselda is infected. But she will not be aware of that fact yet."* R.C-H.]

H19 STORY IN A GLASS JAR
[Note: A one-page typescript is held as part of the R. Chetwynd-Hayes Archive at The University of Liverpool Library.]

H20 STRANGE NEIGHBOURS
[Note: A complete 18pp typescript and carbon are held as part of the R. Chetwynd-Hayes Archive at The University of Liverpool Library.]

H21 THOMAS, EARL OF BLYTHE
[Note: A 3pp incomplete typescript and a one-page carbon are held as part of the R. Chetwynd-Hayes Archive at The University of Liverpool Library.]
(*"The wind chased long-dead leaves over the frost-hard ground, then released a gurgle of delight when a red squirrel went dancing before its billowing advance . . ."* R.C-H.)

H22 THREE CHEERS FOR CATHY
[Note: A 90,000-word romantic novel written in the 1960s and submitted to Hutchinson & Co. and possibly other publishers. A bound typescript and carbon (320pp) are held as part of the R. Chetwynd-Hayes Archive at The University of Liverpool Library.]
(*"A rotten title. It was written just after* The Dark Man *and is in the same kind of mood. I have re-written parts many times and to be frank—for what it is worth—I think it may be the best thing I have ever done. Years before its time when I first wrote it. The story came out of my brain red hot—as did* The Dark Man."* R.C-H.]

H23 VENGEANCE IS MINE
[Note: An 11pp incomplete typescript and variant one-page carbon are held as part of the R. Chetwynd-Hayes Archive at The University of Liverpool Library.]

H24 YESTERDAY'S PHANTOMS
[Note: A TV series proposal written circa 1982 by R.C-H is held as part of the R. Chetwynd-Hayes Archive at The University of Liverpool Library.]

OBITUARY

From the *Richmond and Twickenham Times*,
Friday, March 30th, 2001

OBITUARIES

Prolific horror writer dies aged 81

A SUPERNATURAL fiction writer described as Britain's Prince of Chill died last week aged 81.

Ronald Chetwynd-Hayes died of bronchial pneumonia on March 20th at Homemead care home in Teddington.

During his life Ronald wrote 13 novels, 23 collections of short stories and edited 24 anthologies.

His ghost and humorous horror stories have graced the shelves of nearly every public library in the United Kingdom with some of his works being made into film, notably 'The Monster Club' and 'From Beyond the Grave'.

The Horror Writers of America and the British Fantasy Society presented him with a Life Achievement Award in 1989 and he was special guest at the 1997 World Fantasy Convention in London.

Mr Chetwynd-Hayes was born on May 30th, 1919 in Swan Street, Isleworth and lived and wrote in Richmond and Hampton Hill for the majority of his life.

After losing his mother at a young age, Ronald was fostered in his early years. He then lived firstly with his grandmother and latterly with his Aunt Doris.

He followed his Quartermaster Sergeant father into the army at the start of the Second World War and rose to the rank of Sergeant in the Middlesex Regiment.

He was evacuated from Dunkirk but returned to the beaches of France on D-Day.

On returning from the war he discovered he had a brother Len and they became very close and shared a great love of debating for hours on end.

He landed a job as a trainee buyer in the furniture section of Harrods and then after four and a half years he was showroom manager at Peerless Built-in Furniture Emporium in Berkeley Street.

It was during this period he began to write after he finished work in the evenings.

After selling his first story 'The Orator' to The Lady magazine in 1953 his first book 'The Man From The Bomb' was published by Badger Books in 1959.

When Peerless was taken over and he was let go in the early 1970s, he became a full time writer and began producing a prolific number of ghost stories and gentle tales of terror.

Linda Smith, one of Mr Chetwynd-Hayes' nieces said: "For a man who was effectively an orphan and who received very little education, all he achieved in his 81 years was quite phenomenal. He will be remembered with great admiration by his friends and relatives who will miss the pleasure of his stimulating and witty company."

Stephen Jones, a dear friend and editor who has recently completed a compilation of some of Ronald's short stories said: "Although I guess I had expected the news for more than a year, when I heard about his death I reacted to his passing with more emotion than I imagined and I will miss him greatly."

Dorothy Lumley from Dorian Literary Agency said: "I was privileged as an editor to publish Ron's work in the 1970s, including his best work; in my opinion, 'The Monster Club' and later to work with him as an agent. Personally I shall miss his mischievous sense of humour, his enquiring mind and his fascinating fund of knowledge about the film industry."

A service will be held at Hanworth Crematorium, April 2nd, 12 noon.

STEPHEN JONES' MASTERS OF HORROR SERIES